# CURSED

SIMON & SCHUSTER BFYR

NEW YORK   LONDON   TORONTO   SYDNEY   NEW DELHI

ILLUSTRATED BY
# FRANK MILLER

WRITTEN BY
# THOMAS WHEELER

# CURSED

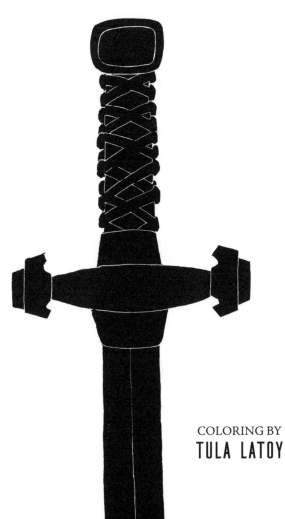

COLORING BY
## TULA LATOY

SIMON & SCHUSTER BFYR

An imprint of Simon & Schuster Children's Publishing Division
1230 Avenue of the Americas, New York, New York 10020
This book is a work of fiction. Any references to historical events,
real people, or real places are used fictitiously. Other names, characters, places,
and events are products of the author's imagination, and any resemblance
to actual events or places or persons, living or dead, is entirely coincidental.
Illustrations copyright © 2019 by Frank Miller
Text copyright © 2019 by Thomas Wheeler
SIMON & SCHUSTER BFYR is a trademark of Simon & Schuster, Inc.
For information about special discounts for bulk purchases, please contact Simon &
Schuster Special Sales at 1-866-506-1949 or business@simonandschuster.com.
The Simon & Schuster Speakers Bureau can bring authors to your live event.
For more information or to book an event, contact the Simon & Schuster Speakers
Bureau at 1-866-248-3049 or visit our website at www.simonspeakers.com.
Book design by Lucy Ruth Cummins
The text for this book was set in Adobe Jenson Pro.
Manufactured in China
10 9 8 7 6 5 4 3 2
Library of Congress Cataloging-in-Publication Data
Names: Miller, Frank, 1957– author. | Wheeler, Thomas (Screenwriter), author.
Title: Cursed / Frank Miller ; Thomas Wheeler.
Other titles: Cursed (Television program)
Description: First edition. |
New York, New York : Simon & Schuster Books for Young Readers, [2019]
Identifiers: LCCN 2018059662 (print) | ISBN 9781534425330 (hardcover) |
ISBN 9781534425354 (eBook)
Classification: LCC PZ7.1.M568 Cur 2019 (print) | DDC [Fic]—dc23
LC record available at https://lccn.loc.gov/2018059662

To Marjorie Brigham Miller

-F. M.

For Luca and Amelia,

The two greatest adventures of my life.

May you both seize the sword in your own stories.

-T. W.

But there was heard among the holy hymns,
A voice as of the waters, for she dwells
Down in a deep; calm, whatsœver storms
May shake the world, and when the surface rolls,
Hath power to walk the waters like our Lord.
—ALFRED LORD TENNYSON,
*Idylls of the King*


Well, said Merlin,
I know whom thou seekest,
for thou seekest Merlin;
therefore seek no farther,
for I am he.
—THOMAS MALORY,
*Le Morte d'Arthur*

THE WATER STIRRED AND NIMUE ROSE SLOWLY FROM THE POND,
THE SWORD OF POWER CLUTCHED IN HER FISTS . . .

# ONE

FROM HER HIDING PLACE IN THE STRAW
pile and through eyes filled with tears, Nimue thought Father
Carden looked like a spirit of light. It was how he stood, back to
the bleached sun, and the way the clouds poured under his draping sleeves and upraised palms, like a man standing on the sky. His trem-
bling voice rose above the din of bleating goats, crackling wood, screaming
infants, and wailing mothers. "God is love. It is a love that purifies, a love
that sanctifies, a love that unites us." Carden's pale blue eyes passed over
the piteous, howling mob, prostrated in the mud, barricaded by monks in
red robes.

"And God sees," Carden continued, "and today he smiles. Because
we have done His work today. We have washed ourselves clean with

God's love. We have seared away the rotten flesh." The clouds of smoke billowing around Carden's arms and legs swirled with flakes of red ash. Spit flecked his lips. "Sawed away the corruption of demonism. Expelled the blackened humors from this land. God smiles today!" As Carden lowered his arms, his draping sleeves dropped away like curtains, revealing an inferno of thirty burning crosses in the field behind him. The crucified were hard to see in the thick black smoke.

Biette, a sturdy block of a woman and mother of four, rose up like a wounded bear and hobbled on her knees toward Carden before one of the tonsured monks in red stepped forward, planted his boot between her shoulder blades and kicked her face-first into the mud. And there Biette stayed, groaning into the wet earth.

Nimue's ears had been ringing since she and Pym rode into the village on Dusk Lady and saw the first dead body on the trail. They thought it might've been Mikkel, the tanner's boy, who grew orchids for the May rituals, but his head had been crushed by something heavy. They could not even stop to check, for the entire village was on fire and Red Paladins swarmed, their billowing robes dancing with the flames. On the fallow hill, a half-dozen village elders were already burning to death on hastily erected crosses. Pym's screams had seemed far away to Nimue as her mind went white. Everywhere she looked, she saw her people being choked in the mud or torn from their homes. Two paladins dragged old Betsy by her flailing arms and hair through her pen of geese. The birds squawked and fluttered in the air, adding to the surreal chaos. Shortly thereafter, Nimue and Pym were separated, and Nimue took shelter in the straw pile, where she held her breath as monks stomped past her carrying blanket bundles of confiscated goods. They unfurled the blankets on the floor of the open wagon where Carden stood, spilling the contents around his feet. The priest looked down and nodded, expecting this: roots of yew and alder, wooden figurines of elder gods, totems, and animal bones. Carden sighed patiently. "God sees, my friends. He sees these instruments of demonic conjuring. You cannot hide from Him. He shall dredge this poison out. And shielding others like you will only prolong your suffering." Father Carden brushed ashes from his gray tunic. "My Red Paladins are eager for your confessions. For your sakes, offer them freely, for my brothers are deft with the tools of inquisition."

The Red Paladins waded into the mob to single out targets for torture. Nimue watched as family and friends clawed over one another to avoid the paladins' reach. There were more screams as children were pried from their mothers' grips.

Unmoved, Father Carden stepped down from the wagon and crossed the muddy road to a tall and broad-shouldered monk in gray. His cheeks were lean beneath his cowl, and strange black birthmarks were blotted around his eyes and ran down his face like streaming tears of ink. Nimue could not hear their words for the shouting around her, but Carden rested a hand on the monk's shoulder, like a father, and pulled him into a whisper. Head bowed, the monk nodded several times in response to Carden's words. Carden gestured to the Iron Wood; the monk nodded a final time, then climbed onto his white courser.

Nimue turned to the Iron Wood and saw ten-year-old Squirrel standing in the monk's path, bewildered, blood dribbling down his cheek as he dragged a sword behind him. At this, Nimue burst from the straw pile and charged at Squirrel. She heard the Gray Monk's hoofbeats getting louder behind her.

"Nimue!" Squirrel reached for her, and she yanked him against the wall of a hut as the monk thundered past.

"I can't find Papa!" Squirrel cried.

"Squirrel, listen to me. Go to the hollow in the ash tree and hide there until it's night. Do you understand?"

Squirrel tried to pull away from her. "Papa!"

Nimue shook him. "Squirrel! Run now. As fast as you can. Are you listening!" Nimue was shouting into his face. Squirrel nodded. "Be a brave one. Run like you do in our fox races. No one can catch you."

"No one," Squirrel whispered, summoning the courage.

"You're the fastest of us all." Nimue swallowed back tears, for she did not want to let him go.

"You'll come?" Squirrel pleaded.

"I will," Nimue promised, "but first I have to find Pym and Mother and your father."

"I saw your mother near the temple." Squirrel hesitated. "They were chasing her."

Ice coursed through Nimue's veins at this news. She shot a look to the temple at the top of the rise. Then she turned back to Squirrel. "Fast as the fox," she commanded.

"Fast as the fox," Squirrel repeated, tensing as he shot furtive glances left and right. The nearest paladins were too occupied with the beating of a resisting farmer to notice them. So without a look back, Squirrel shot across the pasture for the Iron Wood.

Nimue lunged into the road and ran for the temple. She slid and fell in the mud dredged up from horses and blood. As she climbed to her feet, a horseman suddenly swung around from one of the burning huts. Nimue barely saw the ball of iron whip around on its chain. She tried to turn away, but it caught her at the base of her skull with such force it sent her nearly airborne into a pile of firewood. The world unglued as stars burst behind Nimue's eyes and she felt warm liquid stream down her neck and back. Splayed out on the ground, firewood all around her,

Nimue saw a longbow snapped in two pieces beside her. The broken bow. The fawn. The council. Hawksbridge.

Arthur.

It seemed impossible that only a day had passed. And as she lost consciousness, one thought left her choking with dread: this was all her fault.

# TWO

**B**UT WHY DO YOU HAVE TO LEAVE?"
Squirrel asked as he climbed over the moss-covered arm of a
broken statue.

"I'm not going yet," Nimue said, inspecting a bough of purple
flowers growing between the exposed roots of an ancient ash tree. She tried
to think of a way to change the subject, but Squirrel would not let it go.

"But why do you want to leave?"

Nimue hesitated. How could she tell him the truth? It would only hurt
and confuse him and lead to more questions. She wanted to leave because she
was unwanted in her own village. Feared. Judged. Whispered about. Pointed
at. Village children were told not to play with her because of the scars on her
back. Because of the dark stories of her childhood. Because her father had
left her. Because she was *cursed*. And perhaps she was. Her "connection"—

her mother's word; Nimue would call it "possession"—to the Hidden was strong and dark and different from any other Sky Folk she knew. And it came unbidden through her in strange, sometimes violent and unexpected ways, in visions or fits, or sometimes the ground would buckle or tremble or wooden objects near her would warp into grotesque masses. The sensation was like vomiting. And the feelings after were the same: sweaty, ashamed, empty. It was only her mother's prominence as Arch Druid that kept Nimue from being chased out of the village with knives and sticks. Why burden Squirrel with it all? His mother, Nella, was like a sister to her mother and like an aunt to Nimue. So she had kindly spared Squirrel all the dark gossip. To him, Nimue was normal, even boring (especially on nature walks), and that was just how she liked it. But she knew it wouldn't last.

She felt a pang of guilt as she looked over the primordial green slopes of the Iron Wood, buzzing and chirping and chattering with life, and the mysterious faces of Old Gods, faces that pushed through the vines and black earth, faces she had named through the years: Big Nose, the Sad Lady, Scar Bald, remnants of a long-dead civilization. Leaving here would be like leaving old friends.

Rather than confuse Squirrel, Nimue kept up the lie. "I don't know, Squirrel. Don't you ever long to see things you've never seen before?"

"Like a Moon Wing?"

Nimue smiled. Squirrel's eyes were always searching the canopy of the forest for a glimpse of a Moon Wing. "Yes, or the ocean? Or the Lost Cities of the Sun Gods? The Floating Temples?"

"They're not real," said Squirrel.

"How do we know unless we look for them?"

Squirrel put his hands on his hips. "Are you going to leave and never come back like Gawain?"

Nimue glowed inside at the name. She remembered being seven years old, her arms clutched around Gawain's neck as he carried her on his back through these very same woods. At fourteen, he knew the special gifts of every blossom, leaf, and bark of the Iron Wood, remedies, poisons, which tea-brewed leaves bestowed visions and which captured hearts, which chewed barks induced labor and which bird's nests predicted the weather. She recalled sitting between his knees, his long arms draped over her like a big brother's, as kite hatchlings meeped in their laps while Gawain taught her how to read the patterns inside the broken eggs for clues to the health of the forest.

He never judged Nimue for her scars. His smile was always easy and kind.

"He might come back someday," Nimue said with more hope than belief.

"Is that who you're going looking for?" Squirrel grinned.

"What? No, don't be ridiculous." Nimue pinched Squirrel on the arm.

"Ow!"

"Now pay attention," Nimue demanded, exaggerating a glower, "because I'm tired of saving your butt during lessons."

Nimue pointed to a shrub defended by nettles.

Squirrel rolled his eyes. "Osha root. It protects us from the dark magic."

"And?"

Squirrel scrunched his nose, thinking. "Good for sore throats?"

"Lucky guess," Nimue teased. She lifted a rock, exposing small white blossoms.

Squirrel picked for a booger, deep in thought. "Bloodwort, for hexes," he said, "and for hangovers."

"What do you know about hangovers?" Nimue shoved Squirrel gently, and he giggled as he somersaulted backward into the soft moss. She chased after him, but she'd never catch Squirrel. He shot under the drooping chin of the Sad Lady and leaped to a branch that allowed for an unobstructed view of Dewdenn's pastures and huts.

Nimue joined him, a bit out of breath, enjoying the breeze in her hair.

"I'll miss you," Squirrel said simply, taking her hand.

"You will?" Nimue gave him a little hip check and pulled his sweaty head to her ribs. "I'll miss you, too."

"Does your mum know you're leaving?"

Nimue was considering her answer when she felt the hum in her stomach of the Hidden. She stiffened. It was an ugly feeling, like a thief climbing in her window. Her throat went dry. She croaked a little when she nudged Squirrel and said, "Run along now. Lesson over."

That was music to Squirrel's ears. "Yay! No more learning!" He darted between boulders and was gone, leaving Nimue alone with her queasy stomach.

The Sky Folk were no strangers to the Hidden, invisible nature spirits from whom Nimue's clan were believed to be descended. Indeed, Sky Folk rituals invoked the Hidden for all matters great and small. While the Arch Druid presided over the crucial ceremonies of the year and arbitrated disputes between elders and families, the Summoner was expected to call upon the Hidden to bless the harvest or bring the rain, ease a birth, guide spirits back to the sun. Yet as Nimue had learned early on as a child, these invocations, these calls to the Hidden, were largely ceremonial. The Hidden rarely answered. Almost never. Even the Summoner, chosen for their believed connection to the Hidden, were usually left to intuit the spirits' messages by reading the clouds or tasting the dirt. For most Sky Folk, the Hidden came in a trickle, a dewdrop. To Nimue, it was a rushing river.

But this feeling, in this moment, was different. The hum throbbed in her belly, but a calm settled over the Iron Wood, a stillness. Nimue's heart kicked in her chest, but it wasn't only from fear but anticipation. Like something was coming. She heard it in the rattle of leaves, the hum of cicadas, the hush of the breeze. Inside those sounds, Nimue could hear words, like the murmur of excited voices in a crowded room. It gave her hope for a communion that made sense. That gave answers. That told her why she was different.

She sensed movement and turned to a small fawn standing quite close to her. The hum in her belly grew louder. The fawn stared at Nimue with deep black eyes that were older than the dead stump beneath her and older than the sunlight on her cheeks.

*Don't be afraid.* Nimue heard the voice, and it was not her thought. It was the fawn's. *Death is not the end.*

Nimue could not breathe. She feared to move. The silence roared in her ears. An overwhelming awe, like the expanses of a dream, filled the space behind her eyes. She fought the urge to run or squeeze her eyes shut, as she usually did until the wave passed. No, she wanted to be awake to this moment. Finally, after so many years, the Hidden wanted to tell her something.

The sun went behind a cloud and the forest grew dark and cold. Nimue held the fawn's gaze despite her fear. She was the daughter of the Arch Druid and would not flinch from the secret mind of the Hidden.

Nimue heard herself ask, "Who will die?"

She heard the twang of catgut, a whistle, and an arrow thudded into the fawn's neck. A burst of blackbirds erupted from the trees as the connection was severed. Nimue whirled around in a fury. There was Josse, one of the shepherd's twins, pumping his fist in victory. Nimue turned back to the fawn lying in the dirt, its eyes glazed and empty.

"What have you done?" Nimue shouted as Josse pushed through the branches to retrieve his kill.

"What's it look like? I was fetching supper." Josse grabbed the fawn by the back legs and hauled it onto his shoulders.

Silvery vines crept up Nimue's neck and cheek as her temper flashed, and Josse's longbow contorted impossibly, then snapped in his hands, cutting the flesh. Shocked, he dropped the fawn and the bow to the ground, where it writhed on the ground like a dying snake.

Josse looked up at Nimue. Unlike Squirrel, he knew all the dark gossip. "You crazy hag!"

He shoved Nimue hard against the stump as he reached for his ruined bow. Nimue wound up to punch Josse's face in when her mother appeared, specter-like, at the edge of the wood.

"Nimue." Lenore's voice was icy enough to cool Nimue's temper.

Snuffling, Josse gathered the fawn and the bow pieces and tromped off. "You'll hear of this, you bloody witch! They're right about you!"

Nimue shot right back, "Good! Be afraid! And leave me alone!"

Josse stormed off, and Nimue was left to wither under Lenore's disapproving gaze.

Moments later Nimue trailed behind her mother, who walked the smooth stones of the Sacred Sun Path toward the veiled entrance to the Sunken Temple. Though she never seemed to rush, Lenore was always ten steps ahead.

"You will find the wood, you will carve it, and you will string the bow," Lenore told her.

"Josse is a half-wit."

"And you will apologize to his father," Lenore continued.

"Anis? Another half-wit. It would be nice if you took my side for once."

"That fawn will feed many hungry mouths," Lenore reminded her.

"It was more than a fawn," Nimue countered.

"The proper rituals will be offered."

Nimue shook her head. "You're not even listening."

Lenore turned, fierce. "What, Nimue, what? What is it I'm not hearing?" She lowered her voice. "You know what they say. You know how they feel. This sort of outburst only feeds their fear."

"It's not my fault," Nimue said, hating the shame she felt.

"But your anger is your own. That is your fault. You show no discipline. No care. Last month it was Hawlon's fence—"

"He spits on the ground when I pass!"

"Or the fire in Gifford's barn—"

"You keep bringing that up!"

"You keep giving me reason to!" Lenore took Nimue by the shoulders. "This is your clan. These are your people, not your enemies."

"It's not like I haven't tried. I have! But they won't accept me. They hate me."

"Then teach them. Help them understand. Because one day you'll have to help lead them. When I'm gone—"

"Lead them?" Nimue laughed.

"You are gifted," Lenore said. "You see them, you experience them in ways that I will never understand. But such a gift is a privilege, not a right, to be received with grace and humility."

"It's not a gift."

A distant bell sounded. Lenore held up Nimue's torn and muddied hem. "You couldn't make an exception? This one day?"

Nimue shrugged, a little embarrassed.

Lenore sighed. "Come."

She proceeded carefully through a veil of clinging vines and down a set of ancient stairs, slick with mud and moss. Nimue grazed her hands along the sculpted walls, which depicted ancient myths of the Old Gods, to steady her descent into the enormous Sunken Temple. The sun poured hundreds of feet down through a natural vent in the canopy to bathe the altar stone.

"Why do I have to attend this at all?" Nimue said, padding along the tilting path that spiraled all the way to the bottom.

"We are choosing the Summoner who will one day be the Arch Druid. Today is an important day, and you are my daughter and should be by my side."

Nimue rolled her eyes as they reached the temple floor, where the village elders had already gathered. A few of them glowered at her presence, and she made a point of avoiding the circle and slouching against one of the far walls.

Kneeling before the altar in meditation was the son of Gustave the Healer, Clovis, a young Druid who had been a loyal acolyte to Lenore and was respected for his wide scholarship in healing magic.

The Elders sat cross-legged in the circle as Lenore took Clovis's hand and helped him to stand. Gustave the Healer was also present, dressed in his finest, beaming with pride. He sat with the elders as Lenore turned to address them. "As Sky Folk we give thanks to the light that gives life. We are born in the dawn . . ."

"To pass in the twilight," the elders answered in unison.

Lenore paused, closing her eyes. Her head tilted as though listening to something. After a moment, glowing marks, like silvery vines threaded up the right side of her neck, up her cheek, and around her ear.

The Fingers of Airimid appeared on Nimue's cheeks and those of the elders in the circle.

Lenore opened her eyes. "The Hidden are now present." She went on, "Since our dear Agatha passed, we have been without a Summoner. This has left us without a successor, without a Keeper of Relics and without a Harvest Priest. Agatha also shared a deep communion with the Hidden. She was a dear and devoted friend. She will never be replaced. But the nine moons have passed, and it is time to name a new Summoner. And while there are many attributes that a Summoner should possess, none is more important than an abiding relationship to the Hidden. And though we love our Clovis"—Lenore offered a reassuring smile to the young Druid standing by the altar—"we still need the Hidden to anoint our choice of Summoner."

Lenore whispered ancient words and lifted her arms. The light spilling in from above took on a sharpness, like the fires of the forge, and tiny sparks plumed away from the light to dance in the air. The same light drifted from the moss that covered the obelisks and ancient boulders, mixing with the sparks into a flowing luminous cloud.

Clovis shut his eyes and spread out his arms to receive the blessing of the Hidden. The sparks drifted toward him in an amorphous mass, then curled and twisted away from him and the altar, lengthening and stretching toward Nimue, who watched, eyes gradually widening, as the cloud poured over her. She lifted an arm to shield herself, though the sparks caused her no pain.

But what was happening caused a stir among the circle of Elders.

Lenore stood tall, with an expression of wonder, as the murmurs of protest grew into raised voices. Gustave stood up to protest. "This—this ritual is impure."

One of the others said, "Clovis is in line."

And another, "Nimue is a distraction."

"Clovis is talented and kind, and I value his counsel. But the decision to name the Summoner belongs to the Hidden," Lenore said.

"What?" Nimue said out loud. She felt cornered by their accusing stares. Her cheeks burned and she shot her mother a furious look as she tried to escape the cloud, climbing to her feet, but the light particles were determined to follow her, bathing her in light at the very moment she wished to be invisible.

Florentin the miller appealed to logic. "But Lenore, surely you can't suggest . . . I mean, Nimue is too young for such responsibilities."

"True, at sixteen years she would be young for a Summoner," Lenore acknowledged, speaking as though not surprised by the turn of events, "but her rapport with the Hidden should outweigh such considerations. Above all else, the Summoner is expected to know the mind of the Hidden and to guide the Sky Folk to balance and harmony on both planes of existence. Since she was very young, the Hidden have been drawn to Nimue."

Lucien, a venerable Druid, who supported his bent frame with a sturdy branch of yew, asked, "It isn't only the Hidden who seek her out, is it?"

The scars on her back tingled. Nimue knew where this was going.

Lenore's lips pursed ever so slightly, the only sign of her fury.

Lucien scratched his white and patchy beard, feigning innocence. "After all, she is marked by dark magic."

"We are not children, Lucien. They may call us Sun Dancers, but that does not mean we are ignorant of the shadow. Yes, when she was very young, Nimue was lured to the Iron Wood by a dark spirit and would have very likely been killed, or worse, were it not for the intervention of the Hidden. One might suggest that event alone makes her a worthy Summoner."

"That is the story we've been told," Lucien sneered.

Nimue wanted to shrink and crawl into a rat hole. And the light particles would not leave her. Annoyed, she waved them off, but they would disperse only to return to her like a halo.

"What exactly are you suggesting about my daughter, Lucien?"

Gustave tried to play peacemaker and to preserve his son's chances of being Summoner. "Let us simply have another go at the ritual with Nimue not present."

"Do we now question the wisdom of the Hidden if we do not prefer their choice?" Lenore asked.

"She is a corrupter!" Lucien snapped.

"You take that back," Lenore warned him.

Lucien pressed on, "We're not alone in our suspicions. *Her own father rejected her*, choosing to abandon his own clan rather than live under the same roof as she."

Nimue stepped into the circle of Elders. "I don't want to be your bloody Summoner! Happy now? I don't want it!" Before Lenore could stop her, Nimue spun and raced up the winding path as the shouting voices below her echoed off the ancient stone walls.

# THREE

NIMUE COULD ONLY BREATHE AGAIN
when she erupted into the fresh air of the Iron Wood, choking back tears, too furious to let herself cry. She wanted to
drown that old fool Lucien and tear her mother's hair out for
making her sit through that mockery of a ceremony.

Pym, Nimue's best friend, was tall and gangly and was struggling to
carry a sheaf of wheat across the field when she saw Nimue marching
down the hill, away from the forest.

"Nimue!" Pym dropped her sheaf and caught up with Nimue, who
brushed past her. "What is it?"

"I'm Summoner." Nimue kept on charging.

Pym swung a look to the barrow and then back to Nimue. "You're
what? Wait, did Lenore say that?"

"Who cares?" Nimue spat. "It's all a joke."

"Slow down." Pym loped after her, already weary from lugging the wheat.

"I hate it here. I'm leaving. I'm getting on that ship today."

"What happened?" Pym swung Nimue around.

Nimue's expression was fierce, but there were tears in her eyes. She quickly wiped them away on her sleeve.

Pym softened. "Nimue?"

"They don't want me here. And I don't want them." Nimue's voice trembled.

"You're not making any sense."

Nimue ducked into the small wood-and-mud hut she shared with her mother and pulled a sack out from under her bed, while Pym huffed in the doorway. Inside the sack were a heavy woolen cloak, mittens and extra stockings, wood-ash soap, flint, an empty waterskin, nuts, and dried apples. She took a few honey cakes from the table, then was out the door as quickly as she'd come.

Pym followed her. "Where are you going?"

"Hawksbridge," Nimue answered.

"Now? Are you mad?"

Before Nimue could answer, shouts arose. She and Pym looked down the road and saw a boy being helped from a horse. Even from a distance, Nimue could see the horse's white coat was smeared with blood. One of the village men carried the boy in his arms. The boy's skin was light blue, his arms were unnaturally long and thin, and his fingers were spindly, ideal for climbing.

"It's a Moon Wing," Pym whispered.

The villagers hurried the injured Moon Wing boy into the Healer's hut, and scouts rushed to the Iron Wood to inform the Elders. Led by Lenore, they all emerged from the forest with serious expressions. They

passed Pym and Nimue with scarcely a glance, except for Lucien, who gave Nimue a crooked smile as he hobbled to the Healer's hut.

Nimue and Pym knelt down by the shutters as Lenore and the Elders gathered inside the hut. Moon Wings were a rare sight anywhere, being shy and nocturnal, adapted to life in the canopy of the deep forests. Their feet rarely touched the ground, and their skin could take on the color and texture of the bark of whatever tree they were climbing. Besides that, ancient bad blood between Sky Folk and Moon Wings made this boy's appearance in Dewdenn all the more strange and disturbing.

The boy's chest rattled as he spoke, and his voice was weak. "They came by day as we slept. They wore red robes." The boy coughed raggedly, and the rattle worsened. "They set fire to the forest, trapping us in the branches. Many died in their sleep from the smoke. Others leaped to their deaths. For those who made it to the ground, the Gray Monk, the one who cries, was waiting. He cut us down. Hanged the rest of us on their crosses." Another jag of coughing left the boy breathless and his lips wet with blood. Lenore soothed him as Gustave hurried about, preparing a poultice.

"This is no longer a southern problem. The Red Paladins are moving north. We're right in their path," warned Felix, a barrel-chested farmer and one of the Elders.

"Until we learn more about their movement and numbers, no one is to travel," Lenore said.

Florentin spoke up. "How do we sell our goods without market day?"

"We'll send out scouts today. Hopefully this restriction will only take us through one moon cycle. In the meantime we'll make do. Open the fields. Share. And we should reach out to the other clans."

As the Elders debated, Nimue pulled Pym away from the window and headed for the stables.

"What, you're still going?" Pym asked.

"Of course," Nimue said. Waiting would only make things worse. It had to be now.

"Your mother just told us we can't go to Hawksbridge."

Nimue entered the stables, grabbed her saddle from a hook, and prepared her palfrey, Dusk Lady, for riding.

"I'm not letting you get on any ship. I'm not saying goodbye."

Nimue tried to be stern. "Pym—"

"I'm not." Pym folded her arms.

Hawksbridge was a ten-mile ride through rolling hills and dense forest. It was large enough to draw entertainers and mercenaries to its taverns and hold a decent market on every other Thursday, so to Sky Folk like Nimue and Pym, it was Rome, it was all the world. A heavy wooden fort overlooked the town from a northern rise. More than a dozen hanged men fed the crows from the fort's highest wall, a grim warning to strangers and thieves.

Pym shuddered at the sight. She pulled the hood of her cloak tighter around her face. "These cloaks are crap disguises. And I've been doing chores all day. I smell."

"I told you not to come," Nimue reminded her. "And you don't smell. Much."

"I hate you," Pym growled.

"You're beautiful and you smell like violets," Nimue soothed, though she tucked her hair under her own hood just to be safe. Fey Kind wore their hair down, unlike women in town, who wore it under a wimple or head covering.

"This is madness," Pym said.

"It's why you love me."

"I don't love you. I'm still going to stop you and I'm angry you're doing this."

"I bring adventure to your life."

"You bring stress and punishment to my life."

The guards at the eastern gate allowed Pym and Nimue through with little fuss. The girls stabled Dusk Lady in a stall near the gate and walked to the port at Scarcroft Bay, a small harbor for local fishermen and sea traders. Loud gulls hovered about the hulks and small cogs, then dove to the dozens of filled traps of catch lining the docks, fighting over the squirming contents.

As they approached the crowded, noisy dock, Nimue could feel Pym shaking with nerves.

"How do you even know they'll take you on?" Pym asked.

"The *Brass Shield* takes on a few dozen pilgrims every journey. I was told this was the ship Gawain took. It's the only ship that crosses the sea to the Desert Kingdoms." Nimue swerved around a boy with a box of live crabs.

"Of course it's the only ship that goes to the Desert Kingdoms. What does that tell you? That no one wants to go to the Desert Kingdoms, that's what. Honestly, what is the fuss about? Being named Summoner is a huge honor. The robes are glorious and you get to wear amazing jewelry. Where is the problem?"

"It's more complicated than that," Nimue said. She loved Pym like a sister, but she never liked to talk about the Hidden. Pym liked what she could see and what she could touch. It was one area, really the only area with Pym, where Nimue kept her feelings to herself.

"At least your mother wants you home. Mine keeps trying to marry me off to the fishmonger."

Nimue nodded, sympathetic. "Stinky Aaron."

Pym glared at her. "It's not funny."

As Nimue took in the enormity of what she was about to do, she grew serious. She turned to Pym, wanting her to understand. "The Elders won't accept me." It was half the truth.

"Who cares what those shriveled onions think?"

"But what if they're right not to?"

Pym shrugged. "So, you have visions."

"And the scars."

"They give you character?" Pym offered. "I mean, I'm trying to be helpful here."

Nimue laughed and hugged her. "What will I do without you?"

Pym welled up. "Then stay, you idiot."

Nimue shook her head sadly, then turned and marched back to the dock. Pym hurried behind her like a worried hen.

"What if they find out you're Fey Kind? What if they see the Fingers of Airimid?" Pym whispered.

"They won't," Nimue hissed back. "You'll take care of Dusk Lady?"

"Yes. What about money?"

"I have twenty silver." Nimue sighed, exasperated.

"But what if they rob you?"

"Pym, enough!" Nimue half shouted as she approached the bald and sweating harbormaster, who was waving off aggressive gulls at his table.

"Pardon me, sir, but which of these is the *Brass Shield*?" Nimue asked.

The port master never looked up from his lists. "*Brass Shield* left yesterday."

"But I thought—I thought . . ." Nimue turned to Pym. "Gawain left in midwinter. It's only November. It should still be here."

"Tell that to the easterly winds," the harried port master countered, his voice edged with annoyance.

"When does it return?" Nimue pleaded, escape slipping away.

The port master looked up, his eyes drooping, and scowled. "Six months! Now do you mind?" A shoving match between fishermen ensued nearby, upsetting traps and scattering birds. The port master forgot

Nimue and Pym immediately and ran over to the scrum. "Oy! None of that here! Knock that off!"

Nimue turned to her friend, eyes brimming with tears. "What do I do now?"

Pym tucked Nimue's hair beneath her hood. "Well, at least I get to keep you a bit longer."

Nimue looked out to the horizon, trying to contemplate another six months in the village. It felt like an eternity.

Pym wrapped an arm around her shoulder. "You make peace with your mum." She began to drag Nimue back to the stables.

"A pilgrim caravan," Nimue decided, turning suddenly and marching back into town.

"Pilgrims? Pilgrims hate the Fey. That's the very last place you should be seen."

Nimue knew she was grasping at straws, but returning to Dewdenn was not an option.

Pym took her arm. Nimue could tell that her friend was determined to wear her down.

"Wait, I know," Pym said, changing tactics. "I'll be Summoner and you marry Stinky Aaron."

Nimue's scowl cracked. "I'm not—"

"Oh! So your life's not so horrible after all!"

Nimue dashed off, and Pym chased her.

It was market day, and the narrow street was barely navigable for the steers pulling wagons of grain, packhorses hauling blocks of stone for the cathedral under construction, and barefoot farm boys chasing an errant gaggle of geese. A family of four, pilgrims by their dress, scowled at the girls, and the father muttered something under his breath as they passed.

"Pilgrims," Pym pointed out. "Even with our cloaks, they know we're Fey. Why didn't you ask them for a ride?"

Nimue frowned.

"We'll get some bread and cheese for the road and go home while there is still light," Pym said. She pulled Nimue along as the street opened up into the wide city square. Their mouths watered as they walked through a warm cloud of baking bread. The baker's wife had set out a table of fresh king's loaves beside another table of brie tarts and spice cakes. A juggler in a threadbare tunic jumped at them, as players erected a stage nearby.

As Pym applauded, Nimue's eyes drifted across the square and landed upon two horsemen in red monks' robes, observing the crowd with sullen faces. They were barely men, the same age as Nimue and Pym, and wore their hair in matching, bald-pated tonsures. Both were thin, though one appeared to be a good head taller than his fellow brother. Nimue's hand squeezed around Pym's wrist and her eyes directed Pym's to the horsemen. "I think it's them."

"Who?" Pym searched the crowd.

"Red Paladins."

Pym gasped and her hand flew to her mouth.

"Don't make a fuss," Nimue warned.

Pym lowered her hand, but her eyes were wide and frightened.

"I want to get closer," Nimue said, fighting off Pym's efforts to pull her back. She eased her way through the crowd as the Red Paladins spurred their horses into a stroll around the opposite edge of the market square, along a row of craft stalls. They paused at a table of swords. One of the monks said something to the blacksmith, who nodded, then selected a dagger among the blades on the table and handed it to the other monk. He inspected the blade, shrugged his approval, and slid it into a fold of one of his saddlebags, then nudged his horse forward to the next stall. The blacksmith called out angrily for payment. The smaller monk spun around on his horse, trotted up to the blacksmith, and stuck his boot in his chest, shoving the blacksmith into his table of swords and spilling his wares. The Red Paladin circled around, waiting to see if the blacksmith had any more words for him. He did not. He retreated into his stall. The monk snorted and looked around to see if anyone else felt brave. Merchants and peasants alike kept their heads down and walked a wide circle around the monk, who, satisfied, rejoined his brother with the stolen dagger.

"They just stole it," Nimue said, affronted.

"So what?" Pym whispered, stooping to make herself shorter and less visible in the crowd.

Nimue's guts twisted with anger. She pursued the paladins from fifty paces back, mindful to use the pilgrims, farmworkers, and peddlers as cover. But hiding became more of a challenge when the paladins turned onto a narrow street at the corner of the town hall and the weight master. Nimue pulled Pym into an open arcade of vaulted arches, where baskets of herbs and vegetables were for sale. Nimue could follow the bob of the monks' heads between the columns until they rode out of view. She paused a few moments before dragging Pym to the edge of the arcade and then onto the narrow road. Packhorses clogged the street between Nimue and the paladins, who joined another pair of brothers on horseback beneath a three-story scaffold where, high above, tillers patched a weather-beaten roof. Nimue and Pym found shelter in a doorway thirty paces back as the Red Paladins conferred in low voices.

"We've seen them. Now let's go," Pym hissed in Nimue's ear, and tugged on her sleeve.

Nimue exited the doorway, leaving Pym behind, and slid in beside another packhorse lumbering onto the street from the market square. She walked alongside the animal for several paces. A moment later the packhorse interrupted the Red Paladins' conference, the street not being wide enough for them all. A mason atop his wagon of stones winced. "Apologies, brothers," he called as he tried to steer around the group. The monks scowled as their horses backstepped and adjusted around the mason's wagon. Amid this disruption, Nimue walked quickly between the Red Paladins' horses, drew the stolen dagger from the thief's saddle-bag, and smoothly hid it within her sleeve. When the shorter monk turned in Nimue's direction, all he saw was a flash of skirts as she swung around the corner into another alley.

Pym hurried out of the doorway and ran back into the bustle of the arcade. Her breathing had just started to settle when a long blade appeared at her throat. She froze.

"Give me all your coins!" Nimue snarled in Pym's ear.

Pym spun around and slapped at a laughing Nimue, until she herself was laughing.

"Ow! Stop it! You're bruising me!" Nimue covered her head.

"I won't stop, crazy woman!" Pym kept at it until a farm woman shouted at them both for upsetting a pail of cabbages. The girls ran and shoved through the crowd back into the square. Nimue walked up to the blacksmith's stall as a hammer rang in the tent and returned the stolen dagger to its place on the table of blades.

# FOUR

THEY WANDERED TOWARD THE SOUND OF
music. Two young men had propped their swords against a wagon
wheel and were staging an impromptu concert. Nimue took note of
the number of young ladies who were swaying to the singer's voice:

*"With meadows green and skies o' blue,*
*My mistress struck her arrow true,*
*We kissed and danced 'neath Virgo's eye,*
*As the waxing moon fled from July."*

Curious, she fixed her gaze on the singer. He had a boyish face and
was lean with broad shoulders and longish hair that flashed copper in
the sun. His more lumpish friend played an able ruan.

*"Sing high-lolly-lo say my fair summer lady,*
*Sing high-lolly-li-summer-hi-lolly-lo."*

The young singer's voice was pleasing, though he struggled with the higher notes. But there was something about him that fixed Nimue to the spot. The hum of the Hidden swelled in her belly and behind her ear. She touched her cheek to make sure the Fingers of Airimid were not growing. *Who is he?* she wondered. He wasn't Fey that she could tell. But the Hidden were trying to tell her something about this boy. She tried to will the hum away, push it down, but it persisted. Was it a warning? A summons? A mix of both?

Pym clucked her tongue and elbowed Nimue.

*"But autumn gusts do blow cold, summer lady,*
*The swallows fly south from their nests in the bailey."*

The singer's eyes fell on Nimue and the verse held on his tongue.

*"And the warm wine . . ."*

Nimue's cheeks flushed. She looked away, embarrassed, then allowed herself to look the singer in his gray eyes, eyes that reminded her of the wolf cubs of the Iron Wood, alert, playful, and soon to be dangerous. He resumed his verse.

*". . . but there came a maid with blue eyes like ice on the sea,*
*Sing high-lolly-lo say my fair winter lady . . ."*

The singer smiled at Nimue.

"He fancies you," Pym whispered in her ear. Nimue laughed despite herself. But between the hum in her belly and the singer's gray eyes, it was too much, and she turned back into the crowded market, where a juggler danced between a ring of children. He fumbled his balls, and one of them rolled past Nimue and was retrieved by the young singer. But rather than return the ball to the juggler, he offered it to Nimue instead. "Miss, you dropped this."

Nimue took the ball and smirked. "Do I look like a juggler to you?"

The boy considered her. "Ah yes, I know what's missing."

By this time the juggler had tracked down the singer, but he didn't get his ball. The singer stole his player's cap and set it atop Nimue's head. "Perfect!" he declared.

Pym snorted, the player protested, and Nimue allowed his teasing enough to brag, "I only juggle fire."

The singer wagged a finger at her. "I suspected as much."

Judging by his rough manners and hand-me-down tunic, Nimue pegged the boy as a sword for hire. Sky Folk were taught to avoid his type on the forest roads near Dewdenn.

The juggler was losing his sense of humor and stole his ball back from Nimue as the singer plopped the minstrel hat upon his own head. "No more charade. In truth, I am the great juggling master Giuseppe Fuzzini Fuzzini—two Fuzzinis—et cetera! And I am looking for a juggling apprentice to follow in my footsteps." The singer grabbed two turnips from the barrel of a farmer's stall and began his own juggling routine, playing keep-away from the juggler, who now competed with the children in jumping for his hat. Nimue couldn't help but snort with laughter. The young mercenary attempted to kick his heels and juggle at the same time, which taxed his already limited talents to the breaking point. Mercenary and turnips spilled over in a heap.

"Fancy an ale?" the singer asked, leading Pym and Nimue away from the angry farmer and toward a raucous tavern named the Raven Wing.

"Sorry, we should be getting home," Pym said.

"We have developed a thirst," Nimue said, striding past the singer.

"Splendid." He smiled and followed her to the tavern.

"I'm Arthur," the singer said as he set down two mugs of ale for Pym and Nimue and pulled up a chair to a small table in the crowded Raven Wing. Pym's eyes darted all around. The city crowd gave them suspicious looks.

"Nimue. This is Pym." Nimue nudged Pym, who smiled fleetingly.

"That's a lovely name, 'Nimue,'" Arthur said, raising his mug to her. "I must say I like the cloaks, very mysterious. Are you sisters of the convent or something?"

"We're hired assassins," Nimue said.

"I suspected as much." Arthur played along, though Nimue could tell he was still trying to pin them down.

"You live in Hawksbridge?" he asked.

"Near enough," Nimue said, in no rush to answer Arthur's questions. *It's one ale with a local boy, what harm can it do?* She took a sip. Her lips tingled as she swallowed her first gulp. The ale was sour and warm, but she noticed its taste improved the more she drank. "And you?"

"Just passing through, really."

"Are you a sword for hire?"

"Not at all. We're knights," Arthur said. He jerked his head at an unruly table nearby, where several rough fellows played bone dice. A local stood up from the table and snarled, "Bunch of cheats!" The large mercenary with the dice wore a chain-mail shirt and sported a bald pate with several battle dents to match his crooked nose. He stood up with enough menace to hurry the local away, and then his dull eyes kept glancing at Pym and Nimue.

"Bors over there commanded Lord Adelard's host before the old fellow's heart gave out," Arthur said.

Bors was certainly no knight. He and his party laughed and shouted like men looking for a fight. Other locals kept their noses in their drinks. The Raven Wing was growing fuller. The sun flared through the window over the western gate. A bard was tuning his rebec as Pym's voice reached an anxious pitch.

"...by nightfall! Hello? Nimue? Your mother will tan our hides!"

"Then no point carrying on about it." Another local lost at bone dice to Bors. He handed over a pouch of coins as the "knights" jeered at him.

"Nimue, do you hear me? The woods aren't safe at night, and we don't have the coin to stay here. What are we going to do?"

"Don't go just yet," Arthur said, laying a gentle hand on Nimue's arm.

"Arthur! What're you hiding for?" Bors barked. "Bring those fine maids over to say hello!"

Arthur winced, caught himself, then fashioned a smile. He rose as the men at Bors's table muttered and laughed.

Pym turned pleading eyes toward her, but Nimue finished her ale, wiped her mouth with her sleeve, and followed Arthur to the gaming table. *This is what being out in the world is like*, she told herself. *An adventure around every corner.* She imagined herself winning a sack of coins and buying herself a cushioned chair in a luxurious trader caravan headed to the southern seas. Or, more practically speaking, a few coins could buy her and Pym room and board and a chance to weigh her next steps. The ale gave her a swagger as she stepped up to the table behind Arthur.

"Gents—" Arthur started.

Bors interrupted. "Lads, Arthur's found himself some lovely company."

Nimue didn't like the way the men laughed. She saw a table of Josses, a lot of empty heads and bluster.

"Come now, girls, part the robes, let's see the goods." Bors eyed Pym and Nimue like cattle.

"Carry on, boys," Arthur said, starting to escort the girls away.

"I'll have a go," Nimue said, ignoring the laughter. Bors's fat fingers counted coins on the table. The mercenary looked up at her.

"No. Bad idea," Arthur warned.

"Nimue," Pym hissed.

A wide grin broke over Bors's stubbly cheeks. "But of course, my dear." The other mercenaries guffawed loudly and whistled their approval.

"Does the lady have five silver?" Bors asked.

"I don't, I'm afraid."

"No matter, we allow different wagers." He paused and looked her over. "How 'bout we roll for a kiss?"

Pym grabbed Nimue's shoulder. "We were just leaving—"

Nimue pulled from her grasp. "Fine." There was a new round of whoops from the men.

Arthur shook his head. Nimue turned back to Bors. "But if I win, I get ten silver."

Bors chuckled. "That's a deal." He gathered the bone dice into his enormous hands. "Does the lady know how to play?"

"You pick a number?"

"Very close. All you need to do is roll a seven in any combination. Two and five. Three and four. Six and one. You see? The odds favor you, my sweet. It's very easy. I've just had a dumb rush of luck." Bors slid the dice across the table.

Nimue picked up the dice, felt them in her hand. They were weighted, of course. No fool would ever roll a seven with them. But Nimue was no fool. She rolled the dice on the table, and as they landed, she closed her eyes and reached out with her thoughts to the Hidden. She felt the tiniest hum in her belly and a slender thread of silver vine crept up her cheek, mostly concealed by the hood. *The Hidden are answering,* Nimue thought, pleased. Sometimes, in small doses, she could just barely guide the power.

But Pym saw the Fingers of Airimid, and her eyes widened with alarm.

The dice turned up three and four.

Bors stared at the bone dice. The sell-swords sat up. None of them spoke.

Bors looked up slowly at Nimue. "Roll them again."

"Why? I won."

Bors leaned forward and slid the dice to Nimue. "Best two out of three? Seems fair."

"Those weren't the rules," Nimue said.

"Roll again, Nimue, and then let's be off. Please," Pym begged.

"Then it's twenty silver if I win," Nimue demanded.

Bors sat back, chair creaking under his weight. "Can you believe this little maid?" He shook his head and barked with laughter. "You want twenty silver? Then I'll want my money's worth as well."

"Deal."

Pym grabbed at Nimue's arm. "Stop this."

Nimue took the dice, shook them in her hand. Again, the Fingers of Airimid crawled up her neck and behind her ear. She threw the dice on the table. A six and a one. The sell-swords raised up their hands and roared in disbelief, falling silent when they saw the look in Bors's eyes.

"Are you witching me?" he growled.

The Raven Wing was silent. Nimue felt many eyes upon her.

A distant voice in her mind said, *Run, you fool.* Nimue ignored it and smiled at Bors. "Why? Do you fear witches?" Her ears throbbed with the hum and the dam broke. The power spilled out of her and the wooden dice table blossomed with grotesque knobs and spikes and Bors's chair grew branch-like limbs that wrapped around his throat and chest. Bors gurgled and pulled the table down on top of himself along with cups of ale and jugs of wine, and the sell-swords leaped to their feet, terrified.

"Fey witches!" one of the sell-swords yelled.

"Oi! That's it! Off with you!" Pym and Nimue turned to see the bar-keep pointing at them. "We don't want your kind in here!"

"We're sorry," Pym managed. Nimue was in a daze. The magic had left her feeling weak, as if her bones were empty. She felt Pym pull her toward the door, and they bumped into the Red Paladin who had stolen the dagger. Nimue broke eye contact immediately, muttered, "I'm sorry, brother," and hurried out.

For the first time that day, a wave of fear crashed over her.

# FIVE

**N**IMUE AND PYM HURRIED DUSK LADY through the closing city gates. Most of the vendors had returned to their farms hours earlier. Visitors to Hawksbridge after nightfall would have to announce themselves to the watch guard.

A fingernail of moon shone dully through the clouds. Only a mile out from the city gates, the solitary sound on the road was the slow clop of Dusk Lady's hooves.

"Nimue, what was that? You know you can't do magic in town! They'll hang us for it!"

"I didn't mean to. I just—I'm not feeling very well." Nimue's head throbbed. They'd eaten very little, only a few biscuits from the village, and the ale had made her dizzy.

"Why would you pick a fight with those . . . ?"

"They don't scare me," Nimue muttered, still feeling weak. The Red Paladins were a different story, though. Her anger from earlier had burnt itself out, leaving her with only a sick feeling, like she had been removed from her body and was merely watching herself behave so recklessly.

"Half the village is likely searching for us." Pym was worried.

"I'm sorry, Pym. Try to sleep on me. I'll get us home."

Pym grunted, giving in to fatigue, and pressed the side of her face to Nimue's back. Nimue had no illusions about the two-hour ride ahead of them. Dusk Lady was no warhorse, and wolves could easily panic her. And it was no secret the glades were a sanctuary for thieves eager to sack the vendors fresh from market day with their pouches full of new coin.

Nimue's thoughts were interrupted by the sound of a horse approaching from behind. Pym stirred. "What is that?"

"Quiet," Nimue hushed her, and spun Dusk Lady in a circle, searching for a place to hide. Her heart pounded, but Dusk Lady chose that moment to turn stubborn, standing fixed in the middle of the road as Nimue dug her heels into the horse's ribs and a lone figure rode into the moonlight. Desperate, Nimue fished out a cheese knife she had hidden in the saddle. "Come no closer!"

Pym gripped her shoulders.

"I surrender," spoke a familiar voice. A black courser stepped out of the gloom. The young man held up a familiar piece of clothing. "Does this belong to one of you?"

At Arthur's presence, Nimue again felt the hum inside her. Her hand went to her throat, and for the first time she realized she'd lost her cloak.

"You came all this way just to return a cloak?"

"It's a nice one."

"Are you alone?" Nimue glanced into the darkness over Arthur's shoulder.

"Aye. Except for Egypt here." Arthur patted his horse's long neck.

Nimue urged Dusk Lady forward until she was close enough for Arthur to hand her the cloak.

"Never seen anyone treat Bors like that," he said, though Nimue couldn't tell if he was impressed or frightened of her.

She flung the cloak around her shoulders, loath to admit she was as afraid. "Pity. He could use more humility."

"You should be more careful."

"I don't need your advice," Nimue said, doing her best to sound confident but conscious that she'd taken things too far back at the tavern.

Arthur smiled, shaking his head. "Really? You have it all figured out, do you?"

Charming smile or not, his tone annoyed her. "At least as much as a young sell-sword who just does as he's told and keeps his mouth shut."

"Thank you," Pym interjected, "for the cloak. You didn't have to."

"I haven't met your kind before."

"And?" Nimue asked.

Arthur held up his hands. "Maybe you haven't seen as much of the world as you think. For example, there's a fellow name of Ring Nose, likes to set ambushes past the hook turn up the road." Pym looked alarmed.

"And let me guess: you know that because he works for you," Nimue said.

Arthur's ears reddened. "For Bors, on occasion."

"True knights," Nimue scoffed.

"Listen, these are dangerous days for Fey Folk to be witching men in broad daylight."

"We're not witches," Nimue shot back.

"Men like Bors are one thing," Arthur continued, "but the Red Paladins are another. I've seen the burning fields. Have you?"

"I've seen plenty," Nimue lied.

"You don't forget the smell. It hangs in the air for miles. The Southern lords keep inside their walls and give the paladins the run of—"

Nimue hushed Arthur. She listened. There had been a sound on the breeze.

All was quiet.

Then they heard the murmur of voices approaching from the glades.

"Someone's coming. Off the road." Nimue took the reins of Arthur's horse and spurred Dusk Lady down an embankment and into a dark pasture. She made breathy whistles to Dusk Lady, and she instinctively sought shelter in a huddle of young trees, not enough to hide them completely, but far enough. They waited in silence. Dusk Lady huffed and Nimue stroked her neck to shush her.

After an eternity, four riders came into view, pausing at the spot where they'd just stood. One of them held out a lantern and looked around.

"Friend of Ring Nose?" Nimue whispered.

"I don't know them," Arthur said in a low voice.

His hand slid down to the pommel of his sword, and his blithe countenance turned to stone. His muscles tensed.

*More wolf than pup,* Nimue realized.

A sudden hum welled up inside her, and she fought it off. But there was something inside Arthur, a reservoir of energy, barely checked and almost primal, burning like some deep internal furnace. It was unlike any aura Nimue had ever felt, and it made her both curious and deeply afraid. This was no ordinary boy.

Cold laughter brought Nimue's attention back to the road. She could tell by the men's rough voices and poorly fed horses that they were not Red Paladins. After a few moments, the riders moved on. Their lantern light faded and Arthur's muscles slowly relaxed again.

"Follow me," Nimue whispered to Arthur and Pym. She rode into the darkness, farther away from the road.

"Where are you going?" Arthur asked.

"To make camp. We aren't taking that road tonight."

Half a skin of wine later, Pym snored quietly in the grass.

Lit silver by the moonlight, Nimue circled Arthur, aiming the wobbly blade at his nose. Arthur laughed. "What are you doing?"

"Stalking you," Nimue whispered.

Arthur frowned, his short sword dragging in the grass. "Have you held a sword before?"

"I've killed hundreds."

Arthur slid his foot toward Nimue.

"Be careful," Nimue swung with gusto, but Arthur kept creeping forward.

"To the death, is it?"

"If you're careless." Nimue held the sword with both hands.

Arthur feinted left. She swung again, but only sliced air.

"You're fighting with just the blade," he told her. "That's a waste of a good sword."

Nimue lunged forward and Arthur barely dodged. "You talk too much."

But Arthur pivoted inside her reach. "A sword is more than a blade." He stepped between Nimue's legs as she cut at him, but he caught her blade in his cross guard. "It's the cross guard."

With their swords locked and pointed to the ground, he mimed striking Nimue in the chin with his pommel. "It's the pommel."

He bent his knee into the back of hers. "Legs." And then he turned his elbow to touch her cheek. "Body weight."

Nimue sulked.

Arthur smirked.

Then she head-butted him right in the nose.

"Gods!" Arthur stumbled back, pinching his nose to stop the trickle of blood coming from his right nostril.

"Head," Nimue said.

He looked at the blood on his fingers and chuckled. "Tavern brawler, eh?"

Nimue lunged and Arthur raised his short sword in time, deflecting her blow. With two hands, she swung again, too close to Arthur's face. He shook his head. "You are dangerous."

"That is the first intelligent thing you've said all night. Yield?"

"Hardly," Arthur snorted, jabbing the short sword. Nimue pivoted to block him but missed. He slid his blade to the pommel of her sword and spun it hard, flinging Nimue's sword into the grass.

"Luck!" Nimue shouted as she held her smarting wrist.

Arthur sheathed his sword and took her wrist in his hands. "You need to hold the sword loosely, like the reins of a horse."

Pym snorted in her sleep and mumbled. The night air was wet and cold, but Arthur's fingers on her hand warmed Nimue's blood enough.

"What are you doing?" she asked, finding her voice, as Arthur's fingers kneaded her palm.

"Does this bother you?"

"You've lowered your guard."

"Your sword is in the grass. I won."

"Have you?" Nimue snuck her cheese knife from her skirts and brought it up to Arthur's throat.

"Is that a cheese knife?" Arthur laughed.

"It's sharp enough." Nimue pushed the blade against his neck. "Yield?"

"You are a terror."

Nimue let her eyes linger on his. His gray eyes were flecked with green, like flakes of emerald. The hum in her stomach thrummed and rose up her chest and into her throat, overwhelming her before she could resist, and suddenly she was rushing forward. No, something inside of her was locking into Arthur with such ferocity she felt as though she might scream. Then images roared into her mind unbidden: *a blade with the green of Arthur's eyes . . . a hand covered in leprous boils reaching toward her . . . a cave wall of solemn carved faces . . . a woman with red curls wearing a dragon helm . . . an owl with an arrow in its back . . . Nimue herself underwater, clawing to breathe, water filling her lungs . . . and . . .*

Nimue gasped awake, sucking in air, shivering uncontrollably. She fought off a wave of nausea, partly the wine and partly the dread that she'd succumbed to another vision and that Arthur might have witnessed it. She had no memory of falling asleep. She was also wet and freezing. Morning mist drenched her clothes. A weak sun failed to burn through the low clouds. Nimue had never felt so cold. She shook Pym awake.

"Pym, it's morning. We have to go." Pym obeyed with the stupor of the just awakened. They walked softly past Arthur, who slept on one of his saddlebags, climbed onto Dusk Lady, and cantered onto the misty road.

They traveled for an hour, too wet and miserable to speak. The road was empty but for a traveling dentist who had spent the evening serving distant farms and looked like he'd been drinking the entire ride back to Hawksbridge. All the same he offered the girls a complimentary exam, which they politely declined. There was a moment, a curious one, when the dentist observed some totems on Nimue's wrist jewelry identifying her as Fey Kind. The dentist seemed fearful, and he gestured to the road ahead, then stopped short, as though a moment of courage had passed. He bid the girls good day and whickered his horse down the road at a trot.

The mists cleared, and the girls felt their first relief from the evening chill. But as the forest pressed in and the road narrowed, signaling the last mile to the village, an ox dragging its chains but no plow barreled out of the wilderness and into the girls' path. The wooden arm of the plow dragged alongside the animal's shoulder as it lumbered past the girls and down the road, clearly panicked. Nimue followed it with her eyes, confused, and then turned back. In the break of the trees a column of black smoke rose ominously. Flakes of red ash fluttered in the sunlight filtering through the leaves.

Nimue's heart pounded.

She spurred on Dusk Lady, and as the horse cleared the forest, screams ripped the air.

# SIX

THE TALL OAKEN DOORS OF KING UTHER Pendragon's Great Hall groaned open and two royal footmen, wearing the embroidered three red crowns of House Pendragon on their yellow tunics, dragged in a half-conscious mage. His leather slippers dragged on the floor. His brownish-blond beard was stained with wine. They held him up before the young king on his throne.

"Merlin." King Uther calmly smoothed his waxed black beard. "Perfect timing."

"Took a bit, but we found him in the cabbages, sire," Borley, the older, barrel-chested footman offered proudly. "Drunk, I'm afraid."

"You don't say?" King Uther smiled coldly.

Merlin flung his arms away from his captors, smoothed his night-blue robes, and swayed for a moment before steadying himself against a pillar.

"You promised us rain, Merlin. And, per usual, your words have proven hollow."

"Weather is fickle, my liege," Merlin said, fluttering his fingers to the sky.

King Uther dropped a slab of cold mutton on the floor for his wolfhounds.

*He suspects,* Merlin thought through his wine-soaked haze. *He suspects my secret.* But they would continue to pretend, he knew. At only twenty-six years, Uther was a young and insecure monarch and loath to admit error or weakness. That Merlin, his secret counsel, the legendary sage, was a fool and a drunkard, not the feared sorcerer of the ages, was likely too humiliating a thought for Uther to entertain for very long. *Let us end this charade once and for all,* Merlin wished. Merlin the Magician was Merlin the Fraud. His magic was lost and had been for almost seventeen years. It was only spy-craft and will and pride and the gullible nature of men that had sustained the lie all these years. Merlin was tired of it. Yet something within him refused to confess the truth. Fear, perhaps. He preferred to keep his head on his shoulders. Besides, voicing it would somehow make it more real. More final.

Sir Beric, Uther's other counsel, a rotund, plaited-bearded fellow Merlin knew as a leech and a coward, sniffed at Merlin's words and turned back to the king. "The drought and resulting famine are causing wider panic in your northern French provinces as well, sire. Taking advantage of these passions, Father Carden and his Red Paladins have burned several Fey villages."

Uther's eyes darkened and turned to Merlin. "The Red Paladins are not fickle, Merlin. They are quite reliable. How many Fey villages have burned, Sir Beric?"

Sir Beric consulted a scroll. "Ah, approximately ten, Your Majesty."

If the king was hoping for a reaction from Merlin, he was disappointed. The mage simply poured a cup of wine.

Uther chose to speak to Beric as though Merlin were not there. "Merlin is a conflicted creature, you see, Beric. These are his kind being put to the torch, yet he is unmoved. Not that he's ever been confused for a man of the people. He's not fond of the mud of the southern villages. No, he prefers the trappings of our castle and our plum wine." Uther deigned to look over at the wizard. "Don't you, Merlin?"

"It's hardly a mystery what's happening. The Fey Kind are, quite frankly, better farmers. So, in times of want, the mob finds reason to steal their food. Father Carden and his paladins are dull vessels for these old hatreds, nothing more." Merlin wiped some spilled wine from his robes. "However, if His Majesty would allow it, the Shadow Lords may be able to offer some service here."

The king grew quiet and nodded for his goblet to be refilled, and a cupbearer poured.

Uther's paranoia always rose at the mention of Merlin's circle of spies. Merlin could count on that. It was a reminder to the king that Merlin was not a man to cross. The Shadow Lords were more disturbing to the king than Carden's crucifixion fields. The Fey were a nuisance and offered little to the royal coffers, whereas the Shadow Lords were different: a secret confederacy of witches, mages, and warlocks, each with their own networks, guilds, and cells at every societal rank, from the lowliest leper colonies to the royal court, all operating outside the king's grasp.

What Merlin neglected to mention was that the Shadow Lords had become a far greater danger to *him* than to the king. That he had earned untold enemies within the organization, that they smelled weakness and decline, that rumors of his lost magic were swirling alongside rumblings of assassins and black bounties on his head.

And Merlin's response to all this?

*More wine*, he mused darkly, weary of it all.

Servants entered with a tray of food for the king, who was still quietly stewing over the mention of the Shadow Lords. The butler announced, "Supper, Your Majesty."

Uther rose from his throne, eyes never leaving Merlin, and walked to the table, where he sat as the lid was lifted from the tray, revealing medallions of steak on his plate. Upon seeing his food, Uther's mood did not improve.

"We asked for doves," he growled to his butler.

"Deepest apologies, Your Majesty," the butler soothed, "but we seem to have an issue with the dovecotes. Some, ah, dead birds were found."

Merlin frowned at this. "How many birds?"

Unnerved by Merlin, the butler's voice shook slightly as he answered, "Um, nine, sir."

Even a man struck blind can still remember the color blue in his mind. So it was that Merlin, a man robbed of the Sight, recognized an omen.

Nine doves.

Nine was the number for magic but also for wisdom and leadership. The dead doves were a powerful warning of shattered peace and coming war.

Uther sighed. "How appetizing. Go."

The butler and the royal footmen hurried out of the throne room.

King Uther sawed into his meat. "A bit late for your enchanters to help us now."

"Not necessarily, Your Majesty. With the right encouragement, they could—"

Uther slammed the table with his fist, rattling his plate and frightening his hounds to bark. "Drought! Famine! Food riots! We cannot afford to look weak to our enemies! Do you know the Ice King and his northern raiders prowl our coasts, waiting for the right moment to strike? Do you? We want rain, Merlin!"

Sir Beric bowed his head, fearful of Uther's wrath.

King Uther turned to Merlin, eyes aflame. "To hell with your Shadow Lords. Mother doubts they exist at all."

Unfazed, Merlin folded his hands into the long sleeves of his robes. "I would assure the Queen Regent they are all too real. But His Majesty requires rain, and so we shall redouble our efforts."

"Yes, do," Uther bit. But as Merlin headed down the hall in a swirl of blue robes, the king added, "We know how you value your privacy, Merlin. It would be a pity if the wider world learned that you were serving us. Who knows what enemies might crawl out of the woodwork?" Merlin nodded at the warning, and the great doors of the throne room slammed behind him.

However, once he entered the serpentine corridors of Castle Pendragon, he sobered up quickly, no longer swaying, his senses returning and as keen as a fox. He drew a torch from a sconce in the wall and swept into a dark passage. After several steps, he paused and listened. Somewhere up ahead of him there was a scraping sound, followed by small bursts of air. Merlin strode ahead and rounded a corner, his firelight falling upon a magpie, spinning in a desperate circle on the floor, flopping about in its death throes. The magpie was a powerful omen of witchcraft but also of prophecy. Merlin's fathomless eyes drifted toward the ceiling.

Minutes later, his lungs burned as he labored up the last remaining stairs of the castle's highest tower. As he climbed into the turret, the first thing he noticed was the silence. Then he saw the dead birds littering the floor, some of them still twitching. Though the quantity was itself alarming, it was their arrangement that was most disturbing of all. The magpies had all fallen and died in ten impossibly precise patterns of three. Ten arrangements of three.

Ten: a rebirth. A new order. Dead magpies.

*The end of prophecy?*

Nine doves.

Merlin's thoughts swirled. A great magical leader. A new dawn. A great war.

*All of it was coming.*


Dellum the physician had long fingers that sewed flesh together with the precision of a seamstress. Due to the high humidity in his chambers of black stone, sweat dripped from his long nose onto the corpse he was stitching back together. The ceilings were low and without windows. The only light was from two oil lanterns at opposite ends of the room, which shone dully on six wide tables, four of which held naked bodies in varying states of decomposition.

"I'm told you are a collector of sorts. Is this true?"

Dellum yelped. He dropped his instruments onto the floor. "Who goes there?"

"I do." Merlin stepped into the yellow light.

"How did you—?"

"The door was open."

Dellum wiped his sweaty face with a grimy rag that hung on his belt. "You're Merlin the Magician."

"You haven't answered my question."

Dellum's eyes dodged about. "I don't—I was told to not collect—I've stopped all that. Everything is aboveboard here."

"Pity," Merlin sighed. "I was willing to pay handsomely to see some of your more"—he searched for the word—"obscure items."

"Is that so?" Dellum scratched his hands. He glanced to a heavy oak door near the back of the chamber. "What, eh, what sort of item were you looking for?"

"The number three," Merlin answered.

Dellum frowned at this, but after a moment his face lit up. "I may have just the thing."

The heavy door protested as Dellum pushed it open. Merlin stepped past him into a smaller chamber. The lantern he carried spilled light over shelves and shelves of dusty, grim little jars. He gagged at the smell of spoiling meat. Dellum crossed the room. He eagerly scooped a bundle into his arms and brought it over to the examination table for Merlin's inspection. The object was wrapped in a greasy cloth.

"It arrived three days ago," Dellum explained. "Born to a peasant family in Colchester."

He unwrapped the specimen. As usual, Merlin betrayed no emotion. The infant was probably a week or two old, withered and pale green from rot, its small arms curled, tiny fists balled. Its head was divided evenly into two faces, though each shared a misshapen eye just above the two noses.

Merlin turned to Dellum and raised an eyebrow.

"Allow me," the physician purred. He lifted the dead baby from the table and turned it over as though to burp it. This revealed a third face pressing out of the child's tiny back in a silent scream, like a creature trapped between worlds.

"That will do," Merlin said quietly, his thoughts far away.

Dellum gently wrapped the baby back in its cloth. "Might I, ah, inquire as to your interest in the number three?"

"Three is where the past, the present, and the future meet," Merlin said, almost to himself. His robes swirled behind him as he headed for the door. "Something terrible and powerful has awakened. You should be afraid. We should all be afraid."

The door slammed behind him.

# SEVEN

**N**IMUE AWOKE WITH A START TO PITEOUS cries. *How long have I been unconscious?* she wondered, her thoughts sticky and slow. Jolts of agony forked across her skull, and her hand went to a wet patch of hair and a knot just below her left ear where the iron ball had struck her. Numbly, she pulled herself from the woodpile and took in the chaos: village elders roasting on fiery crosses, red robes everywhere, children crying in the mud, every village hut aflame, dogs sniffing dead bodies in the road.

A guttural cry of "Mother!" ripped from her throat. She charged across the road, skull throbbing, racing past bodies and toppled carts. Almost immediately, a Red Paladin took hold of her cloak, but Nimue twisted and it tore free into the paladin's hands.

Nimue lunged onto the hill, the Red Paladin in pursuit. She ran past charred bodies on the crosses, their limbs twisted. The paladin stumbled behind her, and Nimue created some distance. She sprinted into the Iron Wood, dodging between trees until her boots landed on the well-worn stones of the Sacred Sun Path. She flew through the veiled entrance of the Sunken Temple, and from her perch high above the temple floor, she saw Lenore, curled in a ball by the altar stone.

"Mother!"

The pyre loomed like a black tower over Squirrel as he raced along the deer paths of the Iron Wood. He'd grown up hunting with his uncles and grandfather, and now his survival depended on those paths. His cousin's sword bounced painfully against his legs as he caught sight of his uncle through the branches.

"Uncle Kipp!"

Kipp was a farmer with arms like trees. Several other villagers, men Squirrel knew, motioned for quiet. Kipp spied his nephew and hurried toward him. "Squirrel, child, we mustn't shout. We're looking for the bastards we chased into the woods."

"We have to go back," Squirrel pleaded, pulling his uncle's sleeve. "They're all dying!"

Kipp shook his head. The wrinkles on his broad face were deeper than usual. He looked ten years older. "They're already gone, child."

Up ahead, the men came to a full stop at a clearing in the trees. Squirrel and his uncle caught up with them.

Kipp started, "What are you—?" The rest died in his throat as he saw the Gray Monk, with the strange tear-marked eyes, waiting for them in the tall grass like a sun-dappled wraith. His courser grazed nearby.

The wood grew quiet. The monk did not move. Squirrel could smell the sweat of the men turn sour with fear. These were not warriors. They were carpenters and the sons of bakers. Squirrel's uncle was the only one of them who had killed with steel, but that was years ago, defending his family against Viking raiders. But if his uncle was afraid, he did not show it.

Kipp growled. "We're seven and he's one."

They were, in fact, eight. Squirrel's uncle had forgotten to include him. The others drew their swords with a single shining sound. Squirrel swallowed as he tried to lift his own sword, though he stayed a step behind the men who encircled the Gray Monk. The monk calmly drew his gleaming blade.

One of the men, Tenjen, angled himself directly behind the monk, switching sword hands to wipe his sweaty palms on his smock. The monk held his sword low and loose on his left side. He tilted his head slightly as Tenjen shifted his weight from one foot to the other. Squirrel's temples throbbed with tension. He watched the others huff and rev themselves for battle while the monk's breathing never changed.

Tenjen roared and lunged, but the Gray Monk smoothly pivoted away from the strike and in the same fluid motion stepped backward into Tenjen's path. Squirrel never saw the monk's sword move until it stuck out of Tenjen's back, slick with his blood. With a wet sound, the monk freed his sword, and Tenjen pitched forward into the dirt.

On instinct, Squirrel lifted his sword, but his mind was blank. A terrible buzzing filled his ears. His tongue was cat dry. The men's screams were distant and their movements slowed as their swords swung and the monk spun inside their circle, his robes swirling, his blade catching the sun. He wasted nary an inch. His sword struck like a snake and men crumpled in its wake. He cut the tendons in the backs of their legs so they dropped like puppets, then severed throats and punctured hearts. There was no hacking, no cuts, no grazes, no fumbles of any kind.

Ewan, the baker's son, fell onto his knees, trying to hold the blood inside his opened throat with both of his hands. Those same hands had drizzled honey over the crispels in his father's kitchen.

Drof the butcher missed badly, lodging his sword in the earth. He struggled to free it, which was all the time the monk needed to crouch low and launch upward, lifting Drof off his feet, pushing the blade through his body and out his right shoulder blade.

Squirrel's uncle was the first to block one of the monk's strikes. Kipp caught his blade with the hilt. Their steel scraped as their shoulders slammed together. For a split second, the monk was caught up and his flank exposed. Squirrel saw a window to act. He stepped forward to protect his uncle, but Hurst, Tenjen's cousin, also saw the opportunity to strike and lunged ahead of Squirrel. The monk must have sensed his approach, because he wrapped his arms around Kipp and turned him into the path of Hurst's sword, which sank deep into his hip. As Kipp cried out and clutched at his side, the monk whipped around and lopped off Hurst's head.

A mist of blood sprayed Squirrel's cheeks. Kipp stood his ground bravely as blood dribbled down his left leg. The monk circled him, moving fast. Kipp tried to follow him with the point of his sword. The monk feinted twice, Kipp bit on the second, and that was it. The monk stuck him through the chest, and he folded to the ground.

The Gray Monk surveyed the scene of dead and dying men with his strange weeping eyes. He walked among the bodies and waited for signs of life. He nudged Tenjen with his boot. No response. He prodded the twins Kevin and Trey and finished them with a clean stroke through the heart. When it was Kipp's turn, the monk readied the blow and—

"Don't!" That was all Squirrel could say.

The monk barely tilted his head toward the word. He whirled around and . . . hesitated. Squirrel could hear the vibration of the blade beside his ear. His hands trembled as he pointed his cousin's sword at the monk. Squirrel could not see the monk's eyes beneath his deep gray cowl, only his strange tear birthmarks and a smear of blood on his left cheek. With a swift flick, the monk sent Squirrel's sword spiraling into the trees.

Squirrel squeezed his eyes shut and tensed his body for the blow, which he prayed would be clean.

After a few labored breaths, Squirrel opened one eye.

He was alone.

The monk was gone.

Nimue ran down the winding stairs, along the impassive faces of the sculpted walls, until she reached the cracked marble floor. Lenore lay crumpled near the altar stone, her robes wet with blood. Several feet away, a dying paladin writhed on the ground in a puddle of blood.

"Mother!" Nimue collapsed by her mother's body. "Mother, I'm here." Nimue took her mother's head into her lap, revealing a bloody dagger beneath her. She was curled around something wrapped in sackcloth and tied with rope. A large stone had been removed from beneath the altar, revealing what had been a hidden resting place for whatever this was.

Lenore took hold of Nimue's arms. Her hair was wild and her cheeks smeared with blood, but her eyes were clear and her voice steady. "Take this to Merlin. Find him. I don't know how." Lenore thrust the object into Nimue's hands. "He'll know what to do."

Nimue shook her head. "We have to run—Mother! Now! Mother—!"

"This is your charge. Bring this to Merlin. This is all that matters now."

Nimue regarded the bundle with confusion. "What are you saying? Merlin's a story. I don't understand—"

But before Lenore could answer, a paladin with sallow cheeks entered the temple, blood dripping from his sword.

Lenore used the altar stone to drag herself to her feet. She picked up the dagger on the floor. "Run, Nimue."

Nimue clutched the bundle to her breast and froze with indecision. "I won't leave you."

"Run!" Lenore screamed.

Nimue managed to take a few steps toward the stairs, and the Red Paladin moved to block her. His dull black eyes flicked between Nimue and Lenore.

Lenore was pale and unsteady from loss of blood, but she advanced on the paladin.

"Mother!" Nimue cried.

Lenore looked at her daughter with eyes filled with love and remorse. "I love you. I'm sorry this falls to you. You must find Merlin." At this she turned and lunged at the Red Paladin with the dagger, giving Nimue a second to escape.

Through eyes blurred with tears, Nimue clawed up the pathway of the Sunken Temple, fighting the impulse to look back, wishing herself deaf to the sounds of struggle below. Clutching the bundle under her arm, she staggered through the veil of ivy and into the Iron Wood. She ran to the lookout where, just a morning before, she and Squirrel had laughed and wrestled.

From here all of Dewdenn unfurled before her. She saw the hill of burning crosses and paladins on horseback charging across the field from the east to cut off those attempting to escape. At the bottom of the hill, another group of paladins freed huge black wolves from their leashes and set them after the remaining villagers. Nimue spun around and raced back into the forest, praying to the Old Gods of the Sky Folk to guide her.

At that moment, the skies above Castle Pendragon boiled and heaved. The archers atop the gatehouse had never seen a storm come on so suddenly and with such menace. They took shelter in the alcoves as lightning pulsed within the clouds and ripples of thunder shuddered the castle stones.

Hundreds of feet above, in Pendragon's highest flanking tower, Merlin completed painting a large circle on the floor in heavy grease. At the center of the circle lay an open spell book. Out of practice, Merlin double-checked the incantations. He might have lost his magic, but he was still a master scholar of the dark arts. Rising, he pushed aside the feathered talismans he'd hung from the timber in order to position four heavy mirrors, each at opposite angles of the turret. Merlin relit several large candles of invocation that had gone out during the heavy wind gusts. With the candle flames, he kindled a branch of wormwood and waved the smoke about before dropping the branch nto the grease circle, causing it, too, to ignite.

Another peal of thunder shook the castle, and a shout was heard from outside. "We're coming in! This is bloody madness!"

"No!" Merlin barked, swinging back toward the door.

Outside on the wall, footmen Chist and Borley held on to the bricks as the wind swept through with enough force to lift them off their feet. Driving hail danced off the bricks and rattled their helmets.

"You'll do no such thing!" Merlin bellowed as he hurried from the turret into the wind and sleet in a state of manic urgency. He pulled himself onto the battlement. His robes fluttered above a two-hundred-foot drop. The footmen reached for him, but he paid them no mind. Merlin muttered incantations under his breath in a language older than Latin. He tied a pouch of powdered crystal and crushed eggshells, mixed into a paste with his own blood, to a twenty-foot iron pole etched with runes. One end he fastened to a banner housing, with the other end pointed to the heaving sky. *There was a time when I was the storm,* Merlin thought. *When the lightning flew from my fingertips and the winds roared at my command.* Instead he gripped at the stones as the wind tried to rip him over the wall. But Merlin was defiant. *I am no longer the Druid I was, but I am not helpless. I am still Merlin, and I will know the secrets of the gods.*

Merlin had attached a flapping scroll with melted wax to the end of the iron pole.

"You were supposed to be holding this!" he roared back at the footmen, referring to the iron pole, but his words were carried away in the storm. A tremendous bolt of lightning drew his eyes skyward. Inside a mountainous dark cloud, the lightning pulsed like a god's glowing heart, beating once, twice, three times.

Merlin wiped the hair and rain away from his face, not trusting his eyes. Again, the lightning flashed inside the clouds, illuminating unnatural shapes.

"I don't want to die!" Borley howled as he headed for the safety of the turret.

"Wait!" Merlin called after him, leaping down from the battlement. He grabbed Chist by the shoulders and threw him against the wall.

"What—what're you doing?" Chist struggled, but Merlin held him fast, eyes shooting back to the light pulsing in the clouds. There it was again. Three shapes.

Merlin turned to Chist and pressed his hand to the three red crowns of House Pendragon against the yellow of his tunic. Then he turned back to the sky. The lightning pulsed again inside the cloud, forming a halo around *three red crowns*.

"Gods," Merlin whispered. The signs were finally clear.

*A magical child.*

*The end of prophecy.*

*And the death of a king.*

# EIGHT

THE SHELTER OF THE WOOD MUFFLED
the sounds of carnage. Screams faded on the wind, until Nimue
could hear only her own heaving breaths as she darted along
the trails that had defined her since she was born. The map of
her past had now become the slender path to her survival. She passed
the deer grove and the hollow oak where the finches nested. Out of the
corner of her eye, something black shot between the trees. Another flash
of black scurried around the den boulders.

Wolves.

She threw her bundle onto the tabletop rock, a wide flat stone—ten
feet square—that in kinder times served as a stage for child theatricals and
a sun bed for lazy village dogs. Now it was Nimue's last stand. She climbed
onto the rock as the flesh-eaters rushed in from all sides, five of them snarl-

ing at the edge of the rock. One leaped halfway onto the ledge, and Nimue drove her heel into its snout, sending the beast sprawling to the ground. But it wheeled around and leaped again. Nimue backed away, cornered.

Behind her was a ten-foot drop, before her certain death at the jaws of the wolves. Another scrabbled onto the tabletop and snatched her boot in its teeth. Nimue screamed, kicking wildly, until the creature fell away, but it was only a matter of time.

A glint of silver caught Nimue's eye, and she turned to the bundle by her feet. The sackcloth had torn away in one spot, revealing a dark iron pommel carved with a rune of four circles connecting to a center circle inlaid with silver.

"The drought is ended!" King Uther proclaimed, chin held high in victory as servers carried buckets of rainwater and placed them at the center of the feasting table beside the assembled guests. The buckets joined pewter plates of roasted hens, stewed rabbits, pigeons wrapped in bacon, honey-baked partridges, and plump pheasants. The mood was jovial even as the storm continued to rage. Each clap of thunder elicited gasps and applause as Uther stood at the end of the table.

"The gods smile upon us," Uther boasted.

The assembled banged their knives on the table and chanted Uther's name and "The drought is ended!"

One nobleman raised a jug of ale. "To the king!"

Another shouted, "To the rain!"

The guests laughed.

Uther chuckled. "No, friends. We do not drink *to* the rain"—he lifted the bucket that had been placed beside his plate—"instead we *drink* the rain!"

"Hail Uther!" the assembled cheered. "Hail the king!"

Uther lifted the pail to his lips and took a long, sweet gulp. His guests observed, admiring and applauding as the contents dribbled down his manicured goatee and throat, staining his ruffled white collar a bright red.

The room quieted. Uther frowned at the taste and lowered the pail. He smiled at his guests, lips slippery with blood. "I'm afraid I've spilled some."

Ladies covered their eyes as Uther quickly read the faces of his guests.

"What is—?" Uther looked down at his bloody sleeves. "What is this?" He set down the pail and wiped his lips and beard, covering his hands in blood. Uther turned sharply on his butler. "What trick is this?"

Uther's butler was white with fear. "N-no trick, Your Majesty."

Uther tipped over the bucket, and a river of blood flowed over the table. His guests gasped; some screamed and knocked over their benches to run.

The butler cried, "That is the rain that fell upon the castle!"

"Merlin!" Uther screamed as he hurled another bucket, and another, blood rain flooding the pewter plates and spattering onto the floor. The king's eyes were wild with fear as he shrieked to the ceiling, "Merlin!!"

At that moment, atop the battlement, in the full fury of the storm, a single bolt of lightning struck the iron rod. A cascade of energy hurtled through the iron, ending in a searing shock wave that blasted Merlin through the turret door, sending him sprawling—aflame—into the fiery circle. Merlin roared in agony as he fought to free himself from his burning robes. The footmen raced inside to assist him, but the storm followed them in. Sheets of rain met the flames and black smoke choked the air. The footmen coughed and waved their arms until they cleared the smoke away from Merlin, naked as a babe in the middle of the floor, a horrific burn sizzling and bubbling from his right shoulder, down his ribs, and across his thigh and below. Borley and Chist both took a steadying step back, blinking in disbelief, for the burn was in the unmistakable shape of a sword.

✦ ✦ ✦

Nimue reached into the wrapped cloth and tightened her fist around the worn leather grip of an ancient sword. Its wide blade was blackened and nicked by what must have been centuries of combat. She held the mysterious weapon aloft and felt her blood surge as a beast landed cleanly on the tabletop rock. Turning with one swift stroke, she separated the wolf from its head. The body flopped backward and the other dogs scurried aside as it struck the earth.

Nimue stared at the sword. It radiated a cold light and felt feather soft in her hands. The Fingers of Airimid blossomed on her cheek, forming a connection between the sword and the Hidden. The next wolf scratched its way to the ledge, and Nimue divided its skull right down the snout, the blade lodging in the rock a good three inches deeper than the blow. Nimue fought to free the heavy blade as another monster caught her elbow and dragged her over the lip of the tabletop rock.

She flipped in midair before landing hard on her back. Her eyes rolled in her head as she wriggled her body around, and a wolf clamped its jaws on the hem of her skirts. Ripping the fabric free, Nimue lunged for the sword, which lay several feet away in the grass. She reached the hilt just as another wolf leaped at her throat. She cut through the cur's shoulder and the creature rolled over in the dirt, whimpering, unable to climb to its paws. Nimue tasted its blood on her lips as she staggered to her feet. Two thick, bristling wolves remained, barking and snapping at her.

"Come on!" she roared, feeling a surge of power.

One went low for her ankles, and she drove the sword into its back. She wrenched the sword free and slew the last of them with a quick strike to the neck.

It was over. She stood there, panting, in a puddle of blood. She took a deep breath and shrieked at the dead animals.

She left wolf-blood footprints in the mud as she stumbled blindly across the meadow, past the moon rock where her mother had taught her lessons. Her ears buzzed. She could hear Red Paladins gathering in force behind her. Horsemen. Several on foot. She backed into the maze of thorns—a popular hiding spot for children playing "seeker."

Nimue was quickly surrounded. She could see the bald pates of the monks just over the shoulder-high hedges, at the junction of the maze and the clearing. Red Paladins walked softly down every path toward her. She counted seven. The tip of her sword dropped limply to the dirt. Her arms felt molten with fatigue. She sank to her knees, her eyes locked on the monks' dirty feet and simple sandals. *I don't want to go on alone,* she thought. *It's better this way.*

But resignation gave way to a memory of her mother's voice from when Nimue was a child, when the demon gave her the scars: *Call the Hidden, Nimue.* The calm certainty of her mother's voice poured cool water over her thoughts, and Nimue's mind felt clean and washed. In that clarity she reached out to the dirt under her nails, the circling crows, and the wind in the grass. She called out to the stream, thick with innocent blood, and to the wood-chewing ants in the dead trunk of the Old Man— the most ancient tree in the glade. A shudder swept across the hedges of the thorn maze as though they'd been brushed with an unseen hand. The hum of the Hidden throbbed in her stomach. The sword pulsed in her fists. It was as if the two were connected somehow, like the sword was guiding the power of the Hidden through her veins.

The paladin closest to Nimue angled his sword to her head, but his ankle caught on one of the branches. Another tried to free his robes, which had become stuck in the thorns, and still another found his path to Nimue inexplicably blocked by a knot of roots jutting out from the dirt.

Emboldened, Nimue pushed her mind to open more channels of connection. The hum in her gut made hair on her arms stand up as ropy vines looped and constricted around arms, calves, biceps, and necks. The maze of thorns fed hungrily on the Red Paladins, who bleated with panic

*SHE HELD THE MYSTERIOUS WEAPON ALOFT AND FELT HER BLOOD SURGE . . .*

and fear, a music that sang in Nimue's ears and gave her legs new strength. She stood tall as the Red Paladins were strangled to their knees around her. She stared into their bulging, disbelieving eyes and smiled through her tears. She thought of her mother, throwing herself in the path of the paladin to save Nimue's life. She thought of Biette and Pym and Squirrel. Nimue's knuckles squeezed white around the leather grip of the ancient sword. She wanted to savor the moment. She lifted the sword higher and higher, then dropped the heavy blade like a chopping ax. Blood spattered the leaves and vines around her, but she did not stop.

The blade fell. And fell. And fell again. *Again.*

The paladins' wet robes clung to their twitching bodies. Nimue's eyes blazed with righteous fury as she chopped and chopped, unleashing all the loss and the rage and the pain.

## NINE

FATHER CARDEN'S BOOT POKED THE NOSE
of a wolf's severed head. He noted small bloody footprints in the
dirt. The Weeping Monk stood silently behind him. A Red Paladin
had guided them across the meadow to the maze of thorns, and
it had taken an hour of hacking with axes for the Red Paladins to reach
their slaughtered companions.

Father Carden entered the freshly carved path to look upon the bodies
with his own eyes. The Weeping Monk followed. The Red Paladins were
nothing more than unrecognizable lumps of meat cradled in the embrace
of the hedge.

"An abomination," Carden whispered. He pulled the bloody hood
away from one of the paladin's faces, a face contorted by terror. Carden
shook his head and replaced the shroud. Again, he took note of the

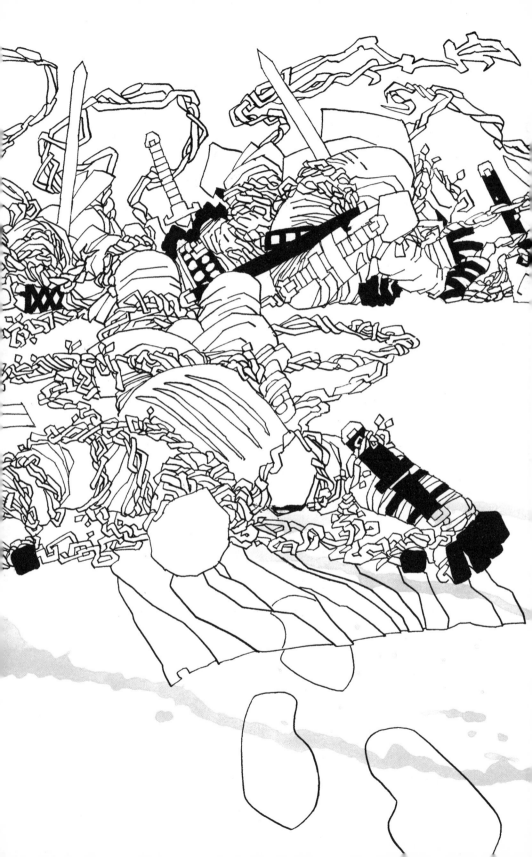

small footprints at the heart of the scene. "One child did all of this?"

The Weeping Monk knelt by another body. "Simon saw a girl leave the temple carrying something." His finger grazed what looked like a burn on the Red Paladin's arm.

Carden joined him. He studied the burn. "Observe. The skin was not marked from the outside. Our brother here was burned from within. This is powerful evil."

The burn had a unique shape: a branch with three stems. "The Devil's Tooth," Carden mused. "This is its mark."

The Weeping Monk looked up at him.

Carden threw back the robes from another dead paladin. His throat bore the same brand. Another Red Paladin wore the mark on his cheek.

Carden stood up, shaken. "We have flushed out the ancient weapon of our enemy. The Sword of Power has been found and is in the possession of one of the Devil's children." He spread his arms to the hedges. "One maid with the power to do this. To pervert God's creations, to make monsters of the earth and air. At all costs this child must be cleansed. The great conflict has begun." Father Carden pulled the Weeping Monk's hooded head into a whisper. "Find the sword. And find her."


Nimue lay against an embankment, in a bed of wet leaves, thinking about Squirrel. The high midday sun was bright but gave off little heat. She had gone back to their hiding spot in the hollow of the ash tree, but he was not there. Instead she had found six men of her village cut down in a nearby field. Left for the dogs.

A cold rain began to fall. It made Nimue's bones ache. Her legs throbbed from running, she'd lost count how many miles. Her only possession in the world was the sword.

Why would her mother conceal it?

If it was important enough to sacrifice her life for it, why had Nimue never been told of its existence?

And was Merlin the same Merlin from the children's stories? Was he a real person? How was that possible?

*No matter*, Nimue thought. She would never last the night. Hunted, without shelter or food or water, her chances were grim. The forest hid thieves and wolves. The city harbored Father Carden's spies. She knew no one outside her clan, and that clan had just been slaughtered before her eyes. Nimue was alone.

She regarded the sword again. The rune carved into the pommel was filled with silver and had to be worth something. Surely it could bring her enough coin for safe passage across the sea? After all, wasn't survival the most important thing? Wouldn't her mother want her to do everything to survive? Nimue turned the sword in her hand, so light. Incredible.

*Mother gave her life for this sword.*

Would Nimue honor that sacrifice by selling it for scraps? What other choice did she have? She was a murderer. She had slain seven Red Paladins. They would hang her for this, or worse. And she had used the Hidden to aid her in the task. She would be branded a witch.

Nimue cried pitiful tears, which were lost in the raindrops. She'd had no time for anything. Pym. Dusk Lady. Her mother. It had all happened so fast. Nimue felt a despair welling up that could swallow her. But before she gave over to it, a name popped into her mind.

*Arthur.*

Nimue thought for a moment. Then she took the sword to her wet blond hair. She sawed through a hank of hair in her hand and let the strands fall to the ground. She needed a cloak. She'd be far too suspicious waltzing into Hawksbridge in her ragged skirts with a valuable sword slung on her back.

Less than an hour later, Nimue crept through a field of wheat toward a laundry line strung up with the clothes of a peasant family: wool stockings, tunics, and shifts. She tore the farmer's cloak and pants from the line and bolted back into the field, running as low as possible so the wheat would conceal her.

As evening approached, Nimue tore strips from her skirts to make a belt that would keep the farmer's trousers around her waist. The oversize cloak concealed the sword on Nimue's back, despite being as long as she was. She needed to reach Hawksbridge before sunset: she doubted she could survive another night of exposure.

Her feet felt like stumps. Her arms hung like iron weights. She ached with hunger. As she approached Hawksbridge, she was panicked to see very little traffic at the gates, and worse still, a Red Paladin stood with the guards.

Suddenly a whistle carried on the air—barely familiar. Nimue turned and saw the traveling dentist from earlier that morning atop his one-horse cart.

The dentist was bald with long brown sideburns and a mustache that curled down his cheeks, giving him the look of a sad hound. His smock was stained dark with the blood of his patients, and though his eyes were still red, with bags under them. Nimue attributed it to fatigue rather than ale. The dentist appeared to be through with his rounds of the local farms and headed back home inside the gates of Hawksbridge.

Without much of a plan, Nimue stepped into the path of his cart. The dentist frowned and pulled the reins. "Everything all right, miss?"

With her chopped-off hair and baggy clothes, Nimue was unrecognizable from the morning. She pressed a hand to her cheek and winced. "It's my tooth, sir."

"Oh? Well, I'm afraid my work's done for the day. Give me directions and I may be able to squeeze you in day after tomorrow."

"But that's far too long! Please, sir."

"Best I can do, miss."

Nimue's eyes brimmed with desperate tears. Given her misery, they were ready to fall at any moment. "But the pain is just shooting, and I can't do my chores, and my mother beats me if I can't work."

The dentist looked her over. He wasn't impressed. "You've got coin, have you?"

"My brother can pay you. He's just inside the gates with his chums at the Raven Wing. I'm sure he'd treat you to a mead for taking pity on me." Nimue grimaced and clutched her jaw. "It's a torment, sir." As Nimue held her cheek, her cloak dropped away from her wrist and the dentist saw the totems on her bracelet. It was then that he recognized her.

"I know you from this morning." He frowned. "You and your friend."

Nimue's mind went numb as she watched the wheels turn in the dentist's mind. He looked over to the gates. They were one cart away from the Red Paladin. After a few moments of conversation, the guard waved it through and walked toward the dentist's cart.

"State your business," the guard said, bored.

The dentist turned back to Nimue.

"Please, sir," she whispered.

Fear, pity, and guilt washed over the dentist's rheumy eyes. He looked at the guard, at a loss for words, as the Red Paladin approached.

"Hello?" the guard asked, annoyed.

"T-t-teeth, sir," the dentist managed.

Nimue noticed the dentist's hands shaking.

"Just—just finishing my rounds," he added.

"And this one?" The guard stared Nimue up and down.

The dentist licked his dry lips. "She's ah, she's . . ." Somewhere deep inside, he found a seed of courage. "She's—she's my patient, sir."

Nimue managed a short breath of relief. She climbed onto his cart.

"One of my regulars," the dentist added.

"Remove your hood," the Red Paladin ordered.

"Yes, sir." Nimue obeyed, pulling down the hood of her cloak, eyes on the dentist's muddy boots.

"Where are you from?" the Red Paladin asked.

Nimue tried to keep her voice light and steady. "Born in Hawksbridge, milord. My mother's a—a laundress for the lord of the keep, and I fetch the lye from the monastery. That is—that is, when my tooth's not ailing."

"What tooth ails you?"

Nimue hesitated before pointing to the right side of her lower jaw. "This—this one, milord?" She tapped the spot.

The Red Paladin looked at the dentist. "The girl is suffering. What are you waiting for? Pull it."

The dentist cupped his ear. "Sir?"

"The tooth. Pull it. Now."

The dentist shook his head, not understanding. "But I—um, I haven't . . ." He looked to Nimue for some kind of guidance.

Her ears rang, and Nimue felt another panicked urge to run. She saw only one course. She shut her eyes and nodded to the dentist.

The guard winced. "What, you want him to do it here?"

"Shut up, fool," the Red Paladin snapped at the guard. Turning back to the dentist, the paladin pressed, "Is that a problem?"

"Not—not a problem."

Nimue watched numbly as the dentist fished out a pair of blood-stained pliers from his weather-beaten satchel. Nimue dared to look at the Red Paladin. His eyes bored into hers. She looked down again.

"Let's—let's see what we have here," the dentist muttered, almost having to pry open Nimue's jaw.

"I'm sorry," he said softly. "Ah yes," he called out. "Here's the culprit." He indicated one of Nimue's molars.

Nimue imagined herself in the brook by the broken statue in the Iron Wood. She thought of the cold water flowing over her legs as the jaws of the dentist's dirty pliers clamped over her healthy tooth. The first twist tore several roots and a guttural sound of pain came up from Nimue's throat. The dentist's hand was strong, and he worked fast. He wrenched left, then right. Nimue's head tried to jerk back, but the pliers held her. She heard the dentist somewhere say, "This will give you relief, milady." Blood filled into a vacuum in her mouth as the pliers did their work and the tooth came free. A rag was stuffed into her mouth. Nimue opened her blurry eyes to the repulsed guard and the smug Red Paladin. The dentist's hand was on her neck and his lips close to her ear. "All done now, child."

The guard waved them on, reclaiming his authority. "Enough already. Away with you."

The dentist whickered his horse, avoiding eye contact with the paladin as Nimue moaned into the cloth, her cheek throbbing. The Red Paladin kept his eyes locked on Nimue as they passed, daring her to look back, but she did not, and she managed a slight breath as they cleared the gate.

## TEN

**N**IMUE SLIPPED OFF THE CART AND hurried into the crowd.

Time was now in short supply. If she could not find Arthur, she risked being trapped inside the walls of Hawksbridge with Red Paladins guarding the city both inside and out.

The shops were shuttering for the approaching evening, but the Raven Wing was filling up. Nimue squeezed between two farmers awaiting entry and shoved her way inside. She took a chair and stood on it, still holding the bloody rag to her mouth, and took in a view of the whole tavern. As she scanned the faces of the crowd, her heart slowly sank. The corner where Bors had fleeced local farmers was filled with sooty boys from the ironworks next door.

"Oy! Get down from there!" Someone pulled at Nimue's cloak.

Another customer gave her a push. Nimue climbed down. At her height, a wall of shoulders surrounded her. There was nowhere else for her to go. Her thoughts went to the sword. Perhaps the ironworks could melt it down for coin? Or the bank might trade for it?

Outside, the stars were coming out above the town square. Footmen were lighting torches. Nimue weighed the wisdom of visiting the ironsmith to cost out the sword. Revealing it in any way would surely provoke questions she could not answer. Her weary eyes began to search out doorways where she might sleep before the watch threw her out the gates.

Then a bell rang and a town crier hurried into the square, accompanied by two Red Paladins. Townsfolk and shopkeepers gathered.

"Oyez! Oyez!" the crier began. "By order of the Vatican, for crimes most foul, including infanticide, cannibalism, and the slaughter of the Lord's servants in conspiracy with demonic spirits—"

Nimue shrank away and searched for a place to hide.

"—thirty gold denarii for the capture or death of the Fey murderess known only as the Wolf-Blood Witch! Any who offer aid or shelter to the witch are heretics punishable by torture and burning under Church law!"

Nimue pulled her hood over her face and hurried in the opposite direction of the town crier, nearly slamming into the hindquarters of a gray charger. The horse lifted a rear leg to kick, and the rider looked back with an annoyed sneer. It was Bors.

"Watch it, you dumb bastard!"

He could not see Nimue's face beneath her hood, and she hurried ahead of his horse, past the other sell-swords to Egypt, Arthur's black courser. She touched Arthur's hand. He looked down as Nimue pulled back her hood.

"Nimue?"

Between relief and exhaustion, her words caught in her throat. She wavered and Arthur swung his leg around and landed beside her to catch her arm before she fell. Glancing to his fellows, he led her a few yards away. They stood beneath a flickering torch.

"I'm—" Nimue tried again, but could only sob.

"What's happened?"

"They're gone," she managed, hating that she couldn't stop crying.

"Who is gone? You're not making sense."

"All of them!" she snarled, rage and panic spilling over. She took his arm, fearing she'd scare him away.

A shadow fell over them. Bors spun Nimue around. She could see him trying to place her, but with her hair shorn, he struggled.

Nimue had no choice. She quickly wiped her tears and changed tacks: "I need to hire you. I'll pay you."

Bors's eyes widened. "You're the witch."

"I'll pay you," Nimue repeated, "to help me find Merlin. I have business with him."

Arthur's eyes flicked between Nimue and Bors. He had no idea what she was talking about. Nor did Nimue, really.

Bors chuckled. "Merlin? Why, she knows Merlin, Arthur. You're a batty little thing, aren't you? I wager you haven't got a pot to piss in."

"Well, I have. I have something of great value that I must deliver to Merlin. If you help me, he'll pay you handsomely." Nimue glanced across the square. The Red Paladins had to be nearby.

Bors grabbed Nimue roughly by the collar of her cloak. "Witch, you've already got debts to pay." As he grabbed her, he felt the outline of the sword. "What's this?" He wrestled it from behind Nimue, who had strung it over her back.

"It's just a sword," she sputtered.

"Let's have a look."

Nimue pulled it from Bors's hands. "I'll show you." She drew the sword. The rune glinted in the torchlight.

Bors rubbed his mouth greedily. "Give it here."

But Nimue hid the sword under her cloak again. "That's enough."

"Where's your friend Pym?" Arthur asked.

"Dead, I think."

"Dead?" Arthur ran a nervous hand through his hair.

There was no time to explain. "I have to bring the sword to Merlin. He'll pay you more gold than you can imagine. But we have to go quickly."

"Maybe I'll just take the sword and we call ourselves even, eh?" Bors grabbed Nimue's cloak again, but she shook him off.

"Don't you dare."

"Bors—" Arthur started, but Bors jabbed his finger in Arthur's face.

"Know your place, boy. You're far too friendly with this wench for my liking." Bors turned back to Nimue. "Now see here, girl. Just give us the sword and be on your way."

"No." Nimue felt the scars on her back scrape against the brick wall of the bakery.

Bors took a step toward her. "Or . . . I can just take the sword, then drag you by the ankles to them Red Paladins. Your choice."

"Listen, I can—" Arthur interjected, but Bors turned and smacked him across the face with the back of his hand.

"You can get back on your horse is what you can do! This don't involve you!"

Arthur stumbled back to Egypt, hand to his cheek. His horse snuffed and reared.

"Now give it here, love." Bors's meaty hand reached for her.

Nimue threw her cloak over her left shoulder. With her right hand she untied the sling knot that held the sword around her. She cradled the blade in the crook of her arm, her hand passing over the iron cross guard.

Bors's eyes shone. "That's a good girl."

The Fingers of Airimid crept up her cheek, and the hum in her belly turned into a sizzling hiss that boiled her blood through her arms to her fists. Nimue tightened her hands around the leather grip, pivoted quickly, and cut Bors's hand cleanly off at the wrist. The force of the blow cartwheeled the severed appendage through the air until it landed in the square thirty feet away. Bors howled and stared at the air above his wrist where his hand used to be.

"Try again and I'll have the other." A wildness had her. Nimue felt ten feet tall and could crush Bors and his screams under her bootheel. The sword felt like a part of her arm, so light, so natural. A hot spring of power moved through her and through the sword. She couldn't help but smile.

Bors recoiled, clutching his bleeding stump, and bellowed, "Kill that witch!"

Nimue shook off the euphoria, though her senses stayed sharp. She ran across the square, shoved Arthur aside, vaulted onto Egypt's saddle, and reached back for him. "Come on!"

"Arthur!" Bors shrieked. "I'll string you up by the guts!"

Arthur leaped onto the back of his horse behind Nimue as she kicked Egypt's ribs and charged across the square.

Townsfolk fled in all directions away from the bloodshed. Footmen ran up the alley from the eastern gate as at Bors's command, the other sellswords spun their horses around and chased after Arthur and Nimue.

"Where are you going?" Arthur shouted.

"I don't know!"

"Give me the damn reins!"

Arthur reached over Nimue and turned Egypt in the opposite direction of the gate she'd entered.

"What are you doing?"

"The western gate! Fewer guards!"

One of the Red Paladins ran up on foot, sword drawn, but Arthur

swung his boot under the monk's chin. The Red Paladin landed square in the sewer ditch as Arthur galloped between two buildings. He took several switchbacks down alleyways to throw off his pursuers, finally emerging into a quiet square where the half-built cathedral loomed over them. A distant bell clanged.

"Damn it. They're sealing the gates." Arthur spurred Egypt down another avenue. Torchlight threw the shadows of their pursuers onto the long walls of the buildings. The sell-swords galloped after them in a furious mass. The western gate was still fifty yards ahead. Footmen hurried to close it.

Arthur spurred Egypt on. "Down!" he roared. "Down!" Nimue pressed her face to the saddle, and they soared toward the lowering gate. Arthur threw his arms around Egypt's neck as they plunged beneath it. The gate's teeth raked their backs and tore at their cloaks, but they cleared the city walls.

They thundered onto the road lit only by starlight.

# ELEVEN

RIVERS OF BLOOD WASHED DOWN THE
pathways of Castle Pendragon as an army of workers put
buckets and brushes to the task of scrubbing the courtyard
walls clean of the cursed rain. Many murmured prayers of
protection as they performed the tasks, word spreading far and wide of
the terrible omen and what it might mean for the king.

No one felt this dread more keenly than Uther himself, who stormed
through the castle in full plate armor. He knew the blood rain was a warning, so he surrounded himself with armored soldiers and the loyal Sir Beric.

"Merlin!" Uther shouted. "Where in the bloody Nine Hells is he?"

Sir Beric jogged to keep up with the king. "We don't know, sire. We've
looked everywhere. He's not answering his door."

"Then break it down!"

Uther led the contingent of torch-bearing soldiers to the inner court-yard of the massive castle. He marched up to Merlin's cottage door and banged with a steel fist.

"Merlin, damn you, are you in there?"

He was.

Merlin shivered in sheets that were soaked with sweat and sticking to the melted skin of the burn. To dull the pain, he poured wine down his throat, cuddling the hide.

"Merlin!" The cottage shook from Uther's blows.

Finally Merlin sat up, grimaced, and staggered to the door, opening it a crack. He thrust his face into the king's.

"Your Majesty."

Uther wrinkled his nose. "Gods, man, are you drunk?"

"All is well in hand, sire, tip-top. I just need a little more time to study the omens," Merlin slurred.

"Study the omens? It rained blood on our castle! Where is the mystery?"

"Expect a full report very soon, Majesty. One mustn't jump to conclusions." And with that, Merlin slammed the door in Uther's face.

The king's cheeks turned a very sour shade of purple. "Break it down. Break the bloody thing down and drag him out."

Two soldiers hurried to the task, ramming their steel shoulders against the oak door. The wood began to splinter.

"Perhaps the rack will sober him up," Uther growled.

Sir Beric bit his lip. "Is that advisable, my liege? Merlin is a curious creature, of course, but he is our creature. Surely we do not wish to further antagonize any dark forces?"

A splintering crack turned them back to the cottage. Soldiers stormed inside. King Uther followed them, only to discover that the rooms were empty and the shutters of the back window opened.

Merlin was gone.

✦ ✦ ✦

Arthur caught Nimue by the arm before she slid off Egypt's saddle. On instinct, she pulled her arm away.

"You fell asleep," he said.

"No, I didn't," Nimue mumbled as she righted herself and weakly gripped Arthur's tunic. Yet within moments, her forehead thumped against his back and her body went slack.

Arthur elbowed her.

"Knock it off," she growled.

"You did it again."

"I'm fine."

"I should let you fall off and be done with you."

That Nimue couldn't muster the strength to retort was a sure sign she'd reached her limit. They would soon have to make camp. Their pace was a crawl. They had ridden south for hours, toward the mountains and the Trident Peaks, deeper into the territory of the Red Paladins, rather than away. Egypt would push on until she collapsed, but Arthur felt her strain. Her lips were flecked with foam. The terrain would worsen from here and the roads would get more dangerous. Only now in the quiet blue darkness before dawn had the enormity of the night's events begun to settle on Arthur's shoulders.

*Where can I leave her?* he kept thinking.

*Who in the Nine Hells is this girl?*

*What was he supposed to do with her?*

He thought the convent at Yvoire might take her, but she was Fey Kind and hunted by Red Paladins.

*And she cut off Bors's hand!*

Arthur was no stranger to bounties, gang wars and blood feuds. He could usually slip his way out of trouble, but this was different. His thoughts raced as he imagined Bors's next move. There were two likely scenarios. First, an immediate pursuit, in which case they would be overtaken within the hour. Bors and his sell-swords were all strong riders and their horses fit, and though Egypt was a superior animal, she was carrying two riders and hadn't had a good rest in over a day. Or, and this was his prayer, Bors's wound would require a surgeon, and that would slow him by hours at least. The cut was clean. In a hundred swings, Arthur wasn't sure he could match it. There was a chance Bors had bled out right there on the street, though Arthur suspected he wouldn't be that lucky. Trysten could make a decent field dressing, and Bors was a hard fellow indeed. He would never forget this. He would never forget Arthur's betrayal, and worse, that a farm girl had taken his sword hand. That tale would fill tavern halls with laughter from here to the North Sea.

Arthur shook his head. He should've left well enough alone. This girl's problems weren't his problems.

*Bors's hand flew thirty feet.*

*Need to get another look at that sword.*

Nimue lurched left again and Arthur reached behind to catch her by the cloak. She murmured a protest and tried to sit up.

✦ ✦ ✦

An hour later, a small fire did its best against the cold mist. Arthur had put a copse of trees between them and the road and prayed their fire was small enough to avoid attention. Nimue slept against a tree, curled up like a child, using her balled-up cloak as a pillow. Arthur bit off some hard cheese and eyed the sword. He rose, careful not to wake her, and eased the frayed cloth sling over her sleeping head.

He drew the blade and turned it in the firelight. A weapon of art, soft, yielding, yet the blade's tip was weighted with a perfect balance of iron and steel for a lethal thrusting strike.

But more than that, the sword hummed in Arthur's fist. His heart quickened. He swung it slowly in the air and crouched to block an invisible blow. He turned faster and the blade whistled past his ear. Arthur studied the nicks in the blackened blade. This sword was a veteran of ancient battles. The strange rune on the pommel, the silver engraving: he'd never seen the like. A royal sword? A ceremonial sword? He did not recognize it as Germanic or Mongol. It wasn't Roman or Genoan. Didn't matter, it was a weapon that would command respect. A weapon of inestimable value.

Arthur glanced at Nimue.

This sword would get him onto trade ships and safely to distant shores. This sword could negotiate with Viking lords, either cutting deals or cutting throats. This sword could buy him his own sell-swords, quality fighters, not dungeon spillovers, and audiences in the courts of barons for respectable work.

Were he to claim it, this sword could return his honor.

Nimue stirred. She turned to Arthur and saw the sword in his hands. "What are you doing?"

"Nothing—I was—"

"Give it back!" Nimue was on her feet. She wrested the sword from

Arthur's hand and thrust it into its scabbard, slinging it back over her shoulder, which pulled the peasant shirt down around her shoulder, exposing her back.

"I was just looking at it—"

"Your 'looking' looks a lot like 'stealing.'"

"Are you mad? Do you even know who your friends are?"

"What friends?"

"The friend who just hung out his neck to save your hide!"

"Was it me you saved or the sword?"

Nimue turned her back to him and flopped down by the tree. She wrapped her arms around her knees.

"You're hurt," he said, walking toward her.

Nimue turned around. "What? No, I'm not."

*He sees the scars.* Nimue's cheeks flushed as she glanced to her exposed shoulder and quickly pulled up the shirt to cover the wounds. "It's nothing." She could barely think for the throbbing of her pulled tooth.

"It's not nothing. You're wounded."

"I'm fine!"

Arthur softened his tone. "I can try to dress them. I have some wine left. Some wrapping. If a rot sets in, you're done for."

Nimue was silent for a long time. "They're not fresh. They just look that way."

"What does that mean?" Arthur sat down by the fire.

"They're just scars. Old scars."

"Scars that never heal?"

Nimue nodded.

"That doesn't make sense."

"It does"—Nimue hesitated—"if the wound is caused by dark magic." She saw unease wash over his face, and it annoyed her.

"Because you're a—you're um, a—?"

"A what? A witch?" Nimue finished sharply.

"No, I'm just, I don't know. I mean, I don't think—"

"No, you don't think, do you? What does that mean to you? That word?"

"Look, forget it."

"I am Sky Folk. My clan was born in the first light. Our ancient queens were summoning the rain, harnessing the sun, and giving life to the harvest while your kind were playing with rocks."

Arthur held up his hands. "I yield."

Nimue rolled her eyes at him and returned to a principled sulk. *Ignorant man blood*, she thought. But the embarrassment ran deeper. She could never escape them. The scars. She was forever marked and forever an outcast. Her own clan feared her. Why shouldn't Arthur? She could see it in his eyes. *He wants to be rid of me. I don't blame him.*

Arthur turned some embers with a stick. After a few uncomfortable moments, he said, "Just looked like it hurt."

"Well, it doesn't," Nimue said quickly. "Most of the time it doesn't." She looked up at him. Their eyes met across the fire.

"Looks like claws."

Nimue nodded.

The memory squirmed in the back of her mind. She could still smell the onions in her father's hair as she slept between her parents. It was the safest, warmest spot in her entire world, or had been until that night, when it all began: the visions, the visits, the spells and the terror, when that sickly sweet voice called her by name: "*Nimue.*"

"I was five years old," Nimue began as she looked into the flames.

"*Nimue*," the voice had whispered again. She climbed out of bed and walked outside their wooden hut.

"Hello?" she called out to the night air. The village had been so quiet.

She remembered her bare feet padding on the dirt and her stomach humming like a fiddle string as the voice said again, *"Nimue, why won't you come?"*

Nimue had asked, "Where are you?" The moon shone so brightly that night it lit a path through the village, past the Chief's Hall and into the Iron Wood.

Unlike most of the children, Nimue had never feared the woods at night. Her mother was the Arch Druid of the village and her father, Jonah, a respected healer, so from a very young age they had taught Nimue about the Hidden. She knew they were very small and hid inside of things, like the dew on a leaf or the bark of a tree. And when they did show themselves, they were invisible to all but a few with special eyes. Lenore could sing songs that teased the Hidden into the light, the way soft strokes made sparks on a cat's back. Nimue had never been given a reason to fear the Hidden. No one had ever told her that just as the Hidden could find her and speak with her, there were other things, darker, more terrible things, that could find her and speak with her too. At five years old Nimue considered the Hidden her friends, though friends she had never quite met. Which was why the voice intrigued her. It was warm. It wanted to play.

Nimue crossed the tree line and felt the pine needles under her bare feet. The hum in her stomach pulled her softly toward the voice.

*Where are you, Nimue?*

*I'm coming. Be patient. I can't find you.* Nimue walked the moonlit path until she reached the dens, a rise of tilting rock slabs that glowed like a pile of gravestones under the moon. Even at her age, she knew the dens were off-limits.

"Why are you in there?" she asked. There was a pause.

"*I need your help,*" was the soft reply.

Nimue climbed onto the rocks that formed the dens, careful not to slash her bare feet on the very sharp edges.

"I'm here," she said.

*"I'm hiding from you."*

Nimue peered into a crevice between two large rock sheets, where the moon shone on a patch of dirt floor some ten feet below. She had always been a very good climber, and her small fingers found grooves in the rock that allowed her into the hole with relative ease. But there she was engulfed in a curtain of blackness that the moonlight could not reach.

"Hello?"

*"I'm here, sweet thing,"* the voice had said from the darkness. *"Come closer."*

The hum in her stomach thrummed painfully as it pulled her toward the darkness. She realized that whatever was inside that darkness had made her come, had somehow drawn her there.

*"You have your mother's eyes,"* it whispered.

Then a hint of black fur swayed into the moonlight, suggesting a creature inside the shadows in the shape of a bear standing on all fours. But it was bigger than a bear. It was bigger than anything she had ever seen. Its shoulders squeezed between the walls of the cave. Claws longer than Nimue's arms slid into the light, and piggish eyes gleamed yellow in a face that looked slashed from a thousand maulings. Loose, bloody jowls hung from its smiling jaws, and patches of flesh were torn out of its long, thick snout.

Nimue screamed for her mother with her mind. The Demon Bear lumbered into the light, whispering, *"Only the seed of Lenore can sate my terrible hunger."*

Nimue turned and slapped her hands against the wall, searching for handholds. Before she could climb, she felt the tips of three swords pin her to the wall. The claws dragged down her back. Nimue howled. They burned where they cut. She dared to look over her shoulder and watched the Demon Bear tasting her blood, like a child sneaking cream from the froth of a milk bucket. Then it giggled at her. Nimue's bloody nightdress clung to her legs and back.

And then she heard her mother's voice in her mind, urgent but composed. *Call to the Hidden, Nimue.*

*I don't know how!* she had thought back to her mother. *Help me!*

*I won't reach you in time.*

This shook Nimue into action. She closed her eyes and reached out. She reached out her thoughts to every rock, leaf, and branch, every grub, raven, and fox. She screamed to the Hidden with her thoughts, as the Demon Bear tasted her scent on the air, then dipped its head low, brushing the dirt with its bloody snout. Nimue could smell its rancid stench of death. The Demon Bear's jaws unhinged and stretched to swallow her whole.

She kept calling to the Hidden.

The crevasse wall trembled under her palms and the hum in her stomach rose to a high pitch. The Demon Bear snorted and looked about as the cave bucked violently and dust filled the air. Nimue had heard a crack directly overhead. She looked up and saw a large slab of rock tilt forward from the pile. It fell, like the blade of a guillotine, so quickly there was no time to react. Nimue shut her eyes as she heard the wet, crunching impact. A terrible wailing filled the crevasse on a gust of hot wind before exploding into a thousand different screams.

After several seconds, Nimue finally found the courage to open her eyes. She remembered staring at the mighty slab standing upright before her. Its sharp edge had bisected the Demon Bear's skull.

Nimue looked into the fire. "Nothing was ever the same after that. The scars never healed, which many in my clan took to mean I was cursed. Even my father's eyes turned cold. He no longer held me. After that night I began to have visions, and sometimes they were so strong I would"— Nimue glanced over at Arthur, who was listening intently—"forget what happened. The spells embarrassed my father. They frightened him. He made me drink sour remedies, thinking they would cleanse me of evil spirits. All they did was make me sick. So he pulled away. Started drinking more wine. His moods became dark and violent."

"What about your mother?" Arthur's voice startled Nimue, but his tone was gentle and without judgment.

"She thought I was special. But I hated her lessons. We fought all the time." Nimue chuckled dryly, then went silent. She felt shame rising up inside of her, and her eyes brimmed with tears. She turned away from Arthur so he would not see. "I don't want to talk anymore."

Arthur opened his mouth to say something but clearly thought better of it. One of the logs on the fire snapped. They sat in silence.

Until screams cut the night.

Wailing. Harsh voices, carrying through the trees.

Nimue stood up and quickly stamped out the campfire, cloaking them in darkness. It was hard to tell how close the voices were. Another round of pitiful screams pierced the quiet. A lull. Then a rise of fierce cries, panicked howls for survival. The sound was dreadfully familiar.

They heard the ring of swords. Then, slowly, one by one the screams went silent. Nimue squeezed her fists against her eyes to fight her rage. They heard a single begging voice and then . . . nothing.

Nimue went back to her tree and slumped to the ground.

The accusatory silence of the faceless victims in the forest hung over them.

THE DEMON BEAR'S JAWS UNHINGED AND STRETCHED TO SWALLOW HER WHOLE.

# TWELVE

THEY HEARD THE FLIES BEFORE THEY SAW
the bodies. The toppled wagons of an ambushed caravan came
into view when Arthur and Nimue rounded the bend of a
sun-dappled trail. A clear, cool November sun fought through
the red leaves of the large beech trees that filled the forest. The lumps in
the road Nimue had first taken as fallen baggage were soon revealed to
be dead bodies. They lay strewn over the path and deep into the thicket,
chased and cut down in panicked flight.

Nimue slid off Egypt's saddle as they approached.

"We don't want to linger here," Arthur warned. But Nimue ignored
him. "They probably camped nearby, waiting to loot the wagons by daylight so they didn't miss anything."

Nimue pulled a woman's bloody corpse over onto its back, revealing a dead toddler beneath her. The mother's body hadn't been shield enough for the paladin's broadsword. The child's face was cherubic and peaceful, cheeks and eyelids tinted blue with death. Nimue stroked the locks that spilled out from under the girl's wimple.

"You're a brave one, aren't you?" Nimue whispered. "I'm very impressed with you. You didn't cry. You stayed strong for your mum." She held the girl's cold hand. She thought of leaving her mother in the temple. She felt so ashamed. "I wish to be as brave as you."

Nimue felt a stir in her stomach. The hum.

The girl's eyes snapped open.

Egypt whickered and turned in a nervous circle, sensing Arthur's tension. For his part, Arthur surveyed the woods, eyes darting for any movement among the trees. He couldn't keep his gaze from drifting back to the bodies.

It looked like the paladins had been too lazy for crosses this time. They'd tied three of the Druid men to separate trees and simply swung away at them with their steel until their bodies were unrecognizable.

Something even more disturbing caught Arthur's eye. It sat by the front of the caravan. Arthur swung his leg around and dismounted Egypt to have a closer look. It was the body of a woman, propped up against one of the wagon wheels. Her head, which lay nearby, had been replaced with a dog's head. Someone had drawn words in blood on the broadside of the wagon.

## DELIVER THE WOLF WITCH

Nimue's heart pounded. Every instinct told her to run, but the hum held her to the spot. It throbbed in her ears. The girl's eyes were absent of light, yet open and staring at her all the same.

"They are watching you." The dead girl's lips barely moved.

Nimue managed to croak in reply, "Who?"

The dead girl stared at Nimue for a long pause, then answered, "Those who seek the Sword of Power. They wait for you to abandon it so they may claim it."

"My mother told me to bring the sword to Merlin."

"The sword has chosen you."

The thought panicked her. "But I don't want it."

"Who in the bloody hell are you talking to?"

Nimue jolted and turned to Arthur looming over her. "Noth-nothing. No one." Nimue looked back at the dead girl. Her eyes were closed. Her cherubic face was still once more.

"There's something you should see," Arthur said softly.

He led Nimue to the woman's propped-up body. Despite all she'd seen in the past few days, her knees still weakened at the almost joyful savagery of the Red Paladins. Stifling an urge to vomit, Nimue growled. "And?"

Arthur pointed out the bloody words on the wagon. "I can only assume this is you."

Nimue stared at the words and then closed her eyes and felt her scars burn under the warmth of the sword on her back. She could sense the steel through the scabbard, and an enveloping fury rose up from her guts, into her neck. For a moment she thought it might blind all her senses, but then she steadied her breath and allowed it to writhe within her like some unchained animal.

"We shouldn't keep them waiting." Nimue turned on her heel and walked toward Egypt.

Arthur turned, confused. "What? Wait—what?"

# THIRTEEN

ARTHUR LED EGYPT DOWN THE PATH
at a crawl, stopping every few minutes to listen for riders and to scan the terrain. Nimue felt Arthur's sidelong
glances but paid him no mind. She felt far away inside
herself. She wanted to unleash the demons. She now knew how to do it.

She could still taste her father's sour brew on her tongue, his paste of
juniper and rue and coal dust. Her insides twisted at the memory of those
sick mornings, writhing on her bedroll, too ill to stand as her mother and
father bellowed at each other. But for all her retching and poison swallowing,
Nimue could not control her episodes nor expel the demons causing them.

Eventually, her father packed his seeds and tools, loaded them on
a wagon drawn by their only palfrey, and rode north. Nimue had been
making dolls that day and came home only to find her mother crying

and her father's wagon turning onto the forest path. He hadn't even said goodbye to her.

Lenore tried to pull Nimue into the hut, but she broke free.

"Papa!" she shouted, and ran after him. It took forever to reach him and when she did, she was so out of breath she couldn't speak. She could only pull on the palfrey's reins.

"Let her go, Nimue," her father had said.

Her stifled sobs made breathing even harder. Again, she had tried to pull on the horse, but her father's switch lashed her on the wrist. Nimue stumbled and fell onto the road.

"You've brought darkness to this family, Nimue. It's not your fault, child, but you've done it all the same. You're cursed."

"But I'm like Mama! The Hidden speak to me, too!"

"Let your mother explain it," her father growled. "Let her give name to the shadow inside you. I'll not speak it."

"I'll fix it, Papa," Nimue had pleaded. "I'll take the medicine! I won't complain!"

"It's in your blood, child. There's no fixing it."

"But you can stay for Mama. You don't have to speak with me, just please don't go!"

Her father's voice was choked with emotion. "Go now." He flicked the switch and the palfrey moved on. Nimue ran after him for nearly an hour, until the moon rose over the trees.

But her father never looked back.

Nor did he come home.

Arthur cursed under his breath and Nimue's attention snapped back to the present. Six horses were tied to a set of pines a hundred paces from the road. Nimue could hear voices in the distance. Arthur clucked his tongue for Egypt to hurry past.

*Red Paladins.* The effect of those words on Nimue was like a torch to oil. It was a fire that swept through her. Her father leaving, Lenore's last dying cries, Biette kicked into the dirt, the mocking eyes of the paladin at Hawksbridge, the demon priest's cold blue eyes, Pym shouting her name.

Nimue slid off the saddle and ran across the road.

Arthur hissed, "Nimue!"

She picked up her pace, ducking under branches, running for the horses. She could hear Arthur's muffled curses behind her. As she approached the horses and drew the Sword of Power, the horses huffed and stepped nervously. With ease she cut the bedrolls, coin purses, food packs, and waterskins from the saddles, letting them drop into the leaves. She ignored Arthur, who was waving his arms like a madman for her to return to the road, and pointed to the stolen goods. Then Nimue turned to the voices. She squeezed the sword's warm hilt.

She felt it. The sword wanted blood.

She wanted blood too.

She felt her rage pouring into the sword like another fold of molten steel, sharpening and hardening the blade. She thought she might vomit. Yet it wasn't a bad feeling, just a monstrous urge. To cut. To kill. To feed. *Like a hunting wolf,* she thought. Unleashing demons.

A path sloped down into what appeared to be a glade, surrounded by large rocks.

Nimue followed the wall of boulders around to the edge of a large green pond, sheltered under generous limestone cliffs, dripping with moss. She crouched in the mud, several feet from the edge of the water. She peered around the leading edge of a rock.

Red Paladins were on the opposite shore, only seventy paces from Nimue. A fury choked in her throat as she remembered the high-pitched screams of the Sky Folk on their crosses while the flames licked their flesh.

*Time to avenge them,* Nimue thought. *Time to avenge them all.*

✦ ✦ ✦

There were two in the water. They splashed, laughing like children. The four on shore shoveled food into their mouths. A blanket of stolen booty was open in the mud, likely the desperate handfuls of the family from the caravan. Religious totems, candlesticks, a few small children's toys.

Nimue heard a stick snap behind her. She turned to see Arthur. He mouthed, "What the hell are you doing?"

Nimue pulled her cloak over her head and took off her shoes, leaving them in the mud as she crawled closer to the water. Arthur shook his head vigorously.

Nimue pressed her chest to the cold mud, dug in her fingers, took a deep breath, and squirmed like a reptile into the pond.

She reached down in the blurry brown darkness for the stones of the bottom and found them. With one hand she pulled herself forward, while her other hand held the Sword of Power, which gleamed emerald. She heard the muffled horseplay of the paladins and then saw their pale, naked legs kicking in the void.

On the water's surface, a monk caught his brother in a choke hold and forced his head down, laughing at his struggle. He caught an elbow in the testicles for his trouble and paddled away as his friend surfaced, gasping for air. They squared off again. The elbowed monk swam at his friend and then hesitated. His brow furrowed. His droopy eyes brightened with awe.

A girl's face hovered in the waters below him. Perfect. A doll's face. Her hair danced and her eyes captured glints of spectral green. The monk took her for a water nymph from one of the pagan stories. He tried to speak as a perfect silver blade entered the bottom of his jaw and tore through the top of his skull. The blade slid back into the water as the monk bobbed for a moment, rivulets of blood pouring down his face, before sinking.

The other monk blinked, unsure of what he'd just seen. He noticed dark pools forming and clouding the pond. His hands cupped the water and came up red. A sliver of emerald surged up out of the darkness. The sword entered his sternum at an angle, puncturing heart and lungs, before biting through his back. The monk coughed a red mist, then toppled into the pond face-first.

One of the brothers onshore looked out and saw only red robes drifting on the pond surface. He slapped the knee of another paladin, whose mouth was full of biscuits, and pointed.

The water stirred and Nimue rose slowly from the pond, the Sword of Power clutched in her fists, paladin blood washing down her stolen clothes. The hum of the Hidden throbbed in her ears. She couldn't feel the chill of the pond for the heat of the blood rushing through her. She laughed. It was a cold, dark chuckle from deep within her. Her wolf howl.

The paladins retreated back to the rocks, convinced that Nimue was some kind of nature demon.

"It's her," one of them growled.

"She's—she's murdered them. Falto!" The youngest monk, Gunyon, shouted to one of the floating bodies. "Now she's come for us!"

"This isn't natural, one girl—" Another paladin, Lesno, was losing nerve.

Thomas, their bent-nosed commander, barked, "Look with your own eyes, you dim toad! She's just touched is all, and it's made her bold!"

At his words the brothers collected their senses and saw the maid, not the rumors, standing before them; a girl, barely five feet tall.

"She's just one Druid whore!"

"Burning's a mercy for this one." The commander loosened the flail from his belt. He let the spiked iron balls hang down to the gravel. He smiled at Nimue.

"I call the sword," Robert, one of the other brothers, blurted.

"The one who kills her gets the sword," Thomas corrected him.

"This will please the Father," Lesno said as he picked his scythe off the ground. They spread out over the length of the shore.

"Come on out, love, let me warm you up," Thomas called to her.

Nimue's eyes darted from one to the other. She waved the sword at them. Its worn leather straps under her palms and the weight of the blade emboldened her. "Who's next?"

"Let's keep her alive, brothers. Never seen a witch like this one."

"Not like those other pigs—"

"I don't see any warts."

"I want to see the rest of her."

Their boots sloshed into the waters.

"Come on, then! I'll gut you all!" she screamed.

Two of the paladins chuckled at the threat. The others were deadly serious.

"Don't be afraid, love, we'll have a nice party before it's all over. Gunyon, pull her out of there!"

Gunyon sounded alarmed by this command. "Why me?"

"I'll have your eyes!" Nimue swung at them as the monks sloshed closer, only ten feet away, encircling her.

Gunyon took a deep breath and plunged under the surface. Nimue hacked at the waters as their commander hurried up behind her and caught her by the hair.

"The sword!" he barked.

Another paladin splashed forward and reached for the blade. But even with her head yanked back by the commander's fist around her hair, she wrenched the sword around and hacked through the paladin's fingers. The monk shrieked and bent forward, clutching his hand as an ax—

intended for him—hurtled past him, headed for Nimue, and she barely got her sword up in time to block it.

But the sword was knocked clean from her hands and vanished into the pond waters, which had been muddied from blood and debris kicked up from the floor.

Nimue saw Arthur cursing his aim and readying another hand ax that he'd freed from the paladins' own horses.

"What did you do?" Nimue shouted at him. Without the sword, her arms were suddenly deadweights. The cold and pain fell on her and she gasped for energy. Fear returned with a mule kick, and she could barely track the shouts and movement and bodies all around her.

Gunyon burst out of the waters and bludgeoned Nimue with a wild swing, catching her in the temple. They plunged back into the water, Gunyon's hands seeking out her neck and squeezing. Nimue sucked in a throatful of water before her air was cut off. She scratched at his bare arms. Where was the sword? Her back hit the rocks of the pond floor, raising another cloud of mud. There was a terrible ringing in her ears. She dug her nails into the paladin's cheeks and eyes, but his grip only tightened. Her mind filled with flashes of white, and in between the flashes she saw images: *tears of blood streaming down lean cheeks . . . Arthur naked and curled up asleep like a babe, surrounded by candles . . . a white owl, impaled by an arrow, flailing in the snow . . . a blue glade, every leaf moving, every leaf a wing, the glade alive, pulsing . . . a sea of banners flapping in a cold wind, their crest a mighty boar's head . . . a ribbon of silver entwining two women's hands . . . the sun turned black and blinding . . . a grassy mound of tilting gravestones rising up, spilling clods of dirt, something underneath, older than time, something terrible . . . a beautiful little girl with green antlers . . .*

Nimue felt herself falling into the white void in her mind, giving over to a dream sleep, when rough hands grabbed her arms and yanked her forward. She inhaled another mouthful of pond water as the cold air hit her cheeks. Arthur dragged her through the pond and flopped her onto the gravel shore, where she vomited. A second later he was on top of her, screaming, though her ears throbbed and she could not make out the words. He shook her, and she coughed up more water. Somehow that brought back her hearing.

"—want to die? Is that what you want? Is it?"

"Yes!" Nimue croaked, slapping at Arthur and shoving him off. She curled over onto her hands and knees and sobbed as she retched on the gravel.

Arthur unbuckled his sword belt and flung his dagger in its sheath at her feet. "Then finish it! And let me be done with you!"

Nimue fell onto her stomach and wept against the cold rocks. Arthur swayed in the breeze, scowling, but did not leave. Instead he sat on the shore, stuffed his shaking hands beneath his armpits, and stared in disbelief at the pond, now a deep red with paladin blood, robes floating like jellyfish on the surface.

Suddenly Nimue slapped at the gravel around her. "The sword. The sword!" Arthur was too exhausted to answer. Nimue crawled into the water, keeping her chin above the blood. She dog-paddled, pushing bodies away until she spied an emerald glint. She dove down and retrieved the Sword of Power.

# FOURTEEN

ARTHUR SAT AGAINST A BOULDER AND watched Nimue throw one of the paladins' saddlebags onto the shore. She sat cross-legged and began to rummage through it.

He bit off a hunk of stale biscuit left over from the ambushed caravan. Every instinct told him to run, to leave the madwoman to her inevitable fate. Yet his eyes drifted to the handkerchief in his right hand, its edges embroidered with purple flowers, the rest brown with old bloodstains. The handkerchief was his mother's, but the blood was his father's. It was the handkerchief that bade him stay.

Tor, son of Cawden, was a restless figure in Arthur's life, an unsteady earner who would vanish for months at a time on grand quests, leaving his wife and children to tend their meager farm in Cardiff. Typically, his father would return home with nothing more than stories of treasures won and lost, of great battles and glorious jousts. He cut an ample figure, with strong appetites for wine and food, and by the time Arthur was thirteen years old, he took to wearing pieces of armor he'd collected through the years and calling himself Sir Tor. He claimed that he'd been knighted during a siege against English invaders in Gwent.

After one journey in particular, Arthur noted a change in his father. His lies were bolder, his stories even more fantastical, and his hands were full of tremors. He took to a chair in the local tavern, the Nag's Head, a bent-over little pub constructed from the timbers of local shipwrecks. His father proclaimed himself the protector of the village and drank wine every day from morning until Arthur's mother, Eleanor, collected him well past the high moon.

For all his many flaws, Arthur still loved his father. He loved his stories of crusading knights and monstrous flying lizards, ghost ships and bloody duels. He knew the local men laughed at Tor. Arthur's knuckles were always scraped, defending his father from the japes and insults of the older boys.

Small children adored Sir Tor, and he was gentle and kind to them. In their wide eyes, Sir Tor was indeed the mighty figure he claimed to be. He also had a beautiful, deep voice and could sing. And by Arthur's sixteenth year, his father had become a local institution, a knight errant, scribing his adventures to song, settling into the comfortable robes of a storyteller.

And so it was until the day three English knights, not much older than Arthur, rode into the village, seeking only thievery and violence, and the harsh truth of the world collided with Sir Tor's imagined one.

Arthur was not there to protect his father that night. He was dancing with a local girl in the next village over. It wasn't until he heard the bells and the shouts and saw strangers on horseback galloping out of town that he sensed something was wrong. By the time he returned, his father had already been carried to an upstairs room at the Nag's Head. Arthur remembered the toppled tables of the inn, the pools of blood on the floor and on the stairs. An inconsolable barmaid explained to him that Sir Tor had stepped in when the knights grabbed her. The boys turned on Sir Tor like wolves.

Arthur thought he would break into pieces when he saw his father twisted in the bedsheets, struggling to breathe. Arthur took his large, soft hand in his own and pulled up a stool. Sir Tor was speaking quickly as though several streams of conversation were passing through his mind at the same time. He repeated the word "dogs" over and over, his eyes gradually coming into focus and seeming to see Arthur for the first time.

"What was—what was I saying? Arthur, where was I, boy? I lost my train of thought." Sir Tor breathed unevenly as sweat dribbled down his round cheeks.

"Dogs, milord," Arthur reminded his father as he pressed a wet cloth to Sir Tor's forehead. The room was so quiet you could hear the flicker of the candles. Blood-soaked rags were heaped by Arthur's feet.

"Dogs, yes, of course, keep a dog. Train him to hunt fowl and you'll never go hungry on a long ride. I had a—but that wasn't—there was something else. Why is it so bloody hard to think?"

"You don't have to speak, Father."

"But I need to, I need to. Never measure your courage by the men you've killed. That's it. Sometimes true courage means avoiding the blow that will take a man's life. Men who judge their worth by the men they've killed are lesser men. Those aren't knights."

Sir Tor grimaced as he adjusted his weight on the cot. Arthur tried not to look at his bloodied shirt.

"No, milord," Arthur answered.

Sir Tor's eyes fluttered; he searched the ceiling for words as his lips moved. "Keep on with the chess. It, it exercises the mind for war, and—and is a good way to meet other youngsters. You need friends, Arthur. You're too solitary for your age. Too serious. I've told you this."

"Yes, Father."

"That's—that's a good boy. I don't mean to be critical. But you're only young once, trust me. What was I saying? What else was I . . . ? There was something I had to, um, with your, with your, with your hunting, your arrows."

"Mark my arrows. Yes, sir."

"Don't waste that iron. Good arrows cost money. Even in battle I never left an arrow if I could help it. Make sure you mark those arrows, boy. And—and don't be so serious. You have fine teeth, you should show them every now and then. The girls, the girls like to laugh. I could always make them laugh." Tor began to pat at his chest and hips, searching for something. "Where is it? Where did I . . . where's my robe?"

Anticipating, Arthur placed his mother's handkerchief with the embroidered purple flowers into his father's hand, and Tor put it to his nose, drawing in a deep breath that gave him great satisfaction.

"She smells like morning. And cherries. Is she here? Is Eleanor . . . ?"

One of Arthur's aunts had taken fever that morning, and his mother had ridden half a day to look after her sister. She had not yet returned. "Not yet, milord."

"She can't see me like this." Sir Tor tried to rise. Arthur gently pressed him back to the pillow.

"Dear Eleanor," Sir Tor sighed, "why does that girl make me wait so?"

"Soon, Father, soon."

Arthur remembered his father's hand in his own and remembered how he'd held it until the tremors stopped and his father drifted away. Now he tucked the handkerchief into the pocket of his jerkin. As a peace offering, he tossed a wedge of hard cheese to Nimue.

She ignored it.

"You need to eat," he reminded her.

"It's stolen."

"What does it matter where it came from? No one will miss it. Look at you, you look sick. When did you eat last? Two days? Three?"

"I don't remember."

"We still have three days' riding to reach the Minotaur Mountains. Shall I feed you then?"

"Try it and I'll stomp you." Nimue found a bundle of scrolls tied together with string. She cut the string and read one of them aloud: "'One hundred gold coins for the death or capture of the Wolf-Blood Witch, who, in agency with the Devil, has transformed herself into animal shapes and drunk the blood of infants and slaughtered women and children in their beds.'" On each scroll a comical sketch of a monster with bat wings and curling horns had been drawn. Nimue snorted and allowed the papers to scatter on the rocks.

Arthur walked over and sat beside her. Nimue stiffened. He picked up one of the pages and managed a light chuckle. "What did you expect them to say? 'Oh, we should mention this maid of sixteen single-handedly skewered an entire division of our best fighters'?"

Nimue humphed. Arthur took the opportunity to cut off a piece of the hard cheese, and offered it to her lips. "I warned you that I would feed you."

Nimue looked sharply into Arthur's eyes. She swung her fist up but Arthur caught it and pressed the cheese into her hand. He then guided the food to her lips. She yielded, opening her mouth slightly, taking the cheese. She chewed, wincing as she swallowed. There were purple handprints on her neck from the paladin's attack.

"Why aren't you furious with me?" Nimue asked.

*Why aren't you, Arthur?* he wondered. *Because she's mad. Because she's braver than I am.* Arthur handed her a skin of wine, which she swallowed in deep gulps. He shrugged. "Fear of reprisal, I suppose."

Nimue choked a little on her wine at this. She glared at him. He gave her another slice of cheese, which she took more eagerly.

*She's like a wild animal.* Yet so beautiful. *Nothing painted or put-on about her.* But then he looked over at the pond and the floating red robes. *A bloody catastrophe. No witnesses, at least.* A cold comfort. They would have to ride fast and far. Nothing and no one would be safe for hundreds of miles. Especially if Nimue kept chopping off hands and murdering Red Paladins.

He tried to reason with her. "I don't know if madness drives you, or voices, but I know one thing: there is little reward for courage in this world. And if you go on like this, you will simply burn like a sky fire and be ashes before the dawn. Is that what you want?"

Nimue took another gulp of wine, not answering, a hint of rose returning to her thin cheeks. She pulled out another batch of scrolls, but this set was different. The parchment was of finer quality, as was the ribbon that bound them. Each scroll had a wax seal: a cross against a two-headed eagle.

"That's Carden's seal."

Nimue broke the seal on one of the scrolls and unrolled it. It was a hand-drawn map with certain villages noted with an *X*. Nimue read them: "Four Rivers, Wick's End, the Hollow, Crow Hill. All Fey Folk villages."

Next to each village was a list of names. Nimue read those, too. "These must be elders. Clan chiefs." Nimue tore open another scroll and read it quickly. It was another set of lists, but Nimue could not divine its purpose. She handed it to Arthur. "What do you make of this one?"

Arthur couldn't believe what he was looking at. He thought about saying anything but the truth, but he knew Nimue would work it out for herself before too long. "These are Red Paladin divisions. You can see their unit numbers correspond to the *X*'s on the map." Arthur pointed to numbers by the village names.

"These are his next targets," Nimue whispered. "We know his mind." She turned to Arthur, eyes brimming with hope.

It was just as Arthur feared. "You have no intention of running, do you?"

✦ ✦ ✦

The road to the Minotaur Mountains was a long and steady climb through dense forests of late November reds and golds. This had been Nimue's favorite time of year, when the colors turned on the ancient barrow and the geese fled the river with shrill cries, ready to fly on an arrow point to the southern lakes. There would be dances at the stone circle, and Mary would fire up her pot, cooking rabbit in almond sauce, followed by honey cakes washed down with bitter ale.

Brisk western winds carried chimney smoke for miles, but traffic was thin.

They rode two horses now rather than overburdening Egypt. Arthur had selected the best of the sad, bony lot the paladins had ridden, a sloe-eyed mare with a coat the color of dirty snow. Nimue couldn't help but despise the nag, innocent and doltish as it was, imagining the blood that stained its hooves, the screams for mercy it had heard. She also resented that Arthur rode ahead of her at least three horse lengths. Though she'd fallen from Egypt's saddle—twice—she missed the comfort of being close to him.

She'd grown used to his smell, a mix of earth and grasses, sweat and something near to cinnamon but more exotic, that she attributed to his bedroll, which had seen many journeys. She'd also memorized the back of his head, the waves of brown hair that lapped over the hood of his tunic and the copper glints it would reveal in the late afternoon sun.

Nimue's thoughts drifted. *What would it be like to kiss him? What would his arms feel like wrapped around me?*

She suddenly and unexpectedly missed Pym so hard her chest hurt. She could see her dear friend's pursed lips and flashing eyes, her *please don't get us into trouble* look. They could break into hysterics over jokes never spoken.

It took one look at her fingernails, rusty with blood, to realize she would never be that girl again, and that her thoughts of autumn romance were as childish as one of Pym's laughing fits.

# FIFTEEN

ORGAN TURNED THE LOCK ON THE back door of the Broken Spear and felt the pain up her wrist. She shifted the bag of spell ingredients she'd collected on her walk that morning to her right shoulder and finished turning the lock with her left hand. Her right wrist was still wrapped in rags to lessen the nagging pain that came from hauling trays of mugs, spilling with ale, for ten hours a day. As she dropped the keys into the pocket of her smock and turned to the road, a swollen rat waddled past her foot. Morgan put the toe of her boot on its tail. The rat squeaked and half rolled onto its back.

"Are you the one that's been digging in my corn?" Morgan drew a small dagger and jabbed it through the skull. She cleaned the blade on her smock, sheathed it, plucked up the rat by the tail, and plopped it into her spell bag.

The white moon was Morgan's torch as she crossed the lone road of Cinder's Gate, a village that was merely a prelude to the actual town of Cinder set deeper into the hills of the Minotaur Mountains. Cinder's Gate was only a handful of farmhouses, a stable with a decent smith, a recently built chapel to the One God, and the Broken Spear for thirsty travelers. The hills on both sides of Cinder's Gate were thick with forests of spruce, larch, and various pine trees as well as a variety of limestone caves.

Morgan pulled her hood up and was about to enter the woods when someone whispered her name from a mound of boulders several feet away. Morgan drew her dagger again and took a few steps back. "Who's there?" She was ever keen to the dangers of the open road and had stabbed holes in more than a few overeager drunks. But her heart jumped just the same as a tall, lanky figure emerged from the shadows of the rocks.

"Morgan, it's Arthur."

Morgan's cheeks flushed with relief and a more complicated stew of emotions. "Arthur?"

He stepped into the moonlight and she shoved him with both hands. "Gods, I nearly jumped out of my skin! That's not funny! What in the Nine Hells are you doing out here?" Though her tone was harsh, she was happy to see him.

Arthur gestured for her to lower her voice. "I'm in a bit of trouble."

"Lost your trousers at dice again?" Morgan scoffed. "Haven't I warned you about gambling?"

"It's not money," Arthur said, not playing along.

"Good, because I don't have any."

"I'm sorry to drag you into this, Morgan. I—truly, I didn't know where else to go." Arthur kept glancing back at the rocks.

Bothered by all the cloak-and-dagger, Morgan changed her tone. "Very well. Get on with it. What have you gotten into now?"

Chagrined, Arthur called over his shoulder, "It's all right."

Morgan frowned, not expecting more company, particularly not the kind Arthur kept.

Slowly Nimue crept out from the rocks. She walked toward Morgan until she entered a shaft of moonlight, then pulled back her hood. Her eyes were dark as pits, her cheeks tight against her bones.

Morgan was unimpressed. "Is she with child or something?"

"Hardly," Arthur chuckled without mirth. "Have the paladins been through here yet? Calling out for rewards and the like?"

Morgan frowned. "I've heard some things. Rumors of dead paladins and witchcraft."

"Allow me to introduce you to Nimue." Arthur hesitated. "The Wolf-Blood Witch."

Morgan burst into laughter. "You shit. What is going on?"

"It's the truth," Arthur insisted.

"Where's your horns, love?" She turned to Arthur. "Her? I think a breeze might blow her over."

"I think you're mistaken," Nimue said in a flat, threatening tone.

"Can we discuss the rest indoors?" Arthur asked, craning his neck to the road, then turning back. "It would be safest."

Morgan took another beat, brow furrowing and mouth slowly opening as she realized: "You're serious."

Arthur nodded. "I am. Nimue, this is Morgan, my half sister."

Morgan took a step back from Nimue as though she suddenly *had* grown horns. "And you brought her here?"

"Please, I'll explain everything, but can we just—just do it inside the tavern?"

Morgan poured a pot of wine into three tin cups and served two bowls of porridge made from beans, peas, cabbage, and leeks with two hunks of black maslin. Nimue gnawed into the hard bread as Morgan studied her. Arthur finished his cup of wine in one swallow and pushed it toward Morgan for another pour.

"She doesn't say much, does she?" Morgan observed, obliging Arthur.

"Normally, she never shuts up."

Nimue kicked Arthur under the table, causing him to grimace.

"There's a girl," Morgan said approvingly. "Arthur definitely needs a good kick now and again. I think I like you."

Nimue turned suspicious eyes on Morgan as Morgan sat down across from her.

"How is it?" Morgan asked, gesturing to the porridge.

"Good," Nimue said with her mouth full. Then she added, "Thanks."

"You're welcome." Morgan sipped her wine, considering Nimue. Then she leaned forward. "Is it true? Did you kill those Carden bastards?"

Nimue looked up at Morgan from her porridge bowl. After a beat, she nodded.

"Good for you," Morgan said with deep satisfaction. She looked at Arthur and then back to Nimue. "How many?"

Nimue thought about it. "Ten. I think. Maybe more."

Morgan sat back in disbelief. "Ten?" She again turned to Arthur, who nodded. Now it was Morgan's turn to empty her cup. She refilled it. "How?"

Nimue looked at Arthur, and he shrugged. "I trust her," he said.

With that, Nimue stood and drew the Sword of Power from the sheath slung on her back. Whether a trick of the candles or something more mysterious, the empty tavern filled with a sudden light before darkening again as Nimue placed the blade on the table under Morgan's wide eyes.

Morgan stood, eyes devouring the sword. She touched it lightly, fingers grazing over the rune on the pommel. "The Devil's Tooth," she whispered.

Nimue frowned. "The Devil's Tooth?"

"Do you know what this is?" Morgan breathed, awestruck.

"I've heard that name. It was the sword from the old stories. The first sword," Nimue said, seeing the glow in Morgan's eyes. "No, come on. This can't be."

Morgan traced the runic symbols. "These are the elemental four circles. Water. Fire. Earth. Air. Bound together in the fifth circle. The root that binds. This is the first sword, forged in the Fey Fires. The Sword of the First Kings. Where did you find this?"

Nimue turned grim. "It was my mother's. She gave it to me when—when the Red Paladins came to my village."

"Incredible. Just incredible. You're Sky Folk, aren't you? Or do you prefer Sun Dancers?" Morgan asked.

"Sky Folk. How do you know?"

"I've become a bit of an expert," Morgan said without elaborating. "Did your mother say where she found this?"

"No," Nimue said. "She bade me bring it to someone named Merlin. I know it sounds mad, but I think she meant Merlin the Magician."

"Not mad at all," Morgan said, staring at the blade. "Something like this, it makes a great deal of sense."

"Wait, are you suggesting Merlin is real? And alive somehow?"

Arthur nodded. "The Arab traders know him. Know of him, at least. They say he spends his days as a black dog and steals away children to some kind of castle underground."

"That's idiotic." Morgan rolled her eyes.

"And you're the big expert on Merlin, are you? Broken Spear regular, is he?" Arthur asked.

"Kiss my ass, Arthur."

Arthur turned to Nimue. "You'll learn quickly that Morgan knows everything and we're all fools."

"Not all, just you," she corrected.

*Definitely brother and sister,* Nimue thought.

"I hope by now you've learned to ignore him," Morgan said to Nimue. "Pretty to look at but not much going on upstairs."

Arthur took an angry gulp of wine.

Morgan looked back and forth between Nimue and Arthur in disbelief. "Aren't you a pair? Merlin is only the most feared sorcerer of this age. Of any age, for that matter. He's mentioned in historical records dating back to the fall of Rome. He's hundreds of years old."

"Fey Kind?" Nimue asked.

"Druid," Morgan answered. "A priest of the Old Gods. I mean, who knows really? Perhaps he has ancient Fey blood or giant's blood or is half god. But he knows Fey magic, of course. And sorcery. And necromancy. And conjuration. He knows all of it. He's the very history of magic in one man. They say he commands the oceans and the skies."

"Now who sounds idiotic?" Arthur chimed back in.

"Well, he's rumored to be a counselor to King Uther Pendragon, for one. So he must think Merlin has something to offer. And he's supposedly, perhaps even more important, master of the Shadow Lords."

"What are they? What are the Shadow Lords?" Nimue asked, feeling more and more ignorant by the minute.

"The great ring of magical spies who secretly control us all," Arthur mocked.

"*Uch*, just get drunk and fall asleep already," Morgan spat. "Arthur fears what he doesn't understand. I believe in them. Since the rise of the Church, the real wizards and witches have all gone into hiding. It is a society of magic hidden within ordinary society. Each Shadow Lord holds a dominion: the beggars or the forgers or the bankers, even."

Morgan's smile faded and she looked upon Nimue's wide eyes with rising sympathy. "Oh, Nimue, you haven't the foggiest notion of what you've set into motion, have you?"

"How do we reach Merlin?" Nimue pressed.

"Wherever he is, I assure you he's far from this forgettable outpost." Arthur smiled at Morgan, then emptied his wine cup.

Morgan thought for a moment, then poured herself another cup of wine. "Perhaps there is a way to make Merlin come to us."

"Come to us?"

Morgan nodded. "If your conditions are met."

Nimue squinted with confusion. "I have conditions?"

"Of course you do. You are the Wolf-Blood Witch and you wield the Devil's Tooth. That makes you powerful. And power is the only thing men crave." Arthur started to interrupt, but Morgan continued, "You are in a position to bargain, Nimue, for your survival, for your people's survival."

Nimue had not thought of any of this. Being branded the Wolf-Blood Witch felt like a death sentence, and until now she hadn't imagined another side to it. For the first time in days she felt the stirrings of hope. This Morgan was not to be underestimated. "If Merlin is as great as you claim, won't he see through these lies?"

Morgan sat up and studied the sword again. She rubbed her hand down the neck of the blade and then showed Nimue the blood stained on her hand. "Is this paladin blood?" she asked.

Nimue nodded.

"What lies? You are the Wolf-Blood Witch and you have brought fear to those red devils. You wield the Sword of Power and you will not part with it unless Merlin meets your demands."

Nimue looked around the simple tavern. "You seem very confident."

"Oh"—Morgan sipped her wine—"you'll find I'm full of surprises, Nimue. But if I help you, I'll expect you to offer something to me in return."

"What is that something?"

"You'll see." Morgan smiled.

# SIXTEEN

MAKING SURE THE ROAD IN CINDER'S Gate was clear of any late-night travelers, Morgan led Arthur and Nimue south into the forested hills. "No torches and no talking," she ordered, then walked ahead of them on sure feet, her brown hood making her difficult to see in between the shafts of moonlight that illuminated the ground like stepping-stones. The only sounds were the soft crunches of their boots over the carpet of pine needles on the forest floor. Nimue had trouble finding any path at all and lost Morgan several times as the barmaid ducked under fallen trees and crossed trickling streams without breaking stride. They hiked like this for close to an hour, at a steady incline, until Nimue's cheeks stung from scratches, her lungs burned, and her feet ached.

Then suddenly Morgan stopped and held up a hand. Arthur and

Nimue waited. The forest was very dark. There were no visible structures apart from the towering pines and unusual rock formations, suggesting they had climbed onto one of the vast horns of the Minotaur Mountains. It was cold, and Nimue pulled her peasant's cloak tightly around her shoulders as something rustled in the branches above their heads. Arthur's hand dropped to his sword hilt, but Morgan shook her head. The "something" leaped with great agility from branch to branch, a dozen feet above their heads, before vanishing into the dark. Too fast for a bear, too large for a bird or a cat.

"What was that?" Nimue whispered.

A distant croak was her answer. It sounded like the frogs in the glade near her home on the barrow. After another set of croaks, Morgan waved them on. As they walked, Nimue sensed dozens of eyes upon them. She wasn't sure if Arthur could sense it too. Shadows rippled near a downed pine. Morgan paid these strange observers no mind as she led Arthur and Nimue to a wall of rock draped in a veil of leafy vines. The floor of pine needles rose up and to the west.

Nimue was prepared for another climb, but the veil of vines abruptly parted, revealing two girls, blanketed in capes of leaves, nearly invisible to the naked eye. Behind the veil was a small cave mouth. Without explanation, Morgan ducked and entered. Nimue followed but kept her eyes on the girls, who looked tired and frightened.

A few steps into the cave it became impossible to see, and Nimue struck her head on a low-hanging rock. On instinct, she reached back for Arthur and found his hand. His fingers clasped hers for a moment before she pulled away.

Nimue followed the sound of Morgan's skirts rustling between narrow walls. Whispers and murmurs echoed off the walls, old voices and young, and as the cave breathed, it sent a gust of smells for Nimue to decipher: pig manure and urine, a variety of highland grasses, goatskins, pepper and cloves, yew and alder, damp leaves, dried lilies and irises, sour ale, tallow, mildew, salted beef, bay leaf, sage and thyme and sweat ripe with fear.

"It's safe," Morgan whispered in the dark.

A black cloth was pulled away from a lantern, casting a flickering orange glow across a sea of faces. Bodies of all shapes and sizes huddled on the floor or sat against the jagged walls. There were at least a hundred, maybe more. The cave was low but wide and reached beyond the light into distant chambers. Nimue's breath left her. They were all Fey Kind. They were all her people, and all were refugees from Carden's pyres.

Her voice choked as she tried to say, "They're so beautiful." It was a painful yet inspiring homecoming to a place she'd never been, to a family she'd never known. Some of the clans were so rare that Nimue had never seen them before. Clans like the shy Cliff Walkers—mountain folk, the men wearing thick helms of ram horn and the women with intricate scar patterns of interlocking circles on their arms. Or the Snakes—who worshipped the night and lived in floating huts on the glade rivers. Their children hid beneath capes of rat skins, and the men and women peered out from masks of stretched bat wings, their faces painted with guano. Storm Crafters were tattooed head to toe and reputed for their rain summoning, while the Moon Wings communed with night birds and were blood enemies of the Snakes. Their young lived in the forest canopy, in rookeries, for ten years before their feet touched earth. One of the children stroked the head of an enormous gray owl as she stared at Nimue with fierce, suspicious eyes. The Tusks worshipped the boar and were equally hot-tempered. Fauns wore antlers, rode giant bucks as mounts, and were outstanding archers. There were even Plogs, tunnel dwellers, who had evolved to lives of perpetual darkness and labor. Their hands were two-fingered, thick, clawed, and calloused, and most were blind. They were the stuff of Fey child nightmares, though Lenore had taught

Nimue that the Plogs were shy creatures who preferred grubs and roots to flesh.

There were still more from clans that Nimue did not recognize. It was all so overwhelming. Add in the combination of the confining cave walls, the warmth and thick air, the fear, and the exhaustion; Nimue swayed, and Morgan had to steady her to prevent her from falling.

Morgan and Arthur led her down a series of tunnels until they reached a small alcove with room for a straw mat and a lantern. Nimue's fists were wrapped tightly around the grip of the sword as she allowed herself to be guided down to the mat. As her eyes closed, she felt herself being swept into a deep and alluring darkness.

She dreamt of fire.

Nimue's eyes popped open. The first thing she saw was Arthur seated against the wall, studying the maps they had stolen from the Red Paladins. He looked up at her.

"You slept almost two days," he told her.

Nimue slapped the ground around her. "The sword." She searched frantically. "Where is the sword?"

"Relax, we're okay. It's here." Arthur showed her a nook in the rock beside her straw mat. Inside was the Sword of Power, wrapped in a cloth. Nimue calmed at the sight of it, though her head was foggy with images from her dreams, curious yet frightening faces staring at her from the darkness.

"I'm glad you're up. They don't really like me here. 'Man blood' and all."

"They shouldn't call you that. My mother never allowed it."

Arthur nodded. "I'm just too human, I suppose. No wings or antlers. I can't say I blame the poor wretches, what they've been through. Oh, and you should be prepared."

Nimue frowned. "For what?"

"You'll see."

She stood up and swept the dirt and straw from her ragged trousers. Together they walked down a long, narrow tunnel that led into a wide, bowl-shaped cavern, partially open to the sky, through which the forest had invaded: fallen trees, gnarled roots, and mossy boulders created a sloping bridge to the outside world.

Nimue marveled at the Fey community that had arisen here as the refugees tried to create a semblance of normal life. The cavern had been divided into tribal areas. Territories were staked throughout the caves. Tusks huddled together, fashioning their unique bone weapons, while high up in the walls, Storm Crafters hung their air beds, and Snakes threw up their unnerving skin tents to avoid contact altogether.

A pall of misery hung over the caves. More than once she had to watch her step for the sick, the old, and the wounded. They crowded the floors, eyes weak and fearful. The caves were a hive of activity as Fey Kind hauled water and baskets of gathered roots and raided vegetables, hung clothes, tended the wounded, and moved the sick to more isolated areas for fear of outbreaks. Even still Nimue could see that provisions were scarce. The cave had an unmistakable edge of tension. She saw a shoving match across the way between Tusks and Snakes. It was broken up quickly, but without enough to eat, tribal and territory minds would eventually take over. It was only a matter of time. She could see that.

Unlike their elders, the Fey children played together, and their laughter was a most welcome sound.

As Nimue and Arthur passed toward the center of the caves, a murmur arose. Nimue felt many eyes upon her. It made her nervous. She didn't know these clans or their customs. She had no idea what sort of welcome, if any, to expect.

"Why are they all staring?" Nimue whispered to Arthur.

"The Wolf-Blood Witch has arrived."

A small Faun girl with tiny antler buds growing from her high forehead ran up to Nimue and touched her leg before retreating to the safety of her family shelter. A few more children of all different Fey clans swarmed around her, pushed to hold her hand or touch her, reach for her, pull at her torn sleeves. Some adults joined the children, encircling Nimue, a dozen at first, then dozens more, then a hundred, surrounding her in a worshipful circle of thankful survivors. Nimue's chest tightened with fear. Part of her wanted to run as the refugees pulled her away from Arthur to put necklaces over her head or to offer her scraps or charms of whatever eager gifts they could. Nimue said over and over, "Thank you, thank you, you're so kind." She turned back to look for Arthur but could not see him in the crowd that had formed around her.

# SEVENTEEN

THE BLIND JUGGLER WAS A GLOOMY, SMOKE-filled tavern with a warped floor that reeked of sour wine. The glowing logs in the central hearth cast a dim yellow glow in the eyes of the men who muttered over their cups, looking for vulnerable travelers to rob of their purses. The women were just as dangerous, skilled at lifting coins as they whispered illicit promises into the ears of lonely strangers.

Merlin was one of those strangers and had chosen a corner table that allowed him to both see and be seen, for he was both hunter and prey this evening. The brutes at the other tables did not concern him. Merlin was trying to lure out more elusive game.

Harrow's Pond was a backwater on the edge of one of the many Wildlands—untamed and violent wildernesses harboring dangers both natural and otherwise—that divided the kingdoms of England, Aquitania, and Francia, making the task of uniting the region the rocks upon which all ambitious kings had crashed. Riders were known to push their horses the extra day's ride to avoid a night's stay, for Harrow's was a thieves' paradise. Its very construction, tightly packed and tilting structures built against a hill to prevent it from sinking into the wetlands, created a rat's burrow of winding alleys, narrow stairways, dead ends, and dark lanes.

It was also the dominion of Rugen the Leper King, Shadow Lord of the Damned. But gaining audience with such deadly company was a delicate dance, even for Merlin the Magician.

A boy with half an ear dropped a hunk of maslin on the table along with a jug of wine and a cup. Merlin flipped the boy a silver piece, and he snatched it like a baby shark. Merlin poured himself a full cup. *It might be a long evening.* He took a long swallow, set down the cup, and froze.

He turned slowly to a veiled woman, dressed all in black, seated in the chair next to him. "Gods, why must you sneak up on me like that?"

"I am the Widow" was her reply.

"Were you followed?"

She tilted her head, curious.

"Foolish question," Merlin said.

"You told us the Sword of Power was destroyed."

His burned skin tingled. "That was my belief. But the omens tell a different story."

"The Shadow Lords consider this a final betrayal. You've lost what little trust remained between us."

"Be that as it may, the sword has been found. And soon the War of the Sword will be rejoined. 'Whosoever wields the Sword of Power shall be the one true king.' Those who believe the prophecy will draw their battle lines. The Ice King's fleets will gather in the north, the Red Paladins to the south, Shadow Lords to the east, and soon King Uther will send his armies. Now shall we spend our energies on internecine struggles or on the true threat at hand?"

"What're you eating? Tables are for supper only." The half-eared boy had returned.

"How is the rabbit?" Merlin asked, hoping it was actually rabbit.

"Sublime," the boy answered with admirable sarcasm.

"I'll have it. And another cup for my companion," Merlin said, gesturing to the Widow.

"What companion?" The boy looked at Merlin sideways.

"You're more distracted than usual," the Widow observed.

"Never mind," he said to the boy, forgetting that to the boy's eyes the seat beside him was still empty. Merlin turned back to the Widow. "I called you here as a friend, not as an emissary for the Lords."

"I tell you this as a friend. If they cast you out, it does not end there. You know too much and have too many enemies. They will hunt you down. And I fear who may rise in your absence."

"Your concern warms my heart."

"This business with the sword has also given new life to the rumors. They say either you are a liar or you truly have lost your magic. Well." The Widow folded her pale hands on the table. "Have you?"

*I am playing with fire,* Merlin mused. He chose discretion. "Are we getting personal now? Shall I ask about your dear husband?"

The Widow tensed expectantly. "Have you heard something? Has someone seen his ship?"

*Stop playing games, Merlin.* The Widow was forever waiting for her husband to return from sea. Her sorrow was so powerful it had kept her alive far longer than any human lifespan and had bestowed upon her the gift to bridge worlds and earn her place as the Shadow Lord of the Dying.

The final three lines of Feadun the Bard's famous "Candletree's Lament" said it best. Candletree breathes his final breath as his brave squire hovers over him:

> *What say you, dear Candletree?*
> *"A gray veil rises," he whispered.*
> *"For it is the Widow's face I see."*

Merlin saw no need to continue to antagonize one of Death's sisters. "I have heard no news. I can only wish for his safe return."

The Widow adjusted her veil. Smoothed her lace sleeves.

He continued. "Your vision, what does it show you regarding the sword? Where will it land?"

The Widow was quiet as she peered into the future. "The sword is finding its way to you, Merlin, but which end—the point or the pommel—is another question."

"Then I must be ready for either."

"And?"

"The sword was forged in the Fey Fires, and to the Fey Fires it shall return. I shall melt it back to its origins."

"You intend to destroy it? And what of the prophecy?"

"They were the hopeful words of a gentler time. I am wiser now. There is no one true king. The sword is cursed and will corrupt all who wield it."

"As always, you choose the most difficult path."

"Few on earth know the sword the way I know it. This is the only way."

"But the forges of the Fey burned out a thousand years ago."

"I am aware. Fey Fire is now a rare, coveted treasure, possessed by only the most discriminating collectors."

"Oh dear, tell me you're not planning to steal from *him*?"

"I am."

"Without your magic?"

"Rumors. Either way, I still have my wits. And my charm."

"I fear you overestimate both."

"Will you help me? Old friend?"

The Widow sighed. "I presume this is why you asked me to bring the necklace?" She slid something to Merlin beneath a black silk.

Merlin took it and hid it quickly inside his robes. "I hate to ask you to part with it."

"I have no need for jewelry." The Widow sighed. "Is that all?"

"I would also like to borrow your horse."

The tavern doors of the Blind Juggler flew open, followed by Merlin. He tried to keep his footing, but the brawny innkeeper had him by the belt and threw him—sprawling—into a pile of manure. The moon was high and bright.

"I should piss on *you*, you sodding dog!" The innkeeper gave Merlin an extra boot to the chest as the mage tried to climb to his knees. Then he turned on his heel and stormed back into the tavern.

"The only reason I relieved myself on your floor is because that sour wine you serve is so bloody watered you have to drink a gallon of it to acquire an adequate drunk!" Merlin threw a ball of manure at the door as it slammed shut. "And, by the way, your 'Mrs.' Innkeeper gets quite over-friendly with the clientele!"

Merlin staggered to his feet, muttering. He weaved along the twisting main road of Harrow's Pond, coins jingling in his purse, half singing and half arguing to unseen companions. He was only a few hundred feet from the Juggler when the shadows began to move along the walls after him.

Merlin took a swig from his wineskin, then cocked an eyebrow as four shambling figures, lepers judging by their boiling, peeling hands and black rags, approached him on all sides. Merlin stood still as the circle closed in around him. A dozen more appeared like wraiths, as though rising from the cracks in the street, while others clawed out of basements and ditches.

Once Merlin was thoroughly surrounded, he threw his wineskin defiantly on the ground and growled, "You know who I am. Now take me to your king."

At this, the mob threw itself upon him and Merlin succumbed to their reaching, scratching hands. Within moments he had vanished inside the ragged swarm. It moved like a single organism, carrying Merlin away into secret tunnels beneath Harrow's Pond, into ancient and abandoned Roman sewers, and into an infernal darkness.

# EIGHTEEN

A FEATHERED ARROW WHISTLED THROUGH the cold forest and struck a rabbit in the haunches, spinning it like a top. A young Faun boy shouldered his bow and hurried to retrieve the animal. His footsteps made no sound on the brittle leaves.

Morgan and Nimue followed behind in hooded cloaks, protection against the chill and against prying eyes. The high gray clouds were flat and unmoving, as though waiting for something. They gave the day an unwelcome suspense.

The Faun boy raised the dead rabbit. Morgan held up five fingers, indicating that the day's hunt had barely begun. He stuffed the rabbit in a sling around his back and set off once more.

"That's a lot of work for one boy," Nimue offered.

"We dare not travel in greater numbers. The rector in Cinder's Gate has been giving me funny looks, and he's recently taken to wearing red robes. It's a miracle we haven't been discovered already." Morgan knelt down to examine a root in the ground, decided it had no value, and left it.

"It's incredibly brave what you've done," Nimue said.

"I suppose. Mind you, I'm no Wolf-Blood Witch," Morgan teased.

"All I've done is run and . . . and fight . . . just to live. I'm no one, I assure you. I hate to disappoint them, but I'm no one," Nimue said, but she felt a rush of warmth at Morgan's words. She found that she was hungrier for encouragement than she'd realized.

Morgan shook Nimue's shoulder. "You're the only one who's stood up to them, who's fought back. These people need to know that. They deserve a little hope, even if it's fleeting."

"Fleeting?" Nimue repeated.

Morgan nodded sadly. "We can't sustain this. Every day brings a new family, new survivors. And now the cold. If the paladins don't kill them, the winter surely will. Up to now I've convinced them not to raid the farms, because once that happens, the game is up, but they won't listen to me for long. And gods, how they argue. Thank the gods for the Green Knight. They respect him."

"Who is he?" Nimue asked, curious.

Morgan chuckled. "I couldn't tell you. He doesn't really speak to 'Man Bloods.' Doesn't trust our kind."

"But you're helping them. That's ridiculous."

"It's a divided world, Nimue."

"But you think this Merlin can help?"

Morgan nodded. "Perhaps. If you're willing to be strong. If you're willing to challenge him."

Nimue felt a pit in her stomach and was desperate to change the subject. "How did you get involved in any of this? You're not"—Nimue saw Morgan's eyes darken ever so briefly—"by that I mean—you owe them—you owe us nothing."

"My bundles were light." Morgan noted Nimue's confusion and continued, "The vegetables I would buy from the local farms were half the weight. The farmers railed on about thieves. This went on for a week. And then I was out gathering herbs for my little 'recipes'—call them potions, if you like; I know it sounds foolish. Sometimes they take me quite far off the road, and that's where I found a family of Tusks, huddled inside a dead oak tree. One of them—an old woman, the grandmother— had been pulled from a burning cross, half-cooked, poor wretched thing. They had carried her for days. She's buried not far from here. And then the floodgates opened. Two families the next day—Snakes, I think you call them. When the Moon Wings arrived, we were able to set up a signal watch in the trees. Scouts were sent to divert survivors from the King's Road. And one sleepless month later we find ourselves here. And you? How did you rope Arthur into all this? He's not exactly known for his selfless behavior. He must fancy you."

Nimue opened her mouth but found no words.

Morgan chuckled. "Oh no, look how red you're getting! We must teach you not to blush. You'll give all your cards away."

"I'm not, that's—that's absurd." Nimue tried walking faster.

"There's no shame in it if you fancy him. He's a beautiful boy, my brother, if unreliable. Here today, gone tomorrow." There was something about Morgan, the way her words seemed to always carry two meanings, that made Nimue think of Pym. Nimue always enjoyed toying with Pym, who wore her feelings so openly. She loved to whisper the foulest thoughts into Pym's ear during lessons, because Pym could never stifle an emotion. Pym's purity always made Nimue feel braver, made her take greater risks, like at the tavern, the day they'd met Arthur. Had she not challenged Bors, had they gone home when the sun was up, would it have made a difference? Would more of her clan have survived? Nimue's chest ached for her friend.

"I owe him my life," Nimue admitted.

"You give him too much credit."

Nimue felt a heat rise around her ears. "Were you there? He showed true friendship and could have left me to the wolves a dozen times."

"Owe him what you like. But ask yourself why he took you south, closer to danger, rather than north? Hmm?"

"We've been running. We barely had a chance to give it much thought."

"*You* never gave it much thought. But *Arthur* did. He brought you here to abandon you," Morgan said matter-of-factly. It stung.

"He wouldn't do that," Nimue said with little confidence. In truth, the thought of Arthur leaving made her legs weak. It touched a deep and remnant pain of childhood.

"Do you think he wants your problems? His feet never touch the ground. Be grateful he got you this far."

"Why are you telling me this?"

Morgan turned on Nimue fiercely. "Because you're too important to tie your heart to any man. You don't owe him anything. It was Arthur's privilege to serve you, and you need to believe that if you want to survive."

Nimue frowned. "I don't—"

"You're not some Fey girl anymore. You are the Wolf-Blood Witch. You wield the Devil's Tooth. Some will worship you, Nimue, and some will fear you, and some will do everything they can to burn you on the cross. But unless you claim this fate, it will eat you alive. You need to know who your true friends are."

"And how do I know that?"

"Look around you. When the paladins come for me, no bards will sing my story. I've thrown in my lot with you and there is no turning back."

"And does that make you my friend?"

"More than friends. Blood sisters. My survival is now tied to yours, Nimue. I will lie and steal and kill for you. But the one thing I won't do is stand by and watch you give up your power to any man." Morgan took her knife and dragged the blade over the edge of her palm, opening a cut of dark blood. She made a fist and got her fingers wet. Then, with the same hand, she clasped Nimue's neck and cheek, smearing the flesh red. "I pledge my life to you. Let me be your soldier. And your student. Teach me." Morgan's bloody thumb dragged across Nimue's lips.

Nimue tasted the salt of her blood.

"I want to learn. I want to hear your voices. I want to see what you see. I want to save the Fey Folk from the wrath of the One God." Morgan smeared blood on her own cheeks and knelt before Nimue.

"Stand up," Nimue said, embarrassed.

Morgan did as asked.

Nimue took Morgan's face in her hands. "I'm no teacher. I'm not what you think I am. You've done more than I have. All I've done is survive."

"You've shown they can die. That matters. You've broken the myth, and that's why they hunt you the way they do. They know your power even if you don't."

"But I can't teach you magic. I don't know any. Mostly, the voices come to me uninvited."

A low whistle drew their attention. Far ahead on the trail, the Faun held up a speckled polecat with an arrow through its neck. Morgan mimed applause as the Faun proudly slung the dead animal over his shoulders.

## NINETEEN

MERLIN WAS HALF CARRIED AND HALF
dragged by a mob of shrieking lepers into the cold and
windswept ruins of the Valley of Maron, home to a
Roman outpost that was now a sanctuary for the law-
less, the abandoned, and the wretched. The marble skeletons of ancient
temples stood as mute witnesses to the Fall of Man, embodied here in
the valley. The Roman laws and codices had been reduced to ash over
centuries of rampant barbarism. There were now only two kinds of men:
the cruel and the afraid.

*Which am I?* he wondered.

*A little of both,* he decided.

The Leper King, on the other hand, was uniformly cruel and ruled
the Valley of Maron as a criminal empire. By embracing the shunned

and the forsaken, he had built a loyal army of spies, thieves, and assassins that reached from England to the Northern Monasteries and to the Viking strongholds of southern France. His private host was known as the Afflicted, and they were a force truly to be feared, acolytes who willingly offered their bodies to the leprosy as payment to the gods of dark magic in return for the Witch Sight. The cost to face and form was often uniquely gruesome.

A mob of lepers formed out of the mists, led by a crone who wore a cow skull over her ruined face: Kalek, the Leper King's closest adviser. Merlin knew her by reputation. She lifted her right hand, a mottled stump but for a single, bony finger, and pointed at Merlin.

"You smell like a woman." Her voice was low and gruff; an obstruction in her throat made her difficult to understand.

"That makes one of us," Merlin answered. Scented oils were a must in the Valley of Maron, and Merlin made no apologies. "Will Rugen see me?"

"His Majesty," Kalek corrected him.

"Of course." Merlin bowed his head slightly. "Will His Majesty, the Leper King, grant his old friend Merlin an audience?" He smiled, and Kalek just stared back at him through her skull helm with a hateful bloodshot eye. Then, with a disgusted wave, the mob dragged Merlin deeper into the valley.

The Leper King had feathered his nest in a cave hewn out of the mountain wall by early Romans, once a part of a larger temple, now crumbled. One simply needed to follow the sloppy mounds of stolen treasure, heaping chests, gems, candlesticks, and torn tapestries that littered the cracked and faded tiles leading into the cave. Skin lanterns gave the cave a sleepy glow. The Leper King's broad shadow fell across the walls.

Merlin was thrown onto the ground like a sack of grain, and the lepers retreated like phantoms into the darkness.

"I can walk, you know," Merlin said, climbing to his feet and trying to swipe some of the filth from his robes.

There was a heavy breath as the Leper King shuffled with the slow lope of a great ape between the smoky lanterns to his wide bed of piled carpets. His heavy, misshapen head, tucked under a deep cowl, sat atop colossal shoulders. Rugen was nine feet high and weighed over a thousand pounds, a testament to the giant blood flowing in his veins.

"Merlin, my dear old friend, isn't this a pleasant surprise." Rugen's voice was low thunder.

A leper girl, barely fourteen, her hands bloody with sores, offered Merlin a cup of thick wine, which he accepted as a courtesy.

The Leper King settled himself onto his carpets with effort. "I'm mortified by the rudeness of my ministers. Please accept my deepest apologies. That is no way to treat a man of your importance, an adviser to King Uther, no less."

It hardly took a wizard to detect the glee beneath Rugen's sanctimony.

"A trifle. Think nothing of it. I'm getting too easily roused in my old age. I blame the travel. The road does not agree with me anymore."

"Nonsense, you look well. Healthy! But there's no denying the world belongs to the young, eh?" Rugen's hot breath puffed in the cold, damp air of the cave. He squeezed his enormous hands into rough, fingerless mittens. Like the other Afflicted, the king was missing several digits on each hand. "Drink, Merlin. This wine is my new favorite. That royal nose of yours might detect hints of cherry and Arabic spices."

"You are a man of culture, as always." Merlin smiled.

"And yet your lips are still dry."

"Just letting it breathe."

Rugen's mouth twitched beneath his draping cowl. "This is an honor, a man of your station soiling those fine slippers to walk among the wretched and the unwashed. We are unworthy."

"I have come here to apologize." Merlin spread his hands.

"Really? What possibly for?" Rugen wore an innocent smile.

"I will be the first to admit, my leadership of the Shadow Lords has been wanting of late."

"No, no, you're too hard on yourself," Rugen said, playing along.

"But I am here to set things right. To pay my respects, to—"

"You embarrass us, Merlin. How can something offend us that does not exist? The Shadow Lords have cast you out. You are a human spy and for years stole our secrets and fed them to an illegitimate king. You are long dead to us. And all besides, the myth of Merlin, it turns out, is entirely that: a myth." Rugen's enormous fingers played with a string on his carpet as he spoke. "After all, the rumors are you've lost your magic."

"Is that what the Shadow Lords will be under *your* rulership? A knitting circle of idle gossips? Are you even capable of a mature negotiation? Have you no interest at all in what I have to offer?"

"I've lost the taste for your honeyed lies."

"I can endorse your leadership," Merlin said.

"Can you indeed?" Rugen smirked.

"The Shadow Lords have grown lazy and contented while a darkness has gathered in the south. If we are truly to guide the destinies of men, then we must reclaim our power. Now, I own my part in placing my hopes in the hearts of humankind. And I am here to set it right. Like me, you watch the skies. You have seen the omens. The Sword of Power has once again revealed itself. All the kings in Christendom are determined it go to them. I am determined it find its way to you."

"To me?" the Leper King growled. "Not to Uther Pendragon? The monarch to whom you have sworn your allegiance?"

Merlin's tone saddened. "Uther is merely warming the throne for a true king."

The walls of the cave shook with the Leper King's breathy laugh.

"Such loyalty. Is this a question of his lineage? His temperament? Or because he's cast you out as well?"

Merlin looked down at his boots. "It's not that entirely—"

"Just some," Rugen chuckled, "a touch. A smidge, eh? Just admit it, Merlin. You're a drunk and a fool, not fit to serve even a bastard king like Uther."

"It is true I am no longer welcome in Uther's court."

"And so you come begging to us."

Merlin could feel the Leper King's temper rising. "We have been rivals in the past, Rugen, yes, but don't let your pride stand in the way of a powerful collaboration. You have me at a disadvantage. Seize that opportunity. There is a reason that five centuries of kings have sought the counsel of Merlin the Magician. With me at your side and the Sword of the First Kings in your scabbard, your empire will rival Alexander's."

The Leper King slammed his fist on the ground. "Why should I believe anything you say?"

Merlin heard the rocks crack under the blow. But within this fury, he detected the frustrated war between Rugen's greed and his suspicion.

"Well, Your Majesty, you'll simply have to trust me. And bitter as that tonic may be to swallow, I've brought along a small token of good faith, to sweeten the drink. It is something I know you have long desired." Merlin opened his hand to reveal a golden necklace etched with runes and bejeweled with ancient sapphires.

Rugen swallowed the spit in his mouth.

"The torque of Boudicca. Around her neck when she led the Iceni into battle." Merlin's eyes twinkled. "Shall we go and put it on her?"

# TWENTY

A TORCH FLICKERED IN ONE OF THE
catacombs that Morgan had claimed. A simple bedroll, a
table and chair taken from the Broken Spear, and some
hanging blankets in place of walls provided the trappings
of a modest chamber.

Nimue sat on the bedroll reading aloud from a parchment as Morgan
listened from the table, tapping a quill on her teeth. "'To the Great Merlin the
Magician.'" Nimue looked up at Morgan. "Is that his proper title? 'Great'?"

Morgan shrugged. "How should I know? It's not like I write him every
day. I thought it sounded official."

Nimue nodded. "Let's stick with 'Great,' then." She went back to reading aloud: "'Greetings from the Wolf-Blood Witch.'" She looked up again. "I
don't know about this."

"You keep stopping. Just go on!"

Nimue took a deep breath, went on reading. "'By now I trust you are aware that I possess the sword of the ancients known as the Devil's Tooth. I assure you that Father Carden knows this, for many of his Red Paladins have felt the sting of its bite.'"

Morgan raised her eyebrows, pleased, as Nimue looked up with a smile. "I like that part."

"I thought it was good."

"You are quite the scribe," Nimue said, and continued to read aloud: "'Be assured my campaign of terror has only just begun. I intend to show Father Carden and his Red Murderers the very same mercy they have shown to the clans of the Fey.'" Nimue paused as though summoning the courage for the task. She went on, "'Yet what I seek most, what we all seek, I pray, is an end to this violence and peace for our kind. I propose an alliance, Great Merlin, and request that you use your wisdom and proximity to King Uther to quell this massacre. In return, I offer you the Devil's Tooth and trust that you will use it to unite the Fey clans and reclaim their lands. Refuse me, and I will muddy every field of Francia with paladin blood.'" Nimue wrinkled her nose. "Doesn't this make me sound a bit monstrous?"

"You have to meet him as an equal or he won't take you seriously," Morgan insisted.

Nimue sighed, trying to take it all in. "But what's the point if there's no hope of getting the letter to him?"

"I've thought of that too," Morgan said, taking the parchment and rolling it, then pulling Nimue into the tunnels.

As Morgan guided them, Nimue asked, "Where did you learn to write like that?"

"The convent," Morgan answered. Seeing Nimue's surprise, she explained, "Oh no, I am no sister of the One God, I assure you. But there was a Sister Katerine who was the sacrist at Yvoire and had access to all the books in the scriptorium: Homer and Plato and even the Runic Tablets, the Druid Scrolls, and the banished texts of Enoch."

They emerged from the tunnel to see that the path before them was littered with mauled trees. Something had pushed through the growth and bent and snapped everything in its path. The ground was turned over for fifty feet or more, as though two plows had tilled the soil.

"What did this?" Nimue asked.

Morgan sighed. "Another family of Tusks arrived last night. And they brought one of their riding beasts with them."

Nimue knelt down to a cloven hoofprint in the mud as wide as a barrel. "By the gods."

"A sight to behold, if you hold your nose. But it certainly complicates our already chronic food shortage."

Nimue gazed at the monstrous print in the ground and the torn-up earth around them. "Still, I'm sure we can find a use for him."

A harrowing squeal rose up from the valley, followed by a succession of fierce snorts. Nimue looked up at Morgan, alarmed.

"Let's hope he isn't looking for a mate," Morgan offered. They walked away from the downed trees, up a hill, and then onto a plateau, where wild-flowers grew in spilling abundance. An ancient live oak, with long and low branches, like welcoming arms, formed a natural shelter for the meadow. Nimue heard a strange murmur of cooing and chirps.

An older Moon Wing woman who resembled an upturned nest, with her disheveled hair and ragged cape of feathers, sat cross-legged in the flowers and autumn leaves. A black tern with a long yellow beak hopped and tweeted at her feet. The woman looked up at Morgan with a scowl. "Someone's eating my birds."

They were surrounded by dozens and dozens of birds of all shapes and sizes: puffins, waxwings, plovers and vultures, quails and turtledoves, sparrow hawks and snow geese, harriers, woodpeckers, tawny owls and peacocks, predators and prey alike.

Nimue's scars prickled. The Hidden were present. Small voices called inside the burble of the many birds.

"We're looking into it, Yeva," Morgan assured the Moon Wing.

"It's no mystery. We have a cave full of Snakes. You warn them, Morgan. Yeva's birds have to eat too. And many fill their bellies on Snakes."

"I'll warn them, I promise."

But before Morgan could say more, Yeva hopped up suddenly, not unlike the tern at her feet, and focused in on Nimue.

"I haven't gotten a close look at this Sky Folk warrior. This Wolf-Blood Drinker." She regarded Nimue down the length of her beak-like nose.

The chatter of the birds rose.

"They have so many questions about you," Yeva confided to Nimue, gesturing to the birds. She held up her hand and shut her eyes. She concentrated. With her eyes still closed, she breathed in sharply. "Oh my." She passed her hand over Nimue's heart and stomach. With both hands she measured something invisible, reaching around and finding its target over her scars. "This . . . this is why you are confused. Here is your power. Not clan. Not Fey." She touched Nimue's back. "This is your bridge to the Many Worlds." Yeva's eyes popped open. "May I see these marks?"

Nimue stepped back, unnerved.

Morgan touched Yeva lightly on the shoulder. "We have a favor to ask, Yeva. A special message we need to send to Merlin the Magician."

Yeva's eyes widened, and she turned to Morgan. "Merlin? What do you want with that traitor to our kind?"

Morgan held up the parchment. "The message is private, I'm afraid. But can you do this? Can you find him for us?"

"I cannot find him." Yeva shrugged. Then she made a guttural call from her throat, and a black kite dove from the branches above their heads, swooping noisily before settling on Yeva's arm. "But Marguerite can find anything."

Nimue approached the beautiful bird. She reached out and stroked its neck.

Yeva clucked. "She likes you."

"How will she find Merlin?" Nimue asked.

Yeva chuckled. "Sky Folk call them Hidden. Moon Wings call them Old Ones. They laugh at all our names. But no matter, they will guide Marguerite."

"At your command?" Nimue asked with wonder.

"Command? No. Request? Perhaps." Yeva took the parchment from Morgan and tied it to Marguerite's leg with a thin strip of leather. She cupped the bird's head in her hand and whispered something, then threw her arm into the air, launching Marguerite into the treetops.

# TWENTY-ONE

ERLIN STOOD, ARMS FOLDED BEHIND
him, and watched as the gargantuan Leper King
fumbled with his clumsy fingers among the keys on his
belt. "Bloody small," he muttered. Finally successful,
Rugen turned the key in the lock and pushed open a vast iron door with
screeching hinges.

Merlin waited for Rugen to navigate his girth through the doorway
before following at a polite distance.

"Well?" Rugen whispered with unrestrained pride.

Merlin's eyes drank in the Leper King's hall of treasures, a famed
and coveted cave of priceless—and stolen—relics. His eyes drifted
past golden chalices and gemstone rings, ruby scepters and ceremonial
shields, and finally landed upon an ancient skeleton wrapped in flowers.

A green light flickered in the skeleton's eyes.

It was a light shed by the Fey Fire burning in the brazier before it.

"Magnificent," Merlin answered.

The Leper King's hand swallowed Merlin's shoulder and some of his back as he pulled him to some favorites. He gestured to a box smothered in jewels. "The reliquary of Septimus the Younger. Pigeon-blood rubies—"

"Mined only in the Mughal Mountains," Merlin offered.

Rugen grunted, pleased. "Very good."

"I am ashamed to admit how I have longed to see this legendary vault," Merlin said. "And is that the Chalice of Ceridwen?"

He crossed the vault to wonder over a warped golden cup.

The Leper King shuffled after him. He seemed taken with the flattery. "The same. The witch who offered it to me claimed it as the Grail. Of course I knew it was far more valuable. Ah, here she is." Rugen sighed as they reached the flowered skeleton. "May I?" he asked, eagerly holding out his hand.

"But of course." Merlin offered him the torque.

Gingerly, the Leper King fastened the necklace around the skeleton's neck. He stepped back to admire it. "Look how the Fey Fire catches the jewels."

Merlin nodded, impressed. "A luxurious flame indeed."

"Nothing but the finest for us, eh, Merlin?"

"Nothing but." Merlin's eyes lingered on the movements of the Fey Fire.

Rugen scratched his chin, relishing the skeleton. "You are complete again, my queen." He nudged Merlin, nearly knocking him over in the process.

Recovering, Merlin nodded. "In life, even more so. Flowing red hair. Skin white as milk."

"You knew her, did you, you old dog?" Rugen chuckled, anxious for the story.

Merlin demurred. "My friend, that is a conversation best had over wine."

A few hours later Merlin was the guest of honor at Rugen's feasting table, an oak monstrosity surrounded by the crumbling thrones of several different eras, attended to by liveried lepers of all shapes, sizes, and deformities.

But the mood had changed. Rugen's expression was sour as he slouched in his great chair. He yawned as Merlin overfilled his goblet, spilling red wine onto the floor and continuing a rant as he slurped. "—but that was always the way with Charlemagne. I told him it was a mistake to trust the Church, that eventually they'd get ideas of their own, try to overrule him, but did he listen to me? No! That's the problem with these mortal kings—"

Rugen's eyes drooped. "Mm-hmm," he answered, not listening.

"—always thinking they know better." Merlin lurched out of his chair and refilled his goblet, apparently forgetting it was still full, spilling more of Rugen's wine onto the floor. "Bloody fools! Whoever tells them what they want to hear, that's who they believe. But no more."

"Yes, no more," Rugen said.

Merlin crept toward the Leper King. "No longer will we dance for them. Or soothe them with pretty lies. Our alliance will topple their false God. We will be their true lords once more!" He slammed down his goblet before Rugen, knocking a wine jug into the king's lap.

"Blast the gods, Merlin!" The Leper King leaped up as servants swarmed.

Merlin tried to help, using his own robes to clean off the Leper King, but managed to tangle himself more. "I am sorry, let me—" He fell into Rugen's arms.

"You're drunk," the Leper King sneered.

Merlin clutched Rugen's shoulders to hold himself up. "And you are surprisingly fit."

The Leper King stepped away, flopping Merlin to his knees. "Pathetic." He gestured to his servants. "Take him out of my sight and let him sleep it off. We'll see if I still have use for him in the morning."

The lepers hoisted the half-conscious Merlin by the elbows and dragged him away.

"Unhand me, brutes!" Merlin slurred dramatically, freeing his right hand and spiriting the Leper King's pickpocketed vault keys into the hidden pocket of his sleeve.

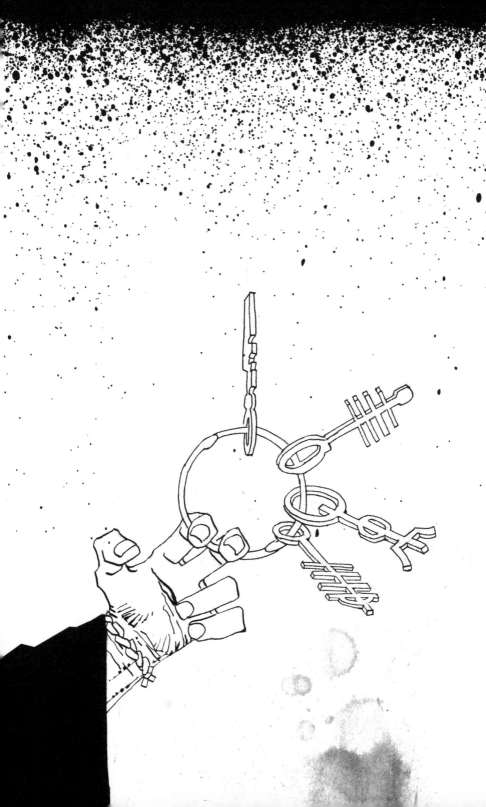

# TWENTY-TWO

L ONGING TO BE USEFUL, NIMUE LUGGED A
bucket of water through the winding tunnels of the Fey refugee camp. Her shoulders throbbed and the burning torches made
the caves stifling and hot. Sweat poured down her cheeks.
Despite this, she told herself this was all temporary, that a semblance of
normal life, or at least a less broken life, was still possible. She feared her
letter to Merlin had been too strident in tone and that she had made an
enemy of the one man on earth who might help her.

*Why him? Why is my mother protecting this legendary sword? Why
does she want it to go to Merlin? A traitor who has turned against the Fey?*

Still another side of her felt the paladin maps burning a hole in
her saddlebag. *We know where they are. We can save Fey villages. And*

*kill more of the red bastards.* But her entreaties had as yet fallen on deaf ears. The needs of the camp were too overwhelming.

As the tunnel opened into the cavern, Nimue saw Fey children dancing in a circle. The sight made her smile, until she heard their song: *"Paladin, paladin, jump in the ditch, hiding from the Wolf-Blood Witch."*

Nimue stopped to listen. *They're singing about me.* It was bizarre and embarrassing and secretly thrilling. The children were holding hands and smiling and falling down with laughter.

*"Paladin, paladin, horse is hitched, sniffed out by the Wolf-Blood Witch."*

Her heart thudded in her chest. She was back in the glade: feeling the push of the blade through the paladin's ribs and the slick pull as she opened him wide, the cold pond turning warm with blood and splashing against her neck like soothing tub water, her ears delighted by his shrill screams.

*"Paladin, paladin, choke and twitch, bitten by the Wolf-Blood Witch . . ."*

While she was lost in her reverie, a Faun woman with small antlers and almond-shaped eyes tried to take Nimue's bucket.

"*Adwan po,*" she said. "*Semal, semal.*"

Nimue gently pulled the bucket back. "No, please. I want to be useful." For the past hours and days, Nimue's every effort to carry, assist, lift, and lug had been thwarted by Fey Kind who wanted to place her on a pedestal.

"*Tetra sum n'ial Cora.*"

Nimue smiled and shook her head. "I'm sorry, I don't understand."

The Faun woman struggled with her English. "Name is Cora."

"Nimue," she answered, touching her chest.

Cora smiled. "Yes, yes. Come." The Faun woman took her by the arm and led her to a circle of Fauns, actively engaged in twisting leaves and vines into decorative shapes, weaving them into salvaged cloth along with boughs of gathered flowers to make dresses of forest beauty.

"Tomorrow night there is *Amala*. A Joining." Cora put one of the dresses up to Nimue's shoulders.

Again Nimue tried to fend off the Fey Kind's generosity. "No, please, not for me. This is beautiful. You should wear it."

"You will wear. You will come." Cora smiled. "You and the handsome Man-Blood boy."

The Faun women chuckled at this.

Feeling her ears and cheeks redden with embarrassment, Nimue hastily thanked Cora, took the dress, and escaped.

She hurried the dress to the cave she shared with Morgan and swung around, only to find Arthur waiting for her in the archway.

"I beg your pardon? This is the ladies' chamber."

"I need to show you something," Arthur said with a cattish grin.

"What about the maps?" Nimue started in again, following Arthur down a new set of tunnels that she had not yet explored.

"We've only just got here," Arthur said.

"But when they find out those maps are missing, they'll change their plans. We'll lose our advantage!"

"Peace, Nimue," Arthur said. Then, lowering his voice, he added, "I've been meaning to tell you, you've gotten a bit whiffy of late."

"I—you what?"

"It's true," Arthur went on. "The Fey children have a new name for you." He turned to Nimue with a serious expression. "They're calling you the Wolf-Blood Stench."

Nimue shoved Arthur into the wall. "Are you wanting to be hurt?"

He held up a warning finger, then pulled her up a small rise and onto a tiny cliff above a grotto. A pool at the center of the grotto was fed by a series of small falls. "It's the snowmelt," Arthur told her. "Comes from the top of the mountain and heats up as it works through the rocks." He handed her a misshapen brown rock.

"What is this?" Nimue stared at it.

"Wood-ash soap. Trust me, you need it." Arthur winked at her as he pulled off his shirt, showing off a lean, muscled frame. His pants were down around his ankles just as quickly, leaving very little to the imagination. Nimue turned away, eyebrows raised, as Arthur whooped and jumped into the hot spring.

"Oh, thank the gods," he muttered as he floated below. "Come on!"

"I'm fine here, I think," Nimue said, stealing glances while Arthur dove and splashed.

"I have seen a woman naked before," he offered.

"How nice for you," she said. Then she flicked her finger, and Arthur dutifully averted his eyes.

In truth, Nimue was eager to shed the rags she'd been wearing all week. They reeked of death. But as she stepped out of her leather shoes, a modesty took over. She'd never undressed in front of a boy. *You're a fool*, Nimue told herself. *After all that's happened, this is what you fear the most?* She tried to shake it off, but her breathing was still shallow and her fingers still shook when she fumbled with the buttons of her stolen trousers and let them fall to her bare feet. She wriggled out of her sleeveless tunic and dropped it to the stones. When she looked down at her body, she could barely recognize it for all the bruises, mud, dried blood, and lacerations. She felt her ribs. She'd barely eaten for days and could see her ribs much more clearly. Both of her knees were torn open. She felt her tangled, knotted hair and her tongue probed the sore, bloody hole where her lower right molar used to be.

Holding on to a smooth boulder, Nimue put her foot in the hot water. It warmed her blood to her cheeks. She slid into the steaming pool and almost wept for the relief of her aching muscles. She submerged into the silence, into a scalding bath that burned away the dirt and blood and sweat. For just a moment, Nimue felt different, like steel melted into a new shape.

Arthur was busy scrubbing himself with his own wood-ash soap, his white derriere above the water for all to see.

"Oy!" he shouted at Nimue when he caught her looking. "Do you mind?"

Nimue rolled her eyes and laughed, her first real laugh since Hawksbridge, since Pym. Arthur plunged back into the pool and popped up nearer to her. She backed away, eyes on his, conscious of facing him. Her scars were a modesty she would allow herself. And Arthur somehow sensed this.

"You don't have to hide them."

Nimue played dumb. "Hide what?"

"We all have scars."

Nimue felt a spasm of embarrassment and swam for the shore.

"Nimue," Arthur started.

"Nothing. It's fine. It's too hot," she said.

"Look! Right here!" Arthur shouted, raising his left leg out of the water and pointing to a pink splotch underneath the buttock. "We used to race and bet on rats when I was a boy. My first race, rat got scared, ran up my pant leg, then panicked and tried to eat his way out. The boys had a good laugh as I cried and ran all the way home with a rat in my trousers. You want embarrassing? You can only imagine the nicknames."

"Arthur," Nimue said, trying to stop him.

He pressed on. "Here." He indicated his left armpit and a puffy scar. "Morgan bit me after I kissed her friend. I was ten and Morgan was eight." He cleared his hair away from crisscrossing scars over the part. "These are from an ale-drinking contest, which, if you are interested to know, I lost. Got so drunk I fell off a bridge onto a pile of cod on a fishing boat. Lucky break, if you ask me."

Nimue smiled. She couldn't help it. Playing along, she pointed to a dark scar along his ribs. "And that one?"

Arthur looked down at the scar. "Oh, that." His smile faded. "That's—that's from the first man I ever killed." He was quiet for a moment. "He stuck me pretty good before it was over."

Nimue settled back into the water as unwelcome memories passed over Arthur's eyes. She swam nearer to him, curious. "Who was it?"

"One of the brutes who killed my father," Arthur said quietly, "or so I thought."

The air was very still, and Nimue didn't look away from Arthur. She wanted him to finish.

"Turns out I'd pegged the wrong gang for it. The fellow was no angel, mind you . . . but . . . Anyway, I was young, drunk, and angry."

"You wanted justice for your father," Nimue offered, wishing there was a better way to show just how much she understood.

"There is no justice. That poor idiot was in the wrong place at the wrong time and died for it. And the sad truth is: it would have broken my father's heart to know I did that."

"Thank you," Nimue said.

"For what?"

"Telling me."

Arthur shrugged. The space between them had dwindled. Nimue moved even closer. She reached out and touched the scar on his rib. He put his hand over hers.

"Nimue."

"Yes?" She was close enough to feel his breathing.

"I don't know what I'm doing." He pushed back a bit. "I can't stay."

The spell had broken. Nimue looked away.

Arthur frowned. "I have debts to bad men. Not just Bors. There are others. You don't need my problems too. I'm sorry."

"Why are you doing this?" she asked.

"You deserve someone good." Arthur's voice shook. "I know I'll never be what my father wanted. I'll never be a true knight. But maybe somewhere I can find my honor. Maybe somewhere I can find justice. And the courage to serve it."

"Are you searching or just running away? They can look the same, you know." Nimue was feeling more and more foolish by the moment.

"Come with me. You don't even know these people. You don't owe them anything. Come with me and we can be across the Iron Peaks in a fortnight. And then we can go anywhere. The Sea of Sands? The Gold Trail? What do you want to see?"

*What do I owe them?* Nimue wondered. But the question also bothered her. She thought of the children singing. What would they think if she simply left in the night? Left them to their hunger and their fear? And what of her promise to her mother? "But what happens to them?"

"I don't know. But I do know a lost cause when I see one. No point in sharing their fate."

"It's only a lost cause when everyone gives up on it. And is that all you care about? Just surviving?"

"No, I told you. I think, out there—"

"A knight doesn't have to search for his honor, Arthur. And he sure as hell doesn't run from a fight." *Morgan was right about him.* Nimue folded her arms, feeling very exposed and vulnerable and angry. "Well, I thank you for your help. Are you leaving soon?"

Arthur shrugged, and that annoyed her even more. *A child's gesture,* she thought. "A day, maybe two. Listen, about the sword. If you're determined to stay, I think the best way to help your people is to give the sword to Merlin. Don't listen to Morgan; she's mad at the world. You said it before: this was your mother's dying wish. She must have known that he would help you."

Nimue shook her head. "She never said a word about him."

"Take my advice for what it is, I guess. But I—I really don't want to see you get hurt."

"You won't," Nimue said, swimming to shore. "You'll be gone."

# TWENTY-THREE

**M**ERLIN COVERED HIS MOUTH WITH his sleeve for the smell and crept past sleeping piles of lepers. He knelt down and left the end of the rope he'd been trailing in the center of the tunnel, then hurried to the iron doors of the Leper King's vault. He freed the stolen keys from the folds of his robe.

It took an eternity for the great hinges of the vault door to cease their screeching. Once inside the hall, Merlin moved swiftly and silently, passing rows and rows of priceless treasures, eyes fixed on the Fey Fire flickering in the brass brazier set before the skeleton of Boudicca.

Merlin glanced at her glowing emerald eye sockets. "Forgive my earlier lies, milady. It would have been a pleasure to know you in life."

With that, he fished a cup of Snake clay from his robes, no larger than the size of his palm. Whispering ancient words, he coaxed the flame into the cup. It resisted at first, as though aware of improper influence, but soon began to yield, bending its flames toward the shiny clay and then leaping over. A new Fey Fire burned in Merlin's cup. Lidding it with another cup of Snake clay, Merlin pocketed the Fey Fire and hurried for the vault door. He swung it open and found Kalek staring back at him beneath her cow-skull mask.

They stared at each other for a moment. *Might she betray her king?* Merlin wondered. Tempting fate, he held the door open and jerked his head to the treasure vault behind him.

This was a mistake.

Kalek lifted her rotting finger to Merlin's face and unleashed a guttural ululation that shook the tombs of Rugen's subterranean castle.

Merlin shoved the witch aside and charged down the tunnel, grabbing a rusted mace from one of Rugen's ghoulish wall decorations. Ragged lepers poured in behind him. They crawled in from out of the floors and the walls and the ceilings. Kalek's unnatural scream swelled in his ears and popped the fragile membranes within. Merlin grunted with pain. Warm blood pulsed in his ears, and the sounds around him became fuzzy and distant.

Three lepers charged him from the front, so he spun the mace and sent one of their melting faces spraying into the walls. He pushed his way past the others, nearly losing his footing. He raced past Rugen's lair as the Leper King's misshapen shadow fell across the walls and his booming voice roared, "Merlin!"

Merlin cursed himself. A quick escape was critical to the plan, for once Rugen was able to employ his magic, Merlin's chances of survival plunged. His path was blocked by three lepers clutching rusted swords.

*I may not have my magic, but I am far from helpless.*

Merlin charged the Afflicted, blocking their blows with his mace and turning their frenzied movements against them. The lepers hacked at one another as Merlin dodged between them, rising up from behind and crushing their spines, shoulders, and skulls.

"*Hashas esq'ualam chissheris'qualam!*"

Rugen was casting. The words of earth magic echoed through the caves. Merlin swung wildly, shattering faces, time running out. The walls shook and the dirt and clay of the cave floor transmuted to a sucking ooze that captured Merlin's boots. He could see the opening of the cave in the distance, dripping and collapsing. The Afflicted were caught as well, flailing and crying out as the ground melted under them. *He'll kill them all to prevent my escape*, Merlin realized, as he fell into the morass, swallowing mud, no longer feeling any solid ground.

*Drowning. I'm drowning.*

Merlin focused his mind despite the bedlam around him. He calmed his movements, which slowed his sinking. His hands searched and searched until they found the wet end of the rope and grabbed hold. The rope was taut. Merlin pulled himself forward, arms burning. The rope pulled back. He kicked his legs, gradually finding traction. He fought off dozens of grasping hands, climbing over the drowning bodies and using them as a platform to escape. *Thank you, Rugen*, Merlin thought, smiling to himself.

He began the muddy climb, the mud-slick rope slowly slipping through his fingers. His boots dug into the slime as he clawed for the distant glow of the dull gray sky, while hundreds of lepers filled the tunnel, squeezing and squirming after him like a rat plague.

Merlin spilled into the light, and waiting for him there, tied around the neck with the other end of the rope, was a black horse with eyes as white as milk, a gift from the Widow. Merlin leaped onto the horse, grabbed the reins, and dug his heels into her ribs. The horse reared and kicked, then surged forward, trampling lepers under her hooves and galloping across the desolate valley, which was swarming with more and more pursuers who were falling farther and farther behind their prey.

After a day's ride through brackish swamps, Merlin found himself back in Harrow's Pond, where, as he expected, twenty soldiers, wearing the seal of Uther's three crowns on their tunics, awaited him.

Merlin took no joy in having left Uther in a state of such fear. The blood rain was a chilling omen but only the first breeze of the Great Storm gathering across the sea. The world could not withstand another War of the Sword, so Merlin was bound and determined to destroy the infernal blade before its blood thirst could topple another civilization, no matter the consequences, no matter the rivals scorned or kings defied.

He would be the first to admit he had been a poor counselor to Uther Pendragon. Notwithstanding the unending schemes of Uther's ambitious and ruthless mother, the Queen Regent, Merlin himself had spent the last sixteen years in a waking sleep of regret and recrimination and disinterest. *And Uther paid the highest price of all,* Merlin thought. But the rise of the sword had awakened his senses. And though his loss of magic left him largely blind to his enemies, he could still read the pieces on the chessboard better than most. Without his intervention, he saw how this would play out. Death and fire would not be his legacy. *Not this time. No matter the cost.*

Still, he knew Uther's temperament well enough to avoid a direct confrontation. Like any king, when Uther learned of the Sword of Power, he would demand it for himself. Merlin had to control that information and manage the king's expectations. The final cut between them was yet to arrive. Until then, Merlin would be walking a tightrope above a floor of cobras. He could only hope that his rivals had not exploited his absence.

As he approached, he tucked the Snake clay with the Fey Fire into the saddlebag of the Widow's horse.

He bent over and whispered in her ear, "When I dismount, fly like the wind, my girl."

The horse snuffed.

At the sight of Merlin, the guards opened the barred door of a dungeon wagon. Several hurried over to take the reins of the Widow's horse as the captain of the guard drew his sword. "Merlin the Magician, you are under arrest by order of the king."

As Merlin climbed down from the saddle, the mare rose up in a kicking fury and knocked the soldiers to the ground. She turned and flew into the narrow swamp trails as though chased by devils.

# TWENTY-FOUR

A GUST OF COLD WIND FLAPPED THE gray robes of the Weeping Monk as he rode across the cattle field of a wealthy dairy farm taken by the Red Paladins as a temporary encampment. Tied to his saddle was a rope pulling a small mare and her riders, a bound and bloodied father and son. The monk knew them as "Tusks," creatures marked by their dark, bristled hair and the stubby horns that grew from below their ears. Their unique prints and musky scents made them easy to track, but that didn't make them easy prey. Far from it. The Weeping Monk took pride that he'd brought in two alive. They were the toughest fighters of the Fey Kind, and capture was a great dishonor in their clan. He had seen more than a few cut their own throats rather than be taken alive.

A group of paladins, bloody to the elbows from the slaughter of the dairy cows, stopped what they were doing to watch the monk. He paid them no mind.

A scouting party kicked up clods of dirt as they galloped into the distance at the command of Father Carden, who smiled and hailed the monk upon seeing him.

"My boy, my dear boy," Carden said as the Weeping Monk dismounted into the priest's fierce embrace. Carden held the monk's shoulders and looked at him with his piercing blue eyes. "Are you well?"

"I'm well, Father," the monk whispered.

"This is very good," Carden replied, still searching the monk's face, but for what he did not say. It was an appraisal as cold as the gusts blowing in from the east. Whatever he saw tightened Carden's jaw. "We're being tested now. All of us. We must be strong. The Beast has awakened and shown his banner. Our resolve must be total. It wants to sow our doubts and our fears. It feasts on these things."

"Yes, Father." The monk nodded.

Carden tightened his grip. "But our love is stronger than its hate. Eventually love wins. It is our unbreakable chain—our bond—that will choke the Beast in the end."

He smiled. The Weeping Monk bowed his head. "Yes, Father."

A tremulous wail of agony carried on the wind from the distant stables. The monk noted a spiral of black smoke arising from the same set of buildings. The next gust of wind brought a sharp, acrid scent to the monk's nose, a familiar scent of burning flesh. Carden noted the curl on the monk's lip and took a deep, satisfied breath.

"The smell of confession. We are very fortunate to have Brother Salt hard at work in his kitchen. Arrived from Carcassonne a few days ago."

The Weeping Monk turned his hooded face toward the stables. His muscles tensed ever so slightly at the mention of Brother Salt.

It was enough for Father Carden to notice. "I need my very best weapons on the front lines. The steel and the fire. Together you are God's flaming sword."

The monk did not respond.

"Now tell me about the Wolf-Blood Witch."

"They went south into the Minotaurs."

"They?" Carden pressed.

"She rides with someone. The injuries on our slain brothers were from sword and ax. They were ambushed."

"She has allies," Carden spat as he paced in the mud. "The sword is a beacon. And every sunrise that passes, every day that she is not nailed to the cross, is a day this plague spreads. Do you understand?"

The Weeping Monk nodded.

All kindness left Carden's face as he said, "I pray you do." With that, he regarded his prisoners. "Now then, what have you brought us?"

"These two"—the monk turned his hood to the wretched father and son on the mare—"were hiding in the brush by the lake."

"Were they?" Carden sized them up. "The Beast's little spies. I've seen their kind before." Carden walked up to the prisoners. "Ah, yes." His thumb wiped the dried blood from the boy's cheeks. "We've been hearing about this. They're painting their faces with animal blood to honor her." Carden turned back to the monk, his lips tight. "To *honor* her."

The monk did not respond.

Carden patted the boy's knee.

At this, the wounded father managed the strength to drive his boot into Carden's arm. The priest stumbled backward.

In a flash, the Weeping Monk's sword was drawn and—

"Hold!" Carden commanded.

Red Paladins were already converging on the scene.

The Weeping Monk's hands twitched to kill as he had been taught.

Carden brushed the mud from his shoulder. "Alive is better. Soon he will feel the full warmth of God's light. Bring them down and strip off their clothes."

Red Paladins pulled the Tusks from the mare's saddle and tore their shirts down, exposing their bare chests to the cold wind. The father had a clean puncture on the left side of his ribs that had gone straight through his back. He coughed wetly and his complexion was gray.

Father Carden poked the wound and the Tusk father winced. "This one doesn't have very long," Carden chided the Weeping Monk. "Your aim is true to a fault, my child." The priest turned to the stables and his eyes brightened. "Well, no matter, this pig will squeal. Here comes Brother Salt now."

Two Red Paladins led Brother Salt from the stables to the well. He dipped his hands in a full bucket, rubbed the water over his shaved head, and poured another handful over his stitched-closed eyes. He dried his hands on his red robe, tightened his belt, and allowed his acolytes to lead him across the muddy pasture to Father Carden. One of the acolytes carried objects in a leather bundle under one arm.

"I heard the hoofbeats on the cold dirt," Brother Salt said with a smile, taking the Weeping Monk's hand and patting it softly. Salt reeked of the sour smoke of his trade. "And I knew it was my brother."

The Weeping Monk removed his hand from Salt's clasp.

"The eyes are weak. We cannot trust what they see, they give away our hearts and they are soft to the touch. That is why I save the eyes for last in my work. A man always cries like a baby when you touch his eyes. This is why I had no use for mine. It makes me a better soldier for God."

The Weeping Monk's hands balled into fists as Carden gently took Salt's arm and led him to the prisoners. "Brother Salt, the monk has brought us gifts."

Brother Salt's hands eagerly sought out the Tusks' exposed skin. His fingers crept into their armpits and around the soft parts of their necks, behind their ears, and around their backs. He found the father's injury and grunted with displeasure. "This one is useless. We'll have to start with the boy. The father will talk when I work on the boy. Do you know me, boy?" Salt asked the Tusk, who the Weeping Monk guessed could not be a day past fourteen. The boy shook from cold and terror but held his grimace. "Have you heard my name? Have you heard of Brother Salt and his kitchen? Let me introduce you to my friends."

Salt's acolytes unrolled the leather bundle, revealing seven iron tools in leather pockets.

"God's Fingers, I call them. Each is named for one of His archangels." Salt pulled out one of the implements, about as long as his arm and tipped with a corkscrew brand. "This is Michael. When I put Michael in the fire, he glows a beautiful white. A white light. The light of truth. For Michael is truth. You can only speak truth to Michael." Salt put the brand back into its leather sheath. He pinched the boy by the nose. "Don't worry, you will meet them all tonight."

"No!" The father lunged for his son, but the Red Paladins easily wrestled him down. "I'll tell all I can! He doesn't know anything!" The father sputtered these words with his face pressed into the mud. At Carden's nod, the paladins dragged the Tusks across the field toward the stables. The boy kept mute the whole time, head hung low as he stumbled along.

Another cold gust rattled the Weeping Monk's robes as he swayed with indecision. Carden noted this with displeasure. He came up close to the monk so they could not be overheard. "You need prayer. We have raised the crosses in the burning field behind the barn. Take the time you need."

The Weeping Monk half nodded, as though embarrassed, and swung up onto his courser, wheeling her around and riding toward the pasture of empty crosses as ordered.

He knelt there for three solid hours, not moving, as his fellow paladins sawed and chopped the wood for several more crosses. They were raised in a crooked line and resembled a skeleton forest around the monk. The temperature continued to drop. The wind lashed at him. The rest of the paladins sought shelter by the fires in the house. The Weeping Monk remained, still as a statue.

When the moon was directly overhead, Father Carden walked into the pasture and knelt beside him. After a few prayerful moments, he turned to the monk, whose cheeks were wet with real tears.

"I'm proud of you, my son. Your gifts bore fruit. They were spies as I suspected, scouts for a secret trail through the woods away from the King's Road, smuggling the Fey Kind who escaped us. The conspiracy leads south into the Minotaurs near Cinder's Gate. There could be hundreds or more crawling around in those caves. This must be where the witch is heading. We can pull this weed from the roots."

The Weeping Monk shook his head. "I failed you."

"How have you failed me, my child?"

"His Grace, I can't feel it. I call to Him, but I reach out and there is only darkness. And I feel . . ." The monk hesitated.

Father Carden rubbed the monk's back. "Tell me."

The monk struggled with his words. "There is a serpent in my stomach. It twists and writhes. It's poisoning me."

"Does it speak to you?"

The monk nodded.

"And what does it say?"

"I fear to give it a voice."

"You have nothing to fear from me, my son. You are the sword of avenging light in pitched battle with the Lord of Darkness. Did you think you could escape his touch? His corruption? The Beast does not tear flesh. It tears souls."

The monk shuddered as he fought off a wave of emotion.

Father Carden's voice was soft. "Speak this poison and expel it before it sickens you further."

"It tells me I am the dark angel."

"Of course it does," Carden chuckled, pulling the monk's hooded face to his chest, "for that is what you are to our enemies. God's cleansing blade. My dear, dear sweet boy." The Weeping Monk wrapped his arms around the only father he knew, balling his robes in his fists. Carden rocked him gently as the wind gusted around them. "I fear I've put too much on you. This work will blacken our hearts, but we must persevere. Channel your strength into that sword and bring me that witch's head and her Devil's Tooth. My dear child," Carden soothed, "my Lancelot."

# TWENTY-FIVE

KING UTHER DREADED THE LONG, winding walk up to his mother's tower. The moment the smell of her pastries hit his nostrils, goose flesh would rise on his arms and his stomach would lurch. He looked down at her slender goblet on the tray he was forced to carry and mused briefly about spitting into the hot water, yet decided against it. Lady Lunette, the Queen Regent, was far too savvy in the dark arts of poison for him to toy with her on that same battlefield.

Still, he resented the summons and knew the cause: three nights before, he had lost three ports and twice as many ships to the Red Spear, a Viking warlord notable for an iron lance, like a great horn, on the bow of his ship, painted with pitch and set ablaze to inspire fear in his victims. The Red Spear was a loyalist to Cumber, the self-proclaimed

"Ice King" and an audacious claimant to the bloodline of Pendragon. This was sure to reignite the murmurings of Uther's illegitimacy to the throne, the type of unjust drivel monarchs were subjected to, Uther could only assume.

Hands full, the king knocked with his slippered foot, hurting his toe on the heavy wood and cursing his mother under his breath for it.

"About time," said a croaky voice from within.

Uther sighed and tried to balance the tray on one hand while opening her door with the other. When he managed to enter, he found her in her usual spot, perched at the tower window to spy over all, endlessly patting her tart dough. The Queen Regent's tower was all white, and a fire burned warmly in the hearth. Trays of candies, cakes, and pies were set atop many tables. By design, there was no lovelier or more welcoming room in the entire castle.

"We're rather busy, Mother, so we hope this doesn't take long."

"Busy, are you? Not as busy as the Ice King, it seems," she scoffed.

Uther allowed his tension to spill over. "Where does this lowly savage find the bloody nerve to claim our name? Our name!"

"Good lords, I hope you didn't blubber on like this at court." She set down her dough and slapped her knees as though preparing to teach a lesson. "It is the pity of princes that no one ever teaches them how to take a punch. Because when someone finally does, they screech like pheasants."

"Right. Thank you, Mother." Uther wheeled around to leave, but Lunette was not finished.

"The first gauntlet of the greatest war in ten ages has just been thrown and you haven't a bloody clue, have you?"

The king hesitated at the door. "What on earth are you talking about?"

"The Sword of Power, Uther. The Sword of the First Kings has revealed itself. Its recovery was likely the very reason for the blood that rained on your castle. I seem to recall a certain trickster in your employ who should have told you about this. What was his name? A famous name, I believe—"

"Just stop," Uther snapped, turning around. The tower was quiet but for the squish of Lunette's dough. He loathed that she was ahead of him on anything. It was the very reason he kept Merlin by his side, to counter his mother's constant meddling. Uther assumed an aloof posture, careful not to betray his urgency to know her thoughts. "Who told you this about the sword?"

"Well, I figured one of us should cultivate acquaintanceships with those who can see the other side. I have my ways, Uther, don't you worry." Lunette smiled coldly.

Uther locked his fingers behind his back, examined some tea cakes, took in the view of the cliffs and crashing sea from the window. Then: "We thought the sword was a story. A child's story."

"Further proof of how ill-served you have been by that mixed-blood Druid." Lunette shook her head and dipped her doughy fingers into another bowl. "I assume you know the prophecy?"

Uther repeated it like a distant memory. "Whosoever wields the Sword of Power shall be the one true king."

"Yes, well, Cumber wants the Sword of Power, and unlike some monarchs I could mention, he appears motivated to actually get it."

"Of course we want the bloody sword," Uther spat.

"Well then, you need a plan, don't you? For instance, it might be nice to know who currently wields it. One might think this falls under Merlin's jurisdiction. Where is he anyway?" Lunette smirked.

Uther gritted his teeth. "Rotting in our dungeons."

"Well, that certainly won't do," Lunette said as she sprinkled sugar over her latest tray of treats. "A Merlin rotting is a Merlin plotting."

Uther feigned a smile. "You do not amuse us."

Lady Lunette wiped her hands on a cloth and got down to business. "Tell me, what loyalty has Merlin ever shown to this crown?"

"Shockingly little, Mother."

"And yet you allow him to lounge about court like an old hound and empty your wine barrels."

"Lest we forget"—Uther turned to face her—"it was you who imposed him upon us when we were ten years old."

"Yes, I confess falling prey to the illusion of Merlin the Magician years ago. But I've learned, Uther. Have you? Kings rise and fall, yet Merlin always survives. What does that tell you about which master he serves? You? Or himself?"

Uther's head was pounding. "Yes, fine, Mother, but what does this have to do with the sword or Cumber and our burning ports?"

"Your weakness," Lady Lunette shot back. "That's what they have in common. And I hasten to add to the mix Father Carden and his Red Paladins, who apparently can march through your lands and burn villages with impunity."

It wasn't just his mother's criticism that galled him but the enjoyment she took in offering it. She made it painfully clear that he was worthless in her eyes. Not wishing to give her any more pleasure, Uther turned his attention to the trays of colorful treats adorning the tower.

"Are they all poisoned?" he asked her.

"Not all."

Uther sighed. "What would you have us do, Mother?"

"Be the damn king," she said as she flattened dough between her hands. "Demonstrate to your court, your subjects, and potential usurpers what happens to layabouts and traitors." She pressed the dough onto a tray. "Kill Merlin."

This shook Uther from his reverie of self-pity. "Kill him?"

Lady Lunette nodded. "Publicly, loudly, so that it rattles in the Ice King's halls."

At first blush, the idea buoyed Uther's spirits. It was tangible. It was real. But just as quickly, fears of the fallout and repercussions from the mysterious Shadow Lords gave him pause. "It's dangerous."

"Even better. It will show there's more than silk underneath those breeches. And it will send a warning shot to his friends the Shadow Lords that you are not to be trifled with and that this Age of Wizards has come to an end."

Her certainty was refreshing. Unlike Merlin, Lady Lunette offered no qualifiers, no equivocations or multiple interpretations. For all her cruelties, she spoke in absolutes, something Uther had been yearning for of late.

"And after?" Uther asked, testing whether his mother had truly thought this through.

She had.

"Embrace the Church. Ally with the Red Paladins against the Ice King and throw him back into the sea."

"And why would the Red Paladins agree to this?" Uther pressed.

Lady Lunette shook her head at Uther. "Because you're the bloody king, that's why," she scoffed. "And Cumber is a heathen, easy to paint as sympathetic to the Fey and loyal to the Old Gods. That will do it."

Uther waited for the slashing comment, the backstabbing, but none came. His mother's advice was sound, shrewd, and strong. Uther straightened. His shoulders broadened.

Lunette chuckled. "It will be easier to claim the sword when there are no kings to resist you."

"Thank you, Mother."

"Indeed, Your Majesty." Lady Lunette bowed her head.

Uther turned on his heel and marched for the door, then hesitated. A twinkle in his eye, he studied the treats on the trays for a third time. He pointed to a powdered sugar cake, but Lady Lunette cautioned against it with a shake of her head. Uther nodded; that one was poisoned. He spied a cinnamon twist and pointed to that one, eyebrows raised to his mother. Again she shook her head. A touch frustrated, Uther examined a tempting gingerbread and again appealed to Lady Lunette, who finally nodded. Pleased, Uther plucked up the cake and took a satisfying bite. He left the tower, a new spring in his step.

# TWENTY-SIX

THE CAVERN WAS AGLOW WITH TORCH-
light in preparation for the Joining ceremony. The air was rich and
sweet, for the uneven floors had been carpeted with wildflowers
of pinks and violets and blues. Fauns had crushed grapes for wine,
and Cliff Walkers had done the same with acorns to make a paste for the
maslin bread Morgan had stolen from the kitchen of the Broken Spear.

The Elders had eased up on the water rationing to allow the refugees
to wash off the dirt, the blood, and the suffering from their bodies as best
they could. There was an atmosphere of expectation, a brief escape.

A few Tusks beat on canvas drums while Fauns answered them with
the lilting harmonics of lyres and hurdy-gurdies. An arbor of flowered
branches stood at the center of the caves, and the Fauns intending to be
joined stood beneath it, holding hands. Cora assumed the role of priestess

and whispered and laughed with the Fauns as everyone took seats on and around the rocks. A soft breeze filtered through the half-dome roof, and the sky beyond the canopy was filled with stars.

Nimue caressed the soft rose petals of her bodice, feeling strangely exposed without her sword slung over her back. Instead her shoulders were bare and threaded vines entwined her lower arms and fingers like sleeves. She wore a corona of laurel around her head, and a braid of autumn leaves spilled down her neck.

A trio of Fey children took Nimue by the hand and led her to a boulder perched above the altar, where they could watch together. Morgan joined her there, wearing her own tiara of raven feathers and a patchwork gown adorned with autumn leaves.

Each clan had its own small rituals and dances for Joining ceremonies, and in pockets around the caves one could glimpse a window into these hidden worlds. The Fauns accented their antlers, twisting their necks in choreographed movements to bless the union with fertility, while the Snakes prowled on all fours in concentric circles, brushing heads and shoulders together, and Tusks stomped their hoofed feet in rhythmic bursts and loud guttural calls. Above their heads, Moon Wings fluttered like moths, spreading fireflies throughout the canopy.

Nimue was thirsty for the beauty of it all but had a sinking feeling. Who would remember these dances? What would happen to these Fey children celebrating birthdays in cold caves with no idea, in some cases, whether their mothers and fathers were alive or dead? Were there other survivors of Dewdenn? Would the stories and rituals of the Sky Folk die with her? The thought was too much to bear.

A Snake child squeezed her hand and smiled at her with tiny, sharp teeth.

What hope could she offer them? She was as orphaned and homeless as they were. But she knew her fate was as "joined" to these Fey Kind refugees as the sweet Fauns under the arbor were soon to be. Could she put her faith in this Merlin to protect them? A man Yeva said was a traitor to the Fey? And if that were true, why in the name of the gods had Lenore implored her to deliver the sword to him?

Nimue saw Arthur enter from the other side of the cave, looking awkward and out of place. His eyes flicked to Nimue, then away.

Morgan saw it too. "I warned you about him."

Nimue shrugged. "He can do as he pleases. He owes me nothing."

"Don't take it personally. He's a lost little boy. He doesn't know what he wants."

Nimue did not answer. Instead she listened as a Cliff Walker Elder recited ancient prayers and Cora translated.

"*Je-rey acla nef'rach . . .*," the Cliff Walker sang.

"Let each soul and spirit here be blended in one sacred space, with one purpose and one voice," Cora repeated.

"*Jor'u de fou'el.*"

"Born in the dawn, to pass in the twilight." The assembled spoke in unison.

A Snake elder bound the hands of the Fauns with a ribbon.

The couple said together, "Under the eyes of the Hidden, under the eyes of the Gods, I join with you and we become one."

The Elders from each clan encircled the couple, reciting ancient prayers, and when they had finished, the Fauns kissed and raised their bonded hands. A horn blew and a shower of leaves fell from above.

Dancing circles formed around the newly joined couple.

Nimue smiled and looked over at Arthur. He returned her smile. She slid down from her rock and crossed over to him. He raised his eyebrows at her, and she frowned. "What?"

"Um, nothing. You look like a . . . dream or something," he said.

"Oh." Nimue flushed. "Well, I just thought, since you're going soon, we could . . ." She trailed off and decided to start over. "I just thought, maybe for an hour, we could simply be us. Without swords or Merlins or debts or paladins."

Arthur nodded. "I would like that very much."

"So what you're saying is: you would like to dance with me very much."

Arthur laughed. "That's precisely what I'm saying, yes. Though I fear I'm a sad comparison to"—he gestured to her dress of rose petals—"this."

"Oh, I don't know, I think you look rather sharp." Nimue took his hand and led him into the circle of dancers, and they were swiftly caught up in the merriment. Cups of wine were thrust into their hands, and they drank as they tried to match the others' fast steps, especially those of the agile Fauns.

Nimue could feel Morgan watching from above.

The dances came and went, and so did the cups of wine, and before long, Arthur and Nimue found themselves in a quieter circle, a lute's soft melody seemingly guiding their movements. Arthur bowed his head to touch hers and at that moment, Nimue lifted her lips to his. The kiss was brief. Arthur seemed about to speak, but she put a finger to his lips. He held her hand to his mouth, then pulled her into another kiss.

This one lasted longer. Deepened.

Couples and families swirled around them, but in that moment they were unaware of anyone else. When the kiss ended, Nimue hid her eyes and Arthur held her head to his chest. They swayed there in the gentle rhythm of the lute. After several long moments, Arthur gently lifted her chin. She looked into his gray wolf eyes as something dawned on him.

"Nimue." He hesitated. "What if it's you?"

"What if what's me?"

"What if you're my honor?" Arthur was serious. "What if you're the justice I'm meant to serve?"

Nimue had started to answer when a commotion near the front of the caves drew their attention. The children were running toward something. New refugees staggered into the cavern, bewildered and exhausted. The music ceased and the Joining was forgotten as Fey Kind hurried water and food to the new arrivals. It took a moment before Nimue noticed a boy covered head to toe in dried mud, hands on his hips, sizing up the cavern with fearless eyes.

"Sq-Squirrel?" Nimue whispered. She took a few steps toward him to be sure. "Squirrel!"

Squirrel turned to Nimue, and a giant smile creased the dried mud on his cheeks. "Nimue!" He dashed to her and leaped into her arms, nearly knocking her over. She swung him about, then checked him up and down for injuries.

"I tried to stay, but the paladins were everywhere—"

Nimue wrapped her arms around him and pulled him close to her. "You were so brave, my Squirrel."

Over his shoulder, she saw two warriors enter the cavern. The first was a woman with long arms, wearing purple robes, the dye as deep as any Nimue had ever seen. Her face was hidden beneath a cowl and she held in her hands a lean staff, carved with runes, made from a smooth wood Nimue did not recognize. The nails on the woman's slender fingers were gleaming black, unnaturally curved, and sharp as knives. Most notable was a lush speckled tail that trailed from under the woman's robe, the tip twitching nervously.

The second was a tall knight in leather armor, with a green, gleaming pauldron across his right shoulder, a broadsword at his hips, a longbow across his back, and a green helm with a chain-mail face shield and curving antlers.

"And is that the one who rescued you? The Green Knight?" Nimue asked.

Squirrel chuckled. "Nimue, you don't know?"

*In that moment they were unaware of anyone else.*

The Green Knight lifted the antlered helm from his head, revealing a sweating face with lean cheeks, a high forehead, and a patchy goatee.

Nimue's lips parted with shock as she processed a face she hadn't seen in almost ten years.

"It's Gawain!" Squirrel shook her arm.

Arthur frowned. "Who's Gawain?"

Stunned, Nimue pulled Squirrel by the arm toward the Green Knight, who took time to acknowledge the Fey children pulling at his gloves and belt. When he looked up at Nimue approaching, he squinted with confusion, unable to place the face after so much time.

"Gawain, it's me." Her voice shook. "It's Nimue."

His face lit up like the sun. "No, no, no, this is not Nimue. This is not her." He laughed loudly and lifted her into the air. They both began talking immediately.

"You have to tell me everything! When did you come back?" Nimue gushed.

"This can't be the skinny little tree climber I left behind! Who is this young woman? Tell me all!" His words tumbled over hers.

Arthur stood awkwardly by until Nimue recognized his discomfort. "Gawain, this is Arthur. We're . . ." She laughed with nervousness. "Friends? Hard to describe, exactly. We've been on quite the journey together."

Gawain looked him up and down. "Sell-sword?"

Arthur nodded. "On occasion."

"Human," Gawain said, not smiling.

"Aye." Arthur shifted his sword belt.

Gawain scratched his chin, considering. "Well, thank you for taking care of our Nimue."

"*Your* Nimue?" Arthur said.

"I am my own Nimue."

Gawain held out his arms, addressing Arthur. "Take as long as you need here to rest up. What little we have, we will share."

Arthur smiled through clenched teeth. "Thank you."

Gawain turned to Nimue. "There's so much to talk about. Come with me." Nimue shot an apologetic look back at Arthur before disappearing with Gawain into the shadows.

# TWENTY-SEVEN

Gawain turned the sword of power in the torchlight, marveling at its design. "Who knows about this?" he asked with concern.

"Arthur, Morgan," Nimue answered.

"The Man Bloods."

"They've proven to be true friends. And you're better than that. The Gawain I knew would never judge others by their blood."

"Times have changed, Nimue."

"Have they? I hadn't noticed." Nimue held out her hand. Surprised by the gesture, Gawain returned the blade to her. She slid it back into the makeshift scabbard she'd slung around her back.

"I'm not the only one who's changed, it seems," he observed.

Nimue stared at the flickering torch. "I watched the Joining and all

I could see was blood. And burning crosses. I have no taste for war. We should strive for peace."

Gawain pointed at the Devil's Tooth. "You say that, but this is the sword of our people. This sword is our history. It's our hope, Nimue." He stood up, frustrated. "And you want to give this to Merlin the Magician? Who turned against his own kind? He's a conjurer, serving a Man-Blood king."

"It was Lenore's wish."

"I loved Lenore like a mother," Gawain said. "But this is wrong. Why him?"

Nimue threw up her hands. "What do you want me to say? They were her very last words to me. She could have said anything to me, but this was what she chose: bring this to Merlin."

Gawain looked puzzled. "A bargaining chip, then. She hoped this Merlin would protect you. But you don't need that, because I will protect you."

Nimue had no time for this. "I don't need protecting."

Gawain softened his tone. "Are you sure? For this sword is also called the Sword of the First Kings. 'Whosoever wields the Sword of Power shall be the one true king.' Uther Pendragon will want this sword, and if history is any guide, he will promise the world, then leave the Fey to the mercy of the Red Paladins."

"Well, I wouldn't know, for I am no king."

"If you don't want the responsibility, then give it to someone else. Someone here. I'll take it if I must. Just not Merlin."

"No one will take it." Her fist was tight around the sword.

Surprised, Gawain sought to calm her. "All I meant—"

But Nimue was embarrassed by her outburst. "No, I just—I won't dishonor her memory." She still felt hot with anger. *What is wrong with me?*

Gawain sat on a rock. "Well, then I guess that's it, then. We put all our hopes and faith in Merlin."

"Not all," Nimue offered. She knelt by her meager belongings, found what she was looking for, turned and scattered the stolen maps across the floor. Curious, Gawain got down on his knees to study them.

"We asked Yeva to send a bird to Merlin, but we haven't yet received an answer. In the meantime, these are Carden's plans. Arthur and I stole them. His maps, his death lists. We know his mind. We know what villages he's targeting and with how many men."

Gawain was stunned. "Gods, girl, why didn't you show me this sooner? We'll ride tonight."

He gathered the maps and was nearly under the archway when Nimue called, "Gawain."

He turned back to her.

"If you're hunting paladins, I'm coming with you."

For a moment, Gawain seemed bemused, but then he sensed her resolve, and his eyes turned a touch sad. He nodded and headed down the corridor.

Nimue headed in the other direction, back to the cavern where the Joining had been, to find Arthur and to apologize. *I kissed him! Or he kissed me.* She wasn't sure. But she was certain she had run off like a fool when Gawain had arrived and that it made her look quite fickle. She hoped to repair that breach and even pick up where they had left off.

She entered the cavern and was sad to see that the beautiful boughs of flowers had already come down and been trampled underfoot by the new refugees. Nimue looked for Arthur amid those tending the wounded, but he wasn't there. After a few minutes, she found Morgan tearing clothes into strips for dressing wounds.

"Have you seen Arthur?" Nimue asked.

"He left."

"Left? It's the middle of the night. Left for where?"

Morgan looked up at Nimue with sympathy. "To wherever Arthur goes."

"What are you saying? You mean he left for good? Without saying goodbye?" Nimue tried to sound calm, but her voice shook.

"I warned you this would happen," Morgan said with an edge to her voice.

Speechless, Nimue hurried down the corridor to the alcove where Arthur slept. His lantern, wineskin, sword, and saddlebags were gone.

Against all her secret hopes, Arthur had been true to his word.

# TWENTY-EIGHT

LED BY THE GLOW OF A SOLITARY TORCH, thirty Red Paladins rode single file through thick woods in total silence along a slender deer path.

Sister Iris carried the torch and led the procession, pleased that she had been chosen as First Fire, an honor Father Carden bestowed upon brothers and sisters considered most pious. It was the job of First Fire to enter the heart of impure villages and set the straw alight, drawing bodies to the flame for easier capture. If some fled, no matter: Sister Iris had her sling and bag of rocks, each rock sanded smooth. Once her prey was hit, Iris would finish the victim with a poke of her two-bladed sword. Or she could spill their brains with her hooked hammer. There were so many ways to purify.

It made Iris smile inside when she learned the Fey Kind had named

her the Ghost Child. This meant they feared her, just as they should. At eleven years old, she was already a spirit of death. Some of the older brothers might still laugh when they met her in person. She was only four feet tall.

But they laughed only once.

Her size was an advantage. That was how the Melted Man won so much gold, tossing Iris into the ring with men twice her size and laughing away as she bit and sliced and gouged them down to her level. Iris despised that laugh as she loathed everything about the Melted Man. He was still the only thing in the world she feared: his monstrous body and face of boils, his stick beatings, his threats of terrible curses, threats of selling Iris to the black network and their secret terrible gods. But he'd taught her to fight and taught her to hate, and now she could use those talents to serve Father Carden.

His face was wide and smiling and cracked with wrinkles like an old statue weathered by storms, as beautiful as the Melted Man was ugly. Almost every night she dreamt she was Father Carden's true daughter, that he took her aside and whispered the truth to her: *you're my real child.* And she would wrap her arms around his neck as a true daughter could.

For now it was enough to be his Ghost Child. One day she might even surpass the Weeping Monk as the favorite in his eyes. That thought warmed her more than the flickering fire she held aloft with her right hand.

The wolves were making a bloody racket with their howling and their chains. Iris shot a look back at the shepherd, who snapped his short whip at the beasts, quieting them down.

Iris was on edge. She did not want to disappoint Father Carden. He seemed more tense of late, the burdens of his task showing in his stooped posture and flashes of temper. The Wolf-Blood Witch was on all their minds. Sister Iris wanted to kill the witch so badly she could practically taste her blood. She so wanted to ease Father's burden by cutting the witch into pieces and consigning her blackened soul to the glorious pyre.

*In time*, Iris prayed, for now she had to focus on tonight's raid.

The village was quiet as they entered. That was good. Sister Iris counted twelve mud huts. These were Marsh Folk, so the air thrummed with frog chirps and the buzz of mosquitoes. For a moment, Iris grew concerned the huts would not burn in the damp air. With her left hand she readied her sling, feeling exposed as the other paladins peeled away to encircle the village and she alone—the First Fire—led her horse to the village center. She was surprised by the lack of dogs, by the lack of any scouts or night watch. Only a single pig rooted through a garden of chard and cabbages. *Where are the dogs?* she wondered.

Sister Iris turned in a few anxious circles outside the Chief's Hall, the largest of the huts, its roof a tangle of swamp branches ringed with animal skulls. She wound up and hurled her torch through the open hatch at the front, then spun and freed her two-bladed sword from her saddle, ready for whoever ran out.

The hall was engulfed in seconds. So she waited, fist tight on the center grip of her sword, yet no one ran out. She lingered well past the time it would take any living thing to roast inside the Chief's Hall, until finally, a scream ripped through the night.

But it was not from inside the hall.

Sister Iris turned as a Red Paladin galloped through the village, a long arrow protruding from his neck. His throat gurgled as he raced past Iris and trampled through the cabbage garden before falling from his saddle into the shallow marsh. More screams cut through the night as an arrow whistled and landed in her horse's right flank. Iris's horse wheeled and blundered backward into the crumbling, flaming wall of the Chief's Hall. Iris was thrown head over heels into a fireball of dead branches.

She screamed and breathed in the flames. Her robes lit up like a torch as she grasped burning coals to pull herself onto her feet. Her eyes swelled shut and the village around her was reduced to distant pinpoints. She was aware of the chaos around her but could not hear anything save for the crackle and sizzle of the clothes she was wearing and the flesh beneath them.

A warrior at heart, Iris had had to manage pain for as long as she could remember in order to think on her feet in the pits. It was this skill she called upon as she tore free of her robes and ran with all her remaining strength into the snake-filled marshes at the edge of the village. As she collapsed into the reedy muck, her body gave off a blast of steam. Iris knew the fire had ravaged her and took no comfort in the numbness of her skin. She knew that was only a prelude to the torture to come.

*The witch. The witch did this.*

Iris rolled over in the mud and smiled with blackened lips as she dreamt of the many agonies she would inflict upon the witch.


Meanwhile, a dozen Red Paladins dodged a volley of arrows and galloped into the forest to meet the ambush head-on.

With their arrows spent, Faun archers scattered and bounded away like deer, their antlers flashing in the light of the paladin torches.

"In the trees!" one of the paladins shouted. All eyes looked up to see shadowy bodies with long arms, framed against the moon, darting through the canopy branches with inhuman agility.

The horsemen rode deeper into the darkness, the leader locking in on an injured Faun, who had separated from the group but who was, even at a hobble, still unnaturally fast. But the Red Paladin had been killing from horseback for months and chopped the Faun's head clean between the antlers without breaking stride.

Having recovered from the surprise of the ambush, the Red Paladins organized and spread out into a wider circle, trapping the Faun archers and several families of Marsh Folk in a ring of trees. As taught, the Red Paladins herded their prey by slowly closing the circle of horses. They barked and yipped like animals to enhance the fear of those trapped. A panicking Faun tried to leap over the horses, but one of the monks was ready and timed his swing perfectly, opening the Faun's guts in midair. This gave the paladins a surge of confidence and they whooped louder, closing in for the kill.

The commander shouted, "Horned devils first!"

Marsh Folk pleaded and covered the heads of their children as the paladins' swords rose into the air.

Yet before the first blow fell, a loud snuff resounded behind the paladin leader, along with a crunching of leaves. The leader threw up his hands, signaling a pause, and carefully turned his horse to the shadows of the glade. He waved his torch in front of him and the spreading light caught upon large, dark eyes concealed in the lattice of swamp branches. What followed was a squeal loud enough to panic the paladins' horses. The commander lived long enough to see the head of a giant boar erupt from the gloom to a chorus of snapping branches. Its saber-like tusks, each the length of a jouster's lance, dipped low, then swung up under the paladin's horse, flipping both rider and mount into the trees, where they were impaled upon the twisting branches. They hung there like scarecrows as blood and leaves rained down upon the others.

The paladins' confidence vanished as pandemonium broke out.

Nimue lunged from her hiding spot in the brush, but Gawain pulled her back.

"Hold. Let the Tusks do their work," he whispered.

Nimue felt hot and feverish, and her teeth were on edge. "I can't." She shoved away from Gawain and charged into the moonlight wearing a chain-mail shirt, two sizes too large for her and belted into a form of skirt;

breeches and high boots for the glade; and the Devil's Tooth slung around her back. A Red Paladin happened to be running directly at her, and she drew the sword and severed his head in a single stroke. She felt like her cage door had risen and she was wild and free. Her fears and anxieties were forgotten. Her hurt over Arthur's departure fled. Instead she reveled in the cries and the desperate, conflicting orders of the Red Paladins.

"*Troch no'ghol!*" Wroth of the Tusks rebuked Nimue as he rode the gargantuan boar and directed the charge to inflict maximum violence upon the paladins. For centuries, the Tusks had trained their war boars for combat with fighters on horseback. The boar kept its nose low, its tusks at ground level, as paladin swords slapped at its thick bristled mane and leather-tough hide to no effect. Then the boar jerked its wagon-size head left and right, sweeping out the horses' legs and flinging paladins into the darkness.

The Tusk fighters had been thrown out of their battle formation by Nimue's arrival, giving the Red Paladins a chance to regroup.

The plan faltering, the Green Knight whistled and hatches opened in the ground. Arrows whisking past their cheeks, Tusks and Fauns hurried the Marsh Folk into the underground Plog tunnels, the shy, strange Plogs tilting their heads inquisitively at the frightened Marsh children as they crawled into the freshly dug corridors, led by Fauns with torches.

"Nimue, stay with us!" Gawain shouted after her as she ran deeper into the marsh, where the Red Paladins were forming a line. A few broke off to engage her. One of them raised his sword high and she swept him low, cleaving his leg off above the knee. An arrow clipped her shoulder. Another buzzed past like a dragonfly. She heard Gawain in the distance, the worry in his voice. But Nimue was not afraid. Her vision was clear. She was a step faster, like she could feel the paladins' movements before they made them. The Hidden enhanced her senses. It was the sword. The sword was the beacon.

Another Red Paladin drove at Nimue with an ax. She parried the blow aimed at her ribs and swiftly countered to his neck. Blood sprayed and blinded the paladin charging up behind her victim, giving Nimue a clean blow to his head.

*Paladin, paladin, choke and twitch, bitten by the Wolf-Blood Witch.*

Nimue smiled. She liked the rhyme.

A flash of movement allowed her to pivot away from instant death, but a dagger still sank deep into her left shoulder.

*Idiot fool!* Nimue cursed her carelessness as agony forked through her head and chest and the Red Paladin's full weight against her toppled them both into a thicket, Nimue on the bottom. She got her forearm up in time to block the paladin's next desperate blow. The paladin's dagger point hovered inches from her eyes. His other hand clawed for her throat and his eyes bulged, ready for death. The Devil's Tooth was useless, pinned beneath her. She scratched at his face, but he bit her hands instead. She tried to knee his groin, but he sat above her waist. His fingers found her throat and squeezed, cutting off her air.

A wet thunk sprayed Nimue's face with blood. An arrow stuck through the paladin's temples. Nimue could suddenly breathe again. She fought off the stars bursting in her eyes, climbed to her feet, and retrieved the Devil's Tooth, roaring at the same time. She turned and saw the Green Knight several yards away, readying another arrow. His face was all fear and fury.

A bold paladin ran past Nimue and speared the giant boar in the side. The beast squealed. Nimue stepped forward, spun the heavy sword in a high arcing circle, ignoring the fire in her shoulder, and—*chuk*—sent the paladin's head soaring through the air, past Wroth atop his boar mount.

Wroth watched the head fly past and splash into the mud, then slowly roll to a stop. He turned back to Nimue with a wide, big-toothed smile.

"The Wolf-Blood Witch!" Wroth bellowed into the night.

Nimue was dizzy, almost giddy, and somewhere, deep down, scared to death.

Wroth and his fighters threw their fists in the air and chanted her name. Her heart pounded and she smiled, despite the lightning in her shoulder. Gawain was checking on her, saying words to her, but there was so much blood rushing in her ears she couldn't hear the words.

She turned and crawled into a mud tunnel. Gawain followed her. Plogs hurried to work behind them, shoveling mud between their legs with their deformed, clawed fingers, filling in the tunnel door and sealing it up to appear as though it had never existed.

# TWENTY-NINE

KING UTHER MARCHED DOWN A FILTHY dungeon corridor, flanked by ten armored guards, until he reached the last cell of the block. Inside, Merlin was chained to the wall, hair and beard disheveled and caked with mud and blood. The soldiers had not been gentle with him.

Uther straightened to his full height. "Merlin."

"Your Majesty," Merlin rumbled, his eyes hidden by greasy locks of hair. "I would stand, but I am leashed to the wall."

Uther's nose twitched at the rank odor of mold and human waste. He posed a simple question. "Why didn't you tell us about the Sword of Power?"

"Well, Your Majesty—" Merlin started.

But Uther interrupted, "Wait, I know. You wanted to acquire it for us first before animating any false hopes."

Merlin's hands gestured in their iron cuffs. "Frankly, yes, Your Majesty."

Uther smiled coldly. "Always the perfect answer."

"I confess the way I left was less than ideal, sire, but you see, the omens—"

Again Uther interrupted. "The omens, yes. Blood raining down on Castle Pendragon. Scary stuff."

"But as I've always said, sire, there are—"

The king cut Merlin off again. "Different possible meanings to signs. Yes, we remember. We are not as stupid as you think."

At this Merlin hesitated. There was no question that their dynamic had changed. He trod carefully. "I never suggested—"

But Uther seemed determined not to let Merlin finish a sentence. "We remember all your lessons, Merlin. For instance: we need not fear omens, but rather we can seize them. Turn them around and examine them until they tell us something new. And then through action make the signs come true." Uther wrapped his hands around the bars of Merlin's cell. "And this thinking was very instructive."

"How so, Your Majesty?"

"Because we decided the blood that fell on the castle was not ours"—all pretense of kindness left Uther's eyes—"but yours."

Merlin peered at the king through his dirty locks, his voice a warning. "Uther—"

"You never believed in us. And now we no longer believe in you." Uther stepped away from the cell and folded his hands behind his back. "The Age of Wizards is at an end. We consider your recent derelictions as treason. And for that there is only one recourse: execution."

"Without a trial?" Merlin growled. "Without a hearing? Who has turned you against me?"

Uther allowed emotion to peek through as he snarled, "You've done that yourself with your disdain, your drunkenness, and your disloyalty." His voice shook. "When you came to this court, we were ten years old. Do you remember?"

Merlin's voice was soft. "I do."

Uther's eyes shone with memory. "We had heard such incredible tales of the great Merlin the Magician. How we awaited you. You see, we never knew our father. There was no one to teach us how to be king." He chuckled. "So we sat at our window for days, searching the hills for you. We wanted to learn the secrets of the world. We wanted to be wise." Uther's smile faded. "The day you rode through the gates, we raced out to see you. And you fell off your horse. You stank of sweat, and your beard was stained with wine. They had to carry you."

Merlin sighed. "You have every right to be disappointed in me, Uther, but if you want the Sword of Power, then killing me is madness. I have it on good authority that the sword is coming to me. Give me one week—"

"I'm sorry, Merlin. But the mob awaits your head. Seize him." Uther turned away, and his heels clicked down the stone corridor as the jailers unlocked Merlin's cell door and the footmen lifted him to his feet.

"Uther!" Merlin cried as they unshackled him and dragged him out of the cell. "Uther, I need more time!"

But moments later Merlin squeezed his eyes shut against the blinding sun as he was led out of the tower dungeon and onto a scaffolding above an assembled mob in a wide courtyard of Castle Pendragon. As Merlin's eyes adjusted, he saw Lady Lunette peering down from her castle window, a satisfied smirk on her face.

King Uther was pale and beads of sweat wet his bare upper lip. He kept glancing nervously to his mother's tower as the footmen forced

Merlin onto his knees before the bloodstained executioner's block.

"Uther, you're not thinking!" Merlin fought with his captors.

Uther snapped, "We tire of your words!"

The king nodded to the executioner. Merlin's neck was pressed into the groove of the chopping block. The king looked up to his mother again. She nodded. Uther took a deep breath and turned to the assembled mob. "Merlin the Magician, you are hereby sentenced to die for the crime of treason against our person!"

Merlin could smell the rusted blood soaked into the block. A resignation overtook him. He chuckled joylessly. In seven centuries, the only pure truth he knew was that death was ugly, sad, undignified, and empty of meaning, and despite what had seemed like great evidence to the contrary, he was proving no exception to this rule. And what difference did it make? In many ways, Merlin was already a ghost. Without his magic, he was little more than a player in a theatrical, pretending to be the great Merlin the Magician to a less and less believing audience. He could not even find anger in his heart for Uther Pendragon, a boy who had never been anything more than a pawn for his cruel, ambitious mother and, to a lesser degree, for Merlin himself.

But as the executioner lifted his ax, an unfamiliar panic swept over him like a rogue wave, a primordial, even embarrassing, scream for survival, and he swung his arms wildly to free himself. But the soldiers held him fast. The blade glinted in the sun and a burst of feathers threw all into chaos.

The executioner stumbled backward from the diving kite as the ax dropped onto the block a whisker from Merlin's nose. The crowd gasped and dozens made the sign of the cross as the raptor lunged and dove at the executioner, ultimately driving him from the scaffold.

Uther had not the slightest idea of what to do. He looked up at the window to Lunette, who gestured to finish Merlin, but before he could order his axman back to his post, the kite landed on the chopping block, a tiny scroll tied to its leg.

"A message, my liege!" Merlin barked, head still pressed to the block.

Uther wanted to escape. His moment of strength was unraveling. Sir Beric took a few tentative steps toward the kite, and his eyes widened.

"It's true, my liege. There is a note!" Sir Beric repeated, compounding the king's misery.

With a sneer, Uther said, "Well? Read it."

Sir Beric hurried over to the bird and carefully extricated the message from its leg. He unrolled it and held it to the sun, his jaw slowly dropping as he read silently.

Uther had had it. "For mercy's sake, Beric, what does it say?"

Beric sputtered, "It is a letter from the Wolf-Blood Witch, sire, offering to bring the Sword of Power, the—the Sword of the First Kings, to Merlin the Magician!"

"Tell her I am indisposed!" Merlin called out.

Uther could feel his mother's eyes burning a hole in the back of his neck. He dared not look up. He bit on his lip, fantasizing about Merlin's severed head falling into the crowd, but he knew when he was bested.

"Get him up. Get him up!" Uther spat as he shoved Sir Beric and a few footmen out of his way and stomped back into the castle, ignoring the jeers and complaints of the mob denied its blood.

The soldiers lifted Merlin to his feet, but he pushed them off and bent over to study the kite, which stared at him with indifferent black eyes. Merlin reached out to stroke the bird's wing and it bit him on the thumb, drawing blood. Yanking his hand away, he realized, "You're one of Yeva's, are you? You tell that old crone this changes nothing between us."

The bird watched him with disinterest as the soldiers pulled him to his feet and led Merlin away.

# THIRTY

A STEADY, UNFORGIVING WIND CHAPPED faces and sandaled feet as Father Carden led a grim procession of thirty Red Paladin horsemen into the foothills of the Pyrenees, where cottonwoods and tall pines had pushed over the marble ruins of Bagnères-de-Bigorre, a Roman outpost favored by the rich for its warm springs. They crossed uneven grassy slopes dotted with boulders that were split by wide, shallow streams filled with brown trout. Even the low peaks of the mountains were snowcapped and were unrelenting funnels for the December winds. Carden gritted his teeth to prevent them from chattering, mindful of being an example to his monks.

The Weeping Monk rode beside him, eyes covered by his draping hood.

As the terrain grew rockier and the slopes grew steeper, the paladins entered a green valley of high firs and a small blue lake, the shoreline of which had been claimed by a massive encampment, declared by the enormous banner of gold and white, the colors of the Vatican. It hung from a crossbeam like the sail of a ship, atop a papal carriage. Several large, red, oval tents, also flying the Vatican colors on long lances, surrounded a grand pavilion, sheltered up the shore from the lake and protected from the wind by a row of old pines.

Servants in religious robes with buckets on long poles ferried hot water from the nearby springs into the pavilion.

The pavilion doors were guarded by the black-robed Trinity, Pope Abel V's personal guard. As Carden and the Weeping Monk rode up to the pavilion doors and dismounted, they could see their warped reflections in the Trinity guards' ghoulish golden masks. Each mask was cast in the likeness of papal death masks, so each Trinity guard was given his own unique death identity. The dead golden faces of previous popes stared back at Carden and the monk with their strange closed eyes.

The Weeping Monk took note of the gruesome flails hanging from the Trinity guards' leather belts, and he coolly tucked his robe behind the pommel of his sword and stood to face them as Father Carden approached the door. The Trinity stepped back in unison and spread the flaps of the pavilion's entrance. Father Carden ducked and entered alone.

A sour mist obscured only the closest items. The air was heavy and scented with incense. Perspiration beaded Carden's brow. Servants continued to scurry back and forth, replenishing the vast wooden tub at the center of the papal tent with natural hot spring water.

Wading in the tub was a human skeleton. Pope Abel weighed no more than a hundred pounds and was mostly hairless. What flesh did cover his bones was sinewy and taut.

"Your Holiness." Carden knelt on the carpet before the tub.

"Rise, Father Carden," Pope Abel answered in his gravelly voice.

Carden stood. He did not react when he saw the pope's face, scabbed with the pox.

"I find these waters quite restorative," Abel said, then asked, "How was your journey?"

"Winter arrives early, Your Holiness," Carden said.

"You must be tired. Let my people draw you a bath. Surely I haven't used all the hot water." Pope Abel smiled. Carden noted that despite the pope's diseased appearance, his teeth were pearly white.

"That is a generous offer, Your Holiness, but . . ." Carden hesitated.

"But the work is too important. I know. I know you. Your work has not gone unnoticed, I assure you, Father Carden. And I know we have taken you away from that work. It must be difficult."

"It is my honor to make the trip, Your Holiness. But yes, I confess there is a feeling that weighs upon me. There is so much to do."

"God sees this work, Father Carden. He sees. How many villages cleansed? Is there a number?" Abel asked eagerly.

"They don't always live in villages, Your Holiness. These sad abominations live in the treetops and mud holes, caves, marshes. It is the rare kind that approximates what we would recognize as a traditional human settlement. The same goes for their appearance. While some might look like us, most of the others have stunted wings or misshapen limbs to afford easier climbing through the branches. Horns. Eyes without pupils that see in the dark. Some are covered in fur, while others live in the dark underground their entire lives and have no use for eyes, so they simply do not have them."

"Extraordinary. How marvelous it must feel to know that you are doing what God planned for you and removing these aberrations from His land."

"I feel this, Your Holiness, I do." Carden felt a swell of emotion at the thought.

Pope Abel swam away and the mists converged around him. He emerged and spat water into the air. "How many Red Paladins do you command, Father Carden?"

Father Carden swelled a bit with pride. "It is difficult to say, Your Holiness. In every town now we are overrun with volunteers. It would not be a boast to suggest that our numbers exceed five thousand."

"You have amassed an army, Father Carden. Incredible. And they are dedicated?"

"They come from different backgrounds, some rougher than others but they are a brotherhood. And a sisterhood as well, I might add."

"Excellent." Pope Abel snapped his hands together and water shot into the air. "And losses?"

The moment Father Carden feared had come. "Some, Your Holiness."

"Some?" Pope Abel replied, still popping water into the air.

"Naturally, there is resistance to our great work."

"A 'resistance,' is it, Father Carden? That sounds formidable. Is that what we call this Wolf-Blood Witch? Hmm? A 'resistance'? All by herself?"

"She is not all by herself—"

Pope Abel sprang up in the tub. "Don't contradict me, you vain farmer's boy!"

Carden looked down at his muddy boots, shamed by the rebuke.

Pope Abel stood there, dripping immodestly, daring Carden to look him in the eye. Then, satisfied, he slowly slid back into the water up to his eyes and waited there, like a crocodile.

"I beg your forgiveness, Your Holiness," Carden whispered.

"She knew our plans, this witch."

Carden nodded. "They found maps—"

"Found? She *stole* them from the Red Paladins she *murdered* in the glade. I know everything, Father Carden. You do yourself no favors by softening the blow. Dozens of Red Paladins slain by this witch, and what has been your answer? Hmm?"

Carden started to answer, but Abel cut him off.

"Nothing! That is what! Your campaign is paralyzed with winter approaching. Weakness is like the pox, Father Carden: it spreads to all who are near it. This witch is making a fool of you. A fool of us!"

"There is—"

"Eh? What's that?" Abel snarled. "Measure your words, pilgrim."

Carden struggled to remain calm. "Your Holiness, we believe we have found where these creatures nest. We are setting the trap. I beg you for time. When we find her, I swear to God, we will make such a chilling example of her it will drive her followers to despair and madness."

"Make it so, Father Carden, or it is *you* who will be made the example."

"Yes, Your Holiness."

"One more misstep and I will send in my Trinity to assume command of this army of yours. Be advised, the Trinity are not famous for their mercy."

"I understand, Your Holiness." Carden bowed and made as quick and dignified an exit as possible.

He was incredibly thankful to breathe the biting cold air again. He strode past the Trinity guards without a glance and was about to do the same to the Weeping Monk, then hesitated. He grabbed the monk at the bicep and hissed in his ear. "This is *your* failure that I have to come here and be subjected to this humiliation. Where is your pride? This witch mocks us. If I burn, mark my words, I will not burn alone." Carden shoved the Weeping Monk aside and marched to his horse.

The monk adjusted his robes and stared at the golden, dead faces of the Trinity standing watch at the pavilion doors.

# THIRTY-ONE

LADY LUNETTE STROKED A SHORT-HAIRED
gray cat in her lap and tipped over a small hourglass on the window-
sill of her tower. The sands began to fall. She gently pushed the feline
from her lap. "Down, down. Work to do." With a tiny
complaint, the shorthair leaped onto a velvet bench and curled into a ball.
Lady Lunette took a lump of fig pastry into her hand and patted it, humming softly to herself, as a knock sounded at her door.

"What is it?" she asked tartly.

The heavy oak door creaked open and Merlin leaned his head into
the small doorway. "Your Majesty Queen Regent?"

An invisible armor of ice settled over Lady Lunette. She smiled
thinly. "Lord Merlin, what a surprise. To what do we owe the honor of
this visit? And may we offer you a fresh cherry custard?"

Merlin admired the tiered trays of colorful desserts that filled the Queen Regent's tower chamber. "I must decline, milady, for I ate my fill at court. Though I hear they are delightful."

"Wine, then," Lady Lunette stated, cocking an eyebrow at a pitcher of wine and two silver goblets. "You must have worked up quite a thirst from such an exciting day."

Merlin scratched his beard, eyeing the wine warily, and demurred. "Exciting day. Yes. Yes, indeed." He sat on a wooden trunk at the foot of Lady Lunette's bed and bowed his head, deep in thought.

Lady Lunette's smile waned. "How may we help you?"

Merlin finally looked up and stared out the window at the setting sun. "For some reason, a day like this reminds me of a story. Perhaps you've heard it. Among the gentry they call it 'The Story of the Midwife.'"

Lady Lunette considered her pastry dough. "I don't believe I have."

Merlin's voice was soft. "They say it was an unusually cold night for May and that a frost had settled over the crops. Yet the people stood beneath the stars holding candles because a king was being born that night. And this was very important, because the old king had died only months before, leaving the queen a regent—not a true blood heir to the throne. But were she to deliver a son, then he would rule as the true king."

Lady Lunette carefully placed the raw fig pastry onto a tray of similar unbaked pastries. Her face was stone.

Merlin warmed to his subject and folded his hands, leaning back to savor the tale. "But as the night wore on, it became clear that the child had not turned and struggled inside the Queen Regent. And though she prayed to Saint Margaret that her child come free as easily as Margaret escaped the dragon's stomach, the baby was stillborn." Merlin paused. "And a boy."

Lady Lunette closed her eyes for the briefest of seconds.

Merlin continued his tale. "Knowing the dead child would snuff out her claim to the throne, the Queen Regent huddled with the midwife and devised a plot. And so, by the light of the moon, the midwife snuck away from the castle to a peasant home that was known to her, one that had recently celebrated the birth of a baby boy."

Lady Lunette began to carefully fold the dough of another tart.

"It is said the mother was paid handsomely in gold coins from the royal coffers," Merlin said. "Yet days later that same woman was found dead from a curious suffocation. Poisoned, some surmised."

Lady Lunette smirked and chuckled softly.

Merlin stood up, folded his hands behind his back, and breathed in deeply. "Indeed, most anyone who might have known of the foul conspiracy met similar ends." He turned to Lady Lunette. "All except for the midwife, who, fearing for her life, fled the kingdom, never to return."

Lady Lunette closed one of her shutters against the setting sun.

Merlin pulled on his ear, thinking. "One imagines that were she ever found, she would represent quite a danger to the king."

Lady Lunette set down her dough. "Which I suspect is why she remained hidden forever, given the grim outcomes of the other characters in the story. Or perhaps the simpler explanation is that she never made it out of the kingdom at all. And shared the fate of that poor mother who sold her child for a few gold coins."

Merlin nodded. "Yes, that has always been my suspicion as well." He walked slowly to the door, paused, then turned back. "There is a third option, of course."

"Is there?" Lady Lunette asked sharply.

Merlin's eyes gleamed. "That perhaps the midwife is alive and well and under my protection. Good day, Your Majesty."

Lady Lunette clenched her jaw as Merlin opened her oak door and stepped onto the tower stairs. When the door closed, it was silent in the tower. Lady Lunette turned to her hourglass. The sands had piled at the bottom.

"*Spspspsps,*" she softly called for the shorthair. "*Spspsspsps,*" she tried again. After no response, Lady Lunette leaned over in her chair. The gray shorthair stared back at her with lifeless blue eyes from where it lay dead on the velvet bench. Lady Lunette smiled with satisfaction. She reached down and plucked the half-eaten cake from the floor and set it carefully back on the tray.

# THIRTY-TWO

RAYMALKIN CASTLE," YEVA MUTTERED
as she fed her kite, Marguerite, a dead mouse in her hand.
"The castle of the lovers Festa and Moreii. Dark spirits
there. That drunkard is up to something."

Nimue stared at the words on Merlin's note as Gawain, his traveling
companion—the woman in purple robes whom Nimue had learned was
named Kaze—Morgan, and Wroth debated their next steps.

"Going alone is too dangerous," Gawain stated. "There are Red
Paladin checkpoints up and down the King's Road. You'll have to take
the forest trails. I'll ride with you."

"*Ech bach bru,*" Wroth rumbled.

Wroth's son Mogwan turned to Gawain. "My father says we need
you here."

"Food runs and finding survivors are the priority," Nimue agreed.

"Why go at all?" Gawain appealed to the others. "The man works for Uther Pendragon. How can we trust him?"

"Agreed," Morgan added.

Nimue stared at the sword. "Arthur would say Uther Pendragon is our best chance for survival." Uttering Arthur's name gave her a small ache in her chest.

"And where's that brave Man Blood now, eh?" Gawain snarled. "And what has this 'king' done for us except sit idly by while Fey have been slaughtered from Cinder to Hawksbridge to Dewdenn?"

"I've seen that slaughter with my own eyes and require no lectures on it," Nimue shouted at Gawain, who took a seat on a rock and simmered. "This was my mother's dying wish. And this Merlin has given me no reason not to trust him."

Yeva chuckled at this.

"You can leave the sword here," Morgan offered.

"He asks me to bring the sword."

"I don't like it." Morgan shook her head.

Nimue decided. "I will go. I will bring the sword." She took Morgan's hand. "And you will ride with me."

"With Kaze as well," Gawain added. "I trust Kaze with my life."

The woman in purple robes simply nodded beneath her cowl. The tip of her leopard tail flicked on the floor.

"It's decided, then," Nimue said, rising and turning to Yeva. "Tell Merlin I will meet with him at sunset in three days at Graymalkin Castle."

Yeva wiped the blood from her hands as Marguerite swallowed the last of the mouse down her throat.

The Widow stood at the edge of a jutting cliff above the freezing green surf of the Bay of Horns. Looming in the distance along the same cliffside, atop a sheer black tower of ancient volcanic rock, were the windswept ruins of Graymalkin Castle. Gulls and blackbirds cried and battled for nests in craggy pockets of the tall sea walls as Merlin rode up behind her, shoulders hunched against the biting winds. He climbed down from his horse and approached.

"Aren't you cold?" he asked her, as she wore only a black dress with a high collar up to her neck, black sleeves and gloves, and her customary veil.

"I like the cold," she said, producing the Snake clay of Fey Fire that Merlin had hidden in the saddlebag of her horse.

Merlin took the fire and placed it in a large pouch on the belt of his robes. "I thank you."

"Do you still plan to use the Fey Fire to destroy the sword?"

"Aye," Merlin said sadly. "I no longer believe in a 'one true king.' Nor in an old Druid's skills to guide him. The sword is too powerful a weapon for this barbaric age."

"You could claim the sword for yourself. And the Shadow Lords could rule once more."

"You know that can never happen," Merlin warned. "In a distant age I once tried to unite humankind and the Fey"—he paused, his eyes clouded—"and failed."

"Well, the Leper King will not forgive your betrayal. By now he's put a high price on your head. Your best course is to disappear for another hundred years."

"Once this business with the sword is complete, that is my intention."

"And what about this Fey girl?"

"Left to her own, she will drown in a sea of fire or Viking swords. I hope to reason with her, but one way or another, this Wolf-Blood Witch will deliver me the sword."

Merlin mounted his horse and turned to the castle, beard blowing in the sea air, unaware of Lady Lunette's spy in the high grasses on a nearby hill. She watched Merlin cross the fields until he dismounted at the perilous walking bridge connecting the cliffs to Graymalkin Tower. Then she crept backward through the grass to send the signal.

Nimue could not sleep. She tossed and turned, but the ground in the low hills of the Minotaurs was hard and full of small rocks. They had agreed to camp without a fire, so it was also miserably cold, though Morgan seemed to sleep without complaint.

Kaze had agreed to stand guard. Nimue had never seen the mysterious woman sleep. She just sat atop a fallen tree, alert to every sound, yellow eyes gleaming in the moonlight, her tail drooping lazily to the ground.

"Your tail is very beautiful," Nimue whispered.

"Thank you." Kaze smiled, baring her white fangs.

"Have you known Gawain for very long?"

"Not very long."

*A waterfall of conversation*, Nimue mused. "Well, I thank you for accompanying us."

"Yes, I am interested to see this Merlin who causes so much argument."

"Have you heard of him?" Nimue asked, curious. Given Gawain's travels, Kaze's thick accent and unique robes, she naturally assumed the woman came from lands far from Francia.

"Not by this name," Kaze said.

"You know him by other names?" Nimue said.

"He live a very long time," Kaze offered. "You must know this. You bring him the sword of your people."

Nimue was embarrassed by her ignorance of the world. "My mother asked me to bring the sword to Merlin. Prior to that, all I'd heard of Merlin had been in children's stories."

"Then he was very important to your mother," Kaze assumed.

Nimue shook her head. "No, she—he wasn't. She would have said something."

"To your father, then."

"My father left," Nimue started, but hesitated. "He left when I was very young."

Kaze stared at the moon. "Your mother kept secrets."

Nimue frowned. "No. Not usually."

"Did she tell you she possessed the great sword?"

"Well, no, but—"

"Your mother kept secrets," Kaze repeated, her point made. As though tiring of the conversation, she leaped lightly down from the fallen tree and vanished silently into the forest.

Cold sweat trickled down the back of Nimue's neck. She felt so unprepared for this. Her heart was fluttering.

*She brings darkness on this house!*

Every time she shut her eyes to sleep, the memory kept creeping in. Her father's voice.

*She's your child!*

And Lenore, furious, throwing a clay jug of water. Nimue could still hear it shatter against the stone hearth.

*I don't know what she is.*

Her parents screamed all night through her fitful dreams.

# THIRTY-THREE

THE BITING, SALTY WIND HIT THE RIDERS
hard as the trees thinned and low, grassy hills opened up to the
sea and the distant towers of Graymalkin Castle. Nimue felt
exposed in the open like this. Perhaps sensing her fear, Kaze
picked up their pace to a gallop as Morgan rode up beside Nimue.

"Offer nothing. Let him make the proposal."

"I know," Nimue said.

*I don't know anything,* she thought. Part of her felt anxious for this
gauntlet to end, anxious to hand the sword over and be done with it.
Yet she felt duty bound to the Fey refugees who were counting on her,
to her friends, even to the sword. *That's absurd. It's only a sword.* Yet the
sword had saved her from the wolves and spared her in the thorn maze.
The sword had given her the courage to challenge Bors and had served

justice in the glade. *It has served me well. And my thanks is to hand it over to a Man-Blood king? Who might use the very same steel to slay what's left of my kind?*

"Make sure your thoughts are yours!" Kaze called back. "Don't let Merlin crawl into your mind!"

*How am to know if my thoughts are mine?* Such a thing had never even occurred to her.

Mists rose from the bottom of the sea cliffs to envelop Graymalkin Castle, making it seem like the castle towers hovered above a bubbling cauldron. For reassurance, Nimue glanced back at Kaze and Morgan holding the reins of their horses. Kaze nodded to her from beneath her purple cowl.

Morgan said, "You're not Nimue. You're the Wolf-Blood Witch."

Nimue turned back to the broken towers looming over her, then glanced down between her boots and the wet boards of the walking bridge and saw only fog beneath her, but she could hear the crashing surf. She crossed the bridge as quickly as she could, holding her breath through most of it, and then walked the muddy path to the rotted draw-bridge and entered into the shadows of the castle.

Her footsteps echoed as she passed under the crumbling gatehouse. She looked up at the rusted chains of the drawbridge. Somewhere water was dripping. The feel of the sword against her back gave her some security as she crossed into the overgrown bailey. Here the vast size of the castle became real. Seven wretched black towers tilted over her like the fingers of a closing fist. Someone whispered behind her, and she turned to a dark doorway of the gatehouse. For a moment she thought she saw a shadow move within.

"Hello?" Nimue called out.

There was no answer.

Unnerved, Nimue backed away from the gatehouse and walked through the mists of the bailey, crossing to the wide keep, which was one of the few structures of the castle still largely intact.

"Is anyone there?" Nimue called as she entered the winding stairway. She detected a flickering green glow above her. She climbed into the darkness, her hand sliding along the timeworn walls until she reached the Great Hall.

Green fire crackled in a large brazier in the center of the vast, empty chamber, offering warmth against the chill of the sea air.

The man in ragged blue robes standing by the window was younger than Nimue expected. His brown hair and beard were unkempt and his cold gray eyes alert and suspicious. On his belt were pouches overstuffed with what looked like various plants and branches. Even from across the hall, Nimue could smell notes of cedar and lemongrass, geraniums and clove. This was not a snobbish, self-important royal envoy but an authentic Druid, a human versed in many magical languages, Fey and otherwise, and a stew of wild energy.

When he saw her, something took him aback, but only for a moment, and he tried to smile, but its effect was not comforting.

"You must be Merlin," Nimue said, hoping he could not detect the wobble in her voice.

"And you are the Wolf-Blood Witch, dreaded wielder of the Devil's Tooth," Merlin said.

Merlin's tone stiffened her spine. "You mock me."

"No," he said, softening, "but you are playing a dangerous game."

A thin, silvery thread crept up her neck and thunder rumbled in the distance. Merlin noted this.

"You think this is a game?" Nimue asked.

Keeping the green Fey Fire between them, Merlin circled the brazier. "How did you come upon the sword?"

"My mother gave it to me." Nimue's lip trembled. "And with her dying breath, she bade me give it to you."

Nimue saw Merlin's face change. He suddenly seemed more present. In a whisper he asked, "You are the daughter of Lenore?"

Nimue's heart beat fiercely in her chest, a revelation dawning. "I am."

Merlin's expression was inscrutable.

Nimue pressed, "You knew her?"

"I did," he answered softly. Then, almost shaking off a reverie, he returned to the sword. "Her instructions to you were very wise. We can—"

"Look at me," Nimue interrupted. She took a step toward him.

"I'm sorry?"

"Look at me."

The ancient Druid's tired eyes looked into hers. It seemed to take an effort to stay locked in her gaze.

"What do you see?" she asked gently.

"You have her eyes," Merlin said through emotion.

"Anything else?" she asked him.

"What name were you given?"

She smiled. "Nimue."

Merlin nodded. "Nimue. That is indeed a beautiful name."

"I have been asking myself, 'Why you?' Why did she ask me to bring the sword to you?"

"And what is your answer?"

Nimue took a shuddering breath.

"She did not wish for me to bring you the sword. She wanted the sword to bring me to you." Nimue smiled. "Because you are my father."

## THIRTY-FOUR

Y ES," MERLIN WHISPERED, "YES, THAT—
that would . . ." He trailed off and turned away, overwhelmed.
"I didn't—"

"You didn't know," Nimue finished for him.

Merlin shook his head, marveling at her, a wry grin cracking his cheek. "You are Lenore made flesh again."

Nimue wiped her wet eyes, her heart warming.

Merlin walked toward her and softly took her hand. He looked at it in his own. They stood there awkwardly.

"Did you love her?"

Merlin nodded. "Very much."

"And did she love you?" Nimue pressed, her questions returning in a flood.

"I like to flatter myself that she did," Merlin answered, a touch of sadness in his voice. He released Nimue's hand and crossed back to the window.

"When did you meet her? Why did you part?"

"I've never spoken of this."

"But I need you to now," she insisted.

"In time, Nimue. What is imperative is that you comprehend the powerful forces gathering to acquire that sword. Right now you stand in opposition to the crown, to the Church, and to northern invaders. Every moment you possess that sword magnifies the danger."

"And yet I have survived."

Merlin turned on her, fierce. "Yes, I see, sustained by a certain boldness that cannot last, which will be snuffed out like a candle flame in the wake of the armies of Uther Pendragon!"

But Nimue was defiant. "You will not frighten me into giving you the sword. For I am no child, I assure you. I've lived lifetimes in these past days." She did nothing to squelch the anger rising in her throat. "You are not trusted by my kind, sir. They tell me you are a traitor and a drunkard and a fraud. If you seek to earn my trust, you will tell me the truth about my past and your history with my mother."

The hall was quiet but for the flickering of the Fey Fire. Merlin weighed Nimue's words. Then a furtive whispering from the stairwell swung her head around. For a moment she thought she saw shapes, figures, slip behind the wall.

"Who is there?" Nimue called out, fearing an ambush. On instinct she ripped the Sword of Power from its sheath and pointed it at Merlin. His eyes shone at the sight of the blade in a way that Nimue could not discern. Was it fear she saw? Or desire? "Who else is with us?" she demanded to know.

The whispers, two young voices, a boy and a girl, seemed to flutter across the ceiling and into the distant canyons of the castle.

"They are the young lovers Festa and Moreii, born of rival clans, who barricaded themselves in this castle more than a thousand years ago and drank hemlock so they would never be separated. It is their voices you hear," Merlin confided. "They are drawn to you for what I sense is a strong connection to the Hidden."

Disturbed by the spirits' presence but no longer fearing attack, Nimue sheathed her sword but remained alert.

Merlin shifted his approach. "Your companions have judged and found me wanting. And it is true I am guilty of many crimes. For this you can neither trust me with the sword nor as a potential father, I understand. But the truth can be painful, Nimue. Are you sure you wish to know it?"

"I do."

"Then perhaps these young lovers will help guide us into memory, so that you may know my story. The story of Merlin."

By Fey Fire torchlight, Merlin led Nimue through the groaning and gusty tunnels of Graymalkin to a narrow gallery above the Great Hall. In the distance, broken shutters banged against the sea winds.

"This is where they died," Merlin whispered, gesturing to a stone corner. "Wrapped in each other's arms."

Nimue felt the familiar hum in her stomach and the presence of others in the room. She froze as a shadow lengthened across the wall.

"*Where are you?*" a girl's voice spoke, from very far away.

The hair rose on Nimue's arms.

Merlin put a comforting hand on her shoulder. They sat on the stones. "Any visions that may come, do not fight them," he advised.

The Fey torch flared and danced as shadows pressed in around them. Nimue fought the urge to panic and, instead, tried to open her mind to the visitors. She saw a young face in her mind, a girl her age with pale skin and freckles on her cheeks, a silver tiara and a long braid.

✦ ✦ ✦

Then Nimue was in the Iron Wood. She was home. But something was different. The light was hazy. She looked at her hands and saw through them, as though they were made of mist. She turned at footsteps and saw Merlin stagger between the trees, collapse briefly, then drag himself up. His eyes were dark pins, he wore rags and animal furs and looked half man, half beast. A foul purplish wound colored his chest and neck and his breathing was thick and wet. To ease his path, Merlin waved his hand and with a thunderclap buckled two oak trees like kindling. Nimue recoiled, stunned. Clutching his side, Merlin came within a foot of Nimue but paid no mind to her, as though she were invisible to him, and stumbled along.

Nimue followed him to the Sunken Temple.

Merlin's legs gave out on the long pathway to the altar. He crawled across the floor, gasping, wheezing, clawing at his side, clearly in agony. Reaching the altar, he curled up into a ball, shuddered, and was still.

The light in the temple changed and the shadows shifted as though several hours had passed. In all that time, Merlin did not move. Nimue was about to reach out to him when a rustle of skirts distracted her and Lenore, in the blush of youth, knelt beside Merlin. As she touched him, he groaned. "Leave me to the Gods. Leave me to die."

"You may die outside if you wish, but not in this temple. Not in the house of the Hidden. This is a place of healing." The sound of her mother's voice brought fresh tears to Nimue's eyes. Lenore wrenched the protesting Merlin to his feet, put his arm around her shoulder, and half carried him to an alcove of the temple, where she laid him on top of a blanket.

The light flickered again. Candles now lit the alcove. Nimue saw Lenore in the corner, grinding herbs with a mortar and pestle, eyes darting nervously to Merlin, who was racked with fever, muttering and shouting, "Fie! Let Alaric have these dead monuments! Burn it! Burn it all! Stack the bodies in the basilica!"

*Again the lights flickered, and Nimue was following Lenore through the Iron Wood as she captured cold stream water in a bucket and carried it back to the temple. Nimue relished watching her mother, watching her confident strides, her beautiful strong arms, feeling her strength and her goodness.*

*She could not help but smile as Lenore dunked Merlin's head in the icy bucket against his protests. She remembered well that her mother's healing arts came with a strong hand. Merlin was learning this firsthand.*

*"Why won't you let me die?" he growled at her.*

*"The Hidden teach us the spirit is not ours to extinguish," Lenore countered, pulling off Merlin's filthy furs and rags. When he was naked and shivering as a babe on the blanket, Lenore's hand slowly went to her mouth at what she saw.*

*It was a hideous, pulsing, deep red and violet wound that curled from his hip, around his stomach, up his back, and up to his throat.*

*A wound in the shape of a sword.*

*"What is this sorcery?" Lenore whispered.*

*Her fingers crept along Merlin's bubbling flesh and pushed down at the top of his ribs. Merlin cried out in pain. For Lenore clearly felt the contours of steel. Probing around his throat, she was able to pull the flesh down so that she could see the outline of a knob like the pommel of a blade.*

*"What is this?" Lenore asked him.*

*Merlin answered through shallow breaths, "My burden."*

*"It is killing you. This is quite obviously what has poisoned you. If it is not removed, you will die."*

*"It is too late," Merlin whispered.*

*The lights flickered again. Nimue stood over Merlin, who was ghost white beneath the blanket, his breathing irregular. Lenore knelt over him, tracing a stone blade across the track of the wound. The silvery vines of the Hidden grew up her neck and cheeks. She whispered an incantation, then pushed the stone blade into the flesh above Merlin's collarbone. Merlin opened his mouth in a silent scream as Lenore reached her fingers into the cut. Nimue could barely watch as Lenore's entire hand searched beneath Merlin's flesh. Her mother's knuckles flexed, and with a grunt, Lenore drew the bloodied Devil's Tooth from the arterial darkness of Merlin's chest. Despite her magical protections, Merlin's agonized wails shook the foundations of the temple walls.*

*The lights of memory flickered ahead several days. Lenore sat beside a sleeping Merlin. His wound had been treated and wrapped, yet his face and beard were soaked in sweat and he hovered between life and death. Lenore took Merlin's hand in hers. She put his fingers to her lips and whispered, "Live."*

*Nimue's eyes drifted to the Sword of Power on the ground, stained with Merlin's blood. Suddenly she felt herself pulled to the sword, falling into the sword.*

*In blackness she heard tortured cries and saw the faces of women and children begging for their lives. She saw severed limbs and torsos in piles. Lightning and fire. She saw rivers of blood flowing through Roman aqueducts.*

Look away from the sword, Nimue! *It was Merlin's voice in her mind.* Do not enter the sword's history. There are only horrors there. Look away! Look away!

*Nimue wrenched herself away from the vision, and she was with Lenore again in a secret crypt beneath the Sunken Temple. Lenore carried the sword across the silent stones to a statue of Arawn, King of the Underworld, a fierce bearded warrior holding leashed hounds that hunted the souls of the dead. At Arawn's boots lay an empty stone scabbard. Lenore slid the Sword of Power into Arawn's sheath.*

*Nimue spoke her thoughts to Merlin:* This must be where she fetched the sword from.

*Merlin's thoughts answered:* I never knew. She told me it was destroyed. She had access to Fey Fire, I assumed. Maybe I just wanted to believe her.

The memories flickered again. Merlin was awake but in a weakened state. Lenore sat beside him with a bowl of porridge. She tried to feed him a spoon of it, but Merlin pushed her arm away. Not to be deterred, Lenore set down the bowl, pinched Merlin's nose, forced his mouth open, and stuffed the spoon inside. Merlin stared at Lenore in disbelief, porridge on his beard. She snorted with laughter.

The lights flickered again and the spirits moved the memories forward to Lenore supporting Merlin as he took a few steps in the Iron Wood, the color returning to his cheeks.

"What is your name?" Lenore asked.

"I have been called many names over many lifetimes. But in these lands I am known as Merlin. May I ask what you have done with the sword?"

"The sword will trouble you no more."

"That is not an answer," Merlin said.

"And you are not my lord, so my answer will suffice."

Merlin smiled at this. "I have met my match, have I?"

"You think very highly of yourself," Lenore observed.

Merlin chuckled. "I am glad to be rid of the sword. For longer than memory, I have been consumed by politics, intrigue, and the Wars of Shadow. I am ready for a different kind of life."

"I have heard this name 'Merlin,' and of your role in these Wars of Shadow. They did no favors to the common folk or the Fey Kind," Lenore offered.

"These conflicts were born from noble intentions," Merlin said defensively.

"Blood begets only blood. And no peace was ever bought at the point of a sword," Lenore said.

Merlin paused to study her. Her eyes danced. "It seems fate has brought me to a house of healing and wisdom."

Lenore lifted her eyes to meet his.

✦ ✦ ✦

In the pink shafts of dawning sun, Nimue caught the last glimmer of the lovers Festa and Moreii, clutched in a final embrace, lips barely apart, hands caressing necks. It was a tender but fleeting image. They vanished in the morning mists.

Nimue wiped her wet eyes as Merlin fixed a pipe.

"I would tell you it gets easier." He blew a savory smoke. "But it does not." He smiled sadly.

Nimue's stomach made a churning sound. She laughed. "You've invited your daughter to this grand castle and brought her nothing to eat."

Merlin flushed with actual embarrassment. "Gods, I am terribly sorry. Give me a moment, just—just one moment." He hurried from the gallery.

## THIRTY-FIVE

ENEATH A PALE MORNING SUN, MERLIN
and Nimue walked through the withered gardens of Graymalkin Castle. Once-thriving cherry trees, pear trees, and
plots of chard, fennel, and leeks were now dried and tangled
husks.

"I fear Graymalkin has left us a meager bounty," Merlin lamented.
"You are the Wolf-Blood Witch. Perhaps you can demonstrate this
powerful connection to the Hidden and produce us a magnificent
feast?"

Nimue shook her head. "It doesn't work that way, at least not for me. It
tends to strike like lightning. It strikes when it will."

"Pity. A gift that rare, enhanced by the Sword of Power, could make
you a formidable sorceress. Yet your fear of it lessens your potential."

Nimue tensed at the slight.

Merlin did not seem to notice. "Your mother was the same. She could have been a real talent rather than a fancy midwife to peasants."

Silvery vines crawled up Nimue's neck and cheek: "Speak ill of my mother again and you shall see dangerous magic, old man."

Merlin took note as a few of the withered plants near their feet coiled like snakes about to strike. He nodded approvingly. "Anger is a start, but it is imprecise and burns out too quickly. Surrender is far more accurate and lasting."

Nimue realized she was being provoked and calmed a bit. She smirked at him.

"Imagine the result you wish to see," Merlin advised.

"I told you, I can't control it," Nimue insisted.

"That is because it is not yours to control. You must simply intend it, then surrender that intention to the Hidden."

Nimue turned away from Merlin and hugged her arms. She breathed the sea air for a moment, calming her temper, and reached out, visualizing a bountiful and vividly green plot. As she did so, the silvery vines slowly crept up her cheek.

Merlin observed a movement in the tangle of brush. Strong stalks pushed through the weeds, tiny buds flowering into leafy chard and cabbages. The branches of the fruit trees assumed a new rigor, rippling with green leaves and shining ripe cherries and golden-brown pears. In only a few moments, Nimue had transformed the brush into a verdant and abundant garden.

Merlin plucked a pear from one of the trees and offered it to Nimue. She took a bite. "My first lesson for you, my young Nimue."

Nimue took another satisfied bite, pear juice dripping from her smile. She allowed herself the smallest bit of hope in all this darkness that had surrounded her.

✦ ✦ ✦

Merlin served Nimue a bowl of stew in the Great Hall. They sat on the floor before the roaring Fey Fire.

"I am known for many things, Nimue, but cooking is not one of them," Merlin admitted. "And I fear we have no spoons."

Nimue saw his eyes drift to the Sword of Power resting in its sheath against the wall. "You still yearn for it, don't you? Even though it nearly killed you."

"The sword was forged as the defending blade of the Fey. It lusts for battle and attaches this desire to he who wields it."

"Or she," Nimue corrected him, though she nodded, agreeing. "I feel strong with it. Invincible, really." She used three fingers as a spoon and took a bite of stew. "I can't imagine giving it up. To anyone."

Merlin nodded. "That is something you'd be wise to resist."

"Why did you leave my mother? How did it end?"

"There are some things that I prefer to remain private, Nimue," Merlin said, shifting with discomfort. "Even between family. I have shared more with you than anyone in five hundred years."

"But I am not only your daughter, am I? I am the Wolf-Blood Witch. And you are not only my father, you are Merlin the Magician, counselor to King Uther Pendragon. If you expect me to surrender the sword to a human king, then I must trust you. And while this visit has meant a great deal to me—a great deal—I am not sure yet that I can do that—that I can trust you."

A sadness crept into Merlin's eyes as the Fey Fire shuddered and the shadows closed in around them once more. Nimue heard the whispering voices of the lovers, and again, they were transported.

*Merlin walked with Lenore in the Iron Wood. She guided his steps. He stumbled and took hold of her hand, then held on to it, bringing it to his chest.*

*"You are progressing well," she said.*

*"Thanks to you. You have saved me," he told her.*

*Lenore blushed. "All life is sacred to the Hidden."*

*"I care very little for my life. The Fates have wasted too many years on me. But you have revived my soul, something I'd feared lost." Merlin touched her cheek.*

*Lenore would not look him in the eye. "I am promised to another."*

*Merlin said, "But you do not love him."*

*"No."*

*Merlin nodded. "I sense you like broken things."*

*Lenore looked into Merlin's ancient gray eyes. "Yes."*

*Merlin wrapped her in his arms, his lips on her neck, her ear, her cheek, her lips.*

*As the lights flickered, the memory shifted forward, to Merlin and Lenore naked and entwined in the blankets, legs enfolded, gilded in candlelight.*

*Another shift forward, and Merlin rose out of sleep in his hut to the sound of voices in the temple. A man's voice berated Lenore.*

*"The Elders question me, and I don't know what to tell them, because the behavior is strange indeed."*

*"Yes, Jonah," Lenore soothed.*

*"There is dangerous talk, and I don't like it. You've isolated yourself, neglected your duties. The medicine gardens are dying. This temple is neglected. Are you keeping something from me?"*

*"I have—no, there is no—I can't speak to childish gossip." Lenore struggled to defend herself.*

*"This embarrasses me. You've spent nights away in this temple. I don't understand it, nor do I approve of it. Return to the village and behave normally. Do you understand me?"*

*"Jonah, you don't—"*

*The lights of memory flickered again and showed Merlin circling the temple garden. Weeds had grown over the herbs and flowering plants. Merlin knelt down and whispered incantations, his fingers conveying ancient symbols to guide his thoughts.*

*And nothing happened.*

*With more effort, he urged the roots to grow and the flowers to blossom, but his words were empty and his gestures futile. The garden was unchanged.*

*"No," he whispered.*

*The lights flickered and Merlin raged through the Iron Wood, frantically sputtering incantations to summon winds and lightning, but the forest was mute, the skies were quiet.*

*Again the lights flickered to find Lenore in the Sunken Temple. She saw Merlin slumped against the altar, muttering to himself.*

*"Merlin?"*

*He turned to her with dark eyes. "Where is the sword?"*

*Lenore took a step back, frightened by his demeanor. "What's wrong? What's happened?"*

*"Did you think you could trap me here in this ugly speck of a village? Hmm? Was that your intent?" Merlin rose to his feet and walked toward her menacingly.*

*"I have no idea what you're talking about," Lenore said.*

*"You took the sword from me! Against my will!" Merlin roared.*

*"The sword was killing you! You were dying on the floor! What is this madness?"*

*"It has stolen my magic! The core of what I am!" Merlin's voice broke with emotion. "Return it to me!"*

*"This obsession has corrupted your mind—"*

*Merlin toppled the altar, breaking the ancient stone. "I demand you return the sword to me! Now!"*

*Lenore stood firm. "The sword is destroyed and your life is saved!"*

*"Liar! You've destroyed me! Deceived me!" Merlin collapsed onto the ground.*

Lenore fled Merlin's raving and entered the temple's secret tunnels. She approached the Sword of Power, nestled under the altar in Arawn's sheath, questioning whether she should return the blade or leave it to the gods. Her hand reached for the grip of the sword. As her fingers clenched around the leather of the grip, she whispered, "Show me," and visions flooded her mind. Her mouth opened to scream as her eyes grew wide and filled with terror.

The lights of memory flickered and moments later, Lenore staggered into the temple. Merlin had regained some composure. He reached out to her. "Lenore, I'm sorr—"

But she cut him off, "Leave this place and never return. I will marry Jonah."

Merlin pleads. "I was not myself—"

"Leave this temple or I will have you torn from it!" Lenore turned her back on Merlin.

"Enough!"

Merlin stood up and backed away as Nimue climbed to her feet. "What did she see? What did the sword show her?"

"I owe you nothing more."

But Nimue was not having it. "There is more to it and you know it. What did she see that so frightened her?"

"I tire of this exercise," Merlin growled. "You have seen enough!"

"Have I?" Nimue turned and grabbed the sword.

"What are you doing?" Merlin asked. "Nimue!"

Nimue held out the sword in both hands and spoke to the blade. "Show me what you showed my mother."

A rush of images suddenly flooded Nimue's mind.

A thousand fires raged unchecked from the Baths of Caracalla to the Mausoleum of Augustus, giving the entire city of Rome a hazy orange halo. Strange blue lightning arced across the billowing black clouds of smoke, obscuring the stars.

Desperate, starving Romans raced for safety as the monstrous invaders poured through the Salarian Gate, nightmares made flesh. They flew on see-through wings like giant insects and prowled like leopards, eyes gleaming in the flames, and stomped on cloven feet, antlers stained with innocent blood.

Legionnaires fell back across the Pons Fabricius and took shelter behind the marble columns of Jupiter's Temple. Across the Tiber, the basilica imploded in a series of pluming fireballs. The cascading lights shone upon the hundreds of drowning bodies in the river.

A centurion on horseback called to auxiliaries when the blue lightning constricted into a single bolt and struck horse and rider, charring flesh and armor.

The invaders howled and shrieked in a celebratory chorus as the conquering dark prince, Myrddin, a younger, crueler Merlin, rode through the flames on his giant silver stag, swinging the Devil's Tooth—the Sword of Power. Myrddin's eyes glowed blue like the bolts he commanded. He pointed the sword at Jupiter's columns, and a conflagration of wind and cold fire obliterated the temple and the women and children who had taken shelter there.

"Leave nothing alive!" Myrddin roared as he galloped across the square, cutting down the fleeing Romans, whether they wore the armor of centurions or not, whether they were old or young, armed or defenseless.

Myrddin screamed to the sky and summoned arcs of lightning, raining javelins of fire on every living thing his gleaming blue eyes could see. Chunks of red ash fell around the hem of his war robes. His black-ringed eyes looked down at the Devil's Tooth, the seed of his ambition, the blade that commanded armies, felled emperors, and bent the knee of barbarian kings. The sword had fused to Myrddin's flesh. There was no hand, no grip, no wrist, only a charred lump of flesh and steel at the end of his arm.

## THIRTY-SIX

**W**ITH A GASP, NIMUE JOLTED BACK to the present, horrified by what she had seen. She turned to Merlin. "How could you?"

"It was the sword," Merlin tried to explain.

"It wasn't the sword. It was you. You killed women and children. You're steeped in blood."

"And you're no different!" Merlin warned.

"Me? Are you mad?" Nimue sputtered.

"How many Red Paladins have you slaughtered with that sword?"

Nimue swung into a fury. "They burned my home to the ground! They killed my best friend! My mother! How dare you compare me to— to that—to that murderer!"

"I was like you. I let the sword guide my hand to justice. And it was like a taste of the ocean. My thirst only grew. And you will feel the same. You already admitted as much. The feeling it gives you. The power. I want to save you from this, Nimue."

"By giving it to a human king?" Nimue said incredulously.

"By destroying it!" Merlin shouted, pointing to the green flames. "In the Fey Fires of the ancient forge. By consigning it to oblivion so that its reign of blood can end forever."

Nimue hesitated. "Destroy it?" She looked at the sword in her hands. "If there is no sword to barter with, then what is to be the fate of my people?"

Merlin sighed. "It was never your charge to save an entire race, only to bring me the sword. And against unthinkable odds you have done this. You are free of your obligation. Now you must trust me as you trusted your mother, to do the right thing."

Nimue stared into the light-swallowing blade of the Devil's Tooth, unsure.

Outside Graymalkin Castle, Morgan paced, eyes locked on the castle. "We should go in. We've waited far too long."

"Wait." Kaze took in the horizon with her inscrutable eyes from atop her chestnut courser, Maha, who grazed on the tall grasses. With her keen senses, Kaze felt the tremble in the ground first, but the rumble came soon after, growing louder than the crashing surf.

Morgan heard it too. "What is that?"

Kaze spun around as an army of soldiers on horseback, flying the banner of Pendragon, crested the nearest hill, less than a mile between them and the castle.

"Nimue!" Morgan shouted as she leaped onto her horse.

Kaze turned Maha, spinning her toward the drawbridge. Leading Nimue's horse, she put her fingers to her fangs, and a piercing whistle echoed off the walls as they charged through the gatehouse and into the wide bailey with its permanent fog.

Nimue and Merlin appeared at the entrance to the keep. Morgan fought with her anxious horse. "Nimue, hurry!"

Kaze pointed her staff toward the hills. "Soldiers!"

Nimue turned on Merlin, dread creeping up her throat. "Who knows we're here?"

"No one," Merlin assured her, though his face was tense. When he saw a flash of Kaze's eyes, he frowned, recognizing her. "You," he whispered.

But events were moving too fast. Morgan threw her hand out to Nimue. "They are Pendragon soldiers! I told you! I warned you!"

Nimue lurched away from Merlin as though by an invisible force, a repulsion. "You lied," she said, shaking her head in disbelief. "You lied to me."

"Nimue, this is not my doing!" Merlin insisted.

"How could you?" she screamed at him, as she turned and ran to her courser and pulled herself into the saddle.

Merlin ran after her, protesting, "I've been deceived! Nimue, please!"

But Nimue pointed the sword at Merlin, freezing him in his tracks. "You will pay dearly for this!"

Morgan's eyes gleamed with pride.

Kaze gave Merlin a strange, knowing smile before spinning Maha around and galloping back through the gatehouse. Morgan and Nimue followed after. Kaze dug in her heels and the wind flew through Maha's white mane as she leaned her neck forward and they tore a path across the fields, galloping in a horizontal line against the wall of steel barreling down the hill toward them. Even from a quarter mile they heard calls of "The sword! Get the sword!" as dozens of riders peeled away from the main cavalry.

Kaze drove them into the thickest, darkest heart of the forest to lose the soldiers. The trees grew in tight clusters, and Nimue ducked her head and clutched her courser's neck to prevent being ripped from the saddle by reaching branches. But Maha was an extraordinary animal, barely losing a step as she made switchback after switchback, blazing a trail for Morgan and Nimue but confusing the same for their pursuers. They plunged down a steep hill, until they reached a wide stream. Maha stepped easily into the shallow water, further muddying their path.

Soon the soldiers' voices faded in the distance and the forests opened up to the stormy cliffs of the White Hawk Sea. The three women allowed their horses to rest and graze, their coats covered in sweat and mud.

Nimue walked to the cliff, where the waters' namesake raptors dove for the crabs exposed by the retreating surf. She slung the sword from her shoulder as thoughts of betrayal and lies churned her guts. That she had opened her heart to Merlin in the slightest galled and enraged her. She was stupid. Stupid and naive. Why did she think she knew better than Gawain or Yeva or Morgan? Why would she ever think she could trust that drunken monster?

The memories of her mother and Merlin together disgusted her to her core. What cruel point had Merlin been hoping to make? He was only planning to steal the sword in the end, so why torture her with memories? And why in the name of the gods would Lenore send Nimue to Merlin? She'd been tricked as well. She was as big a fool as her daughter.

Nimue felt more lost than ever, the unwilling custodian to the Sword of Power, the Devil's Tooth, the Sword of the First Kings, sacred relic to the Fey Kind. She stared at her fist clenched around the frayed leather grip of the sword and imagined her flesh seared to the metal, imagined slowly consuming the sword until its sharp sides sawed at her guts as she, too, devolved into a muttering, murderous wraith. She hated the sword for stealing everything from her. Lenore might have lived had she not felt compelled to protect it. The sword tore her parents apart and poisoned her father's very soul. The sword had made Nimue a murderer. She could still taste the drop of Red Paladin blood that had fallen on her lips during her slaughter at the glade. Maybe Merlin was right about one thing. Maybe they were the same. A murderous father, a murderous daughter. But no, she would make a better offering to Ceridwen, Goddess of the Cauldron.

Nimue took the sword in both hands and swung back to heave it into the White Hawk Sea when a pair of strong hands stopped her. She turned angrily to Kaze. "Let me go! This is none of your concern!"

"That is the sword of my people, so it is my concern," Kaze said calmly.

"Take it, then!" Nimue threw the sword at Kaze's feet. "It has brought me nothing but misery."

Kaze shook her head and walked away, passing Morgan and muttering, "This witch is not right in the head."

Morgan picked up the sword and then presented it back to Nimue, pommel first. "Perhaps you won't suffer so much if you stop trying to give it away."

"What am I supposed to do with it?" Nimue asked, exasperated.

"What did you want Uther Pendragon to do with it?"

"Save the Fey!" Nimue shouted. "Proclaim himself First King and stop the slaughter!"

"And why not do this yourself?"

Nimue scoffed, "Because I am no king."

"Of course not. You are a woman."

Nimue hesitated, a mocking smile frozen on her lips. "Are you saying I should proclaim myself queen?"

Morgan did not laugh. "I am saying the sword came to you. Not to me. Not to King Uther or Merlin. Not to Kaze and certainly not to Arthur. If you want a great leader to save the Fey Kind with the Sword of Power, then I say: do it yourself."

"But I don't want it," Nimue whispered.

"I don't believe you. I think you fear the opposite is true. That not only do you want it but you might actually have the power to achieve it."

Nimue was quiet at Morgan's words. The gulls called and the wind buffeted them both.

Morgan took Nimue's hand and put the sword in it. "Now we must ride before the soldiers catch up to us."

Without another word, Nimue slid the Sword of Power back into its sheath and slung it over her shoulder.

# THIRTY-SEVEN

**D**RUUNA TILTED BACK IN HER CHAIR
and rubbed her shaved head as she considered Arthur with
a gold-toothed smile. "Still easy on the eyes you are, boy."

"And that gold truly becomes you. Is that a new pinkie
ring?" Arthur flashed his easiest smile and leaned over the table, letting his
hair fall over his eyes.

"It is indeed." Druuna waved her gilded fingers at him. She wore a great
deal of jewelry, mostly gold. She wore rings on every finger, men's breeches
held up by a Germanic belt buckle carved with a golden octopus, a silk
blouse, high leather boots, and four gold rings in her nostrils.

"What happened to Bors? Thought you had a good thing there."

"Yeah, falling-out. Left him a bit shorthanded, I'm afraid. Looking for
a new crew, maybe some sword work?"

"Are you square with Bors?"

"Square?" Arthur repeated.

"Do you owe him money? Any debts? I don't need any of that trouble."

"No, Druuna, we're good. All clear." Arthur regretted lying to Druuna, but he needed coin and needed it fast. He'd ridden south for days in hopes of outpacing word of his run-in with Bors or dead paladins. He took no pride nor joy in his flight. He felt sick most of the way. But he'd grown used to the gnawing in his guts every time he ran when the fire grew too hot. A dull disgust with himself. He'd felt it ever since he was a boy. Ever since he let their uncle, Lord Hectimere, take Morgan away from him to put her in the convent. Arthur could still hear her beg and scream. But Arthur had been ten years old and saddled with his father's debts. What could he do? But Morgan never forgave him.

True, this was different. He owed nothing to the Fey. He felt terrible for their lot, but that was the end of it. He was a "Man Blood" and not even accepted by their kind. *Why should I put my neck on the block for them?*

He tried not to think about Nimue. *I tried to save her. I asked her to come with me.*

"I might have something," Druuna said, fingering a gold denarii. Druuna was a priceless resource in the trader port of Rue Gorge, placed strategically between the foothills of the Iron Peaks and the River of Fallen Kings. Her area of expertise was acquiring sword escorts for illegal caravans. "I've got some wagons of exotic items, dyed silks, rare spices, I don't know where from and I don't want to know. Need to cross the Peaks. They'll only pay for one sword, so it might be dangerous. Leaves tomorrow. Interested?"

"Done," Arthur said without hesitation. He wanted nothing more than to put the Iron Peaks between him and his shame.

That night he drank too much ale and slept poorly.

The next morning he met the traders he was meant to accompany,

Dizier and his wife, Clothilde. They were travelers, judging by their colorful foreign clothes and their heavy accents, and talkative about all things but the contents of their five wagons, which were heaped with blankets and straw.

Arthur couldn't have cared less. He was eager to get moving into the mountains before nightfall. Most thieves were too lazy to climb into the Peaks and would instead ambush on the road out of Rue Gorge. He and Bors had done it a dozen times back in towns like Hawksbridge.

Luckily, Dizier seemed just as eager to get on the road, and by midday they had loaded their supplies, left Rue Gorge, and were only ten miles from Doroc's Cross, which spanned the River of Fallen Kings and marked the journey into the Iron Peaks.

From his position at the back of the convoy, Arthur spied two Red Paladins atop a wagon—a checkpoint—down the road. *Red bastards are everywhere*, he thought. He noticed Dizier's posture change and a series of nervous looks between him and Clothilde.

A squeak turned Arthur's head to the wagon beside him, the last wagon. *Was that a sneeze?* He sidled closer to the wagon, drew his sword, and with the flat end of the blade lifted the corner of a set of heavy carpets.

A terrified Faun child looked back at him. Her small antlers had been sawed off in what Arthur assumed was a sad effort to make her easier to disguise. He looked back at the road and the Red Paladin checkpoint fast approaching. He looked at the five wagons he hadn't bothered to inspect. *Gods, are they all hiding Fey families?*

Dizier glanced back at Arthur as though reading his mind. The traveler's eyes were strained and worried. Arthur cursed his bloody luck. He turned and looked over his shoulder at the empty road behind him. If it came down to a pursuit, Egypt could outrace them. And that would leave Dizier and his cargo to the mercy of the Church, and there was very little question of how that would play out.

When Arthur turned back around, Dizier was waving his hat to two Red Paladins in a friendly manner. The paladins approached on their skinny horses. The caravan gradually rolled to a stop. Arthur missed the first bits of conversation as he numbly whickered Egypt forward toward the front of the convoy. There was little to distinguish the Red Paladins up ahead. They both seemed to be young and ugly. One of them had a tonsure that flowed into a patchy black beard filling his cheeks and neck. The other kept his brown locks neatly trimmed. Both of their exposed pates were sunburned.

"What goods are you moving?"

"Just carpets, my brothers. Very, very fine. A family tradition. Four hundred knots per finger. I can make you a very nice deal."

"We don't want your gypsy rags. Get down from your horse. We'll have a look."

"No need for that, my good man." Arthur rode up. "I'll vouch for them."

The Red Paladins regarded Arthur with dead eyes and curled lips. "No one asked you, friend."

Dizier watched them intently.

The bearded paladin turned to Dizier. "Get off your horse."

"Don't move, Dizier," Arthur advised. He turned to the paladins. "Why doesn't Dizier here make a Church donation and we'll be on our way?"

"Here's how it goes, boy," the clean-cut paladin said to Arthur. "We look through these wagons, take what we like, and you shut that shithole of a mouth."

The bearded paladin added, "There's been a lot of hedge pigs and blood beaks getting secreted through these hills."

Arthur knew those vulgarisms for Tusks and Moon Wings. "Well, that's not us, brothers. Just carpets and a desire to reach the foothills before dark. These roads can be dangerous at night, as you know."

"You're a real funny one." The clean-cut paladin drew his sword. "Lose the steel, boy."

"I—I have gold," Dizier sputtered.

"Aye, the field is yours, sir," Arthur said as he unbuckled his sword belt and dropped it on the dirt road.

With a smirk, the clean-cut paladin dismounted and picked up Arthur's sword. He snarled at Dizier and Clothilde. "Get down, both of you. Now."

As the clean-cut paladin walked past Egypt's saddle, Arthur drew a dagger from his boot, caught the Red Brother by the throat, and jammed the blade into the back of his skull, giving it a twist as he whispered, "I send regards from the Wolf-Blood Witch."

The bearded paladin fumbled for his sword as Arthur yanked the dagger free, flipped it between his fingers, and threw it hard, spearing him under the chin. The bearded paladin gurgled and clutched his throat, blood flowing between his fingers, as his horse turned in nervous circles before rearing and dumping him onto the dirt.

Arthur dismounted in a flash and retrieved his sword. "Help me!" he shouted to Dizier as he grabbed the clean-cut paladin by the boots. Dizier helped Arthur drag the bodies to the side of the road. Arthur's eyes darted in the direction of Rue Gorge, praying for time. He took Dizier's arm. "Dump the saddles and take their horses. Get to Doroc's Cross. Once you're over the river, you'll be safe in the hills."

"Wh-what about you? You're not coming?" Dizier asked.

"There's no time. I've got to clean this up. Hide the bodies before the next shift and hope they assume the post was abandoned. If the Church hears that paladin blood was spilled here, they'll tear down the Iron Peaks looking for you." Arthur took Dizier's shoulders. "Go. You'll be safe." His eyes drifted to the wagons. "And so will they."

Dizier's eyes welled with tears of gratitude. "Born in the dawn."

Arthur smiled grimly. "To pass in the twilight."

# THIRTY-EIGHT

**A**TOP A HIGH CLIFF IN THE MINOTAUR Mountains, the Weeping Monk dipped his arrow into a bucket of pitch at his feet, then fed it to a burning torch stuck into the dirt. Arrow alight, he lifted his longbow and fired high into the air. The flaming arrow soared three hundred feet across the gorge and landed in a pasture of wheat far, far below, within a hundred yards of several more arrows, which had lit the entire field ablaze.

Drawing another arrow, the Weeping Monk repeated the process, pivoting his foot a few degrees to face another set of farms just to the west. Already, dozens of cones of smoke were visible across the Minotaur Valley.

✦ ✦ ✦

Nimue felt a pit in her stomach when she smelled the burning wood. What at first appeared to be a thick mist in the rolling hills of the Minotaurs was, she realized, actually smoke.

"Something is on fire," Nimue said, riding beside Kaze, who steered Maha to a promontory from where they could overlook the entire mountain valley.

Morgan rode up behind them. "Do you smell that smoke?"

Nimue nodded. She'd expected to see fiery crosses, but what they found instead was more confusing.

There were multiple fires raging over the wide pastures, filling the sky with a swollen, mushroom-shaped black cloud and giving the air a sickly yellow hue.

"A wildfire. Maybe from lightning," Kaze offered.

Nimue sensed a greater malevolence at work. "No, those are farmlands. Barns. Look how the fires are spaced apart. Those were set on purpose."

Nimue and Morgan shared a look.

"Our food," Morgan said.

"They're burning the farms."

Kaze nodded. "They cannot find us, so they will starve us out."

Nimue could taste the smoke on her tongue as tiny embers fell around them from the sky.

The population of the refugee camp appeared to have doubled overnight. There was no space on the floor for the new arrivals. On every rock and patch of dirt, three or four Fey Kind huddled, eyes tired and dull. The children were no longer singing, for there was no space to dance. The altar of the Joining ceremony had been broken and dismantled, the wood used for fires and to create new totems for clans to stake out smaller and smaller territories. The air was hot and thick with the stench of illness

and blood and unwashed bodies. And unlike before, where the suffering was shared, there was a new sense of hostility as Nimue noticed frightened human families mixed in with Fey Kind. Nimue guessed they were farmers caught harboring Fey Kind. Regardless of their sympathies, young Snake males and young Tusk males, always quick to temper, paced around the Man Bloods in a threatening manner.

A child took Nimue's hand as she entered the cavern. Nimue was unnerved at first by the sackcloth the child wore over her face, except for a small tear to allow her sight through one blinking eye. Nimue could only imagine the disfigurement beneath, and what horrors must have caused it. She squeezed the child's hand and knelt beside her. "And what's your name?"

The child was silent.

"Oh come now, if you don't answer, what do I call you?"

"Ghost," she whispered, though her voice was muffled.

"Ghost, is it? I'm not sure that's the name your mother gave you, but it will suffice for now." Nimue took her shoulders. "You're safe here, Ghost, do you understand? I won't let anyone hurt you here."

Ghost nodded. Winking at her, Nimue stood and led her through the oppressive atmosphere of the camp, and within a few moments they found Squirrel tucked in a nook in the wall. He hopped down and gave Nimue a hug, glancing sideways at Ghost.

Nimue made introductions. "Ghost, this is Squirrel, who often gets into trouble but is otherwise a lovely little fellow. Squirrel, can you show Ghost around?"

Squirrel looked up pleadingly at Nimue, who smiled at him sternly in return.

"Fine," Squirrel sighed. "Come on, I found some dead rats this way." Ghost was reluctant to let go of Nimue, but after a brief tug-of-war, she resigned herself to Squirrel's care.

Squirrel dashed ahead of Ghost, who struggled to keep up, although Squirrel jabbered as though she were right next to him. "It's gotten crowded, so I keep to the deep tunnels. This cave is huge! I must've crawled a mile. I found a spider as big as my fist. He tried to run straight at my face. My papa told me all the animals get quite fierce in the caves because there isn't enough food, so they're hungry and mean all the time." Squirrel got down on his hands and knees, preparing to wiggle into a dangerously narrow crevice. He turned back to Ghost. "Do you want to see the rats or not?"

Ghost hesitated, then climbed down onto her hands and knees to follow Squirrel. Together they squeezed along for several feet until the caves opened up, allowing them to sit upright. All along, Squirrel kept talking: "I mean, it's the same as around here, isn't it? The Tusks are mean to begin with. Now that we're down to one bowl of porridge a day, they'll fight with anyone. I'd never met Tusks before. Have you? You're not Tusk, are you?"

Ghost shook her head.

"So, what clan are you with?" Squirrel asked.

Ghost shrugged.

"You don't know?" Squirrel said, incredulous.

From the way they were seated, Squirrel could see strange scars on Ghost's right calf. Four slashes and a half moon. They looked man-made. Like a branding.

"What're those?" Squirrel asked, pointing to her leg.

"Squirrel, are you in there?" called a familiar voice.

Squirrel sighed. "It's Morgan. That woman gives me no rest." As Squirrel turned his head to address her, Ghost picked up a sharp rock and raised it to strike the back of his skull. "What is it?" he shouted back.

"You were supposed to fill these water buckets while I was gone!" Morgan answered.

Squirrel began crawling back the way he'd come and Ghost missed her opportunity. She lowered the rock. "You said it could wait!" he argued.

"I never said that!"

As Squirrel wriggled back to the main cavern, Ghost pulled the sackcloth from her head to breathe easier. The flesh that had melted over her mouth and her ruined nose made breathing difficult, just as her burned left eye kept her vision weak, but Sister Iris smiled all the same. She had found the witch's nest, and now she would kill her.

## THIRTY-NINE

NIMUE, MORGAN, AND KAZE ENTERED the chamber where tribal elders weighed camp decisions. The mood was tense. The farm fires had pushed the camp to its breaking point. Cattle had been slaughtered and hundreds of barns were burning and with them any hope of food for the starving refugees. Making matters worse, the fires were spreading to the surrounding forests, the smoke driving deer and smaller game out of the Minotaur Valley, forcing the Fey hunters to travel farther and farther into Red Paladin territory.

Morgan returned from giving Squirrel his orders and stood in the back, ignoring the glares of some of the Fey Kind about the presence of Man Blood at their tribal meeting.

In the meantime, Gawain tried to find common ground with the Elders. "Staying here is no plan," he reminded them.

Wroth of the Tusks slammed a fist upon the boulder that had become the Druids' council table. The blow echoed through the uneven ceilings of the caves. "*Gar'tuth ach! Li'amach resh oo grev nesh!*"

One of Wroth's sons—Mogwan—interpreted: "He won't lead what's left of his kind to slaughter on the open road."

Cora of the Fauns stood her ground. "And what you suggest? That we sit and starve like newborns?" Cora, like Nimue, was the daughter of her clan's Arch Druid and had become the de facto leader of her kind. She also shared her clan's deep antipathy for Tusks.

Wroth slammed a fist on his chest. "*Bech a'lach, ne'beth alam.*"

"We forage. We survive," Mogwan said.

"On our land! Stealing our food!" Cora rebuked.

Gawain pinched the bridge of his nose as the arguing between clans resumed. At issue was a Faun proposal to escape to the south by hugging close to the King's Road and using Moon Wings and Plogs as scouts and spies to spot Red Paladin checkpoints. The only problem was, there was no guarantee that Fey refugees, having safely crossed the Minotaurs, would be met with any less violence by the Viking warlords who held the southern ports and therefore the Fey Kind hopes of exodus by sea.

Nimue found the debate difficult to follow, given the varying dialects and clan languages and the occasional English speaker.

"We'll take our chances in the peaks," groused Jekka, Cliff Walker elder, her sagging arms covered in tattoos.

A tall Storm Crafter who, like his kind, was hairless and unmoved by the cold, snarled in his native tongue, "*Awl nos chirac nijan?*"

Nimue turned to Kaze, who translated: "What of the rest of us?"

"I've lost fifteen of my own blood. A generation wiped away. My people have to come first. We can't hide you all." Jekka shrugged, weary of the struggle.

Nuryss of the Snakes spat, "*Klik kata ak took!*"

Kaze whispered, "He says, 'Just like a Cliff Walker to look down on the rest of us.'"

Jekka bristled. "And what has your kind ever done for any of us, except sow discord? And now you want our help?"

"We agreed to stay together," Gawain reminded everyone, but he wasn't heard above the shouting. Fear and rage and sorrow boiled over and found fuel in tribal disputes older than the caves that sheltered them.

A piercing light and a sub-aural hum silenced them all. Every head turned to Nimue, holding the Devil's Tooth in her fist. She walked forward and set the sword on the boulder. The other Fey Folk brooded on the sword and remained silent.

Nimue's voice shook and her skin tingled as she felt the presence of her mother beside her. Regal. Forthright. "We're not running, not hiding, not abandoning our own kind. Shame on the one who turns her back on her brother. Or sister. We've all lost mothers and brothers, sons and friends. We are all we have. We are all that stands between our kind and annihilation. Our languages, our rituals, our history, we're the only thing that keeps Carden's river of fire from washing them away."

The caves were quiet but restless. Nimue knew the moment wouldn't last.

Gawain nodded at this. "And what do you propose?"

"How far is the town of Cinder?" she asked, her voice steady.

"Ten miles south from Cinder's Gate," Morgan answered from the back.

Gawain shook his head, anticipating her proposal. "It's no refuge for us. Red Paladins occupied it a fortnight ago."

"And what gives them that right?" Nimue asked.

Gawain gave her a quizzical look. "They have no right. They just take."

With Lenore clear and beautiful in her mind, Nimue spoke. "This is our land. These are our trees. Our shadows. Our caves. Our tunnels. We know these lands and these trails. Why should we leave? Carden is the invader. His paladins are the invaders. Let us treat them like the invaders they are."

Lenore's voice was quiet but firm: *Then teach them. Help them understand. Because one day you'll have to help lead them. When I'm gone—*

A few of the Fey Kind nodded in accord, but Gawain tempered Nimue's argument. "Carden has thousands of fighters. We cannot take him head-on."

She felt the Hidden act as a bellows in her stomach, coaxing the growing fire, a power not lashing out but yielding to her will, awaiting her command. The Sword of Power seemed to glow under her gaze. She spoke with Lenore's certainty. "I agree, we cannot win a war with Carden. But we can frustrate him, thwart him, put him on the defensive, and in the meantime save as many as we can from his crosses. I say we turn the land against him. Make him fear the cliffs." Nimue looked at the Cliff Walkers. "And the glades." She glanced at the Snakes. "Make them fear the shadows. I've seen these paladins up close. They aren't devils. They're men. Flesh and blood. They scream and bleed like we do. So let's make them. They've taken our land, so let us take it back!"

Wroth of the Tusks pounded his fist upon the boulder again, this time in approval. The Snakes stomped their feet along with the Storm Crafters. Morgan smiled, eyes shining, as gradually all the Fey Kind were slamming their fists or stomping their feet in approval. Gawain turned

"WE'RE NOT RUNNING, NOT HIDING, NOT ABANDONING OUR OWN KIND."

to Nimue, concern etched on his brow, but she felt a strange serenity. Part of it was the certainty of having the sword, and the vast power of the Hidden beyond it. But the other part was relief. There would be no more running. They would take the fight to the Red Paladins, and come fire, death, or torture, the Wolf-Blood Witch would have her blood.

# FORTY

CINDER WAS A LARGER TOWN THAN Hawksbridge, numbering almost five thousand residents, and was tucked in a valley of low mountains at the southern end of the Minotaurs, attracting immigrants and laborers from both the port cities and the northern lands: Aquitania, Francia, and England. It was surrounded by steep and dramatic waterfalls that fed a number of streams meeting at the Boar River, which wended its way through the heart of the small city and fed the moats of the town gates and the smaller moats of the lord's castle as well as feeding trade to the rest of southern Francia.

The smoke of the farm fires loomed over Cinder like a yellow storm cloud and curled around the merlons of the ramparts. The Red Paladins patrolling those walls held their hoods over their mouths to avoid breathing the acrid air.

It was just past dawn and the gates were already raucous with peasant workers seeking shelter, and farmers and their families begging for food, not to mention the herders with their dozens of bleating sheep and goats, horses, and cows rescued hours before from burning barns. Where normally oxcarts and trade wagons would form a line half a mile long, only a handful of sellers arrived for market day. They were hastily led inside while Red Paladins and the footmen of Lord Ector, Cinder's chief magistrate, argued with the gathering mob, most of whom were demanding reparations for, and protection from, the spreading fires.

Into this chaos, a single hooded rider emerged from the smoke and the dense green forest about a quarter mile from the road and the gates of Cinder. The Red Paladins atop the wall took notice as the rider paused and flipped back her hood. Nimue stared at the Red Paladins on the wall. Then she threw aside her robes and drew the Sword of Power, raising it above her head, the blade flaring in the sun like a torch. *See it, you bastards? Come, then. Come and take it from me.*

"The witch!" one of them cried. Another quickly grabbed a longbow and fired an arrow at Nimue, who did not move as it landed in the brush a dozen yards away.

"The Wolf-Blood Witch! The sword! She carries the sword! It's the witch! It's her! The Devil's Tooth!" These calls were now racing up and down the walls, and in a matter of minutes one hundred Red Paladins galloped through the gates, blasted past the bereft farmers and their livestock, and stormed across the road and into the brush. Nimue wheeled around, tempted to charge them. *Stay with the plan, fool.* And instead she bolted into the forest, luring them into a chase.

Anax was the commander of the Red Paladin company and a seasoned killer, with bony features and a coarse black tonsure to match his beard. He feared no witches and bemoaned the bed-wetters he led, with their superstitions and silly gossip. Anax believed in the god of steel and felt the comfort of his bastard sword banging against his leg as he rode deep into the forest.

"Spread out!" he barked, and red robes fanned out on his right and his left. The smoke and the mists cut down on visibility. The witch appeared to be weaving between the trees some two hundred yards ahead. "Watch the trees!" he ordered, assuming the witch was organizing an ambush. But Anax felt little fear of it. True, some paladins had died at the witch's hand. *But that's what you get for putting a child in command,* Anax thought with disgust. *The Ghost Child.* The Green Knight had sparked a tiny rebellion in some of the lower hills, a few archers here and there; some had been decent shots, but for the most part the Fey Kind were a cowardly lot that showed little will to fight, from his experience. And he had plenty of experience. Anax had personally seen twenty villages burned and had cut down more than a hundred of the monsters, some with horns coming out of their throats, others with strange, almost see-through skin, others covered in slime who lived under the mud. They died all the same and begged all the same and burned all the same. The witch would be a nice prize, he mused. The sword alone would earn him great credit with the pope, a nice assignment with the Trinity, perhaps, somewhere out of the mud and the cold.

As the trees closed in, Anax noted stick figures hanging from hundreds of branches throughout the wood. They brushed against the paladins' shoulders as they passed. Some of the figures were wrapped in entrails, others had feathers and blood stuck to their limbs, others were smeared with animal feces. Anax heard his boys starting to mutter in frightened whispers. "Quiet!" he hissed.

*Thump!* Something large scampered above their heads.

"Trees!" several Red Paladins shouted. A few of the archers nocked arrows to their bows and fired into the canopy.

Anax saw nothing. The smoke was thick above their heads.

"Commander!" Anax turned to the voice, very far away. One of his own. "Commander, where are you?" another Red Paladin shouted.

"Oy, who is that?" Anax swung around to his company.

But he was alone.

Fifty Red Paladins had vanished in the smoke.

"Commander?" Another frightened Red Paladin yelled for him from somewhere deep in the trees.

"I'm here!" Anax called back. "Ride to my voice!"

Had he ridden off course? Only seconds had passed. Where was his company? He drew his sword and swiped at the totems dangling all around him. "Ride to my voice!" he called again, hurrying his pace.

"Commander Anax!" This voice came from behind him. Anax turned his horse and saw a group of red robes fifty yards away. "Stay in formation!" he yelled. "I'll come to you!" He whickered and dug in his heels, urging his mount forward, but she fought him and reared up as a rushing sound stirred in front of him. It sounded like a diverted river, turning into a roar as hundreds of shrieking ravens flooded the wood from all sides, their heavy bodies thudding against Anax and his horse, sharp beaks drawing blood on his cheeks and arms and calves. Anax struck the ground hard, struggled to his feet, and chopped blindly, severing birds in two all around him until, finally, the swarm relented, hundreds of them perching on the skeletal branches above his head. His whinnying horse, its eyes gouged out, dashed wildly into the mists in a panic.

Then Anax heard the screams. They were all around him. Through glimpses in the fog and smoke he saw red robes hurtling upward into the trees. How?

"They're in the ground! They're in the ground!" came more panicked cries. Anax stumbled toward the tortured voices, though he could not place them. Begging calls for help echoed through the wood. The gurgle of men drowning.

"Sound off!" Anax commanded. He stumbled ahead and saw half of one of his men, arms flailing, the rest trapped in the ground, in quicksand, Anax assumed. He ran to the boy and grabbed his arms.

The boy had blood in his mouth. "It's eating me!" he screamed, before succumbing to the sucking earth and vanishing away.

Anax shielded his head as branches crashed noisily above him and a Red Paladin struck the dirt like a bag of rocks. The monk's head had been twisted front to back. Dead eyes stared up at Anax, and his own eyes darted to the treetops, where shadows bounded behind the smoke.

"Show yourselves!" Anax spit.

The dirt buckled upward around him and Anax stabbed at the mud repeatedly, falling backward and kicking away. He turned and fell into a run, chased by the panicked and agonized cries of his Red Paladin company.

Suddenly a root caught his foot, and Anax fell face-first into the dirt. He looked up at the Wolf-Blood Witch. She walked toward him. So small. Just a waif. Anax snarled and tried to swing his sword, but a tree root had wrapped around his arm at the elbow. He turned, horrified, as another root wormed out of the mud and constricted around his bicep like a snake.

It was her. She was doing it.

"P-please," he said to her as she raised the Devil's Tooth high. "Please!" And then she cut off his head.

On the walls of Cinder, above the meager marketplace, a skeleton crew of Red Paladins huddled with concern as close to an hour had passed with no sign of Commander Anax or his company.

Finally one of them took command. "Close the gates! Close the gates!"

At this cue, Gawain, Wroth, Kaze, and a dozen Fey Kind fighters threw off their peasant robes and grabbed their smuggled swords,

hammers, and longbows from underneath the fruit and vegetable baskets in their wagons.

Wroth and Kaze ran at the Red Paladins manning the gate, catching them by surprise and cutting them down, while Gawain sent two arrows through two throats atop the wall. The Red Paladins pitched forward and plunged through the thatched awning of a bakery, kicking up clouds of wheat flour.

The crowds of peasants, farmers, and traders ran in all directions, some wisely hiding behind their trade wagons. The Red Paladins were caught flat-footed. Wroth charged one skinny monk headfirst, butting him into a cart of turnips and crushing his skull with an overhead hammer blow.

Expert Faun archers tipped over vegetable stalls and used them for cover as they plucked Red Paladins from the ramparts, while across the yard a Cliff Walker fell to the mud with a slashed-open stomach. His clansmen overwhelmed his Red Paladin assassins, chopping them to death with their rock axes.

But the Red Paladins on the wall regrouped and laid down a volley of arrows that sent Fey Kind sprawling into the mud. Gawain took cover behind the guard tower as Kaze found herself in a melee with three Red Paladins.

Paladin reinforcements poured in from the garrison on the northern wall. Wroth and his Tusks met them head-on, and the fighting was pitched and gruesome.

Gawain felt their advantage slipping away. He braved the arrows whipping by to cut into the Red Paladins slashing at Kaze. An arrow grazed his ear as the ring of clashing swords turned his eyes back to the gate.

Arthur galloped through the gates on Egypt, sword slashing and Red Paladins falling in his wake. He vaulted from Egypt and ran up the stairs of the western wall, hacking at Red Paladins as he climbed.

With the archers distracted by Arthur's arrival, Gawain and Kaze gutted their paladin attackers and ran to the aid of Wroth and his Tusks.

The rout was on. Arthur fought like ten men atop the wall, sending a steady rain of paladin bodies onto wagons, barrels, and rooftops.

The footmen of Lord Ector, having already endured the occupation of the Red Paladins, surrendered without a fight. So, with the bulk of their numbers lost in the forest, the remaining Red Paladins grabbed what horses they could or took flight on foot and fled through the gates of Cinder.

Gawain shouldered his bow and leaped onto a soldier's courser. Arthur ran at him, waving him off. "Forget them! It's not worth it!"

"I'm happy to see you, Man Blood, but you don't give me orders!" Gawain shouted at Arthur. "Secure the keep!" Then he bolted through the gates after the fleeing Red Paladins.

"I will go after him!" Kaze shouted to Arthur, seizing one of the local horses crowding the square, and galloped after him.

It was left to Arthur to gain control of the situation, which was rapidly devolving. With no Red Paladins left to fight, the Fey Kind warriors turned on Lord Ector's footmen, who until now had been waiting out the battle, unsure which invading force to support. Arthur threw himself between an eight-foot-tall Storm Crafter and a terrified soldier. "They're not the enemy!" It took effort to pry them apart, but the Storm Crafter finally relented. Arthur shouted, "We're not here to slaughter!" He turned to the soldiers. "Drop your swords and you won't be harmed, I promise you!"

The soldiers turned to their captain, who was bloodied from a tussle with a few Cliff Walkers. He nodded to his men. Swords were thrown into the square. But the citizenry were panicking, some farmers grabbing pitchforks and fallen swords to protect their children from the "monsters" in their midst. Wroth snatched a spear from one of the farmers and broke it in two with his bare hands. He was about to gore the poor farmer when a murmur rippled through the crowd of Fey Kind, soldiers, urban workers, and peasants.

Nimue entered the gates of Cinder trailed by dozens of Fey Kind: Fauns, Snakes, Cliff Walkers and their kin, Moon Wings, and Man Bloods.

Arthur staggered out of the smoke, exhausted, sword dragging in the mud. Nimue stood in place and said, "You're here."

"Aye. I'm no knight, that's clear enough. But if you'll have me, I pledge my sword. And my honor. To you. I think there's still some good left in Arthur."

"There is." Nimue took him into her arms. She could smell the blood and smoke in his hair. She wiped the grime away from his eyes and cheeks and kissed his mouth.

Arthur held her face in his hands. "I'm glad you're here."

Nimue turned to the frightened populace. She could feel the violence about to erupt. They knew who she was and they feared her. She climbed onto a toppled wagon. Her heart raced.

"I am Nimue of Dewdenn from the clan Sky Folk! Daughter of Lenore, Arch Druid to my people! To my enemies"—she searched the crowd for Red Paladins—"I am known as the Wolf-Blood Witch." She softened. "But I am not your enemy. I want you to know that as of this moment Cinder is free! You are free to live. To raise your families in peace. To work. To love. And to worship the gods you choose, so long as those gods seek no dominion over any other." Nimue felt her mother with her, guiding her words. "All we want is peace. To return to what's left of our homes and rebuild. We did not ask for this war. But that does not mean we cannot fight this war! That does not mean we cannot win this war!"

*"QUEEN OF THE FEY! QUEEN OF THE FEY!"*

The Fey Kind roared their approval; even a few farmers slapped their hands on the wagons, drumming their support.

Nimue lifted the Sword of Power to the sun. "This is the sword of my people, the sword of my ancestors, forged in the Fey Fires when the world was young. Let this sword be our courage, our light in all this terrible darkness, our hope in all this despair. They say this is the Sword of the First Kings! But I say the kings have had their chance! For I claim it as the sword of the First Queen!"

"Queen of the Fey!" Wroth bellowed. His clansmen followed suit: "Queen of the Fey! Queen of the Fey! Queen of the Fey! Queen of the Fey!"

Arthur watched with amazement as the chant spread across the square, a rising tide of voices, Fey Kind and human, farmers, families, even some of Lord Ector's soldiers. He turned back to Nimue, holding the sword aloft like an avenging goddess, beautiful and frightening. Despite his reservations, Arthur pumped his fist with the rest. "Queen of the Fey! Queen of the Fey!"

## FORTY-ONE

GAWAIN AND HIS HORSE WOVE between small, leafy trees in pursuit of a fleeing Red Paladin. He squeezed the saddle between his legs and released the reins to grab his longbow and nock an arrow. He targeted the flapping red robes, aimed for the center, and fired. The Red Paladin's arms flew wide and he arched in a way that Gawain knew he was dead. The horse rode on, the paladin bobbing in the saddle before finally crashing into the brush.

Gawain slowed his charge. His horse was coated with sweat. He followed the sound of a stream to a small stone bridge, its walls blanketed in soft moss. He led the palfrey to the stream below, where she could drink before he saddled up for the ride back. Gawain knelt and drank the cool water in handfuls. Out of the corner of his eye, in the reflecting mountain stream, he caught a glimpse of spectral gray robes above him and lunged to the left as a barbed arrow sank into his right hip. Gawain scrambled for tree cover, knowing from the wound's depth that it was a swallowtail arrowhead, used to hunt larger game, designed to maximize bleeding and injury. He threw himself against a crooked ash tree and snapped the arrow in two. He heard the *shing* of a sword being drawn and spun around to see the Weeping Monk vault the bridge wall and land silently in the mud. His sword was long and thin, its slight curve reminding Gawain of the sabers he had seen on the belts of Asiatic warriors in his desert travels, but more elegant, the hilt shorter and more square, a weapon of finesse and speed.

Ignoring the fire flaring down his right leg, Gawain drew his long sword and ran onto the stream bank, roaring and slashing with two hands. His leg buckled slightly on the charge, but it was enough to force the monk back on his heels, though he wasted no movement and sidestepped into a cut that Gawain barely got his blade up to block. The Weeping Monk took the advantage, and steel on steel rang through the forest as he lunged and swung, pushing Gawain into the stream, where his bad leg gave out on the slippery rocks. It was only his green pauldron that prevented him from being cut in half by a savage blow. All the same his skin split under the damaged armor, and he felt warm blood trickle down his shoulder. He rolled in the water away from multiple blows. Gawain had never met a fighter as fast.

He finally braced himself against a rock and took his blade in hand, blocking the monk's sword and clubbing him with the pommel. Gawain used his height advantage to drive the monk up against the high stream bank and tried to force him down into the mud, but the monk grabbed the edge of the broken arrow in Gawain's hip and twisted. As he cried out, the monk pivoted free and slashed the back of his thigh, hobbling him further.

The monk took him by the ear and reared back for the fatal cut when Kaze dove from the trees, with a leopard growl, tackling the monk into the water and rocks and knocking his sword loose. They fought wildly. Her tail whipped the air as she slashed with fang and claw. The monk kicked her off but she fell onto him again, teeth at his throat. Somehow the Weeping Monk slipped her grip and scrambled on top of her, his arm locked across her throat, choking her. As she struggled, her claws dug deep grooves in the monk's cheeks beneath the strange birthmarks around his eyes. He held fast. Her fingers made spell forms and she tried to speak conjuring words, but her cat eyes rolled back into her skull and she slumped in his arms. He threw her against the rocks. The Weeping Monk picked up his sword, flicked it dry, turned, and stabbed Kaze through the back.

Gawain wrenched himself to his feet. "Kaze!"

Then the monk came for Gawain, who pulled himself onto the bank by the branches of an overhanging elder. He clawed through the dirt, up to the bridge, the Weeping Monk walking steadily behind him, smoothly, with no urgency.

Gawain fell onto the ancient wall, his hands sinking into the moss. His slashed thigh would take no weight. His armor was soaked in blood and a chill racked his body, yet as the air whistled he got his sword up in time to parry the Weeping Monk's cut. They clinched, and Gawain, locking his sword grip against the monk's, swung him against the bridge. They fell into a test of strength, Gawain trying to force his blade across the monk's throat. The monk threw his hand against the moss to brace himself. Gawain's eyes darted to the hand, anticipating attack, but instead what he saw stunned him.

The Weeping Monk's hand, its texture and color, was entirely invisible against the moss. It had blended to the bridge surface like some lizard's camouflage. Gawain gasped, "You're one of us?"

The monk bared his teeth and shoved Gawain across the bridge. Gawain dropped to one knee and tried to keep his sword up against a merciless rain of blows, but the monk was enraged and Gawain had lost far too much blood. As his arm weakened, the monk took advantage and stuck him in the ribs.

*Death will come soon,* Gawain mused grimly, his thoughts turning to Kaze in the stream. Yet as he awaited the fatal blow, the Weeping Monk cracked him across the skull with the grip of his sword. The world spun. Gawain collapsed against the wall.

He heard the monk hiss, "They want you alive," as another blow fell and all went dark.

# FORTY-TWO

LORD ECTOR'S CASTLE WAS SMALL AND compact and capable of a worthy defense, with four rounded flanking towers protecting the curtain walls, a chained bridge, murder holes in the gatehouse, and machicolations along the parapets, but when the Red Paladins fled, the remaining guards, having been vanquished once, surrendered it without a fight.

Ector's disarmed guards huddled in small groups, talking in low voices, as Wroth led Nimue, Morgan, and Arthur into the Great Hall, a vast space held aloft in a point by crisscrossing timbers and by stone columns of black and gold, the colors of Lord Ector's seal. His banner of a gold dragon against a black background hung behind his modest throne.

Morgan and Arthur walked a few paces behind Nimue.

"What angle are you playing, brother?" Morgan asked.

"Well, clearly I've been missed. It's nice to see you, too, dear sister."

"Are we to believe you are suddenly the defender of the Fey?"

"Isn't it enough to be a friend to Nimue? What is the problem? Are you disappointed you don't have her all to yourself?"

"We've actually made progress without you. I just don't want you filling her head with foolish ideas."

"Like proclaiming herself Queen of the Fey?"

"You doubt her?"

"I doubt the strategy."

The four of them paused before the empty chair as huge logs snapped in the wide fireplace along the western wall. Then Nimue walked forward, climbed the four steps, unslung the Sword of Power, and hung it on the corner of the chair.

Then she sat on the throne.

Morgan smiled and nodded. Arthur's expression was less joyful. Wroth pounded the end of his war hammer on the stone floor and barked, "Stra'gath!"

Two Tusk soldiers led Lord Ector into his hall. His round, soft features showed the strain of the past weeks. His cheeks were patched red from drink and his eyes were heavy with bags. But he comported himself with dignity as he approached Nimue.

"Lord Ector, I want to thank you for this sanctuary," said Nimue.

"Well, it was not offered, milady, it was taken," Ector answered darkly. Wroth growled.

Ector shot a look at Wroth and added diplomatically, "I have no argument with your kind. And I have no love for the Red Paladins, I promise you that. But when you say that Cinder is free and then take your seat in my hall, I must question your sincerity, milady."

Nimue glanced at the damp imprints her hands left on the arms of the throne. She spoke slowly. "All we want is to go home. We want our land back. As you know, we are not city folk. But my people were starving, and it appears that to deny us food, the paladins set fire to your lands. If we can support each other through this, if you can let my clans recover here, then perhaps we can attack Father Carden and stop his paladins. Nothing would make me happier than to return your keep to you and to have my people return to their homes in peace."

Lord Ector smoothed his mustache and sized up Arthur and Morgan and Nimue. "You're practically children," he said in disbelief.

"Easy now," Morgan advised.

"Do you think you're safe here? Is that what you think?" Ector pressed, assuming the adult voice in the room. "You were safer in your caves or your trees or wherever the hell you were hiding. You're the most hunted woman alive, madam. And you've just painted a brilliant white target on your back. You will never leave Cinder with your life."

Arthur was quiet.

Morgan was not. "Is that a threat?"

"It's reality, girl!" Lord Ector spat at Morgan. "The witch is here. The Sword of Power is here. Soon the armies of Uther Pendragon and the Vatican and the Ice King will be here, and then what? Then they will rain fire on Cinder until even the rats are dead. So eat lightly, for these provisions you crave will have to last a long and bloody winter." Ector gave Nimue a dark look before turning on his heel and marching from the hall.

But his words lingered. Nimue felt cold sweat trickle down her back. In truth, the walls of Cinder had felt like a shield. She had fought for this, urged against other plans for escape, used the trust of her people to force this action. But what if she had been wrong? What if the walls of Cinder were not their shield but their cage, entrapping them until the slaughter?

"You all right?" Arthur asked her, perhaps reading her face.

"I'm fine," Nimue lied.

She turned to the Tusk soldiers. "Is there any news on the Green Knight?"

Mogwan was one of them and shook his head. "No, my queen."

She winced at the word "queen" but nodded crisply.

Mogwan added, "What do you want us to do with the prisoners?"

"Prisoners?" Nimue asked, struggling to catch up with events of her own making.

Mogwan led Nimue and Arthur to the gatehouse and down several curving stairways to a claustrophobic and reeking corridor of cells. Glancing through the small barred windows in the doors, Nimue saw dozens of bleak, frightened eyes blinking back at her. The dungeon was full to bursting.

"Free them," Nimue said, sickened by it all.

"All?" Mogwan asked.

"Some may be dangerous," Arthur offered.

"They've been treated as poorly as we have. Let them pledge their loyalty to us, if necessary, but free them."

"And what of these brutes?" Mogwan asked, pushing open the door to one of the last cells in the hall. Inside, four broad-shouldered, scruffy warriors lay in chains against the walls. Their beards and long, embroidered woolen tunics and baggy pants identified them as Northmen. One of them was shirtless and had been beaten bloody and burned with torches. He was barely alive, his breathing shallow.

"Raiders," Arthur warned.

Nimue entered the cell. The Vikings regarded her with sullen looks. She knelt by the tortured prisoner. She took his hand in hers.

Nimue thought of Lenore kneeling by Merlin's bedside. She remembered her prayers. She wondered if she might have the same healing gifts.

A thread of silver wound up her neck, and the raiders' eyes shone with fascination. She reached out, silently asking the Hidden to bind the raider's wounds. After a moment of contemplative listening, Nimue gently placed the man's hand down. "Your friend is beyond my help," she told them. "He's joining the Hidden soon. The most I can do is ease his pain."

"That's a mercy," one of them murmured.

Nimue put one hand on the tortured prisoner's shoulder and took his hand with the other. The vines of the Sky Folk on her skin lit the dark cell silver. She whispered her mother's prayers as the Northman's breathing deepened. She bade the Hidden to surround and embrace the dying man. His limbs relaxed. His comrades bowed their heads and murmured words to their warrior gods. After several minutes, the prisoner's breathing slowed and then gradually ceased.

"He drinks from the Horn now," one of the raiders said.

Nimue struggled not to betray emotion, though the death of the prisoner had moved her. "You are far from home."

Their leader with a long blond ponytail nodded. "Aye, we came to these shores with the Ice King. Fell into some trouble with these monks. They dragged us south to here."

"You are welcome to join our cause," Nimue offered.

"Wait, they are?" Arthur asked, incredulous.

"The Northmen are no friend to Tusks," said Mogwan. "Father will not like this."

Arthur subtly pulled Nimue aside. "I'm with Mogwan. These raiders are murderers, pirates, and thieves. They kill everything. You don't want the fate of the Fey to be in the hands of the Ice King, I assure you."

"We could use some murderers, pirates, and thieves," Nimue said. "An enemy of the Red Paladins is a friend of ours." She turned back to the raiders. "Will you join us?"

"As you say, we're far from home. And besides, our dead brother is relation to our captain. We should return him to the sea."

Nimue nodded. "Then we wish you safe travels. We can spare a week's rations and two horses."

Arthur started to interrupt, "A week's rat—?"

But Nimue cut him off. "I'm sorry we cannot offer more."

"That will suffice," the blond raider answered.

Nimue ordered the Vikings freed. Mogwan unchained them. They thanked Nimue, and as they left the cell, the blond raider turned to Arthur and clasped his arm. "You've earned the thanks of the Red Spear, brother."

Arthur eyed the raider warily. "If you say so," he said, grasping the raider's arm in return.

The Vikings bowed their heads to Nimue. Then frightened voices rang down from above. "My queen! Milady!"

Nimue and Arthur hurried past the raiders.

They were quickly led out of the keep and a few hundred yards into the town square, where a group of Fey Kind huddled around a blood-stained horse and a mound of purple robes on the ground. Nimue pushed her way through the crowd and got down on her knees to Kaze, who was covered in blood.

"Kaze? What's happened?" Nimue assumed the worst.

"They took him, milady," Kaze whispered, fluttering in and out of consciousness. "They have Gawain."

Nimue's hand went to her mouth. After what she had just witnessed, capture by the Red Paladins seemed a far worse fate than death.

# FORTY-THREE

THE ENERGY IT TOOK TO OPEN HIS EYES made Gawain want to go back to sleep. The steady movements of the horse sent shock waves of pain through his ravaged leg and hip. His lungs felt heavy when he breathed, and his clothes and armor were cold and damp. Looking down, he realized they were wet with his own blood. He realized he'd fallen unconscious in the saddle. His hands were bound and the Weeping Monk rode his own horse to his right. They were at least a few miles from Cinder, judging by the position of the Minotaurs peaks, and out of the fire zone given the taste of the air. He knew they were headed to a Red Paladin encampment.

"Why?" Gawain asked.

The Weeping Monk rode in silence.

"You're one of us. How could you?"

"I'm nothing like you," the monk answered.

"I saw your hand change. What are you? An *Asher*? There haven't been *Ash Men* in these lands for centuries. They had marks too. Like your eyes—"

Instantly the monk's sword was under his chin. "Say it again, devil."

"Do it, *Asher*," Gawain said through clenched teeth, the blade still at his throat. "Kill me if you're so brave. Or better yet, free my hands and we'll see how good you are. I took your arrow, coward. Why was that? Were you afraid to face me up close?"

The Weeping Monk considered Gawain's words, then returned his sword to its sheath. "In a few hours, you'll wish I'd killed you."

Gawain felt numb at the sight of the first Red Paladin torches flickering a dull, hazy light. The forest had been sheared with clumsy haste, leaving jagged stumps, like a field of broken teeth, for hundreds of yards in all directions. A noisome odor of burning flesh shook Gawain's bold countenance as they entered the muddy field of tents. Dead-eyed, tonsured monks standing around campfires followed their progress until the Weeping Monk slowed to a stop. Gawain followed the monk's eyes to a small army, a hundred or more black-robed warriors. They were the Trinity, Gawain surmised. He'd heard the rumors of their fighting prowess and cruelty. Their golden death masks gazed impassively at the Weeping Monk as he resumed his ride, pulling up to a larger tent, where, judging by the scowls and puffed-out chests, the tension was thick between Father Carden's Red Paladin guard and the Trinity soldiers.

The monk dismounted and dragged Gawain from his palfrey. Against all his efforts, Gawain screamed when his feet struck the ground and he buckled to his knees, his wounds tearing wider after the long ride. At the monk's orders, two Red Paladins grabbed Gawain roughly by the shoulders and dragged him into the large tent.

Father Carden stood at a table covered in maps, next to a man in Trinity robes with a shaved head and a black beard worn in a French fork. Brother

Salt was also present, swaying in the corner, ever smiling, stitched eyes turned to the ceiling.

Even in his wounded state, Gawain could feel the edge in the air. Carden's face was pinched, but upon seeing the Weeping Monk and his prisoner, some blush came to his cheeks. Relief, it seemed.

"My son, you are a sight for sore eyes," Carden said.

"Is this him?" the man with the forked beard asked, circling around the table. "Is this the famous Weeping Monk?"

The monk turned to Father Carden with a look of confusion at their new visitor. "This is Abbot Wicklow. He's here to . . ." Carden trailed off.

"Observe," Abbot Wicklow finished for him.

The Weeping Monk bowed his head respectfully. Wicklow folded his arms behind his back and studied the monk's face, studied his eyes. "I've heard a great deal about you. A great deal. They say you're our best fighter. Possessed with *unnatural* speed and grace—"

There was something in the way Wicklow said "unnatural" that made Carden stiffen. He interrupted. "Speak, my son. What have you brought us?"

"The Green Knight, Father."

Wicklow turned to Carden, surprised. "The rebel leader?"

Carden came forward. "This is welcome news." He put his hands on his hips, taking in Gawain's condition. "The Green Knight. Well? What do you have to say, hmm? Perhaps if you tell us where to find the Wolf-Blood Witch, you can save yourself."

"What do I have to say?" Gawain repeated. Then he turned and looked at the Weeping Monk, who did not return his look. "There is much I can say." He let his words hang in the air. "There is much I have learned."

Abbot Wicklow frowned.

Father Carden grew testy. "No matter, we are very skilled at making your kind sing."

As he regarded the Weeping Monk, Gawain had a change of heart.

Instead he turned back to Father Carden. "I'll tell you this much, old man. The Queen of the Fey has taken back Cinder and left five score of your Red Brothers dying in the wood."

Carden's cheek twitched.

"Are these lies?" Wicklow asked Carden, who did not immediately answer. Wicklow turned to the Weeping Monk. "Is this true what he says?"

"The town has fallen," the monk said without emotion.

"She's taken the damned city?" Wicklow said to Carden incredulously. "How did this happen?"

"Brother Salt," Carden said, eyes burning with fury, and ignoring Abbot Wicklow, "take this abomination to your kitchens."

Gawain's face went slack and he fell into the arms of the Red Paladins supporting him. He struggled as they led him away. The Weeping Monk turned, and their eyes met for a brief moment before Gawain was dragged outside.

Hundreds of yards away, Squirrel crept across a high branch in an old black alder, pushing aside the wide leaves, eager to get a better view of Gawain. He was careful not to shake loose any seeds onto the heads of the Red Paladin patrol beneath him. He had been upset when Nimue had not allowed him to join the other fighters in the market wagons at Cinder. But when he saw Gawain break away from the gates in pursuit of Red Paladins, Squirrel had seen a chance to play a part and gave chase. He'd only arrived in time to see the Weeping Monk lift a bloodied Gawain onto the saddle. Now he watched as Gawain was half dragged across the muddy encampment by two paladins, followed by a blind old man, also in red robes, to a square pavilion with two entrances and an open hatch at the top that belched a thick gray smoke. The coppery, sickly-sweet taste in the air told Squirrel what happened inside that tent. With his eyes he plotted his course between the tents and the campfires. There would be three near misses with Red Paladins before a final sprint to the torture tent and to Gawain's rescue.

# FORTY-FOUR

I N CROW HILL A RED PALADIN CHECKPOINT
was desecrated with wolf blood and the heads of farm dogs. Farther
east, still in the French provinces, many peasant farmers have turned
their loyalties to the Wolf-Blood Witch, believing she is some kind
of savior. They've burned several Red Paladin outposts and driven them
out of the villages of Gryphon and Silver Brook. A church was put to
the torch in Gray Moor. And then of course there is the case of Cinder, a
large town in the hills of the Minotaurs"—Sir Beric smoothed one of his
thick eyebrows—"previously occupied by the Red Paladins, quite against
Your Majesty's wishes. It was taken four days ago by the witch and an
army of various Fey Folk with grave paladin losses—"

"What is the population of Cinder?" King Uther asked in a low, menacing voice. His fingers were white as they gripped the arms of his throne.

"Perhaps five thousand, sire?" Beric guessed.

"Gods, that's a small city! And who is the lord of that keep?"

"A Lord Ector, sire, a distant cousin to the Baron of Thestletree. I believe he attended your games in the—"

"We don't care what games he attended. We want to know how he's lost his city twice in a fortnight! Wine!" Uther held out his cup to a footman, who hurried to fill it.

Sir Beric lowered his parchment and drew a line on the stone floor with the toe of his leather shoe, considering his words. "It would appear the keep was surrendered willingly, Your Majesty."

"Willingly?"

"It would seem what Your Majesty faces is a popular uprising in favor of the Wolf-Blood Witch. She has become a symbol of defiance against the Red Paladins, who seem to have overplayed their hand, the final straw being the burning of miles of farmland in the Minotaur Valley, apparently in an effort to starve out the witch and her kind—a strategy that has most definitely backfired."

"I can walk on my own, thank you very much," Lady Lunette snarled, pulling her elbow away from her footmen escort. Her shoes clicked as she marched to the throne. "What is the meaning of this, Uther? I don't like being summoned. I don't like leaving my tower, you know this."

Sir Beric hurried as quickly out of Lady Lunette's way as dignity would allow.

Uther sat up rigidly in his throne. "Mother, did you order soldiers to follow Merlin to his meeting with the witch?"

"Of course I did," Lady Lunette scoffed. "And what of it?"

"That was not our wish, and those are not your soldiers to command," Uther fumed. "Prior to your interference, we had Merlin in check and the sword in our grasp, and now we have neither!"

"I would advise you to lower your voice when you speak to me."

"We will speak to you as we like because we are the crown!" Uther roared.

"Clear the hall, please," Lady Lunette ordered.

Sir Beric and the footmen headed for the door.

"Stay where you are," Uther countermanded.

Sir Beric and the footmen hesitated, caught between the two monarchs.

Lady Lunette sighed. "Yes indeed, stay where you are. But a warning: those in the past who have heard the words I am about to speak have a terrible habit of winding up dead."

After a few tense moments of silence, Beric sputtered, "With your leave, Your Majesty," but hurried off without actually receiving permission, only to be followed in short order by the footmen. The door closed soundly behind them.

Lady Lunette and King Uther were alone.

"I'm done coddling you, Uther. It's done you no favors."

"'Coddling' is not how we would describe your parenting, Mother."

"Yes, well, I was never meant to raise children, Uther. You see, I was meant to rule. That was my talent. But in this world of men and their bloodlines, that was not meant to be. Instead it was my task to make you king." Lady Lunette's words hung in the air. "And it seems I have failed in that task."

"You undermine us and then sit in judgment. How rich."

"I wasn't about to sit idly by as you crawled back into Merlin's lap. I've given you far too much rope, and now the kingdom hangs for it. From this moment on, I am the throne and my words will flow from your lips like a fountain statue as I pour them into your ears, or you will suffer the consequences."

"We lost track of the outrages in those last few sentences, but we have noted, with great concern, that your faculties seem impaired, Mother. You are not yourself. A good rest by the sea, perhaps." Uther savored the thought.

But Lady Lunette was wistful. "Sadly, Uther, this is my truest self. For it is you who are the lie."

# FORTY-FIVE

**S**ISTER IRIS TURNED TO THE RAMPARTS
that grew out of the castle and surrounded the town, and
where Faun archers patrolled. Without a word, she headed
back into Cinder. The influx of Fey refugees had created
congestion and confusion through the streets. Many of the villagers of
Cinder were frightened by the different Fey races and had shuttered their
shops to hide in their homes, only to discover that shy and anxious Moon
Wings had taken up residence in their rafters and spun themselves into
silk cocoons; while the more generous residents—the innkeeper of the
Seven Falls, Ramona the baker's wife—struggled to meet the demand
of the starving invaders. The roads were almost impassable by wagons
thanks to the divots dug up by burrowing Plogs. Loud, shoving, anxious
lines grew in the square as Fey and humans struggled to work together

per the queen's orders. Iris walked past the stone church and its smashed windows. The words *Wolf-Blood Witch* were smeared on its walls with calf's blood.

She approached a pair of Fauns stealing swigs from a pilfered wineskin in between their shifts on the wall. *"Talaba noy, wata lon?"* one of them said about Iris, nudging his friend, who laughed.

"I don't understand," Iris said flatly.

"Forgive my friend. He is rude," the laughing one said to Iris in English touched by his melodious accent.

Sister Iris ignored him and looked at their bows. "How far does the arrow fly?"

"With a Faun longbow? This is the strongest bow in the world." The laughing one made a *swoosh* sound and an arc with his hand, suggesting very far.

Sister Iris turned, measuring the distance from the wall to the keep. "Would it go from here to the castle, for example?"

"And then double that," the Faun bragged.

"Can you show me how?" Iris asked, gazing up at the Faun through her sackcloth hood with her one good eye.

The Faun frowned. "Can you see, little one?"

"Well enough."

"Why do you want to learn this so bad?"

Iris shrugged. "I'm hunting a dog."

The Fauns looked at each other, *this strange kid,* and laughed together. The nice Faun bent down to her. "Yes, little one, I will help you kill this dog."

Nimue couldn't sleep. She gazed down at the many campfires the Fey Kind had lit in Cinder's main square as they slept out in the open air. Not a hardship, for most of them preferred the outdoors to cramped caves or human dwellings. The fires gave the small city a gentle orange glow. The moon was half-full and gauzy through a sky veiled by smoke.

She heard whispers, looked down, and noticed that she was holding the sword. Curious. She hadn't realized. She was so tired. She rested the blade in her hand and studied its clean lines, how the steel seams caught the moonlight. The whispering grew louder. Like distant screams. *The memories of the sword, of course,* Nimue thought. The sword was speaking to her. It was recalling victims and their cries. Some of the screams she recognized. They were Red Paladin screams. But strangely, she was not horrified. They quickened her heartbeat and warmed her blood. Her tired muscles felt revived by a current of energy flowing between her and the blade. Her doubts of the earlier day felt small and silly.

Why did she doubt herself? She was the Wolf-Blood Witch. Queen of the Fey. She possessed the Sword of Power and dared any man king to take it from her. She would inspire more of her kind, more of humankind. They would rally to her calls of freedom and fight for her, bleed for her, and together they would crush the Red Paladin plague and send them scurrying like rats back to the Vatican. *And then let the Church itself tremble,* Nimue thought. *Let them fear me. I will pile their crosses into a bonfire and—*

"Nimue?"

She whirled and the sword flashed and pointed at Arthur in the doorway, holding a lantern.

"I surrender," he said, calling back to their meeting on a dark forested road. It seemed like ages ago.

Nimue lowered the sword and turned to the window.

"I can come back," he said, wavering at the door.

"No, it's fine," she said softly.

Arthur entered. "I saw your torch."

"I can't sleep," she said, feeling strangely annoyed by the interruption, not wishing to share her time with the sword.

Arthur regarded the blade in her hand. "Expecting trouble?"

"It keeps me warm," she said without thinking.

Arthur frowned, then smirked. "There are other ways to keep warm."

Nimue did not respond. Instead she looked at the blade in the torch-light. "Do you think Red Paladins have ghosts? When they die? Do you think their spirits live on?"

"I suppose." Arthur shrugged. "If any of us do. Why?"

"I hear them in the sword. I hear their screams."

Arthur was quiet for a few moments. "You're tired. A lot has happened."

"What do you think is happening to him?" Nimue asked, referring to Gawain.

Arthur shook his head. "Don't think about that."

"I have to," she said angrily.

"We don't have the fighters to march on their camp. The fighters we do have are injured." Arthur paused, as though afraid to provoke her further. "I take it the meeting with Merlin did not go as planned."

"My people were right. He's a liar."

Arthur nodded, accepting this. "Then we should consider escape routes to the sea. Scavenge what coins we can from this town and try to buy our way onto a ship." He joined her at the window.

"Surrender. Of course," Nimue said, the campfires reflecting in her eyes. "I thought you'd changed," she scoffed.

"What does that mean?"

"Nothing. It means nothing. Run. Go. What's stopping you?"

"Do you want my advice or don't you?"

"I don't know. How can I trust your advice? How do I know if you'll be here from one moment to the next? How can I trust you when all you want to do is run away?"

"Survive and fight another day," Arthur corrected.

"Why don't you believe in us?"

"Who is 'us'?"

"I meant me. Why don't you believe in me?" She turned to him.

Arthur put his hands on her shoulders. "Believe in what? What is the alternative? Storm the gates of Castle Pendragon? Wage war on the Church? Let them call you Queen of the Fey all they like, you are still one woman with a sword."

"Not just any woman." Her eyes flashed.

"Trust me, I need no convincing. But you've done enough, Nimue. Don't you see? You've given them a chance to live. You flushed the Red Paladins from the Minotaurs. That is a great success. But don't think for a moment they won't respond and with far greater numbers, and before they do, you need a plan to get your people to safety."

"Then I'll find an army. The Northmen."

"Do you think the Ice King will follow a peasant girl with the Sword of Power rather than taking it for himself?"

Nimue was about to answer in anger. But a calm settled over her. "The Hidden will guide us. It's not your fault, but you could never understand."

"Why is that? Because I'm a Man Blood?"

Nimue's silence spoke volumes.

Hurt, Arthur withdrew. "With respect, *my queen*, you're acting the fool."

"That will be all," Nimue shot back.

Arthur bowed at the door, turned, and marched down the corridor.

# FORTY-SIX

LADY CACHER SAT IN THE LORDLY GARDENS
of House Chastellain and listened to the sound of her family's
laughter. Against the setting sun, servants set out the next
course on the outdoor feasting table, consisting of
roasted pheasant and capons with lemon sauce, ragouts of swan, and eel
pies. Lady Cacher's cup of spiced wine was refilled. She touched a purple
rose to her lips as her husband and their grandchildren played dancing
games while a serving girl played a fiddle.

"Catch him, Marie, he's a slippery one!" Lady Cacher warned as Lord
Cacher dodged the children's hands. She sat back, contented and smiling,
as the dogs barked in the distance. Their maid trekked across the grounds
from their stone keep, made beautiful by the vines of rare purple roses
that grew up its walls.

"What is it, Mavis?" Lady Cacher asked.

Mavis looked flustered. "A visitor at the gates, milady. Asks for you specifically."

"Do you know him?" she asked, confused.

"No, milady, but he says that you will."

Lady Cacher paled and set down her spiced wine. She steadied herself a moment before rising and smoothing her skirts. She began her walk to the gates, Mavis at her side, but she stopped her. "No, Mavis. I'll go alone."

"Are you sure?" she asked her.

She smiled thinly. "Yes, just make sure the babies eat. And that Lord Cacher doesn't overexert himself."

Mavis agreed reluctantly. "Yes, milady."

Lady Cacher resumed her long walk to the gates of House Chastellain. When she arrived there, she saw Merlin through the steel bars, feeding grass to his horse. Both man and animal were filthy from road dust and sweat. He and Lady Cacher stared at each other for long moments.

Finally Merlin asked, "Your family is well?"

Lady Cacher nodded. "All of them. Indeed, I have seven grandchildren."

"Yours and their every need tended to?" Merlin questioned.

Lady Cacher's face tightened. "Every last one that a peasant girl could have ever thought to ask for."

Merlin stroked his horse's mane. "Now it is time for you to keep your promise to me."

Lady Cacher took a deep breath, then produced a ring of keys from her skirts and opened the lock of the wicket gate. "Please," she said to Merlin, and led him into the orchard and to a bench beneath a pair of plum trees. They sat together in a long silence. Then she offered, "I always knew this day would come. But somehow it still seems too soon." A wave of emotion passed over her. Tears quietly fell. She wiped them with a kerchief and composed herself. "May I host you for the evening? It would give me the opportunity to spend one last evening with them."

Merlin shook his head. "The hounds are at my heels. We must go now. I will wait for you to say your goodbyes."

Lacy Cacher read Merlin's face and saw no yielding there. She nodded crisply and rose to her feet. She walked to the edge of the orchard, where she could see her husband rolling in a heap with her grandchildren. Nearby, her own children laughed and sipped wine in chairs beneath the old chestnut tree. She smiled and savored every detail. Then she slipped into the main house and returned minutes later with a soft leather drawstring bag of clothes. "No goodbyes," she said to Merlin. "Let them play."

Rising in the distance, the keep at Dun Lach seemed to have grown right out of the craggy rocks of the shoreline of the Beggar's Coast. Its towers tilted, and the walls were surrounded by a natural barrier of spiked sandstone, which shielded Dun Lach not only from invaders, but from the punishing tide as well. The coastline was clogged with slender warships. Merlin searched for the Red Spear's famed vessel, with its fiery lance fused like a horn to its prow, but it was not to be found. Northern archers paused their patrols on the wall to watch Merlin and Lady Cacher ride up to the gates. After a few rounds of muted conversations and dark looks in Merlin's direction, the warriors at the gate shouted to lift the portcullis.

Shunning offers to freshen up after such a long journey, Merlin requested an immediate audience with Cumber, and so he and Lady Cacher were led up several winding stairwells and into the Great Hall, where the warmth of five roaring hearths painted a far different picture from the grim war camps beyond the walls. It was not only the warmth but the sound: Merlin heard laughter. There was never laughter in Uther's court. But when Merlin and Lady Cacher entered, Lord

Cumber's booming laugh was shaking the walls, a joy derived from the energetic play of a wolf pup with a hunting falcon, who displayed her wings and clicked her beak and hopped along the stone floor, frightening the pup. The Ice King was barrel-chested and wore a black cave-bear cloak over one shoulder with his sword arm free, Viking-style, pinned by a platinum brooch inlaid with amber, gold, and blue glass. His face was tanned from the sea wind, his auburn hair pulled into a ponytail and his beard close-cropped.

Cumber's four grown children—two brothers and two sisters— seemed more entertained by their father's amusement than by the pup's antics. A history of observing courts gave Merlin the ability to read conditions quickly. Unlike their warrior father, Merlin surmised, Cumber's children had been raised in courts as political animals. He suspected they would be most resistant and suspicious of newcomers.

And quietly watching all was Hilja, the Ice Queen, regal but understated in her pale blue underdress. Her hair, once the color of straw and now graying, was finely braided. She drank wine from a horn as she spun silk for an embroidered robe. But she missed no details.

Confirming some of Merlin's theories, Cumber allowed his eldest daughter, Eydis—raven-haired, pale-skinned, with green pigment painted around her blue eyes—to address the new arrivals. "Merlin the Magician. A wizard with no magic sent by a king with no claim." She turned, smiling, to her sister and brothers, pleased with herself. Dagmar, the eldest brother, and the most like his father in bearing and look, grunted his approval. The smaller Calder rolled his eyes, and Solveig, blond and bejeweled, stared daggers at Merlin.

Merlin ignored the slight. "May I have some tea or sweet wine for Lady Cacher? She is frozen to the bone and has ridden the night through."

Hilja nodded to one of the butlers, who aided Lady Cacher to a bench along the wall, while footmen brought over a horn and some wine.

"My thanks, Lady Cumber," Lady Cacher said.

"Shall we also make you a bed or will you state your business?" Eydis asked, chin high.

"Young lady, I am not here to make beds but to make kings."

Eydis stiffened. "You stand before the one true king, conjurer."

"Perhaps, if your nights last six moons and all you walk on is snow."

Cumber's children looked agitated, their eyes darting to the Ice King, who distracted himself with the nipping pup.

Merlin scratched his beard and regarded Eydis. "Now you have regal bearing. And I have no doubt that someday you will make a fine queen. Unfortunately, you have the manners of an ass."

Eydis gasped. "How dare you?"

Hilja threw down her spindle.

Dagmar stood and drew his sword. "I'll have your tongue, dog!"

Calder sat back to watch the spectacle about to unfold.

Only Cumber chuckled, a rolling sound that warbled in the timbers of the ceiling. "You Druids don't have children. I think that's why you live so damn long. I indulge mine. It is a weakness you wouldn't understand."

"You might be surprised," Merlin answered. "And while I am happy to act as your daughter's political quintain in more peaceable times, the war winds blow. Have you a plan, Lord Cumber? For it was a bold stroke taking these ports, but now you seem content to squat upon this foul beach like a hen reluctant to drop her eggs."

Eydis seethed. "Honestly, Father, are you going to allow him to mock you like this?"

Cumber's eyes narrowed to slits. "Does Uther put up with this nonsense, Merlin? I have no ear for it. I don't recall asking your opinion on my military strategy."

"Let us assume then, for the sake of argument, that you actually do have a military strategy. Was it wise to send your dreaded Red Spear against paladin camps along the Granite Coast, given that Pendragon forces already outnumber you by a hundred to one? One might assume it best to encourage Father Carden to remain neutral in this struggle rather than antagonize him."

"Now, that is a fine question, Merlin. Bravo. Who does command the Red Spear, Father?" Calder smirked.

Cumber turned to his youngest son. "Shut your hole, boy, or my ax handle will." Then, turning back to Merlin, Cumber growled, "What the Red Spear does is none of your bloody concern. Now, I am a simple man. I've no desire to play games or match wits with dark creatures like yourself. Speak plainly your reasons for coming here, and for your dear sake I hope they please me."

"I would like to know the character and intellect of the man I am about to put on the English throne," Merlin stated simply. "Is that plain enough for you?"

Cumber paused, then set the pup down on the floor. "Bold words," he said. "You've turned on your Liar King."

"I am my own man," Merlin countered.

"A traitor is always a traitor."

"If only the world were so black and white," Merlin mused. "I suspect you waver here on these frigid shores because you enter a land unknown to you and ignorant of your claim as the true Pendragon—a charge that can be proved only by the one living witness to the stillbirth of the Queen Regent's son."

Cumber stood up, stunned. "Is this . . . the midwife?"

Merlin nodded gravely. "She is. And now we shall discuss what you will give me in return."

# FORTY-SEVEN

**N**IMUE STARED DOWN FROM LORD
Ector's throne at a sullen Tusk by the name of B'uluf, slender
for his kind, with a broken horn beneath his right jawbone.
His arms were held behind his back by Arthur and two Faun
archers. Wroth stood to the side with a fearsome glower, arms folded over
his broad chest, and across from him stood Lord Ector. Morgan stood to
Nimue's right.

Nimue and B'uluf were the same age, and his unimpressed smirk told
her that he was among the few Fey Folk who still viewed her as a willful
girl and not a queen. She knew him from their battle in the marshes,
where he had distinguished himself for bravery. She also knew him as a
troublemaker who saw signs of disrespect everywhere and caused a lot of
headaches in the caves.

He stood before her now for the murder of a Cinder resident, a carpenter, from the poorer section of town. B'uluf and three other Tusks had beaten the man to death outside his home in full view of his wife and children. Nimue could see the man's blood on B'uluf's furred knuckles. The mood in Cinder had already been dry tinder seeking a spark. *This wasn't a spark*, Nimue thought, *but a torch and a barrel of oil*. That evening alone, Arthur and his ragtag guard of Storm Crafters and Fauns had broken up a group of Cinderians trying to force their way into the armory for their confiscated blades.

"What could possibly have possessed you to do this?" Nimue asked B'uluf, her voice shaking with rage. She yearned in that moment for Gawain's steady temperament, for she could feel the Sword of Power hanging beside her, compelling her hand to reach for it.

B'uluf shrugged without remorse. "He made comments to us many times," he said in his thickly accented English. "And has the cross painted on his door. He is not one of us, he is one of them. One less of them." B'uluf glanced at Wroth, who turned his baleful eyes on Nimue. She knew the young Tusk was confident of Wroth's protection. The Tusks were their best fighters, and they were already stretched woefully thin.

Nimue could not afford to lose any of them.

Lord Ector wore an equally furious expression.

"You are aware that the Red Paladins took this city first, are you not?" Nimue asked him sharply.

Again, B'uluf shrugged. The conversation did not seem to interest him.

"And that non-Christians were singled out and hanged on stakes and burned to death? As a result, most of Cinder's people painted crosses on their doors to protect their families."

B'uluf's attention drifted.

"Look at me," Nimue demanded.

"This outrageous crime must be answered blood for blood," Lord Ector spat. "More violence will result if this is not dealt with swiftly and harshly."

Before Nimue could answer, Wroth spoke up. "*Deh moch, grach buur. Augroch ef murech.*"

As always, his son Mogwan interpreted: "Wroth says Tusks have 'war blood.' It flows hot long after a battle." He listened to more of his father's comments, then added, "He says he will discipline B'uluf."

"By doing what?" Nimue asked.

Wroth glared at Nimue. "*Negh fwat, negh shmoch, gros wat.*"

"We give him less food, less water, more work."

Lord Ector scoffed, "That's it? Unacceptable!"

Wroth barked something at Lord Ector.

Nimue shouted, "That is enough!" The hall grew quiet. Nimue's head throbbed.

She heard the sword whisper to her. She refused to listen. Her skull felt like it was going to crack.

"Bring him forward," she said in a low voice. Arthur and the Fauns led B'uluf to the steps of the throne. "I made it clear when we took this city that no human blood was to be spilled. It was not a request but a command from your *queen*." B'uluf glared at her with defiance.

The sword hissed in her mind. She fought it off. Rubbed her temples. She blinked, trying to clear her eyes and her thoughts. Her eyes drifted to B'uluf's hands. "What is that on your fingers?" she asked him. "Hold them out," she told Arthur and the Fauns. They held B'uluf's bloody hands out for Nimue to see. "What is that?" she asked him again, pointing to his rust-colored knuckles.

"Man blood," B'uluf said with a sneer.

"You wear your guilt on your hands. Along with your defiance."

B'uluf shrugged.

With effort, Nimue said, "You will spend a week in our dungeons and then be given over to Wroth for what I expect will be severe punishment. That is all."

Lord Ector cursed under his breath.

Wroth nodded, satisfied.

B'uluf held out his hands. "Man Bloods have to know their place."

At that, Nimue turned, drew the Sword of Power, and in a single stroke severed both of B'uluf's hands at the wrist. The Tusk's mouth was open a full second before his guttural scream, and he fell back into Arthur's arms.

"Defy me again at your peril!" Nimue screamed.

Wroth lunged at Nimue, and the Fauns threw themselves in his path only to be tossed aside like rag dolls. Only Mogwan had the strength to hold his father back as Wroth spat every Tusk invective he could at Nimue. As B'uluf wailed on his knees, Arthur drew his own sword and swung it around at Wroth. Nimue held the Sword of Power in both hands, aiming the point at Wroth, who struggled against Mogwan before relenting. He marched over to B'uluf, yanked him to his feet by his unbroken horn, and stormed out of the hall.

Morgan took Nimue by the shoulders as the sword dropped from her shaking hands and she muttered, "I—I can't—I'm sorry—" Her thoughts exploded. *I'm a monster. You are Queen of the Fey. A monster. I'm a monster! Your people need you. They need you. It's just blood. He's just a stupid boy. I can't. I don't want this. You wield the Sword of Power. I don't want it!*

"You did the right thing," Morgan reassured her, though her voice shook.

*I'm turning into Merlin. The sword will fuse to my hand.*

Arthur sheathed his sword and also went to Nimue's side. "Now we've lost the Tusks," he warned.

*This isn't me. I don't know who I am. You are Queen of the bloody Fey!*

"What in the Nine Hells was she supposed to do!" Morgan shouted at her brother.

*Paladin, paladin, choke and twitch, bitten by the Wolf-Blood Witch.*

"I don't know! I know we have fifty bodies at best who can use a sword. And—gods—" Arthur gestured to the clenched, bloody Tusk hands on the first stair and called to the Fauns, "Pick these up."

Lord Ector shook his head at the display and marched from the hall.

"Have they found Squirrel, Arthur?" Nimue asked, tears streaming down her cheeks, her voice suddenly small.

"Not yet."

"She's exhausted," Morgan told Arthur. "She hasn't slept or eaten for days."

"We're all exhausted," Arthur shot back, running his hands through his hair.

"Milady! My queen!" Cora ran into the hall, the torchlight catching on her chestnut antlers. "Come quickly!"

Moments later Nimue, Morgan, Arthur, Cora, and several Faun archers hurried along the ramparts of Cinder's northern wall, joining several Fey Folk soldiers already shouting and pointing into the Minotaur Valley.

A hundred yards farther down the wall, Sister Iris saw the commotion and stood up. She had become a fixture on the ramparts, the Faun archers finding her quirky manner amusing. She had pestered them into longbow training and they had relented, even allowing her to shoot between the crenels at sparrow hawks and ospreys as long as she ran out and retrieved the arrows. Her talent shocked the Fauns, who were renowned archers. After only a week or so, Iris could neck-shoot a raptor, in flight, from two hundred yards. She had become so adept, so quickly, that the Fauns had called over others to watch their young prodigy shoot. They had even given her a bow of her own to practice with, though the catgut was frayed and the wood slightly warped. Fluency with weapons had always been the way with Iris. It was a life-and-death necessity in the fighting pits. At this moment, while all eyes were on the activity beyond the wall, Iris was focused on Nimue. She took her bow in her hands and slid an arrow from her quiver. The catgut creaked in her ear as she nocked the arrow and followed Nimue with her front knuckle. From this distance, Iris could guarantee a neck shot. Her finger slowly eased off the string when dozens of footsteps thundered toward her.

"To the walls!" This order was repeated up and down the ramparts as Fauns shoved past Iris and took up offensive positions. Iris turned back and Nimue had been swallowed into a crowd.

When the archers saw her coming, they cleared a path for Nimue, who climbed onto the wall. Then her breath left her.

A sea of torches, mounted cavalry, and wagons flying the colors and crowns of House Pendragon washed across the vast farmlands only a few miles from the town of Cinder.

Nimue felt her throat go dry. Lord Ector's words of warning rang in her ears. She had painted a target on their backs.

"To the east! Look to the east!" a Faun shouted.

All heads swung to the eastern farmlands and another army marching into the valley, this one displaying the red banners and white crosses of the Vatican. A thousand torches lit the night, as wave after wave of Red Paladins emerged from the tree lines and farm roads, swallowing up acres and acres of countryside. For the next hour, Nimue and the others could only watch helplessly as the two glowing armies filled in the entire valley between the Minotaurs peaks.

They were completely surrounded, with no chance of escape.

*THEY WERE COMPLETELY SURROUNDED, WITH NO CHANCE OF ESCAPE.*

# FORTY-EIGHT

K ING UTHER ENTERED THE ROYAL
pavilion shoulder first so as not to disrupt the tray of goblets and the pitcher of spiced wine he carried. Lady Lunette
looked up from her tray of cakes, surprised.

"Uther, where were you? What is all that?"

"A bit of honeyed wine to celebrate," Uther said, smiling, as he set
down the tray and poured their cups.

"Celebration, you say?"

"We just met with the famous Father Carden. Turns out he's quite
the reasonable fellow."

Lady Lunette's face tightened. "We were supposed to meet with him
together, Uther. That was the plan."

"Yes, well, that is true. But we preferred in our first contact with the rebel leader not to play second fiddle to our mother." Uther sat down, satisfied. "We are sure you understand."

Lady Lunette's gaze did not soften. "If this new arrangement is to work, Uther, you will have to get over such trivialities."

"Indulge us this once. We think it worked out quite well."

She sighed, relenting. "And what did you and Father Carden discuss?"

"An alliance. We will allow the Church to keep a majority of the lands seized—as long as a generous tax is paid for the rights, of course. In return, the Red Paladins will support our claim to the throne and lead the siege on this 'village.'" Uther waved his hand dismissively in the direction of Cinder. "No sense in losing any good men to the cause. When all is said and done, they will burn the witch and we will get our sword, countering this Ice King's slanderous lies. Cheers, Mother." Uther clicked his goblet against hers.

Lady Lunette's eyebrows were raised as she sipped, dubious of Uther's claims. "You were never much of a negotiator. Did you have the good sense to get any of this in writing?"

"Our scribe was present. We think you will find all the terms quite agreeable."

"Well, we'll certainly see about that," Lunette smirked, clearing her throat. "Have him come over here. I have a number of questions for this Father Carden, questions I'm sure you forgot to ask." She cleared her throat again.

"Yes, Mother, we expect nothing less."

"Who will define these borders, for example? They've scourged half of Aquitania. Are we supposed to—" Lunette paused and stared at the table. She cleared her throat again.

"You were saying?" Uther pressed.

Lunette opened her mouth slightly and touched her throat. "The wine is not agreeing with me."

"Yes, the borders. We may have missed some details. No doubt you will clean it all up."

Lady Lunette cleared her throat more violently. Her hands shook as she pushed away the goblet. "Fetch the Healer, Uther," she gasped.

Ignoring his mother, Uther gazed into his goblet of spiced wine and swirled the contents.

"Uther, do you hear me?" Lady Lunette said, her lips reddening.

Uther looked back up at her, his smile fading. "Yes, Mother?"

"Fetch the bloody—" Then she paused, her eyes widening as she realized.

"Fetch what?"

Lady Lunette tried to speak, but all that came out was a grinding croak and a mist of blood. She clawed at the table, clutched her throat, and fell onto the carpet, then rolled onto her back, struggling to breathe.

All the while, Uther watched impassively. "We forgot to mention, Mother, we had Sir Beric inquire, quite discreetly, of course, into the circumstances of our birth. It was not easy, we assure you. You obviously went to very great lengths to conceal your tracks. However, with the resources of the crown, we found a single record of a peasant girl named Sylvie who worked on a farm quite close to the castle. She died, rather mysteriously, after drinking some spiced wine. She was only nineteen years old. Was this she? Was this our mother you had killed?"

Lady Lunette struggled to crawl as blood dripped down her chin, but she lost her strength and collapsed beside Uther's boots.

"These last few days we've thought very often of this young Sylvie and the sort of mother she might have been to us. You said you paid for us in gold coins. Obviously, you wanted us to have the impression that this peasant girl was eager to trade her newborn son for riches. Yet we wonder. Was she really given a choice? You knew your intentions. There was no way that woman could live, given the enormity of your secret. Nor do we find it very surprising that you gave birth to a stillborn child. We imagine it would be very difficult for any babe to live inside you. With all that cold blood."

Lady Lunette was turned face up, eyes open, face the color of chalk, mouth stretched wide. The only sound coming from her was a soft rattle. Uther got down on his knees and took Lady Lunette's face roughly in his hands. He shook her as he spoke.

"But whatever fantasies we entertained in these past few days of a life we will never know, of a loving mother we will never see, of a kindness we will never feel, let this final toast between us remove all doubt: I am now and forever *your* son." Hateful tears streamed down Uther's cheeks as Lady Lunette's breathing ceased. Yet before her eyes glazed over, they softened and cleared and brimmed with a feeling Uther had never experienced from her. Her eyes shone with *pride*.

The king wept over Lunette's body for several moments. Then he furiously wiped his tears and cried out, "Beric! Beric!"

Moments later Sir Beric and a footman raced inside the pavilion. Sir Beric gasped when he saw Lady Lunette on the floor. "Your Majesty!"

Uther stood and turned away from the body. "She fell over. We were talking and she just collapsed. She's gone."

Sir Beric snapped his fingers to the footman. "Quickly, quickly! Get her to the Healer, there may still be time!"

Uther took Sir Beric's arm. "Don't bother, she's gone."

"There may still be—"

But Uther tightened his grip on Beric's bicep. "She's gone."

Sir Beric flinched at the look in Uther's eyes. "Yes, yes, sire." He turned back to the footman, who had lifted Lady Lunette into his arms. "Take the body to her tent and await further instructions."

The frightened footman nodded and hurried out of the pavilion.

Beric's shaking hands reached for a wine goblet, but Uther placed a hand over it. "Some water, perhaps."

Sir Beric quickly connected the dots. He straightened up and struggled to compose himself. His eyes betrayed fear.

Uther savored it. "We need to arrange another meeting with Father Carden. There are new terms to be discussed."

"Yes, Your Highness." Sir Beric bowed more deeply than usual and made a hasty exit.

# FORTY-NINE

**O**NE HUNDRED SIXTY BARRELS OF ALE, forty-five barrels of wine, several hundred bags of wheat flour. We've salted the fishes and meats, we're drying the fruits we can, and the wells should give us fresh fish until they manage to spoil it. And we have plenty of waterbirds in the moats. Unfortunately, the fires have left us in quite a state as far as wood is concerned. We just won't be able to feed the fires. Available wood may be our greatest need." Steuben was Lord Ector's captain of the guard: tall, bald, and rail thin with a quiet, reassuring voice.

"We may need to sacrifice a few structures to the cause," Arthur noted. Around the table in the Great Hall were Nimue, Lord Ector, Morgan, Arthur, and Cora. Wroth had not been heard from since the incident with B'uluf.

"Aye, though just whose structures pay the price may prove complicated," Steuben offered.

"How much time," Nimue asked carefully, "do we have? Before we—"

"Starve, milady?" Steuben finished for her.

"Yes," Nimue said.

Steuben scratched his chin. "Well, before all of you"—he paused—"newcomers came about, I would have said a month or two before we ran out of food, but given our current state and just how much some of your kind eat . . . Well, I'd say a week at most. Even without the siege, we just have too many mouths to feed."

"A week," Nimue whispered, repeating it to allow the reality to sink in.

"There is no choice but surrender," Lord Ector said bitterly.

"Surrender for you," Nimue said darkly. "The fires for us."

"Or death for us all," Lord Ector shot back. "In a day or two the siege engines will be upon us. Let's see how bold you all are when they send the burning pitch over those walls."

"My queen!"

Nimue turned to two Faun archers standing at the entrance to the hall. "Yes?"

"A rider is at the gates. He says his name is Merlin."

Minutes later the archers led Merlin into the Great Hall, where a scowling Nimue waited on the throne with Morgan and Arthur standing on either side of her.

"Milady Nimue." Merlin bowed his head slightly. "It is a pleasure to see you again."

"That's Queen Nimue, sir. She wields the Sword of Power," Morgan corrected him.

"Let us not become too attached to our titles," Merlin said, "for I fear that blade is about to become a bargaining chip in a much larger war."

"Arthur, Morgan, I would like to introduce you to Merlin the Magician." Nimue's tone was tinged with frost. *"My father."*

Arthur and Morgan both turned to Nimue, shocked.

Morgan said, "Your what?"

Ignoring Morgan, Nimue said to Merlin sarcastically, "Wasn't this your plan all along, Merlin? To find a human king to wield the Sword of Power?"

"I had every intention of destroying the sword in order to prevent this very thing: the petty struggles for incremental power, the seizing and reseizing of lands that were formed before time and belong to no one."

"Pretty words that do not match your actions," Nimue accused.

"What sort of fool would I be to ambush you with Uther's soldiers as you claim? Why not kill you on the road? Why the charade? Why show you my most intimate thoughts if my purpose there was to simply betray you? Think, Nimue."

"I saw them with my own eyes!" Nimue scoffed.

"As did I, confirmation that we both have enemies. I was betrayed. And now his army stands against you, shoulder to shoulder with the Red Paladins. We are at a precipice and must either prepare ourselves to work together and make very difficult choices or risk the very extinction of our people."

"*Our* people?" Morgan interjected. "Since when have you been a friend to the Fey?"

Merlin took a few menacing steps toward the throne. "For seven hundred years I have stood in the breach between men and the Fey Kind, giving all my blood and toil to keep them from tearing out each other's throats. I have lost more than I have won, but it is an effort that has cost me dearly in my heart, in my mind, and in my very soul. You would be wise to know your history before you ask such questions."

"Morgan is a loyal friend," Nimue said, while putting a hand over hers to compel her silence. "Continue," she said, not wishing to betray the gnawing, trapped feeling gripping her heart, urging her to run, flee, and escape it all.

"The sword has its grip on you, Nimue. I know you feel it. I've felt it too. It wills you to slaughter. To conquer. But this is the path to oblivion. The sword has power but no answers. A leader must be not only brave but wise."

When Merlin spoke of the sword, Nimue's stomach twisted with anger. *How dare he? He wants to steal it for himself.* She sensed the sword's influence pushing her mind like winds on a sail. Feeding her passion. Her rage.

But she pushed back. The Fingers of Airimid flared briefly; *the Hidden checking the sword,* Nimue observed.

"What is it you propose, Merlin?"

"Very recently I brought a gift to the court of Cumber, the Ice King, a Viking lord who claims to be the true blood heir to the throne of House Pendragon. This gift will go a very long way to affirming his claim, or at the very least, diminishing Uther's. This was something I had hoped I would never have to do. These matters inevitably lead to the deaths of innocent men, women, and children. Nor have I any desire to wound Uther Pendragon. He has been ill-served by those he trusted most. Let us leave it at that," Merlin said ruefully.

"And yet?" Nimue asked.

"I had to do it," Merlin continued. "So that I might bargain for your life."

Nimue folded her hands in her lap, unexpectedly moved by his words.

But a troubling thought snuffed the light. "And what of the Fey Kind?"

Merlin's eyes darkened. "The Ice King has offered you sanctuary in his court. As a prisoner, of sorts. To be treated very much as a guest, but a prisoner all the same. That is as far as the invitation goes."

"What kind of invitation is that?" asked Morgan. "You want her to be a hostage?"

Nimue was about to object, but Merlin pressed. "I would encourage you to journey with me to the Beggar's Coast and take an audience with the Ice King. Together we can plead the case of the Fey and attempt to turn his mind."

"And leave my people to the mercy of the siege?" Nimue asked incredulously.

"I don't know who has put these ideas in your head," he said, glancing pointedly at Morgan, "that you are the savior of your race. That was not Lenore's charge. She bade you bring me the Sword of Power. You've done all you can, but now you must think rationally. To stay here is to die. The only hope for the Fey is for you to plead their case to the Ice King and seek his protection."

Nimue imagined what it would feel like to hand off the responsibility to someone else. The burden lifted. Like a dream. She turned to Arthur. "What do you think?"

"Quite a risk. The raiders aren't known for their mercy. But if Merlin has shown him a path to the throne, perhaps it's a risk worth taking."

"Morgan?" Nimue asked.

"You know my answer. The sword is where it should be. With you."

Nimue could feel the heat of the sword on her back, resisting her. Memories arose of the hot wind that blew as Dewdenn burned, as the timbers of the barn crackled and the horses fled in panic. The Ice King would never feel this. The Fey and their plight would remain what they always were to human kings: an inconvenience, a distraction, an obligation.

*There is no human savior. We can only save ourselves.*

"I am sorry that you have gone to so much trouble on my behalf, but I cannot leave them," Nimue said.

"I implore you, take the evening and think on this. There is no other way."

Nimue rose from her throne, dizzy with exhaustion and the crushing pressures of the day. "You may stay if you like. But my decision is final."

With that, Nimue took the Sword of Power and left the hall.

# FIFTY

I DID THIS," NIMUE SAID TO ARTHUR AS SHE stared from the tower window at a horizon aglow from thousands of campfires. "I trapped us here."

Arthur sat at the window beside her. "We all did this. It was the best of a lot of bad options."

Nimue smiled sadly. "You should have stayed away when you had the chance."

"We can still leave." Arthur took her hand. "Just you and me. Throw the damned sword over the wall and let's run. We stand a chance out there. Get to the sea."

"I would like that," Nimue said, running her hand over Arthur's knuckles. But she turned back to the small city of Cinder below, the barrel fires, the motion of the crowds. "I'm not what they think. I feel like such a fraud. They must think or hope that I know what to do. But I don't. I don't even know myself. I feel less and less control." Nimue's eyes turned to the Sword of Power, slung over a chair by the bed. "Perhaps it's best if I die tomorrow."

Arthur took her arm gently. "No, that's not happening."

"At least then I won't turn into something horrible." Nimue's eyes were locked on the sword. "You don't understand what it can do."

"It's just a sword, Nimue."

"It's more than that," she said, her voice shaking.

"Your rage is your own. They took everything from you. Your mother. Friends. Loved ones. You've earned that rage, but don't let it— You are Nimue. Not the savior. Not the Queen of the Fey. That sword is nothing more than the coin that buys your freedom."

"It's the sword of my people," Nimue protested.

"You won't have a people unless you bargain the sword."

Shouts below drew their attention. There was activity at the gates.

"Someone's here," Arthur said.

Moments later Steuben appeared at the door, slightly out of breath. "A representative of King Uther requests an audience with the Fey queen," he said.

Nimue took this in. "Is that the title he used?"

"It is, milady." Steuben nodded.

Sir Beric was shown into the Great Hall. He wore a pinched expression as he stood alongside a Pendragon footman holding the banner of his house. Before him sat Nimue on the throne, flanked by Arthur and Morgan, while Merlin stood by one of the roaring fires. Sir Beric made a point of ignoring the magician.

"King Uther sends his regards to the Queen of the Fey and congratulates you on your recent military successes. Surely, you have proven yourself a formidable leader."

Nimue was caught off guard by this approach. She was not sure she had heard it all correctly until Morgan elbowed her.

"Thank you," Nimue sputtered, knowing she sounded absurd. She had once heard that royals spoke of themselves as "we" and wondered if that was something she should try, then thought better of it for fear of confusing herself. "That is nice of King Uther to say . . . to . . ." Nimue paused. "Me."

Morgan winced.

Sir Beric went on. "His Majesty would prefer to end matters peacefully and has authorized me to present the terms of your surrender."

Nimue felt the back of her neck go hot. Slender vines crept up her cheek. "My . . . surrender?"

"You are surrounded and outnumbered. Until now, His Majesty has rejected Church entreaties to besiege the town as a united army, though the opportunity still exists for such an alliance. There simply is no other choice for you. Accept His Majesty's terms or be annihilated."

Nimue took a deep breath to marshal her temper. "And what are those terms?"

Sir Beric folded his arms behind him. "Your Fey army must surrender its weapons and leave this town within twenty-four hours, at which time you will give yourself over to His Majesty's custody, whereupon you will be tried for treason and, if found guilty, be held in his dungeons for the remainder of your life. A mercy His Majesty offers in return for the Sword of Power."

"Might I suggest what you can do with your offer?" Merlin growled from the wings.

"You may not," Nimue shot at Merlin.

Sir Beric sniffed in Merlin's direction. "I assure you that is as generous an offer as you will receive, milady."

"And what about my people?" Nimue asked. "What assurances of their safety can you give me when they leave this town? For the only reason we are here at all is because they were forced from their homes with only the clothes on their backs, after their families and friends were put to the torch."

Sir Beric shifted awkwardly. "His Majesty promises no Fey Folk will be harmed by Pendragon forces."

"But what about Red Paladin forces, who have done this massacre under the king's nose with no sanction at all? Will King Uther stop this rampage?" Nimue asked, her voice rising.

Sir Beric shook his head, annoyed. "His Majesty does not command the Red Paladin forces."

"Then what sort of king is he if he cannot protect his own people?"

"You are in no position to make any demands."

Nimue drew the sword, filling the hall with a ghostly blue light. "This is the Sword of Power. It is said that whosoever wields the sword shall be the one true king. It was forged by my people when the world was young. If King Uther believes he is worthy of this sword, then let him prove it. Let him be the protector of men and Fey alike."

Sir Beric spread out his hands. "I am afraid that is all I am authorized to offer, milady. Is there a message you would like me to convey to His Majesty?"

Nimue sat back on the throne, deflated. "Tell him there is still time to be a king worthy of his people."

Sir Beric nodded. "Very good, milady." He turned to go, then hesitated. "Just to be clear, if King Uther were to guarantee protection for your people from Church forces, you would deliver yourself and the sword to him?"

Morgan turned to Nimue, panicked.

Merlin stepped forward. "Don't answer."

"I would."

# FIFTY-ONE

GAWAIN HAD TO BREATHE IN SHALLOW
gusts. Holding his breath seemed to be the only defense
against the searing pain. His hands were numb and tied
behind his back in the chair, and his feet were tied to the
legs. They had stripped him to a loincloth to ply their burning tools. The
blind man had taken his left eye. The skin felt stuck together. With his
good eye he tried not to look down at his burned flesh. He flinched when
he sensed movement at the tent entrance, fearing the return of the blind
man with his leather roll of tools. Instead Gawain saw a dark angel. *No,
not an angel,* he realized. The Weeping Monk.

"Don't be afraid, *Asher,* I won't bite," Gawain mumbled through swollen lips.

The monk entered but kept close to the walls.

Gawain was overwhelmed by agony. His head drooped and he moaned for several long moments. Then his breathing became very fast.

The monk lowered his hood. His marked eyes regarded the torture tent.

When the wave passed enough for Gawain to breathe again, he tilted his head at the Weeping Monk. "Have you come to watch me die?"

"Why did you keep silent?" the monk asked.

"When?" Gawain's thinking was dulled by pain.

"The tent. When I brought you in. You could have"—the monk paused—"told them what you knew about me. Why didn't you?"

Gawain tried to chuckle. "Because all Fey are brothers." His good eye welled with tears of pain and sorrow. "Even the lost ones."

The monk approached. "This suffering, it will cleanse you."

"You don't believe that. You know it's all lies, brother."

"Don't call me that," the monk warned.

"Look at you." Gawain tried to hold his head up to stare at him. "They turned your mind inside out."

"Through suffering you will see the light of truth."

"Why does your God want the little ones to die? I've seen the paladins chase down the children with horses. Why them?"

"I have no argument with the children. They don't know what they are."

"You kill children."

"I don't kill children," the monk said, his voice rising.

"All right, then you stand shoulder to shoulder with men who do. Who do it for the same God. And you let it happen. You've seen it with those weeping eyes. That makes you guilty."

The monk shook his head and turned to leave.

Gawain implored, "Brother, you can fight. I've never seen anything like it. You could be our greatest warrior. We need you. Your people need you."

"You're not my people," the monk growled.

"Then tell them the truth," Gawain said, jerking his head to the encampment. "Tell your Red Paladins, if they are your people, if they are your family, tell them what you are and see how they react."

As the tent flap was pulled back, the Weeping Monk swung around as though nervous they had been overheard.

A Red Paladin poked his head in and addressed the monk. "Father Carden wishes to see you, sir."

The Weeping Monk nodded. He turned to Gawain. "I'll pray for you."

Gawain was grim. "And I for you."

With that, the Weeping Monk swept out of the tent.

Squirrel spotted the Weeping Monk riding from the Red Paladin encampment and followed him at a sprint into the thick woods that divided the paladins from Camp Pendragon.

After a few miles, the Weeping Monk caught up with Father Carden, Abbot Wicklow, and an entourage of twenty Trinity and Red Paladin guards as they entered the muddy Pendragon encampment. The king's soldiers regarded them with more curiosity than aggression. Most had only heard stories of the Red Paladins and especially the Weeping Monk, whose lethality had grown to legendary status. The Trinity death masks were another exotic touch, and as they passed each campfire, there were murmurs and sidelong glances.

Squirrel snatched a discarded Pendragon tunic from a wagon and threw it over his head as he darted between tents, eyes on his sworn enemy.

When the monk and his party reached the king's sprawling pavilion, only Father Carden, Wicklow, and the monk were allowed entry.

Squirrel waited several minutes behind a half-built siege engine. As the Trinity guards drifted to the front of the royal pavilion, Squirrel dashed to the side of the tent and gently lifted the flap.

He saw the back of the throne. Abbot Wicklow and Father Carden faced the king, whom Squirrel could not see.

The Weeping Monk lingered in the background.

Squirrel could sense a thick tension.

Abbot Wicklow spoke. "We all desire an agreeable end to this uprising of the Fey. How do you, King Uther, envision such an ending?"

"With the Sword of Power in our hands," Uther answered.

"The Devil's Tooth is a very powerful and symbolic Fey relic," Father Carden spoke up, reasserting his authority, "highly coveted by the Church. Indeed its capture would be a crushing defeat to the Fey. Were we to relinquish our own claim to the sword, we would insist, at the very least, that the Fey witch be delivered to us alive, so that she can be made an example of, and to answer for her crimes before Almighty God."

The king answered him, "Had you coordinated from the start, such an outcome might be acceptable to us. Unfortunately, this Fey girl has aroused the passions of the mob. Burning her at the stake will only enflame those passions. Therefore, we have decided to accept the Fey witch as our prisoner, to be housed in our dungeons, until such time as we feel these passions have subsided sufficiently. Only then might we be willing to discuss her exchange with the Church."

"Weeks? Months? Years? What sort of time are we talking about?" Carden asked, agitated.

Abbot Wicklow put a quieting hand on Carden's arm as he said, "And what of the Fey inside those walls, Your Majesty? These are murderous creatures with paladin blood on their hands."

"They will be given ships to journey north. Let them settle in Denmark or Norway or fall off the face of the earth for all we care," Uther said.

But Father Carden seethed. "This will be viewed as a victory for the Fey over the Church. Unacceptable."

Abbot Wicklow folded his hands beneath his draping sleeves and assumed an air of deep sobriety. "I share Father Carden's concerns, Your Majesty, and I know Pope Abel's mind on these matters well enough to assure you he would be greatly alarmed by this leniency shown to such licentious and demonic creatures."

"It saddens us to upset the Church. You would have known our intentions sooner had you not presumed to negotiate with the Queen Regent behind our back. If the Church takes exception, we have conveniently assembled five thousand soldiers to answer your grievance."

Father Carden practically spat, "This is an outrage."

Suddenly Squirrel's legs were lifted into the air and he was dragged out from under the tent. He wriggled his body around to stare into the dead faces of the Trinity guards. One of them took his neck in an iron grip and walked him around to the front of the tent as Carden, Wicklow, and the Weeping Monk exited in a fury.

Carden growled to Wicklow, "All you've done since you've arrived is undermine this cause—"

Wicklow interrupted, "I wouldn't bloody be here if you had smothered this rebellion in its crib and not turned this Fey whore into an icon! Now I have to clean this up."

Their attention was drawn to Squirrel, who kicked and thrashed in the guard's arms.

The Weeping Monk recognized him.

"What is this?" Carden asked the guard.

"We caught him trying to sneak into the king's tent," the guard said behind the death mask.

"I'll have your eyes, you—" Squirrel threw every wicked, awful curse he had ever heard at the Red Paladins.

Father Carden curled his lip. "Have Brother Salt take his measure. And tell him to start with that foul little tongue of his."

The Red Paladins nodded, but the Weeping Monk stepped forward. "He's just a boy," he said to Father Carden.

Wicklow stopped and stared at the Weeping Monk.

Father Carden shook his head, turned, and slapped the monk with a force that nearly knocked them both over. The monk's hand went to his cheek as Carden straightened his robes.

Wicklow turned to the Trinity guards. "Well? What are you waiting for? Take him away!"

The guards obeyed and dragged Squirrel away to the Red Paladin camp.

Father Carden turned and grabbed the monk's arm. "Why would you embarrass me like this? Why?"

The Weeping Monk shook him off and stalked away into the maze of tents.

In the moment afterward, Wicklow gave a silent order to two of his Trinity guards. They nodded and headed off along the same path taken by the Weeping Monk.

When Father Carden returned to the Red Paladin camp, he entered his tent and found that a woman was already there, standing with her back to him, her cloak of snow-leopard pelts spilling over his carpets. She turned, lowered her hood, and gazed at Carden with cold blue eyes painted with green pigment. "Father Carden, I am Eydis, first daughter of Cumber, the one and true blood heir to House Pendragon. I believe we have mutual interests and mutual enemies."

# FIFTY-TWO

N O!" MORGAN CRIED AS SHE RACED
down the corridor to the Great Hall. When she entered,
Nimue, Merlin, Arthur, Lord Ector, Steuben, Cora, and
several Fey Elders were gathered at a table, discussing a tiny
note just delivered by raven. "Is it true? Is it?" Morgan demanded.

Nimue's answer was written all over her face. Her eyes were defeated.

"No!" Morgan howled, running at the table. "You can't give it to him.
They'll kill you. They'll kill us all!"

"Morgan—" Arthur started.

"Shut up!" Morgan said, turning fiercely on Arthur. "Are you happy
now? Do you think he'll make you a knight now, you fool? Do you think
King Uther will make you his pet? He doesn't care about you! You're
doomed like the rest of us."

"And what is your answer, Morgan!" Arthur bit back. "What's your brilliant solution? Oh, I know! Fight the bastards! Fight them all!"

"Yes!"

"Yes, brilliant! That's all you know! That's all you ever do!" Arthur shouted. "And where's that gotten you, sister? Hmm? Nowhere. You just burn it all down and move on."

"How dare you?" Morgan snarled.

"Stop it!" Nimue snapped. She turned to Morgan, softening a bit. "This is my decision alone." She held up the note. "King Uther has offered us ships to the north."

Morgan put her face in her hands.

Nimue put her hand on her friend's shoulder, fighting her own emotions. "This is the only way, Morgan. All these lives"—she waved to the entire city—"are my responsibility. I don't want to leave you, but I see no other way."

"We can sneak you out, tunnel you out," Morgan said, grasping at straws. "You can rally other towns, cities even."

"And what happens here?" Nimue asked. "What happens to these children?"

Morgan persisted. "If they find out you're gone, they won't care anymore. They'll lose interest in Cinder."

"Really?" Nimue said. "That is not my experience of Father Carden. Something tells me that were I to leave, he would more likely take out his wrath upon all of you."

Morgan turned to Merlin with tear-streaked eyes. "Can't you do something? You're Merlin. Can't you turn her into a bird or change her face to hide her? Can't you do something? Anything?"

Nimue had a glimmer of hope as she turned to Merlin, curious for his answer. But in that moment, Merlin almost looked his full seven hundred years. He shook his head sadly. "Were it even in my power to do so,

King Uther's conditions demand Nimue as his prisoner. Furthermore, she has rejected the Ice King's offer."

"Only because he makes no allowance for the Fey Kind at all," Nimue reminded him. "I have to be sure they are protected."

The table was quiet and somber as Nimue weighed her decision. In barely a whisper she asked Merlin, "How would it work?"

Merlin considered this, then offered, "Someone must lead the Fey Kind out of Cinder. That will be the first very dangerous task. There's no predicting how the Red Paladins might react. I can't imagine they are contented by King Uther's offer. It's a job for a soldier."

Nimue took Arthur's hand. "Arthur?"

"No." His voice shook. "I want to stay with you."

"I don't trust anyone else with their lives. Please," Nimue pleaded.

"I don't want to leave you," Arthur insisted. Then, revealing his shame, he added, "*I don't want to run.*"

"You're not. This isn't the same." She took his face in her hands. "Listen to me, Arthur. This is your path to honor."

"Another way, please," Arthur begged softly.

"It has to be you."

Merlin continued, "It will be a day's march to the sea. When the Fey Kind are aboard Uther's ships, Arthur will send a raven informing you of this." He paused. "And that is when you will surrender yourself and the Sword of Power to King Uther."

"How does that happen?"

Merlin scratched his beard, not entirely sure. "I suppose a royal escort. Outside the gates. The note demands that you surrender yourself unaccompanied."

Morgan shook her head, horrified.

As Nimue absorbed this chilling idea, she added, "And Gawain. They must return the Green Knight to us. Alive."

Merlin did not appear hopeful. "We can certainly ask. But if this Green Knight is in the hands of the Red Paladins, I fear the worst."

"These are my conditions," Nimue said flatly.

Merlin repeated, "We can ask."

"Will you write the reply?" Nimue asked, feeling foolish and young. "I don't want to sound . . ." She trailed off.

Merlin nodded, understanding. "I will write the note agreeing to the king's revised terms and bring it to you for your approval."

Nimue turned away from the table, and headed to her chambers without another word.

An hour later Nimue was at her window, staring out at the glowing twin camps of Pendragon and Red Paladin. A distant squawk turned her attention toward the northern gate, where a blackbird soared low over the heads of the archers on the wall. Moments later she heard a knock. "Yes?"

Merlin entered. "The raven has been sent to Uther with your reply."

"I saw." Nimue smiled bravely.

Merlin swayed awkwardly at the door. "I'll leave you," he started.

"No, please. Join me."

He closed the door and approached the window where Nimue sat.

"You must think me very foolish," she said.

"Not foolish at all, no." He shook his head, amazed. "You are Lenore to your very bones."

Nimue managed a smile.

Then he added, "With a touch of Merlin as well. A very combustible combination, if I may be so bold."

Nimue laughed. "It explains a lot, yes."

Merlin smiled. He even covered it with his hand, so rarely did a smile appear on his lips. "I can tell you this: she would be deeply proud of your choices here." He hesitated, then added, "As I am."

This meant more to her than she realized, and she was caught off guard by the tears that streamed down her cheeks. She quickly wiped them away. She had never had a father, not truly. And though part of her yearned to reach out to Merlin, another part of her feared his rejection. "But I don't know what I'm doing."

"And that is how courage is found. When the path is least clear." He started to say more but looked away.

"What?" Nimue noticed this.

"I'm sorry," Merlin said simply. "I'm sorry that I couldn't save her."

Nimue nodded, accepting this.

"And I was wrong about the sword," he said.

"What do you mean?"

Merlin suddenly turned, a revelation forming. "It wasn't Uther's blood that rained on the castle, nor was it mine. And I daresay it was not portending death but great transformation. It was Wolf Blood that rained on that castle."

"I don't understand."

"All this time I've been chasing the sword, believing that somehow it was turning events, but it was never the sword. It was you. The Wolf-Blood Witch." Merlin grew sad. "I could have helped you. I—"

"You are here now."

"I will ride ahead to seek audience with King Uther. To smooth the path in whatever way I can. Please be under no illusions, the king has gone for my head already once in these past days, and my actions since have only served to heighten his animosity. I could very easily be dead before you even arrive."

Nimue regarded Merlin. His tired eyes met hers. She saw no calculation, no chess game, no manipulation there. This was a very human Merlin. This was her father. "You don't have to," she told him.

"Yes, I do," he answered.

# FIFTY-THREE

ARTHUR PUSHED OPEN A CREAKY BARN
door on the fringes of town near the southern wall. He
turned back to Nimue. "Are you sure about this?" She
brushed past him. The air was thick with musk and it was
very dark. Nervous horses whinnied in their stalls. Nimue held out her
torch as a Tusk lunged from the shadows, barking and baring chiseled
fangs.

Arthur drew his sword, but Nimue stood fast. "Where is Wroth?"

The lunging Tusk settled into a grimace as a low bark came from
the back of the barn. The young Tusk thrust his jaw horns at Arthur but
allowed them to pass. As her torchlight spilled over Tusks squatting and
huddling in the straw, she was reminded of their uncanny night vision
and their preference for total darkness. They found Wroth slouched on a

hay bale, chewing on a gypsum root. A pale and silent B'uluf lay nearby, his bloody stumps tucked under his arms.

Mogwan stood and approached. "You are not welcome here."

"What would you have done, were you in my shoes?" Nimue addressed Wroth directly. "If you wielded the sword and a Sky Folk defied you?"

Wroth spat a few words at Nimue and waved her off.

Mogwan was impassive. "We'll never know, he says."

"I don't need your love or worship. I don't even need your respect. What I do need is your strength to protect the Fey Kind in my absence," Nimue said.

Arthur added, "She's giving the sword and her freedom to King Uther." He allowed that to sink in. "She is sacrificing herself so that the rest of us may live. So that Tusks can survive to the next generation."

Surprise flickered over Mogwan's face and he began to interpret, but Wroth cut off his son with his own response. Mogwan said, "My father says it is not like you to give up."

"I am not giving up. The Fey Kind have been through enough. I won't subject them to a slaughter. If my life buys you freedom, then it is well spent."

There was a rustle in the back and Wroth suddenly emerged into the torchlight, broad-chested and fierce. His deep-set black eyes studied Nimue closely. Then he growled, "*Gof uch noch we'roch?*"

Mogwan suppressed a smile.

Nimue frowned, curious. "What did he say?"

"He says are you sure you are not part Tusk?"

Wroth allowed a grin that showed off a golden fang. "*Brach nor la jech.*"

Mogwan translated, "You are harder woman than his first wife. My mother."

Wroth snarled something at Arthur and swatted him in the chest, knocking the wind clean out of him.

Mogwan said to Nimue, "My father says when you are tired of this chicken-legs Man Blood, you can be his third wife."

"Let's not rush things," Nimue said with a smile. She took Wroth's hand in hers. "But I do need champions. I need you and Arthur to lead the Fey Kind to the Pendragon ships. Will you do this for me?"

Wroth enclosed her small hand in his giant ones. She felt his great warmth and his rough skin. His nails grazed her arm. "Gr'luff. Bruk no'dam." Then his mouth struggled to form words she could understand. "Born in the dawn."

"To pass in the twilight," she finished, touching her heart in thanks.

Wagons, sheep, donkeys, palfreys, screaming Fey Kind children, carts, a dozen oxen, shouting Fauns, buzzing Moon Wings, crying babes, and hundreds of refugees both Fey Kind and Man Blood alike swarmed Cinder's main square by the western gate. Half a dozen rumors of treacherous plots had set off near riots throughout the day, and it had taken all Arthur and Wroth's determination and discipline to ward off disaster. The mob was not stupid. They knew they were marching defenseless into Red Paladin territory. Nerves were on a knife's edge.

Emotions ran just as high at the wicket gate, where Nimue and Morgan went to see Merlin off on his mission. Nimue had never seen the mage so rigid and unsure. "Wait for the raven," he told her for the twentieth time. "Be sure it's Arthur's writing."

"I will," Nimue assured him.

"Have him leave you the very same letter so that you might compare them. Uther has the means to devise adept forgeries."

"Already done," Nimue told him.

"That's good." Merlin pulled at his beard. "If I sense a plot, I will do all I can to warn you. But I—"

"I know you will." Nimue smiled.

Merlin started to say more but could not find the words. Instead he merely nodded and ducked through the gate, climbing onto his freshly saddled horse. With a meaningful gaze at Nimue, he yanked the reins and wheeled around onto the path, galloping off toward the king's campground.

Nimue turned to Morgan, who appeared to be preparing to say her goodbyes. "No, not yet," Nimue said, and took her arm, leading her away from the mob and down a series of narrow alleys, hugging close to the ramparts.

"What is happening?" Morgan asked as Nimue pulled her down one switchback after another. She would not answer until they came upon a goateed Faun lounging on a wagon in a dark corner between two sagging buildings, picking his teeth with a piece of straw. "Where in the Nine Hells are we?" Morgan asked, finally yanking her arm free.

Nimue gestured to the Faun. "Morgan, this is Prosper." She nodded to Prosper, who hopped off the wagon and pushed it aside. Beneath the wagon was an empty sack. Nimue pulled the sack away, revealing a tunnel in the ground. Morgan leaned down, fascinated, as a dark-skinned Plog popped out of the opening, chittering in its strange language. "Gods!" Morgan leaped backward. Prosper chuckled.

"And this," Nimue continued, gesturing to the Plog, "to the best of my ability to pronounce, is Effie."

Morgan swung around, beaming. "You're escaping!"

Nimue shook her head. "No, my love." And she unslung the Sword of Power from her shoulder. "You are."

# FIFTY-FOUR

THE POPULAR CINDER TAVERN WAS KNOWN as Red Eye's Lonely Horse, but Nimue had decided to take it over as her own Great Hall in order to stay closer to the preparations for the Fey exodus. Arthur was sweating and filthy as he entered, surprised to find Nimue nearly alone, apart from the harried barmaid, Ingrid, the great-great-granddaughter of the original Red Eye, an unsmiling woman who nodded curtly at Arthur as he pulled a chair over to Nimue.

"Quiet in here," he observed.

"Not as quiet as that ghastly keep," Nimue said, sipping a cup of wine. She added, "The Elders have all gone to their clans." She took another sip.

The enormity of Nimue's sacrifice kept crashing down on Arthur in fresh waves. "You don't—"

"Stop," Nimue interrupted. "I do." She laughed, fighting back tears. "Trust me, I really want to go with you."

Arthur clutched her head to his chest. He pressed his lips to her ear. "Don't make me do this."

She held his cheek to hers. Their mouths touched. "Are you sorry you came back?"

"Enough sorrys. You're not my queen. You don't command me. You're my friend." His thumb swept away her tears.

"I have a secret," she confided. "I've never been on a ship. It was always my dream. To be on the ocean. To be somewhere that never ends. To sail to that point where the sea meets the sky. Just to be a speck in all that stillness."

"Not very Sky Folk of you," Arthur teased.

"I'm a traitor to my kind," she admitted. Then she snapped her fingers. "I missed it by a few days. My ship. It was the day we met, actually."

"Meant to be, then. Just think of all the fun you would have missed," Arthur said.

Nimue put her face into her hands and chuckled darkly. She reached for Arthur and he cradled her, in silence, for long minutes. She gave him one last lingering kiss, then slowly stood up. She offered her hand. He took it, and she led them out of the tavern.

The cacophonous mob of Fey Kind quieted and parted as Nimue and Arthur moved through the crowd, hands locked. Those who understood Nimue's sacrifice reached out to her, touched her arms and her shoulders, while the children tried to walk in beside her and hold her hand. Others bowed or murmured prayers in their native tongues. Nimue smiled to them all. She couldn't let them see her fear.

When they reached the front, she turned Arthur to her and kissed him deeply. She touched his face, his eyes, his wet brow, his neck, and his

sweaty hair matted over his ears, trying to remember every detail. When she softly pulled away, he put the heel of his hand to his eyes and climbed onto Egypt. Her long neck twisted to Nimue, and she gave Egypt a kiss on the nose and a scratch.

There was a thunderous squeal and Wroth emerged from a side road atop the giant boar, leading his Tusk warriors. The crowd wisely made room for the fearsome beast, which jerked angrily at its reins. Riding up beside Arthur, Wroth nodded to Nimue. *"Budach ner lom sut! Vech dura m'shet!"*

From his horse, Mogwan translated, "If the paladin scum give us any trouble, we'll be sure to make them pay."

"I have no doubt of it," Nimue said, touching her heart, and Wroth answered with a fist to his own.

Nimue gave Arthur's hand one last squeeze and then backed away, nodding to the Fauns at the gate. There was a groan of steel as the portcullis rose, and the procession began its march. Nimue watched them, waving to some, bowing to others, acknowledging every face she could as they passed under the gates of Cinder and onto the King's Road. Nimue's heart was in her stomach. Her own fate seemed very far away. All she could think about were the Fey's trusting eyes and how she might be leading them to a burning cross.

It wasn't until the last of the carts had vanished through the gates and the portcullis had been lowered again with a grinding of chains that Nimue felt the crush and scope of her decision. *What have I done? I've sentenced them to die.* How had it come to this? That she felt like a mother to her entire race? She had never been accepted by her own kind, had always been shut out, judged for her scars and her uncontrollable connection to the Hidden. *We're not perfect,* Nimue mused. Like B'uluf and her village Elders, the Fey were capable of tribal hatreds and carried ancient grudges. Like Man Bloods, they feared what they didn't understand. But they were the exception. Nimue thought of the torchlight spilling over all those wondrous and unique faces in the cave on that first night with Morgan and Arthur. The beauty and creativity of the Hidden had been on full display that night. These were races attuned to the beating heart of the earth, to their lands, to the animals that shared those lands, and their curious faces were both a mirror and a window into those worlds. Where Father Carden saw monsters, Nimue saw families in a deep, abiding and ancient connection to the Hidden and the Old Gods, all with their own dances and magic, languages, crafts, and stories. The Red Paladins wanted to burn all the Fauns and Moon Wings and Tusks and Sky Folk, burn all the colors and textures away until everything was gray like the ashes of Dewdenn. Nimue would not abide such a tragedy.

*If I die, it's still worth it,* she thought. *It's worth protecting.*

*From outcast to queen.*

She looked over the trampled dirt of the square and saw only human faces staring back at her with fascination and fear, curiosity and disgust. Lord Ector grimaced at her and turned his horse back to his castle, a castle he was about to reclaim.

The first mile the caravan traveled was eerie for its silence. Arthur could not detect a single birdcall, could not hear a fly in the brush. It was cold but still. Even the steady and biting Minotaur winds seemed to pause for their crossing. There was only the slow rumble of the wheels and hooves and boots behind him, the steady clops of Wroth's boar. Ahead there were only barren trees and the rising hills.

The first sign of trouble was a Red Paladin checkpoint. Five tonsured brothers stood by a Vatican banner, shouldering flails and heavy maces, and watched them approach with murderous eyes.

"Easy, Wroth," Arthur whispered, knowing the Tusks would take their cue from their prideful leader and knowing how difficult it was for

Wroth to walk away from a fight. For his part, Wroth was quiet. That worried Arthur more.

As the caravan came within fifty feet of the paladins, the name-calling began. The paladins had different names for different clans: squealers, roaches, twisters, blood beaks, hedge pigs. They hurled them all, trying to goad the warriors into a conflict that might give the excuse for an all-out assault.

Wroth kept his eyes locked on the road, but as they passed the checkpoint, he dug in his heels, and the boar gave a squeal that shook the cliffs of the Minotaurs and sent the Red Paladins scurrying into the forest. Arthur feared reprisal but saw no sign of the monks. He smirked at Wroth, who let out a satisfied *huff*. But the good feeling was short-lived, as the next mile led them into the heart of the Red Paladin camp.

A quarter mile behind Arthur, Sister Iris had slowly been letting herself drift to the back of the caravan. She didn't belong to any clan. No one had claimed her. No one particularly wanted her. She had played the vagabond between clans for days. So no one cared when she wandered off on her own. When eyes were ahead, she ducked into the high grasses and slid onto a wet embankment. She slung a stolen longbow out from under her sackcloth cloak, slipped an arrow between her fingers, and darted into the forest, curling back toward the town of Cinder.

At the front of the caravan, Arthur saw that spears had been lit aflame and were stabbed into the ground in symmetrical rows along the road, and hundreds of paladin horsemen filled in the spaces between the trees of the forest that surrounded them on all sides. This was a terrible sign. Arthur's heart sank. They'd never survive a direct assault. He vowed to take as many with him as he could, but it was impossible not to let some of the hopelessness in. He felt an ache in his heart knowing he would never see Nimue again. A growl rippled in the boar's throat. It could feel the threat all around them. Arthur's hand drifted to the pommel of his sword.

"Keep moving," he called back to the caravan, sensing the building panic.

Wroth grabbed his war hammer.

"No, Wroth," Arthur whispered.

The paladin horses grew agitated in the woods. Arthur saw their swishing tails and jerking heads. One spark was all it would take. Someone had ordered the paladins to stand down, but Arthur could feel it was a tenuous hold. They wanted any excuse to charge and would do so at the slightest provocation.

A rumble of horses pulled Arthur's attention to the road ahead. Another column of horsemen approached from the north, about to meet them head-on.

*It's over*, Arthur thought.

"Not them," Wroth said in broken English.

It was true. The approaching horsemen carried the banner of House Pendragon.

*I don't believe it.*

The caravan moved forward and the column of soldiers split around them, forming a barrier on both sides between the Red Paladins in the forest and the caravan of Fey Folk.

Arthur thought he might cry as one of the king's soldiers nodded to him and he nodded back. He swallowed the lump in his throat. The murmurs of fear turned into a burbling relief as the Fey Kind families realized the king's men were shielding them from the Red Paladins. Some cheered, others wept, some took the opportunity to hurl invective at their tormentors. As the caravan rolled along, the horsemen turned and rode beside them.

King Uther had kept his word.

*I never should have left her. I pushed this. I pushed her to give the sword to Pendragon.* Arthur looked across a sea of grateful families who'd had so little to celebrate in the past few months. This was victory. Arthur had been right. The Fey would live and a human king had done it. *Still too high a price.* To barter for the sword was one thing. But not Nimue. *Not her. I should go back.* The Fey were not safe, not yet, not until they were on the ships. He had promised her. But he couldn't help playing things out in his mind. *She arrives at Uther's camp. They seize her. Take the sword. Deliver her to Father Carden and the Red Paladins. And then?* The thought made him sick. They had fed their wolf to the lions.

The rest of the journey was a strange, bittersweet dream. The Fey Folk were uplifted, even celebratory, setting aside the unknowns of their future to relish the peace and mercy of the present as the caravan rolled through the lowlands and the air misted from the nearing ocean. The sandstone cliffs took on jagged, violent forms, shaped through the ages by the battering coastal winds, and the forests leveled out, becoming undulating fields of wild grasses.

Arthur and Wroth rode to the edge of the bluff, climbed down from their mounts, and gazed out upon the churning green seas of the Beggar's Coast. A heavy fog had settled offshore, whiting out all but the rocky beach and the nearest lapping tide. Their eyes searched the horizon for signs of life, but all they heard were the gulls. A heavy silence fell over the Fey Kind as expectancy turned to fear.

A mast cut through the fog, followed by a sail emblazoned with the three crowns of House Pendragon. A joyful whoop erupted from the Fey Folk, and even Arthur was caught up in the rush of the moment. Wroth threw his arms around Arthur, nearly crushing him with joy, as up and down the cliffs, Fey clans embraced, children pointed and shouted, and mothers and fathers wept from relief and gratitude.

As Arthur wiped his own tears, all he could think about was Nimue.

## FIFTY-FIVE

TWO PENDRAGON FOOTMEN ESCORTED
Merlin into King Uther's pavilion and shoved him before the
throne. Sir Beric shook his head in disbelief as he rose from a
table filled with parchments to stand beside the king.

"He rode into camp and surrendered, Your Highness," the older footman explained.

As Merlin smoothed his sleeves, the king regarded him with reptilian
calm. "Hello, Uther," Merlin said, nodding.

Uther smiled coldly. "Dispensed with the formalities, have we?"

"What are your intentions with the Fey girl?" Merlin asked, cutting
to the chase.

"Are you here on behalf of the witch? We thought you served the
Ice King? Honestly, Merlin, you have to be careful or you'll earn a repu-

tation as a loose wizard." Uther made an effort to control himself. "Your audacity coming here is the vilest affront of all. Do you presume us so castrated that you can stand before us after your crimes and survive?"

"I've given up trying to survive, Uther. It just happens," Merlin offered.

"Oh, we shall test that theory."

"I would have expected to find you in better spirits, considering that we are on the eve of your greatest victory as king. You've stopped the Fey slaughter, subdued the Church, negotiated a firm but just peace with the leader of the Fey rebellion, and, despite all my best efforts to destroy it, the Sword of Power is within your grasp."

Uther's eye twitched. "We swear, Merlin, if you are about to claim credit for this, we will have you quartered here on the carpets before our eyes."

"Not at all. The victory is yours and yours alone. After all, Beric here could hardly negotiate his way out of a sack of turnips, so one might argue you have done this with one arm tied behind your back."

"Indeed!" was Beric's indignant reply.

Uther smiled despite himself. He always enjoyed when Merlin poked at Sir Beric. However, his smile faded into a snarl. "But unlike you, Beric is loyal to us. Whereas you, while professing friendship, rode to an enemy camp and delivered the dagger to slay this monarchy."

"Where is your mother?" Merlin asked, defiant in the wake of Uther's murderous rage.

"Dead," Uther spat.

Merlin quickly did the math. "My condolences," he said.

"Don't be too sad. You'll join her soon enough, and together you can scheme for eternity in the Nine Hells."

"The midwife was your mother's crime, Uther, not yours. And fight it all you like, but the light of truth will always burn away the shadow of lies. Be that as it may, you are finally your own man. If you want to be recognized as the one true king, now is your chance to finally earn it. Chop my head off tomorrow if you like, but let us finish this business with the sword today. So I will ask you again: What are your intentions with the Fey girl?"

"As stated," Uther replied.

"And do you trust Father Carden?"

"About as much as we trust you," Uther countered.

"Then you have made arrangements in case he betrays you? The Wolf-Blood Witch is in his reach. I assure you he hasn't come this far only to cower before you now, unless he's planning something," Merlin warned.

"How dare you interrogate us after your numerous treacheries? Your gall has no equal. Guards, put Merlin under watch until the Wolf Witch arrives. Once we have the sword, kill him."

The guards took Merlin roughly under each arm and led him out of the royal pavilion.

Nimue sat in her quarters, staring at the eel pie on the plate before her, and listened to her stomach growl. She had no appetite. The hours of waiting for word of the caravan had left her ragged with worry. Ector's wife, Lady Marion, had taken it upon herself to make sure Nimue was fed.

She hovered over Nimue, taking away the eel pie. "We have some lovely guinea hen with an almond glaze on its way."

"No, please," Nimue protested.

But Lady Marion sat beside her and held up her hands, suggesting it was beyond her control. "You won't die on my watch. You are too pale, my dear."

"I'm very grateful for your hospitality, Lady Marion. Considering . . ." Nimue trailed off.

"That you stole Lord Ector's throne?" Marion finished.

Nimue smiled softly. "Well, yes."

Lady Marion thought about it. "Why shouldn't a woman sit on the throne?"

Nimue's hand shook as she reached for her cup of wine.

Marion gazed at her with deep sympathy. "What you've done for your people is very brave."

Nimue was about to speak when a distant squawk echoed down the corridor. She stood suddenly. "Was that a raven?" She broke into a run, Lady Marion following far behind. Nimue searched frantically. "Hello!" She rounded a corner to find Steuben climbing the stairs, a note in his hand.

"The bird came, milady," he said, handing her the message.

Nimue unrolled the small parchment. She read it aloud: "'Ships are here. Boarding now. The king has kept his word. The Fey Kind will sail to the point where the sea meets the sky. Thanks to you, my love. Giuseppe Fuzzini Fuzzini.'" She dropped the note and put her hand to her mouth, fighting her tears. "They're safe," she said.

"This pleases me, ma'am," Steuben said, putting a hand on her shoulder.

# FIFTY-SIX

**T**HE PORTCULLIS ROSE NOISILY UNTIL IT
locked into its mooring in the top of the gate. Nimue nudged her
palfrey forward and passed under Cinder's northern wall, riding
alone onto the King's Road. A cool breeze rustled through the tall
grasses and caused the treetops to sway and rattle the last of their orange
leaves. The woodlands hummed with life. Nimue detected the tight peeps
of thrushes and the looping whistles of blackbirds. Her clenching fear, the
gnawing worry of the past days and weeks, sank away and a serenity fell
over her. She felt the Hidden very close. *Don't be afraid.* She remembered
the fawn in the Iron Wood. *Death is not the end.* This was not the life Nimue
had imagined for herself. So fast. So brutal. And yet so full. Of course there
was more she wished for: to see Arthur again, for one. To unravel his mys-
teries. To sleep in his arms. To travel the seas and explore the world together.

To one day raise a family. Nimue took a shuddering breath but fought back the tears. What she had known, she was thankful for. The rest was known only to the Hidden. *Born in the dawn, to pass in the twilight.*

The tranquility was broken by the sounds of approaching horsemen, Nimue was jerked back into the present, and a chill poured down her spine. A dozen men in full plate armor emerged from the wooded road, presenting a banner of three crowns. They slowed to a trot as Nimue approached, forming a steel barrier in the road before her. One of the armored soldiers lifted his faceplate. The eyes behind it were cold, the skin pocked, black mustache groomed.

"You are the Wolf-Blood Witch?" he asked her.

"I am."

"I am Sir Royce of the king's personal guard. Have you the sword?"

Nimue forced herself to look Sir Royce straight in the eyes. "I do not."

The soldiers exchanged looks at this. Sir Royce frowned. "Is this a jest, madam? The king has kept his word to you. Have you been false to His Majesty?"

"The sword is near. But I have conditions of my own." Nimue hated the way her voice shook.

Sir Royce's face contorted with anger. "You're a bold wench, aren't you? Where is the sword?"

"Grant me an audience with King Uther. To him only will I share its location."

Sir Royce twisted his reins in his gloved fist. Nimue assumed it was her neck he was imagining. "This ends poorly for you, girl," he warned. "Keep up." With that, he wheeled his horse around. The soldiers fell in around her as they rode to Camp Pendragon.

Nimue's saw the ocean of black-and-gold tents reaching across a vast plain and speckling onto the low hillside. She had never felt quite so small or unimpressive as she passed glowering soldiers with muddy faces, some regarding her with suspicion, others making lewd faces or gestures. A cold hand squeezed her guts when the sprawling royal pavilion came into view and she saw six Red Paladins and six Trinity guards stationed outside. Her heart was thudding as Sir Royce dismounted, took her palfrey's reins, and allowed her to climb down. Her legs were weak, but she straightened herself and glanced into the paladins' murderous eyes as the flap was opened and she entered.

She wondered if they would grant her some water. Lush carpets covered the ground. There were tables of abundance and luxury all around her: heaping bowls of fruits and cakes and breads, jugs of wine and golden candlesticks. King Uther sat on a throne, a thin golden crown over his narrow forehead. He was younger than she'd expected. Standing to his left was the man she knew as Sir Beric. Next to him was a small and dark-eyed man in exquisite black church robes, and across from the king was Father Carden, tall with a warm, round face that belied the evil that lived within. He gazed upon her with thin pity.

Sir Royce brushed ahead of Nimue and knelt before the king. "Your Majesty, the witch requested an audience. She doesn't have the sword. She claimed she would only reveal its location to you, sire."

"She mocks your kindness, Your Majesty," Father Carden said. "Why waste another breath on her? We are more than capable of drawing out the sword's location from her. Indeed, it would be a privilege." Father Carden turned and smiled at Nimue.

"I concur, King Uther," the little man in the rich robes offered. "Give us the witch and the Sword of Power will be yours by sundown."

"Girl, we fear you presume too much mercy from us," the king said to Nimue. "You are aware what awaits you should we hand you over to the Red Brotherhood?"

"Aye, very aware, Your Majesty," Nimue said. She looked at Father

Carden. "He had my mother killed. My family. Those who raised me. My best friend. He burned them all. Burned our village down. I know him well."

Nimue saw Carden's jaw clench while she felt a heat rising through her.

"We will humble you before Almighty God, child, I swear it," Carden replied.

"That's what your boys in the glade thought," Nimue heard herself say.

Father Carden took an aggressive step toward her, and on instinct, Sir Royce stepped in his path. Nimue turned back to the king, a fury building.

King Uther studied her. "You promised us the sword. Now where is it?"

"I will deliver you the sword, Your Majesty, when the Green Knight is released and returned to me." Nimue turned to Father Carden. "Alive," she finished.

Father Carden scoffed, "The Green Knight is ours, and we will continue to purify him until his soul is clean."

"Then you will never have the sword," Nimue promised Uther. "And you will never be the one true king."

Sir Beric's eyes grew wide. "How dare you speak to the king in this manner?"

"Please, Your Majesty," the man in black robes implored the king, "it pains me to see this witch degrade you so."

"I believe you are fair," Nimue said to Uther, "and merciful. You would not have sent your ships for my kind were you otherwise. You have me. I will pay for whatever crimes I must. But in return for my life and the sword I beg you, free the Green Knight."

"More lies," Carden said.

"I am ready to die. Are you?"

"Is that a threat, girl?" Carden asked.

"Torture me all you like, strip me to the bones, I will never reveal the sword. It will never be found. Never," Nimue said directly to the king.

Uther sighed. "Gods, it will give us great joy to be rid of you all." He pinched the bridge of his nose, thinking. "Royce, take the witch to a tent while we deliberate."

Steel hands took her arms and led her away as heated voices erupted behind her.

Arthur stood on the beach, suffering through the interminable wait as the rowboats transporting the Fey Kind to the two-masted hulks offshore fought the wintry tide. Over and over again, the waves bashed the boats back ashore and the Fey passengers would need to unload into smaller groups. Complicating matters still more were the Fey's unfamiliarity and discomfort with the open seas. Many panicked as the rowboats left the sands, and it was only fear of Wroth and his war hammer that made them scurry back to the boats. In twelve hours, they had only loaded half the refugees, and the rest shivered on the beach, huddling near the large rocks by the cliff wall.

Arthur hurried to corral two crying Faun children who were nimbly avoiding efforts to get them into the rowboat. He scooped up one from behind, enduring a series of jabs from the young Faun's budding antlers, and plopped him into the arms of a Faun elder. As Arthur fought to keep the boat steady through a series of strong waves, shouts arose above the rush of the surf. Arthur glanced to the hulks, where people were rushing toward the bow, which was pointed out to sea. He heard them scream, "Raiders!"

Arthur's heart sank into his belly as the shadows of Viking longships appeared like wraiths in the fog. They peeled out of the mists like predatory sharks, flying the white axes of Eydis, encircling the hulks and volleying hooks and arrows onto their decks. Mass panic ensued aboard the already overloaded hulks. Arrow-filled bodies began to leap from the decks into the frigid waters, where it was easier for the Viking archers to finish them off.

Arthur and dozens of Fey Kind floundered into the ocean to receive the survivors, many of whom washed up drowned and riddled with arrows. There was absolute mayhem aboard the Pendragon hulks as panicking sailors held up a weak defense against the dreaded Vikings, who were as at home in sea battle as they were curled up beside a warm hearth.

Arthur was swallowing gouts of seawater, dragging heavy bodies ashore, when a shaft struck the sand beside him. He looked up at the cliffs at another cohort of raiders firing arrows onto the beach. *We're ducks in a barrel,* Arthur realized as another two arrows thudded into the sands, dangerously close. Fey Kind scattered blindly, fleeing in all directions, and Arthur watched several cut down, Viking arrows in their backs. His eyes searched desperately for cover. He spied an outcrop, nearer to the raiders' cliff, but its proximity would actually make them harder targets.

"To the rocks! The rocks!" Arthur screamed, pointing to the jutting sandstone a hundred yards away. He spotted Wroth hurrying Fey Kind toward the shelter, an arrow in his shoulder, as Fauns tried to return fire and a few raiders cartwheeled down the steep cliff, shafts through their necks.

Arthur plucked a Snake child into his arms and attempted to sweep a pair of elderly Storm Crafters along as arrows zipped past their ears. He turned back with dread to see the shoreline blackening with bodies. When he looked out to sea, he saw raiders had already taken one of the hulks, its deck belching smoke, dead Pendragon sailors being thrown overboard. The heads of Fey and men alike bobbed in the four hundred yards between the hulks and the sands. There were still nearly two hundred Fey Kind on the beach, only forty or fifty capable of defense, and Arthur felt dizzy at the thought of the impending slaughter. He raced under the sandstone abutment, where dozens of Fey had already found shelter, thanks to Wroth. Luckily, it was deeper than Arthur had first assumed, reaching fifty feet into a small cave, and would allow protection for most of the Fey, at least until the Vikings landed on the beach.

# FIFTY-SEVEN

NIMUE'S BRUTAL HOURS OF WAITING ended abruptly as two Red Paladins barged into her tent supporting Gawain, his arms over their shoulders, and they dumped him, naked but for a loincloth, on the ground. His horrendous wounds glimmered wetly in the torchlight.

"Here's the bag of shit you ordered," one of the paladins spat as they exited the tent.

A gust of horror fell out of Nimue as she dropped onto her knees next to Gawain and put his head in her lap. "Gawain?" She felt his neck and chest for a heartbeat, put her ear to his lips. Small breaths rattled in his chest. "No, no, no, no, no," she repeated over and over as her hands traced over the terrible burns, gouges, and cuts that riddled Gawain's body. "Not you, no, no, no, Gawain," she whispered through tears.

His fingers twitched. His good eye tried to open and his lips struggled to form words. Again, she put her ear to his lips.

In barely a whisper he said, "Squirrel." He took another shallow breath. "They have Squirrel."

Nimue sobbed at this as Gawain ebbed. His eye rolled back and she held his cheeks. "No, hold on. Hold on." Vines of silver crept up her cheeks and filled the tent with light as a rage pushed through her entire body and erupted through her mouth. It was a deafening roar that blew out the early evening torches of Camp Pendragon and shuddered through the trees of the surrounding forests.

Morgan swung around from her hiding place in a thick copse of trees above the royal campsite. Nimue's scream hung on the air like a ghostly echo. Tears welled in her eyes. She knew what this meant and knew her orders: if Nimue were killed or conditions turned for the worse, she was to spirit the Sword of Power back to the Fey Kind. Morgan's horse became agitated, disturbed by the unnatural scream, and Morgan's eyes fell on the pommel secured in her saddlebag. If there was a chance she was alive, Nimue would need the sword. Morgan had seen her do incredible things with it. She hadn't come this far to abandon her now, had she? She had not.

Morgan dug in her heels, the horse shot forward, and she galloped through the trees, hurtling down the winding deer path toward the Pendragon camp.

Squirrel shivered in the darkness. He'd been in the tent for hours, maybe even a day. The cry he'd heard, unnatural as it was, sounded like Nimue. It had somehow blown out the torches in the torture tent, and Red Paladins struggled to relight them. Squirrel's hands were tied tightly to the arms of a wooden chair that was cold and wet with Gawain's blood. He could not move his feet either, as his ankles were similarly bound. His heart fluttered like a bird's as Brother Salt shuffled into the tent.

"We're working on the torches," one of the two Red Paladins said, entering with Brother Salt.

"I don't need them," Brother Salt chuckled, his silhouette moving closer to Squirrel. He set an old leather bag on the table in front of Squirrel and unrolled it, revealing an array of torture tools.

"Don't you need the fire to"—one of the Red Paladins hesitated, choosing his words—"do your work?"

"No," Brother Salt said quietly, selecting a heavy iron screw and a set of thick pincers and holding them in front of his stitched eyes. "I can do other things."

Squirrel could not breathe. He jolted as Brother Salt touched his leg.

"Shall we play now?" he asked Squirrel.

The boy closed his eyes. He heard a wet gasp and two thumps, which confused him, so he opened his eyes again.

Brother Salt tilted his head, listening. "Brothers?" he asked.

Squirrel could barely see in the darkness, though he could make out someone else in the tent. A moment later a gray hood loomed over Brother Salt, who smiled uneasily. "Have you come to watch, my Crying Brother?"

"No," the Weeping Monk answered as thin, wet steel punched through Brother Salt's chest, stopping inches from Squirrel's nose. Then the blade was retracted quickly and the torturer slumped backward, his sandals flopping into the air. The monk shoved the body aside with his boot, examined Squirrel's restraints, then freed his hands with two swift chops to the arms of the chair. Two chops later and Squirrel's legs were free.

The Weeping Monk took him by the collar, almost lifting him into the air. "Can you walk?"

"I—I think so," Squirrel sputtered.

"Stay close," the monk advised as he went to the entrance, his gray hem sliding across a dead paladin's shocked face.

When they emerged from Brother Salt's tent, it was very dark. Thanks to a half-moon, Squirrel could make out the tent shapes, but that was about it. The Weeping Monk pulled Squirrel by the arm through a winding maze of tents, then paused. They both heard the sounds of chains. Squirrel looked behind him and saw the moonlight fall on the dead man's face of a Trinity guard. And another. And another. He turned his eyes forward and saw another wall of Trinity, their gruesome flails dangling by their legs. Squirrel counted ten Trinity.

Abbot Wicklow parted two Trinity guards to address the monk. "We have suspected for some time that your true sympathies went against the Church. Why is that, we wonder?"

"He's just a boy," the Weeping Monk answered.

"Yes, a Fey orphan. Perhaps he reminds you of someone," Wicklow mused. "Give him to us, Lancelot."

"Behind that barrel," the Weeping Monk ordered Squirrel in a calm voice. Squirrel ran and ducked down beside a water barrel as the monk drew his sword. He addressed Wicklow. "I don't want to fight you."

The abbot folded his hands behind his back. "The Church has reclaimed its supremacy over this embarrassing episode. The Fey witch will burn as she must. As we speak, her kind is being exterminated on the Beggar's Coast. And finally, Father Carden's corrupting weakness will be expunged. Surrender, brother, and I promise a clean death. You know the skill of my Trinity guards. Don't make this any bloodier than it needs to be."

The monk's answer was to stand utterly still, fists wrapped around the grip of his sword, the blade of which he held before his closed eyes.

Abbot Wicklow understood. "So be it." He nodded to the Trinity, who converged around the monk in a circle. Several flails spun. On their first advance, the Weeping Monk sprang into the air and kicked out, sending two Trinity sprawling through opposite tents. As he landed, he severed another's arm and lopped the head from a fourth. But a flail captured his blade and yanked it from his hands.

Squirrel watched with terrified awe as the monk took a boot under the chin, snapping his head, and a flail ripped the back of his neck. He was shoved forward and used his momentum to tackle a Trinity guard, rolling over him and locking his arm around his neck. As the monk stood up, he cracked the man's spine and dropped him like a sack of bricks. He leaped and vaulted over a shearing wave of flails to reclaim his sword, which had fallen into the mud. He somersaulted between two Trinity guards, blade sticking out to one side, cutting their legs, then faltered, his strength seeming to leave him.

As the Weeping Monk knelt on the ground, Squirrel could see dark blood soaking the monk's hood from where the flail had torn him open.

As the monk tried to rise, he suffered a drubbing. Spiked balls rained down on his arms and back and head as the three remaining trained hand-to-hand fighters cracked his ribs with vicious kicks. Two of them grappled and held him as the third Trinity guard slashed him right down the cheek and chest with his flail. Blood sprayed everywhere and the monk buckled in their arms. They lifted him up again, and the Trinity guard reared back to strike, but the monk managed to wrap his legs around the man's throat. With masterful body control, his left foot locked behind the man's neck as his right foot wedged under his jaw and pushed up, snapping the bone. The man flopped down like a pile of laundry. But more flails from the last two guards rained down on him and the Weeping Monk crashed down hard onto the ground.

Squirrel covered his eyes for what came next.

✦ ✦ ✦

Across the Minotaur Valley, at the Pendragon camp, shouts and calls were rising everywhere. Cries of "Where is the king?" and "Prepare for battle!" filled the air.

Merlin was a lion in a cage, pacing back and forth in his tent prison, as the two footmen guarding him grew more and more alarmed by what they were hearing outside. Finally they flagged down an out-of-breath archer.

One of the footmen, his gut hanging over his belt, asked, "What in the bloody hell is happening!"

The archer gasped, "His Majesty's ships are attacked! The Church has made alliance with the Vikings!" With that, the archer flew out of the tent.

"God's blood," the other footman said, running his hands through his greasy locks. This one couldn't have been older than fifteen. "They mean to attack us."

"Stay here. Watch him," the portly footman growled, throwing the tent flap back and entering the growing chaos.

The greasy footman turned around to set the rules and Merlin was on him, tightly wrapping his arms around the footman's mouth and neck. As the boy struggled in his arms, Merlin tried to remember who had taught him the hold. He thought it might have been the Bedouin chief Mohammed Saleh abu-Rabia Al Heuwaitat, or Charlemagne's sword master, whose name he had forgotten. Both were excellent fighting instructors. By the time Merlin had decided it was the sword master who'd taught him the hold, the young footman was asleep in his arms. Merlin laid him down, stole his broadsword, and flew out of the tent.

## FIFTY-EIGHT

NIMUE WEPT OVER GAWAIN'S DEAD
body. His skin gleamed with frost and the vines of the Sky
Folk shone on his neck and cheeks. But he was gone. Nimue
had poured all she had into him but to no avail. His wounds
were raw and open, his body still scourged with burns. Somewhere in
the back of her mind she heard the growing chaos outside, the panicked
shouts of Pendragon soldiers. She sat back on her knees, almost drunk
with sorrow. But the hot tears gave way to a hot blood that rose up her
throat and into her skull, boiling like a pot. She threw out her arms and
opened herself to the Hidden, heart, mind, and soul. Her mouth opened
wide and a fog poured forth, washing over Gawain, filling the tent and
flooding out the door.

The fog also rolled in from the surrounding forests in gargantuan waves, barreling down the Minotaurs hills and swallowing the tents in a thick and oppressive gloom, only heightening the bedlam.

Before they even knew what was happening, Nimue walked past the guards posted outside her tent, enshrouded by the mists of the Hidden. Frightened soldiers brushed past her without a second glance. She heard others crying, "Where is the king?" and "The king has abandoned us!"

However, back in the tent that had sheltered Nimue, Gawain's resting place, something was happening, something that Nimue did not see. Tiny blades of baby grass were forming like a strange web between Gawain's body and the ground itself. Within a matter of minutes the baby grasses had lengthened and reached over Gawain's shoulder and across his chest until they had formed what could only be described as a shroud over his entire body, mummifying him beneath an undulating sheet of grasses.

But outside, the camp erupted with the screams of the murdered as hundreds of Red Paladin horsemen invaded Camp Pendragon, their torches burning away the fog, cutting down the king's men with the same practiced brutality they had used on the Fey. Father Carden led the charge, eyes fixed on vengeance. "Bring me the witch! Find her! Hunt her down!"

Nimue threw herself against a tent as two Red Paladin horsemen blew past her. She ran back onto the pathway but had to duck down again as a cluster of Pendragon soldiers surged out of the mist, fighting back on their heels against Red Paladins on foot and on horseback. She was trying to get her bearings when hands snatched her from behind. Nimue swung her fist around but Merlin caught it with his hand.

"The camp is overrun. Follow me. Sure and steady." Merlin turned to go, but Nimue yanked her arm back.

"We're not leaving."

"Nimue, don't be a fool!"

But she would not hear it. She turned back into the fog and into the heat of the fighting. Merlin cursed and had no choice but to pursue her.

"Father Carden! Father Carden!" A trio of Red Paladins waved the mist away as they dragged a beaten Morgan into the torchlight. "We've got the witch! We've got her!"

Father Carden pushed through a crowd of Red Paladins to see what they had brought him. When he saw Morgan, he grimaced. "Fools, this is not her."

"She has the sword!" one of the Red Paladins claimed. Another brought forward the blade she had kept in her saddle.

"No, no! You bastards!" Morgan cried, fighting wildly in her captors' arms.

Curious, Father Carden took the sword and freed it from its binding. The blade gleamed in the moonlight. "Gods," he whispered. He turned it and examined the filigree on the blade and the rune on the pommel. "It is the sword," Carden said, smiling, eyes blazing. "It is the Devil's Tooth!" he proclaimed, and the Red Paladins gave up a roar as Father Carden held it aloft victoriously. "We have it!"

"Carden!" Nimue screamed.

Father Carden and the Red Paladins turned—stunned—to Nimue, who stepped through the fog, Merlin trailing behind her, still instinctively, yet futilely, pulling at her arm to prevent her from walking into the mouth of the lion.

Father Carden twirled the sword in his hand in a mocking gesture. "Blessings be upon us, brothers. The good Lord rains gifts upon us." He turned to Nimue. "Whatever will you do without your precious sword? Seize her," he said to his paladins.

As Red Paladins took hold of her and Merlin, Nimue snarled, "I don't need a sword to deal with you!"

A rat suddenly ran over Carden's boot. He kicked it off, startled.

Several more rats ran out of tents and out of the fog, darting between the Red Paladins' legs. In the air, the torches became beacons for clouds of bats, fluttering angrily. The rats grew more aggressive, climbing up the robes of the paladin holding Nimue and biting through the cloth.

"Ah! Ah!" the Red Paladin screamed, and Nimue wriggled free of his grasp.

"Nimue!" Merlin shouted.

But she fought her way across the mud as the rats parted around her boots and hungrily swarmed the legs of the Red Brothers.

Father Carden could not see Nimue approach because a wave of biting flies had gone for his eyes. He furiously tried to wipe them clean as the flies invaded his ears and mouth and nostrils. He coughed and gagged. "Kill her! Kill her! Strike her down!"

Then Nimue locked her hands over Carden's. She fought him for the sword.

"No! No!" Carden gagged, opening his mouth to speak and allowing another handful of flies to fill his throat. He croaked to vomit as Nimue wrenched the Sword of Power free. She screamed with primal rage, spun around and cleaved Father Carden's head from his neck.

Merlin swung around and pulled his captor's sword. The Red Paladin shielded his face and lost his arm to Merlin's blow. Merlin stepped aside for another paladin lunge and drove him headfirst into the carpet of rats at their feet. Merlin fought past the other flailing monks and slashed his way to Morgan's captors. They battled the mage despite the dozens of rats hanging on their robes and the bats fluttering in their faces but were ultimately no match as Merlin plunged the steel through their hearts and tore Morgan free. "Now! Nimue, now!" he cried.

Nimue stumbled away from the sight of Carden's head on the floor, gradually becoming a meal to the teeming flies and rats.

But another cohort of Red Paladins thundered around the distant bend of tents. Sensing the enormity of the moment and drawn to the panicked cries of their brothers, they poured on the speed and Merlin, Morgan, and Nimue were forced to take flight.

Arthur ran out from under the shelter of sandstone and grabbed the longbow of a fallen Faun archer. Using the body as cover, he took an arrow from the dead Faun's quiver and fired at the charging raiders, who had cleared off the cliffs and were now charging on horseback across the sands to finish them off. Pendragon sailors and Fey Kind were still washing onto the beach, bloodied and nearly drowned, easy prey for the approaching Vikings. Arthur emptied the quiver, but he was almost alone in the battle. Half his best fighters were dead or wounded on the beach. Hundreds of Fey Kind huddled in terror beneath the sandstone. Arthur knew the raiders would not be taking prisoners. They were there to annihilate. Out of arrows, Arthur drew his sword and stumbled into the path of the horsemen. He vowed to take a last few with him before he was cut down. The pounding hooves roared in his ears. The raiders were close enough for Arthur to see their bloodthirsty smiles. He tightened his grip as a strange whistle came from the east. Something flashed in the corner of his eye, and a massive fireball of burning pitch blasted into the first dozen raiders of the oncoming charge. Bodies flew everywhere. The impact threw Arthur backward. The air was filled with black smoke and swirling sparks. Burning horses stumbled about on broken legs or heaved and screamed in the sands. The confused Vikings circled around the resulting crater in the earth as another whistle cut the air and a second fireball tore through the raiders' back end of the charge. Another ten riders wailed in a mass of broken and charred limbs.

Arthur turned to the sea and the raider ships, as one of them suddenly split in two, torn in half by a Viking longship augmented by a burning lance fused to its prow. Arthur felt caught up in a dream. "The Red

Spear," he whispered. He recalled the raiders in the dungeons of Cinder, Nimue's healing magic, and a promise made with a handshake. A volley of fireballs exploded onto the raider ships, thanks to the ballista and customized trebuchet aboard the Spear's fleet.

The raiders on the beach were having second thoughts about their charge as the Spear's ships took a head-on position for the shore. Huge fighters in bearskin capes leaped into the shallow surf armed with axes and met the raiders on the wet sands in clanging fury.

Arthur could not reason through the Viking on Viking violence but was thrilled to be the beneficiary. And as the first wave of ships fled back into the deep seas or burned and sank, the Red Spear's longship rode the surf toward the shore, ably turning the ship in the churning waves. The Vikings aboard waved to the survivors on shore and Arthur sprang into action, shouting to the Fey Kind. The Tusks gathered the refugees into columns and led them into the surf as the Red Spear's invading force made short work of the raiders on the beach.

More of the Red Spear's ships rode the surf near to shore to receive the Fey Kind. Arthur plunged into the waves, fighting the brutal cold to help the weak or the small or the aged. He stayed in the biting surf for more than an hour, sloshing up and down the coastline to help the Fey get aboard the longships until his arms were frozen, dead weights and his lips were blue. Before he sank under the waters, a rough hand took hold of the back of his neck and Wroth half lifted him onto one of the ships. Arthur collapsed onto the deck, vomiting seawater and racked with chills. He looked up at a pair of steel-toed boots lined with sealskin. A set of axes hung from a belt over leather breeches. A leather-and-steel-gloved hand reached out to him. Arthur saw circular dragon carvings on the gauntlet. He took the hand and noted the size of it. He stood to his full height and looked down slightly at a fierce dragon helm.

"I'm told I owe you a debt," said the voice within.

"I'm glad to hear it. And by the gods consider us even," Arthur gushed.

The Red Spear removed her helm and red curls spilled over her shoulders. Her green eyes flickered with mischief. "You're an easy one, aren't you? I'm Guinevere of the court of the Ice King—a court now under siege by traitors."

"I'm Arthur," he answered. "And we'll do all in our power to help you."

# FIFTY-NINE

THE WEEPING MONK WHEEZED HEAVILY. Something was broken inside him. His left arm hung useless at his side, and his sword dragged in his right hand. The ground was thick with twitching Trinity bodies. One Trinity remained. His death mask had been knocked aside, revealing wide, fearful eyes behind it. He spun his flail. The monk walked forward, fearless of the weapon. The Trinity guard shouted and swung his flail. The monk caught the spiked balls in his ribs, grimacing through the agony, and locked his elbow down over the chains, trapping it. The Trinity yanked to no avail as the monk drew him in and stuck his sword directly through his throat. The guard coughed blood and pitched forward as the Weeping Monk jerked his sword free. The monk spun around as his legs buckled under him.

Squirrel raced to him. "Come on now. Up you go." He pulled on the monk, who rose on instinct alone, allowing Squirrel to guide him to a nearby horse. The Red Paladin camp was largely empty. The sounds of battle from the Pendragon camp echoed across the Minotaur Valley. Squirrel knew that Trinity guards were still at large and would soon discover their dead brothers.

The Weeping Monk tried to mount the horse but was too weak. Squirrel fitted the monk's boot into the stirrup and wedged his shoulders under his backside, then pushed up with his legs. The monk lay over the saddle clumsily, and Squirrel hopped up behind him. He reached over the monk for the reins and urged the horse forward, turning them toward the wood. Several times Squirrel had to throw himself against the monk to keep him from pitching over the side. The bloody night had ended and a burning pink dawn was rising.

They rode for an hour in silence across a hillside of tall pines.

"What . . ." The monk tried to speak. He took several breaths, summoning the strength. "What is your name?"

"Squirrel," he answered.

"That . . ." Again the monk lost strength. He tried again. "That is not a name. A squirrel is an animal."

"That's what they call me," Squirrel said, shrugging.

"What did your parents name you?"

"I don't like that name," Squirrel protested.

The Weeping Monk was quiet for several seconds. Squirrel wasn't sure if he was about to die or not. He figured it was not the most unreasonable question.

"Fine. They called me Percy," he said, annoyed.

The Weeping Monk grunted. "Percy?"

"It's short for Percival, I think." And this brought up another question. "Do you have a real name?" Squirrel asked.

"Lancelot," he answered. "A long time ago my name was Lancelot."

✦ ✦ ✦

Across the valley, the Red Paladins invaded the forest to hunt the Wolf-Blood Witch, hell-bent on vengeance for the death of Father Carden.

Only a half mile ahead of their hunters, Merlin and Morgan battled with Nimue, who fought with them to cross the fields to the Vatican camp. "I can't leave him again! They have Squirrel! You don't understand!"

Morgan took her friend's face in her hands. "I do. I do understand. But he's gone, Nimue. He's gone. They won't leave him alive. You're alive and your people need you!"

"They attacked the ships," Nimue said through tears. "They never made it, they never made it, it's my fault. I can't lose him, too."

She pulled away from Morgan and stumbled back down the trail.

"Nimue!" Merlin shouted.

She wavered on the lip of the rise and looked down and saw a wave of red washing through the woods. More than a hundred Red Paladins were closing in on them. Because of this, she allowed Morgan to pull her back to where Merlin studied the terrain.

"If we make it to the Rabbit Cross, we can lose them in the Narrows. This way. Hurry. It's less than a mile." Merlin hurried them down the hill. Several minutes later they could hear the sound of rushing water and came upon a swiftly moving river and a tilting wooden bridge, covered in moss. A hundred yards farther on, the river pitched over a deep falls, marking the start of the dark canyons of the Minotaurs. They ran to the edge of the bridge, the sounds of the falls drowning out the rumble of the paladin horses behind them.

"Hurry now! Now!" Merlin pulled Morgan onto the bridge and had taken several strides before realizing Nimue wasn't among them. He turned back.

Nimue lingered at the end of the bridge. "I'm sorry. I'm going back for him," she said to Merlin.

The mage heard her words, but his eyes noticed a movement near the trees, on the opposite end from where the Red Paladins were pursuing them. Nimue was turning back in that direction as a small figure emerged wearing peasant rags and holding a longbow far too tall for its tiny frame. An arrow was nocked.

"No," Merlin whispered.

Nimue thought she recognized the child, though she wasn't wearing her disturbing mask. "Ghost?" she asked as the first arrow struck her in the right shoulder, knocking her to one knee. Sister Iris smoothly loaded a second arrow, still marching toward the bridge, and fired again. *Thud.* Nimue fell onto her back and looked down at the second arrow, sticking out of her ribs on the left side. She clawed the dirt, struggling to stand, as Sister Iris nocked another arrow and fired. *Thud.* The third arrow caught Nimue in the center of her back as she turned toward the bridge, propelling her forward. She caught herself and stood there a moment, swaying, as Merlin and Morgan rushed back across the bridge toward her.

The Red Paladin horsemen cleared the rise, saw Nimue, Merlin, and Morgan, and thundered down the hill.

Nimue's eyes fluttered as she drew the Sword of Power, only to have it fall limply from her hand and clatter onto the bridge. She faltered, tried to catch herself, and slid over the slick, wet moss covering the low warped wall. She tipped over and somersaulted fifty feet into the rushing river, the current swallowing her like a drop of rain.

Morgan threw herself against the bridge wall. "Nimue!"

Sister Iris slung her bow over her shoulder and watched the Red Paladins storm the bridge.

In that moment, Merlin looked down at the Sword of Power at his

feet. He knelt down and wrapped his fist around its grip. It felt as easy and warm as a heartbeat, and it opened a channel that flooded Merlin with energy. It was his magic, returning to his blood with molten heat and power. His blue crackling eyes gazed up at the Red Paladins, and with the sword he drew a glowing sigil in the air. The effect was immediate: the clouds overhead turned black and roiling and tempest winds swung up through the Minotaur Narrows, colliding with such fury, they flung and spun the horsemen into the air, breaking them against the trees, hurtling some hundreds of feet into the air or dropping them onto the sharp rocks of the falls.

Sister Iris wisely retreated to the shelter of the trees as another wave of Red Paladins crested the hill only to be bludgeoned by the gale-force winds. Merlin roared and held the sword aloft as a series of lightning bolts struck the sword and the bridge in a succession of deafening blasts, culminating in a fiery explosion that uplifted a massive column of black smoke. Gradually the winds died down and the surviving paladins crept down the hillside. When the smoke finally cleared, the Rabbit's Cross was nothing more than blackened, charred, and sparking pieces.

And there was no sign of Merlin or Morgan.

Nimue drifted in a cobalt-blue void. The gentle currents danced her arms at her sides as ribbons of blood encircled her. A tiny stream of bubbles escaped her slightly parted lips as she turned in a wide, descending spiral toward a pulling blackness.

*The sword is still close.*

She couldn't touch it. She couldn't see it. But she sensed it, and the idea warmed her cold body.

Her eyes fluttered briefly and her body convulsed as she swallowed water. She flashed to the fawn in the Iron Wood. *Death is not the end.*

Would the light of the Sky Folk reach her in these depths? Would

*Nimue drifted in a cobalt-blue void.*

Lenore be waiting for her? She hoped so. She longed to feel her mother's arms around her. And Pym. Mad, wonderful Pym.

*And Arthur. My young wolf. My heart. Will I see him again?*

Her body convulsed again, with less force. She was yielding to the dark and the cold. The Fingers of Airimid slowly branched up her neck and cheeks.

*This was my vision.*

*I will keep the sword safe. Neither the Church, nor Uther, nor Cumber will have it. The War of the Sword dies with me.*

*Until a true king rises to claim it.*

# EPILOGUE

POPE ABEL WORE HIS CEREMONIAL TIARA, a three-tiered crown, his flowing mantum and his falda skirts to emphasize the importance of the occasion. In his right hand he clutched the papal ferula, a shepherd's crook topped with a crucifix. The torchlight of the small cathedral San Pietro in Vincoli shone on the golden Ring of the Fisherman, which he wore on his left third finger. He gazed out upon mute columns of Trinity soldiers. Abbot Wicklow stood to the side in his ceremonial robes, hands folded in prayer.

Pope Abel smiled to the congregation. "Out of the darkness there always comes a light. Blinding in its clarity. Searing in its strength. Innocent like a child. Pure as our Lord God is pure. For make no mistake, to smite the abomination of the Wolf-Blood Witch, God has sent us his own avenging angel, her humble origins a model of saintliness and duty, her conviction indomitable. Today we add to the ranks of the Trinity a new warrior of God. Rise, Sister Iris."

Sister Iris looked up at Pope Abel with her melted eye. She stood as he draped her own unique death mask over her head. She turned to the Trinity brotherhood as they bowed their heads to her.

Pope Abel whispered in her ear, "We shall accomplish great miracles together, my child." His breath smelled like dead men's bones.

Nimue's body washed up on a sandbar in the shadows of the looming canyon walls of the Minotaur Mountains. The arrow in her back had broken off to a stump. The other arrows were bent under her weight. Her breath came in heaving intervals.

Something moved near her. Footsteps on the gravelly sand. Black robes swept around her. More footsteps were followed by hissing and whispering voices. Dozens of bodies swayed over Nimue. Blistered hands, some missing fingers, pushed and probed at her. After some debate in a secret, ancient language, the ghoulish hands reached underneath Nimue's body and lifted her into the air. The leper mob swarmed her limp body and spirited it into a dark and foreboding tunnel.

I WOULD LIKE TO THANK ARTHUR RAKHAM, A. B. Frost, Al Foster, Wallace Wood, John R. Neil, Thomas Wheeler, Silenn Thomas, Madeleine Desmichelle, Tony DiTerlizzi, Angela DiTerlizzi, Jeannie Ng, Chava Wolin, Tom Daly, Justin Chanda, and Lucy Ruth Cummins.

—F. M.

# I REMEMBER DRIVING DOWN MOORPARK STREET

in Studio City, California, when Frank's first sketches of *Cursed* hit my phone. I won't lie; I temporarily lost control of the steering wheel. I had the presence of mind to pull over, and it was then I realized—as I scrolled through lustrous dark fairies and a dream-like image of Nimue, with her back to us and her face turned away to reveal her Demon Bear scars— that, oh my God, this was really happening.

I'm a lifelong Frank Miller fan, and this collaboration has been the unlikeliest of bucket listings. He's one of a handful of creators whose work helped shape my creative voice through the years, and it has been my high honor to tell this story with him. I'm so thankful for his trust, his wisdom, and his idea to ally Sister Iris with an army of killer children (a *must* for book two).

This project also would not exist without the tenacity and creative passion of Frank's partner in crime, Silenn Thomas. She was there at the very beginning as we shined a light on the idea-seedlings that would grow into the thorn mazes of *Cursed*.

Phillip Raskind at WME was an early believer in *Cursed*, and when he sets his mind to something, the wisest thing to do is dive out of the way and let him do his thing.

So, through Phillip, I was introduced to Dorian Karchmar and Jamie

Carr at WME New York, and their early enthusiasm, encouragement, and outstanding notes helped shape *Cursed* closer to the form it takes today.

Dorian and Jamie were instrumental in bringing the amazing Justin Chanda and Simon & Schuster to the party. I feel quite blessed to have benefited from Justin's experience and heartfelt guidance through the editorial process. For me he was the ideal and necessary combination of cheerleader and field general to help power me to the finish line. With the keen eye of designer Lucy Ruth Cummins, they are a team extraordinaire. Thank you also to Alyza Liu, Chava Wolin, Jeannie Ng, and all the folks at S&S who made this possible.

From there, Cori Wellins at WME took on the idea and dreamt it into the novel-TV-Netflix-series extravaganza that it is today. And my attorney, Harris Hartman, managed to make some kind of contractual sense out of it all.

And on that note, I express my eternal gratitude to Brian Wright, Matt Thunell, Ro Donnelly, and Coral Wright of Netflix for locking into Nimue's story early on and refusing to let go. Their ambitions for *Cursed* have exceeded my wildest dreams. Frank and I could not ask for better partners or truer advocates.

While the book was baking nicely, I was thrust into a writer's room with a number of very talented and intelligent writers, and together we kicked the story tires of *Cursed* over several months, yielding some excellent scripts and ideas too good to pass up. So, I would be lying if I said some of those ideas hadn't wandered back into the novel in certain areas. To my outstanding team of Leila Gerstein, Bill Wheeler, Robbie Thompson, Rachel Shukert, Janet Lin, script coordinator Michael Chang, and writer's assistant Anna Chazelle (whose mother, medieval historian Celia Chazelle, offered great insight into the customs, culture, and diversity of the Middle Ages)—thank you from the bottom of my heart. Their collective fairy dust is sprinkled throughout these pages.

And while the *Cursed* novel and the *Cursed* Netflix series are two related but separate endeavors, the spiritual bridge between them was built by three people, starting with the extraordinarily talented Katherine Langford, who brings Nimue to heroic life every single day. Zetna Fuentes, our first block director, inspires all who are around her with her imagination, vision, and joy. And lastly, our producer, Alex Boden, juggles a colossal production with style and an unwavering commitment to quality.

My assistant, Micaela Jones, has been a lighthouse in a storm and her able coordination of script drafts, network notes, multiple copyedits, intercontinental relocations, editor's notes, numerous novel drafts, and my occasional whining has helped me keep the important bits of my sanity.

And finally, my wife, Christina Wheeler, has such a beautiful smile and has managed to keep it, even as the *Cursed* train rumbled thrillingly and noisily through our lives, moving us thousands of miles apart for long stretches, and yet she remains my muse, my love, and my closest, dearest friend. I trust her creative instincts first and foremost, always and forever.

—T. W.